BY BERNIE SU AND KATE RORICK

The Secret Diary of Lizzie Bennet

THE EPIC ADVENTURES OF LYDIA BENNET

Kate Rorick and Rachel Kiley

Touchstone

New York   London   Toronto   Sydney   New Delhi

Touchstone
An Imprint of Simon & Schuster, Inc.
1230 Avenue of the Americas
New York, NY 10020

First Touchstone trade paperback edition September 2015

TOUCHSTONE and colophon are registered trademarks of Simon & Schuster, Inc.

For information about special discounts for bulk purchases, please contact Simon & Schuster Special Sales at 1-866-506-1949 or business@simonandschuster.com.

The Simon & Schuster Speakers Bureau can bring authors to your live event. For more information or to book an event, contact the Simon & Schuster Speakers Bureau at 1-866-248-3049 or visit our website at www.simonspeakers.com.

Interior design by Akasha Archer

Manufactured in the United States of America

10 9 8 7 6 5 4 3 2 1

Library of Congress Cataloging-in-Publication Data

Noble, Kate, 1978-
  The epic adventures of Lydia Bennet / Kate Rorick and Rachel Kiley.
      pages cm
  1. Sisters—Fiction. 2. Video blogs—Fiction. 3. Life change events—Fiction.
4. Self-actualization (Psychology)—Fiction. I. Kiley, Rachel. II. Austen, Jane,
1775-1817. Pride and prejudice. III. Title.
  PS3614.O246E47 2015
  813'.6—dc23
                                                            2015022363

ISBN 978-1-4767-6323-1
ISBN 978-1-4767-6324-8 (ebook)

To all the Lydias out there.

Chapter One

COUNSELING

There's one scene at the end of almost every made-for-TV movie.

You know the one: the big dramatic emotional confrontation happens, fade out, and before the credits speed by with a promo for the next show, you're forced to watch a minute of the super-traumatized young woman (and it's *always* a young woman) sitting in a cozy office with wood paneling and dead, dried flowers, being prompted by some cross-legged PhD to start telling her story and working through her issues so she can get on with her life. That one.

I've always hated that scene.

But I guess that's my life. A low-budget cable-channel movie you watch half-asleep at 3:00 a.m. because you're too hungover to remember where the remote is.

Pretty freaking lame, huh?

I mean, it could be worse. At least my life has the unmistakable benefit of starring the one and only Lydia Bennet, aka me. Not some former Disney channel star struggling to prove she can handle "real drama" so one day she might be "taken seriously" as an "actress."

Fine, and therapy—okay, *counseling*—isn't all that bad, it turns out. It's actually kind of nice talking to someone about your life and knowing they aren't going to act like you're some stupid overemotional kid or butt in with dumb opinions when they don't even know anything about you.

In real life, anyway. I still think that's an idiotic way to wrap up a movie. Because that's not the end. If anything, it's the start of the sequel.

Problems aren't magically solved just because you throw out

some societally approved ideas for how to fix them. Putting things back together is always harder and more complicated than breaking them.

I should know. I'm excellent at breaking things.

"Have you heard anything about your college application?"

So, yeah. Counseling. I'm in that. Like, right now.

I shrugged. "They sent me some more forms. Still collecting my thoughts about it."

My counselor, Ms. Winters, reminds me of my oldest sister, Jane, in certain ways. As kind and patient as Ms. W can be, like Jane, you just get this feeling she could break someone in half for looking at her wrong if she wanted to.

Although Ms. W is overall less prancing chipmunks and double rainbows than Jane. And she's never once offered me tea.

I miss Jane.

Ms. W seems to be pretty good at what she does, and she's freakishly insightful sometimes. It's that insight that made me think I might be good at counseling, too—from the counselor's side of it, I mean.

So I thought if I wanted to go into psychology, maybe become a counselor or a therapist or whatevs myself, it couldn't hurt to try to learn a few techniques from her. Learn . . . copy right in front of her during our sessions . . . whatever you want to call it. She's never said anything about my mimicking, but I sometimes wonder if she thinks I'm crazy. Like *The Roommate* crazy (that's *Single White Female* crazy for those not versed in popular teen movie rip-offs about stalking people and taking over their lives). Either way, that could be a fun twist.

I probably shouldn't mention that to anyone.

"I've just been really busy getting ready for summer classes tomorrow and prepping for Mary to move in, and with Lizzie leaving today . . ." I could already hear Ms. Winters in my head as I rambled (*I see. So it's all external factors holding you back, then?*), but it was the best I could do. "I've still got a few weeks. Nothing to worry about!"

Yep. Summer classes. Such is my curse. You see, I kind of . . . didn't finish up all the credits I was supposed to during the spring semester. It sucks, but it's not like the end of the world. I had my reasons for missing classes. But now I've gotta spend the summer taking two more courses so I can claim my associate degree and transfer to Central Bay College in the fall. Happy summer vacation to me.

Ms. Winters scribbled something into her notebook without looking down or away from me at all. She kept staring, most likely trying to read my mind or some other counseling voodoo (seriously, not convinced there isn't witchcraft behind it all—and I *so* better get to learn that in college if there is). I wasn't sure if I was supposed to say something else, so I just waited.

"Lydia, you know I'm not here to tell you what to do." *Yes, you are.* "But as challenging as some of your classes here have been, if you're serious about going into psychology, this next level of work is going to be even more difficult. And the one after that, and the real world after that. I want to make sure we're setting you up with the tools you need to succeed."

I wrinkled my nose. Did she think I couldn't do it? Wasn't she, like, paid to believe in me?

"It isn't that I don't think you're absolutely capable of this, because you are." (Okay, seriously? Mind voodoo.) "I just want to make sure you understand you're going into something that's going to take a lot more effort and preparation than just filling out an application."

"Pfft. Don't worry, Ms. W. You and I both know there's nothing to this whole psychology/counseling thing. I've got it down."

"Oh, there isn't?" Ms. W said, smiling. "Then let's try something. If you think you've 'got it down,' try putting yourself in my shoes. If you were acting as your own counselor, what questions would you ask yourself?"

"Like, how can the world handle *two* doses of mega-adorbs without imploding?"

"Something like that," said Ms. Winters. "But maybe at least a few questions you think would lead to answers that could help you. Or maybe just a list of questions that would help, in their own way. Do you think you'd be up for that?"

"Please. Lists are my specialty." I corrected myself: "One of many."

"Good. I'll see you here next Sunday? With the questions?"

"Don't we have that special session on Tuesday?" I asked.

"That's right," she said, as if she'd forgotten, but she definitely hadn't. I normally only have counseling on Sundays, but this week being this week . . . "See you Tuesday, then?"

I nodded and grabbed my things as Ms. Winters went to hold the door open for me on my way out. She always does that. I haven't figured out what kind of psychology trick it is yet, but I will.

"Oh, Lydia? If you need to pop in unscheduled this week, don't be afraid to, all right?"

"I know. Thanks."

"And you can always text, too. You have my number."

"That I do."

I stepped out into the hallway and heard that generic click of a door closing behind me.

It's strange to think of summer classes starting tomorrow, seeing as how I've still been coming to the school for these counseling sessions every week since the spring semester let out. It feels like everything is running together, no clearly defined end and beginning with a break in between. I guess that's what life will always feel like once I'm finally done with school.

Not that that will happen any time soon.

I've been at this lame community college for three years now. More than three, once you count the upcoming summer session. I'm not a ditz or anything; school was usually just so *boring*. Academics were always my sister Lizzie's thing. Art and fashion and that sort of creativity is Jane's. And mine is . . . partying. Interacting with humanity. Socializing, drinking, going out. The fun stuff. The cool stuff.

Or was. I haven't really done that in a while.

It's just that, being a third-year student in a two-year school, literally all my friends have left town at this point. And I mean, how can you party alone? Solo partying would basically be the definition of lame. If it wasn't for that, I'd so be out there painting the town pink (a way better color than red; "painting the town red" sounds like you're bleeding everywhere, and I certainly don't see how that sounds like anything fun or cool).

That's all. NBD.

So I just gotta rededicate. "Hunker down," as my dad always says. Do well in these last summer courses, (*finally*) move on to a real college near where Lizzie will be, and make awesome *new* friends I can party with—while still proving myself to be a responsible college student/kind of technically an adult.

That's the plan, anyway. Sounds easy enough, right?

And the first step is preparing for class. Which means school supplies. Which I should probably go buy.

See? Responsibility. What up?

Chapter Two
School Supplies

Shopping for school supplies is, hands down, the best part of being in school. What's the easiest way to make something mega-dullsville like chemistry or geometry a tiny bit more exciting? Glittery notebooks with cats all over the front. Obvs! I never understand classmates who just grab whatever plain notebooks and cheap ballpoint pens they see first and call it a successful shopping trip. Like, way to be sheep.

Even Lizzie isn't that basic, and that's saying something.

So I took Jane's car—now *my* car (I may miss Jane, but I loooooooove having my own wheels!)—through Main Street and turned into the pharmacy/pet shop/school supply store that has kept me in strawberry pencil sharpeners and scratch 'n' sniff stickers since I was old enough for my parents to think I knew that just because something looked or smelled like food didn't mean that it was. (Keyword: *think*.) It's the *only* place to shop.

No, seriously. There's nowhere else in this town.

I made my way down the aisle, keeping an eye out for anything that popped—glitz, glam, bright colors, unique and fun crap other people won't have. That's how I roll.

Tossing some gel pens and a bedazzled pencil bag into my shopping basket, I reasoned that using different color pens for each book we discuss in my Gothic Literature class will for sure keep my notes properly organized. And of course I need something cute and pleather to carry them in.

"Lydia?"

I stopped and turned toward the unmistakable voice of my fourth-closest BFF from the prior school year, Harriet Forrester.

So maybe that whole thing about everyone I know having left town wasn't entirely truthful.

"OMG!" She strode over to me, her dangly earrings clinking against themselves amid her glossy brown waves. Though we were never super close before last year, I've known Harriet since we were little kids running around giving ourselves cootie shots on the playground.

And I haven't seen anything about her look remotely out of place since then.

Her arms wrapped tightly around my neck.

"I thought that was you! It was just difficult to be sure with this color." She brushed her fingers through my fading red hair, examining it. "Or lack of." I guess it usually is more lively. Must've forgotten to do anything about it the past few weeks. Or months.

"Never mind that! How have you been?" She let out a small gasp and looked around the aisle. "Are you doing summer classes, too? I got my associate degree in the spring like everyone else, but I thought it would be a good idea to take a few easy things before I move on to USC—that's the University of Southern California, not South Carolina, of course. Get ahead so I have time for extracurriculars, God knows we didn't have any good ones here." She leaned in closer, and I could practically taste her Marc Jacobs perfume. "Besides, my parents said I'd have to get a *job* if I wasn't taking classes. Can you imagine? The only place even hiring is that weird coffee shop near campus. A service job. Cleaning up after underclassmen and, heaven help us, high schoolers. I shudder."

She actually didn't.

"My cousin Mary just got a job there," I told her.

"I didn't know you have a cousin who lives here!"

I opened my mouth to explain that Mary, who previously lived maybe an hour away—and whom Harriet had met numerous times over the years—was moving in with us for the summer now that Jane's and Lizzie's rooms were more or less free (the "more" being that no one was sleeping in them, the "less" being that my mom always managed to find some exotic use for any spare inch of space in the house—her brief foray into meditation when Lizzie was gone for a month earlier this year was proof of that).

"Irregardless, let's leave that kind of demeaning work to those who are in need of the money, shall we?"

I felt a twinge of discomfort at her words (one of which I'm pretty certain isn't real), unsure if maybe they were a jab at my family, who, at this point, everyone knows has fallen on somewhat rough times. Or it could have just been an offhand, thoughtless remark with no intended underlying meaning.

Like the thing about my hair.

"Now, which class are you taking? I'm enrolled in some goth book course. My brother took it a few years ago before he transferred and said it was such an easy A. And you know if *he* says something's easy . . . although that was before they had all this ridiculous plagiarism-detection software, and I can't imagine Zach getting through anything without copying someone else's work."

"I'm in that one, too. Gothic Literature? With *Dracula* and Edgar Allan Poe, that kind of stuff?"

"Exactly!" Harriet beamed. "Won't that be fun! We haven't been in the same class since . . . well, I suppose we were both in Classics with McCarthy during the spring, but that hardly counts, seeing as how you disappeared for most of the second half of the semester."

There. There it was.

I wanted to think of something clever to say, or at least redirect the conversation. But instead I just bit my lip, locking in the words that weren't coming to mind, anyway.

"Oh! Not that anyone blames you," Harriet continued, as if the tension undoubtedly radiating from me like a freaking Bat-Signal somehow surprised her. "Honestly, I'm impressed you're staying in town for the summer at all. If it had been me, I'd have just packed my bags and finished up school a town or two over. Or state, just to play it safe." She considered this for a moment. "Though with the Internet being so permanent and *everywhere*, that wouldn't likely make much of a difference, would it?"

"I'm also taking Intro to Psych."

Harriet wrinkled her brow. Yeah, way to segue there, Lydia.

"Cute," she finally replied. "Speaking of!" Her hand shot past me and snatched something off the shelf. "Isn't this notebook just the most precious little thing you've ever seen? Cats and lasers! It's *so* you!"

It definitely fit my adorbs quota. Sure, it was lasers, not glitter, but nothing's perfect.

I tentatively reached toward it, but Harriet immediately dropped her hand, and the notebook, to her side.

"Anyway, it was so good to run into you, Lyds. Everyone started to wonder if you were just locked away in your room or something. I mean, I told them that wasn't your style, but I guess if there's one thing we've learned this year, it's that sometimes you just don't know people the way you think you do, right?" She tucked the shiny array of cats and lasers under her arm and smiled. "I'll see you tomorrow?"

Without waiting for a response, Harriet flicked her wrist in a quick wave and disappeared off into the main aisle.

That was a sign of control. Having the last word, making your exit, not waiting to see—or caring—what the other person had to say.

See, Ms. W? I totally get this psychology stuff.

Besides, I'd taught Harriet that, back when we were friends.

Were we still friends? Yeah, we'd always done this hot-and-cold thing—granted, usually with a little more give-and-take—but that's how it's supposed to be, right? Girl friendships and all. That's how it is on, like, every TV show. Then again, this was the first we'd really interacted since before I started skipping classes, and that didn't seem . . . friend-y. She hadn't talked to me on the days I did show up, and I hadn't heard from her on the days I opted to stay home.

But to be fair, I hadn't heard from anyone.

Chapter Three
STORY TIME

My sister is kind of famous. Well, Internet famous. I've decided recently that being Internet famous doesn't count as being real famous. Some people would disagree with me, but that's my opinion and I'm keeping it.

I have to. Hopefully you'll understand why.

I have two sisters. The tea-bearing, awesome Jane, and the nerdy, academic middle sister who wears a lot of plaid, Lizzie. I'm the youngest. Obviously when my parents had me, they realized they'd achieved perfection.

So my sister is kind of Internet famous. Lizzie, not Jane. Though Jane kind of is, too. And so am I, but in a different way now, I think.

Lizzie and her best friend, Charlotte, started a video blog for a grad school project last year. She's not any good at stuff like makeup or video games or being funny, like you're supposed to be when you have a video blog (okay, that sounds so stupid, I have to start calling them vlogs), so she just decided to dress up like people we know and talk about her life.

The vlogs were actually pretty cool. And me and Jane and Mary and other people we knew got to be in them, too. Lend our awesomeness to Lizzie's somewhat-less-awesomeness.

A lot of people watched her videos.

And followed her on Twitter.

And followed her on Facebook.

And then they started following all my stuff, and Jane's, and Mary's, and everyone else's. Even my cat, Kitty, had a Twitter following.

And then . . . I started my own videos.

It's this thing you sort of get caught up in. You don't really think too much about sharing your life with strangers online, because you aren't thinking about them as strangers online. It starts with just a few people, and then a few more, and a few more, and before you know it, it's this giant network of fans telling you how awesome and cute you are and how invested they've gotten in your life, and defending you when you get into fights with your sister or when people are being mean to you. They're like friends. And non-Internet-famous people have online friends, so it's totally legit.

Except when there are so many, they aren't your friends. They don't actually know you, and you don't know them. They're just strangers, watching like you're in some sort of glass cage. Only, you're the one who put yourself there, and you don't think about trying to get out because you don't even notice the walls surrounding you. In reality, you're just existing, raw and exposed, on display for everybody's amusement. To dance when they scream for you to dance.

So you dance. And you flip and you twirl and you get caught up in the music —

And then you trip.

And all the applause and laughter goes dead silent. And before you know it, the silence has morphed into heckling, a taunting audience that doesn't resemble the one you thought you knew, shrieking about how much you deserve whatever karmic retribution you're about to get. It throws you. And as you keep tripping, as you keep screwing up, you can't help but wonder if you've always been dancing on two left feet. If their amusement has always been at your expense and the only difference now is that for whatever reason, nobody's amused anymore.

You're not amused, either. Not by them, not by yourself. Not by much of anything. All you can do is try to stop tripping. Try to stand still.

But they've already seen so much of you. Too much. Everyone has. And anyone who wants to for the rest of existence will be able to because, like Harriet said, that's how the Internet works.

Everything gets remembered. Forever.

And people . . . they aren't afraid of using stuff against you. Of taking your lowest, most regrettable moments and saying that's all you are.

All you ever can or will be.

Ms. W says it's to make them feel better about their own failures. But I think it's because we've made it easy to think of people online as *not* people. If they aren't, we can never be them. We can't make the same mistakes, fall into the same ugly traps. I guess what me and Ms. W think aren't that different. It's all about distance. Us versus Them. Me versus You.

Everyone at my school versus Lydia Bennet and George Wickham.

Who's George Wickham? Yeah. He's . . . well, that's a good question.

I can tell you what I know.

- George Wickham was this guy my sister Lizzie dated for like six seconds.
- He was super hot and had great abs and was really nice. Seemed really nice.
- Lizzie and I got into a huge fight. We went our separate ways for a while.
- My way accidentally crossed with George's way.
- We started dating.
- We didn't tell Lizzie.
- He said he loved me.
- I think I loved him.
- We made a tape. The kind you don't want to get out.
- Except he did. Want it to get out. And tried to sell it on the Internet for money, using my pseudo Internet fame. And my videos. And my face. Pictures of us.
- Lizzie's new boyfriend and George's childhood-friend-turned-nemesis, William Darcy, cleaned it all up and nobody's seen or heard from George since.
- I don't know why he did it. George, I mean. I don't know.

Oh, and all of this? Happened on camera.

So, there you have it. There's my very own personal tale of the consequences of televising my private life across social media. I'd have given you a PowerPoint presentation to go along with it but you can just Google me to get the gist. Even watch it happen—all my videos are still online.

I thought about taking them down. Lizzie wanted me to, even

offered to take some of hers down—and she believes in the public record. She said she didn't want me to ever go back and relive any of that. But I haven't. Taking anything down—videos, tweets, all of it—wouldn't change what happened. What it meant.

But the point is: everybody knows about it. Everybody at school. Everybody in the whole town. All of it, right up until the moment the site that would have sold the video to anyone with PayPal was shut down.

Everybody knows.

Anyway, that's why I missed some classes last semester. That's why I'm in counseling. That's why Central Bay College took pity on me and is allowing such an extremely late application for fall enrollment (well, that and Ms. W put in a good word for me. And it didn't hurt that Darcy is a long-time benefactor of the school and made a few calls "suggesting" they allow me to apply). That's why I haven't been out partying with my friends, and why I'm not convinced I even have any friends left here to party with.

And that's why I'm not entirely thrilled to head home right now. I love my family, but they've been so overbearing since all this happened. Not in a bad way. They just want to make sure I'm *okay*.

All the time.

Sometimes I want to ask them how I can be okay if they keep treating me like I'm about to break.

But I guess sometimes I wonder if I am.

Texts with Lizzie

Lizzie: Didn't your session end at 1? It's almost 2.

Lydia: I got kidnapped and trafficked into Canada. Oops.

Lizzie: Figures.

Lizzie: I have to leave earlier than I thought. Meet me at Crash in 20?

Lydia: Omw

Lizzie: OCSYS

Lydia: That sounds like a disease. Leave the acronyming to the pros, nerd.

Chapter Four

LIZZIE

Crash is this ancient twenty-four-hour diner across the street from our bestest local bar, Carter's. It's not actually called Crash, but that's the only name people remember. Ask anyone in town how it got its name and you'll hear a different story. The one they tell at the diner is that a couple was arguing about where to eat lunch and the wife was so insistent on getting a specialty burger from Crash that she yanked the steering wheel to turn into the parking lot and blasted right through the sign out front.

I'm old enough now to realize they probably just tell it that way to sell more burgers, but when I was a kid it seemed like the coolest story in the world. I always wanted to get a Crash burger because I thought if someone wanted one so badly that she'd risk her life to make it happen, it must be pretty epic.

They're okay. Once, Lizzie found a grasshopper leg in hers.

Either way, the sign really was plowed halfway down and never replaced, and everyone started giving out directions by pointing to "that diner where someone crashed into the sign" until eventually it just became easier to call it "the crash diner." Which was still too much effort, hence, Crash.

Lizzie was messing around on her phone in a booth by the window when I got there.

"Sexting DarceFace?" I threw my bag onto the seat and slid in after it.

"What? No." Lizzie blushed through her obvious lie.

I rolled my eyes. It is almost cute how she still acts like a preteen with a crush. Almost.

"You're allowed to text your *boyfriend*, dummy."

"Okay, fine," she said, pushing her phone away from her. "But I'm not anymore."

Bzzzt. Her phone disagreed.

Her eyes flicked to the lit screen and I raised my eyebrow, waiting. When she didn't reach for it (I totally saw her fingers twitch), I sighed. "You can answer him, it's no big deal."

"Nope!" She snatched the phone up and shoved it into her purse. "I'll see Darcy when I get to San Francisco later tonight. Right now, I'm getting lunch with my sister."

Lizzie's been treating me differently since everything happened with George. I mean, everyone has, but Lizzie's the most noticeable. She's been more attentive, more patient, more interested in my life. Which is great! Don't get me wrong. But she's also the one who wants to make sure I'm the most *okay*. Sometimes it's a little much.

We fought before George and I crossed paths. We argued more often than not to begin with, but that fight was worse than the usual "siblings who are super different bickering over dumb stuff" kind of fighting. That was the longest I think we've ever gone without talking. I know she feels partly responsible for everything that happened. And yeah, maybe if we hadn't fought, I wouldn't have gone to Vegas and I wouldn't have run into George and I wouldn't have made out with him and . . . et cetera. But that doesn't make it her fault. The choices made were George's, and mine.

It would be great if she'd realize that.

While the waitress came, took our order, and brought our food back far too quickly for it to be fresh, I managed to coerce Lizzie into at least talking to me *about* Darcy, even if she was still refusing to talk *to* him while we were together. (Added bonus: we weren't talking about me. After talking about myself for an hour with Ms. W, even I was a little worn out on the topic.)

"So, is Darce ready for cohabitation?" I teased. "Has he stocked the fridge with your favorite Ethiopian food and artisanal cheeses?"

"Okay, one: Who has a favorite artisanal cheese? And two: We aren't cohabitating. I'm house-sitting for Dr. Gardiner's friend, remember?"

"Whatever, you're still gonna see the inside of his . . . fridge." Lizzie threw a straw at me. "Fine. Are you guys ready to be living in the same city? Giving up the strain of long-distance sexting and webcam convos?"

"Yes," she said, blushing again. I can read Lizzie like a book. No, like a tweet. And thinking about Darcy made her so adorable it was gross. "But, um . . . we've lived in the same town before. *This* town, in fact."

"Yeah, but you weren't exactly starry-eyed lovers back then."

Actually, I'm pretty sure if they'd have stayed in the same town for much longer, the universe would have imploded from frowning and visibly uncomfortable dances.

But now? He makes my sister happy. She doesn't say it, but any idiot can tell. And Lydia Bennet is way more observant than your average person. I don't think I've seen her smile this much since her science teacher let her do weekly extra-credit assignments in eighth grade. Which is great—I was really starting to worry about her getting premature forehead wrinkles.

"How was counseling?" Lizzie asked. Oh, goody, talking about me again.

I shrugged. "I think Ms. Winters is threatened by how totally easy it would be for me to take over her job."

Lizzie laughed but didn't look up at me as she pushed her salad around with her fork. Probably looking for grasshopper legs. "I think she's got a few years before she has to worry about that."

"Pretty much what she said. It's fine, though. Same as always. She told me I could come by this week if anything gets weird at school."

"Do you think it will?"

I shrugged again. "I don't think so. I hope not. I mean, I think everything will be fine."

She waited, eyes focused on me.

"I just want to get through summer and move on."

"Of course," said Lizzie, setting down her fork. "But if anything gets to be too much . . ."

"I'll talk to Ms. Winters. Or Mary, or you, or Jane, or whoever."

"It's okay if that happens. We don't mind."

"I know!"

"Okay!" Lizzie held up her hands in surrender. "I'm sorry. I'm just trying to help."

I took a breath and steadied myself.

"I know, I know. I'm sorry," I replied. "Everything's going to be fine."

"I'm sure you're right."

I picked at the remains of my burger while Lizzie finished up her salad.

"Lydia . . ."

I didn't look up. Lizzie had that hitch in her voice that I knew meant she was having a hard time finding the words for what she wanted to say. The conversations that followed were always serious. I was tiring of serious. Serious was hard. Serious meant things weren't back to normal.

"I don't know how to do this."

Was she waiting on me to respond? Did she want me to ask what she doesn't know how to do? Hey, you know what's fascinating? This crack in my plate. It kinda looks like the outline of Kentucky. Or maybe Virginia, or Iowa, something like that. I never paid much attention to geography.

"I don't want you to think I don't trust you, or that I think you can't handle being on your own—" Montana, maybe? A European country? As little as I know about American geography, I know less about European. "But I'm not sure how to leave and not worry about you. I feel like we're just starting to get on the same page, but I still don't really know what's in your head most of the time."

No, definitely Kentucky.

"I know it sucks for me to ask this, but I need you to tell me it's okay that I'm going."

The waitress chose that moment to swoop in and snatch Lizzie's plate and my Kentucky off the table and leave the check in their place. No, we didn't want coffee or dessert, thanks for asking.

With nothing else to properly distract me, I met my sister's eyes, finally. "Lizzie, it's not okay that you're going. It's more than okay. It's great. I want you to be happy. I don't want to hold you back from that."

"You're not—"

"I know I'm not," I cut her off. "Because you're going. You're gonna go start your life, really start it, the same way Jane did, the same way I'm going to in a few months. I'll be up at Central Bay before you know it. Everything. Is. Going. To. Be. Fine. Got it?"

"Okay," she finally agreed. "Got it."

"Good. I assume you also mean this meal, so, you pay for that"—I shoved the bill at her—"and I'm going to do the one thing we never do here." I looked off toward a dim hallway with a noticeably crooked and likely never dusted sign that read RESTROOMS with an arrow pointing into the darkness.

"Really? Are you sure?" Lizzie cringed, and with good reason. The bathrooms at Crash are notorious for never being cleaned. Carter's—a *bar*—gets a lot of traffic from people who walk across the street after dinner and buy a drink just so they can use the bathroom.

"I'm feeling adventurous," I told her. "Back in a minute."

I made my way toward the hallway, dodged a cobweb, and pushed open the squeaky door.

I turned the faucet on, letting the water run for a moment to clear the rust (ew), and rinsed my hands underneath it. Just to have something to do, I think. I just needed to get away. Needed a minute out from under Lizzie's eyes. She's right; she still can't read me all that well. I don't let her. But I know that could change at any moment. And this is not the right time for that. I meant every word I said about Lizzie needing to start her life, and about me being okay. Or at least, I want to be okay. And I need her to leave in order to try.

But at the same time, as irritating as Lizzie's vigilance can be, it's been a constant over the past few months. A part of me can't help but wonder: *If I'm not feeling annoyance, what will that leave me open to feeling in its place?*

Nothing, I decided. Well, that sounds incredibly emo. Not *nothing* nothing, but not the things I'm afraid of, at least. I'll do just as I said, keep my head down, finish classes, and move on. Things will be fine once I get out of this dumb town.

I'm not worried.

I am worried.

But I won't let myself be.

That's all there is to it, right? Have a plan. Follow through with said plan. And . . . something. I'm not sure what. Something decent and rewarding. Worry about that later.

I combed my fingers through my hair. I smiled into the mirror. I straightened my top.

One step at a time.

And the next step was saying bye to Lizzie.

She was waiting for me by her car when I came outside.

"You survived. You may be the first. What was it like?"

"Peeling flower wallpaper. Couple of ghosts. Pretty much what you'd expect."

"Poor ghosts. They deserve better."

"Are you leaving straight from here?" I asked, peering into the window of her fully packed car.

"Yeah. Dad doesn't want me driving too late."

"Okay."

"Call me tomorrow? After classes?"

"Okay."

"I'll see you soon. Don't say 'okay.'"

I grinned. "All right."

She shook her head. "I won't overwhelm you with more overprotective sisterly stuff, but I love you."

"Yeah, I know. I love you, too, Lizzie."

We hugged. She got in her car. And she left.

I know it's melodramatic to see someone leave and think of every time anyone's left you, but as Lizzie drove out of that parking lot, I can't say it didn't cross my mind. Lizzie, Jane, all my school friends, George . . . there's been a lot of leaving. A lot of leaving me. I know that's life. I do. I know that. But I still can't help but feel there's been a pattern lately of watching people disappear out of, if not my life, at least my town.

I'm not entirely sure what it meant, but the next thought to cross my mind wasn't that I wanted them all to come back.

I wanted to be the one leaving.

Chapter Five

DINNER

"You're here!" I squealed as I came into the house. Mary was busy unpacking her ugly army duffel bag into Jane's old dresser. Unlike Lizzie's room/Mom's new Zen garden/aquarium/whatever, Mom had kept Jane's room exactly the same, like a shrine to everything Etsy.

"Okay, I can't breathe now," Mary said, squished beneath me. It's possible I tackled her. You can't prove anything.

"I'm just so glad to see you!" I said, helping her up. (She could have just fallen over in her excitement to see me. You still can't prove anything.) "We're going to have such a blast! All-night slumber parties! Ragers at Carter's! Getting you to wear colors!"

"I'm not here for slumber parties or color," Mary replied, stone-faced. "I thought you weren't 'raging' these days, anyway."

"I'm not," I said. "I'm all study, all the time. I'm basically you, minus"—I looked her up and down, trying not to cringe at the tattered Evanescence shirt and cargo shorts—"all the you parts. Scout's honor."

I was a Girl Scout once. Heavy on the *once*. Mom didn't make me go back after I realized I couldn't use the badges as currency at the mall.

But Mary's not here to jump back into the party lifestyle with me, like she said. She's here because the coffee shop next to my campus (called Books Beans and Buds—the buds are from the adjacent flower shop. Many a confused college kid has thought it meant something else) pays double what the pizza place in her hometown does. So she'll save up cash and work for Lizzie's new company remotely doing accounting stuff until I graduate and we can ride off into the sunset.

The sunset in this scenario being an apartment of our own near campus for me and near Lizzie's still-unnamed-and-somewhat-fictitious New Media start-up company for Mary.

That's the goal. I go to school, Mary is Lizzie's person in charge of numbers, and we share an apartment with Kitty, who will rule over us all.

"Girls! Dinnertime!"

And in the meantime, this gives Mom someone else to feed.

✻   ✻   ✻

Dinner is one of those rare things we had always done as a family, even as we got older. Sure, sometimes Dad worked late and sometimes Jane and Lizzie and I were out doing extracurriculars or hanging with friends, but without fail, Mom always made a meal for the whole family and anyone who was able to would stop whatever we were doing and sit down and eat. Even when she was sick. Even when no one else was going to be home at the same time. She'd call it her "mom duties," and Lizzie would inevitably go off about antiquated gender roles, but Mom would just tell her to be quiet and warm up some leftovers later if she couldn't make it to the table when food was served.

There are three times I can remember Mom being home and *not* making dinner:

1. When she refused to step away from the TV during coverage of the Royal Wedding.
2. The week after Jane's kind-of-then-boyfriend-but-definitely-current-boyfriend Bing left town and Mom was convinced Jane would never get married.
3. The morning she found out about me and George.

When Lizzie found out, she thought I'd made the tape to get back at her, that I was proving my irresponsibility and lack of foresight. I understood why she thought that. I still do. When Dad found out, he just felt guilty. Guilty that he hadn't been paying more attention or been more involved in our lives.

I didn't know how Mom would react, and I wasn't sure I could deal with it. So I asked Dad to tell her. Maybe that was cowardly of me. But Ms. W says I have to look out for myself. She also says things about how I have to face my fears and take responsibility for my life, but all those things seemed to kind of cancel each other out in this instance, so I went with having Dad talk to Mom.

He stayed in the kitchen after breakfast one Saturday and waited for Mom to finish cleaning up. Just waited at the table. He tried to help, but she wouldn't let him. It took longer that way.

I'd been sitting on the stairs, listening, like we used to do as kids. It was the perfect place to hear things happening in the kitchen without being seen. But then Dad started telling her everything.

Well, not everything. She still didn't know about Lizzie's videos at that point (although she knows now, and watching her try to figure out YouTube was like watching her be the first contact for an alien invasion). But the stuff about George, and me, and . . . *that* everything.

But the minute I heard my mom's voice break when she said "Lydia?" I knew I couldn't stay. So I grabbed my keys and drove to Mary's. We sat in the backyard and I flipped through the same magazine for hours while she read some Russian novel that didn't look nearly as captivating as she seemed to think it was, but at least I wasn't home.

So I don't know what he said. I don't know how Mom reacted, in that moment. I just know that when I got home that evening, Lizzie was poring over our collection of rarely used takeout menus, and we ordered Thai for the three of us. Me, Lizzie, and Dad, who'd said Mom had overworked herself cleaning and gone to bed early.

I couldn't sleep that night, so I snuck back downstairs after the rest of the house was dark and quietly turned on a marathon of bad reality TV. An hour or two into it, my mom walked through the living room and into the kitchen, not even looking at me. I almost thought she was sleepwalking. But ten minutes later she came back with two mugs of hot chocolate, set one down in front of me, and settled in next to me on the couch. It wasn't long before she was asking me questions about the show and we were poking fun at how awful the people on it were.

I guess I drifted off somewhere during episode five, because when the sun came out a few hours later, I felt fingers idly slipping through my hair and realized I was lying down with my head on my mom's lap.

The next dinner she made had included all my favorite foods. And she hasn't mentioned George since.

Now that I think about it, I haven't been the one to tell anybody. Everyone's just found out, some way or another.

It wasn't as strange sitting down at the dinner table after Lizzie left as I had expected it to be. But the absence of Jane, the awkwardness of Lizzie introducing Darcy to the family, and the general uncomfortableness that had permeated everything right after the fallout of the tape had kind of already made all our recent family dinners weird.

Mary impressed me during dinner. She sat staring straight down, silent, dark hair shielding half her face. She was like a misplaced member of the Addams Family, transported directly out of the TV and straight to our kitchen table.

I knew the reason she sat that way was because she was hiding a book in her lap and reading through whatever conversation she found completely disinteresting. I think my dad knew it, too. Yet absolutely any time Mom attempted to engage her or asked for her opinion, she could parrot back whatever had just been said, without fail.

"So, Mary, where is that lovely boyfriend of yours these days?" Mom said, spooning some peas onto Mary's plate.

Mary's head came up. Barely. Just barely. Enough to convince Mom she was engaging.

"Nonexistent. We broke up. In January."

Mary's head went back down.

"Oh no! Such a tragedy!"

Up.

"Not at all."

And down. End of questioning.

See? Mad avoidance skills right there.

And, yeah, in a different situation, I would have been dying to pry into Mary's love life like Mom, but I wasn't.

Mostly because I already knew Mary's boyfriend drama.

Last year, Mary—who never likes *anyone*—liked Eddie.

They dated. Yes, Mary dated. It happened. I saw.

Eddie started a band in his garage. It was him and his friend Todd, and they both played atonal synthesizer and wrote songs about roadkill. Oh, and they never left the garage. Ever.

Stunningly, Eddie thought Mary was getting in the way of his music, and he broke up with her.

He. Broke up. With *her*. I mean, Mary may be quiet and emo and into bass guitar, but at least she doesn't write songs about dead animals. As far as I know.

Anywho, it was still Mary's first boyfriend. First breakup. So the fact that she's avoiding the topic of dating is not a surprise.

Also, she's Mary.

Without Lizzie or Jane to ruthlessly question about their reproductive prospects, Mary's avoidance skills, and my being off-limits, Mom gave up and started talking about her upcoming tennis lesson.

I helped clear the table after we all finished eating (and after Mom shooed Mary away from the kitchen, insisting she's still a guest and can't help with anything), and as I was rinsing off my plate in the sink the conversation finally shifted to what it kept shifting to no matter where I went: me.

"Are you ready for school tomorrow?" Dad asked, still sitting at the table.

"It's the same as always."

Out of the corner of my eye, I saw Mom hesitate as she scraped some leftovers into a Tupperware container. Just for a moment, but I saw it.

"Mm-hmm, it is your last set of classes at this school, though."

I shrugged, even as I realized nobody in the room was actually looking at me during this conversation. "Sure. No big."

"It's good that counselor of yours is right down the hall if anything comes up."

"Lizzie already grilled me on everything, Dad. There's nothing to worry about."

Mom buzzed around behind me, loading the dishwasher. It's not often she's quiet and Dad's the one speaking. It was kind of unnerving. Like she was biting her tongue.

I don't know when my dad moved from the table, but I felt his hands on my shoulders as he leaned down and kissed the top of my head.

"We're allowed to worry, peanut. That's what parents are supposed to do."

I didn't say anything this time. The "supposed to" hung in the air, a reminder of the guilt I knew he felt over thinking he hadn't been there for us over the past year. It was silly, his feeling guilty, but I knew sometimes feeling guilt didn't make sense.

I heard him leave, and the remainder of the cleanup was only silent for a moment before Mom started telling me all about the phone call she had with Jane last week. She had filled me in the day it happened, but I pretended it was all new and fascinating. I passed her the soap for the dishwasher and wondered who she'd talk to about my sisters' lives when I was gone, too.

Maybe I should get her a parrot.

Chapter Six

The Night Before

This is one of those times I would have vlogged.

Sitting up in my room, getting ready for the first day of class, showing off my fancy new school supplies (if I had gotten fancy stuff), wondering who would be in my classes, what failed careers my community college professors had attempted before ending up here, what boy (or boys) I'd pursue for the summer.

This is one of those times I would have vlogged, if I still vlogged.

I thought about it. Picked up my phone, switched over to the camera, flipped it around, stared at my face. A pimple was forming over my right eyebrow. Perfect. I'd have to put toothpaste on that later.

People kept tweeting me to make at least one more vlog. I saw that. It took me a couple of weeks before I decided it would be better to turn off my Twitter notifications and delete the app from my phone. But during that time, I saw everyone saying how awful it was that my last video—before everything came apart—was about how I had fallen completely in love with George Wickham, and that I really needed to post just one more, at least one more.

They weren't being mean. I know that. They pitied me. They wanted me to rise up and be this strong, independent woman and show that I was going to be okay. They wanted a proper end to my story.

It frustrated me that I couldn't do it. It frustrated me then, and it frustrates me now, sitting in my room, finger hovering over the record button.

It isn't that I'm not that person. I'm freaking Lydia Bennet. I'm awesome, and I can do anything.

Except when I can't.

A knock on my door interrupted my failed attempt at vlogging.

"It's open." I put down my phone, crossing my fingers that the slow, heavy knock meant it was Mary on the other side of the door and not one of my parents. Room visits often meant serious conversations, and I could only handle so much from them in one night.

"I finished unpacking. And I finished my book."

Definitely Mary. Thank God.

"I'm glad hanging out with your favoritest cousin comes second to reading," I teased.

Mary shrugged and plopped herself down across from me at the foot of my bed.

"I can't believe you only brought one bag of stuff," I said. "You're living here like all summer. I mean, you didn't even bring your bass guitar."

She shrugged again. I swear, if she could get away with only communicating via shrugging, she absolutely would. "The rest of my stuff is only an hour away. Besides, I have to wear all black for work, anyway."

"Oh, that will be so hard for you." Like anyone's ever seen Mary in color.

"I start tomorrow," she said.

"I thought you had another week before they needed you?"

Shrug. "Manager called this morning. Someone quit, so they upped me to this week."

"Well, I hope it doesn't get in the way of your grand plans to get a library card and sit in Jane's closet all day with the light off."

She cocked her eyebrow. "Why would I do that?"

"All of Jane's windows get direct sunlight. Ooh! I can come visit you in between my classes. I get free drinks, right?"

"Let me at least get through the first week before I put my job in jeopardy handing out complimentary lattes." Mary sighed. "But you can still come visit, if you want." She paused, fidgeting with her sleeve. "I don't know how things will work out with taking breaks and talking to customers and whatever, but I *will* be right there, so if anything comes up—"

I cut her off with a groan. "Not you, too. Did Mom and Dad put you up to this?" She shook her head. "Lizzie?" Again. She opened her mouth but I barreled through. "Well, either way, seriously, I'm super fine and I will continue to be super fine. Everyone constantly asking me about whether I'm fine isn't going to make me any more fine than I already am because I. Am. Fine."

Mary looked at me. I waited for her to shrug, but she didn't.

"Okay."

"Okay?" She nodded, still not looking away from me. "Okay."

"I've got some spreadsheets I want to set up for Lizzie, so I'm gonna get started on that."

"Seriously? Lizzie just left a couple of hours ago—she's probably not even there yet."

"Still. She should have them before she meets with investors again." Mary got up and made her way back to the door. "'Night, Lydia."

"'Night," I called as the door shut behind her.

Part of me knows it wasn't easy for Mary to make that kind of offer. But I just can't anymore.

I looked at the clock on my phone and realized I still had some time to kill before I could justify attempting to sleep. So I dragged myself off my bed, over to the computer on my desk, and sat in the not-as-comfortable-as-I'd-have-liked chair I snagged from Lizzie's room after she left. I tapped the mouse to wake up the screen so I could scroll through my email and found the latest one from Central Bay College.

It came in last Friday. And when I saw the subject header, CENTRAL BAY COLLEGE FALL SEMESTER APPLICANT, I thought, *Oh! Is this it? My formal acceptance? Will my student ID and cafeteria pass be attached?*

Nope.

Dear Miss Bennet—

We received your transcripts and financial aid information, so thank you. However, we discovered part of your application was missing.

   Please complete the attached forms and return to the admissions office by—

Immediately, I'd checked the document, slightly freaked that I'd somehow missed part of the application. Slowly my heart rate returned to normal. It wasn't so bad. It was just a form asking for my name, social, a lot of the same stuff on my other forms. The only new things they wanted were two letters of recommendation (yeesh) and an essay.

If Mary's working tonight, so can I, I decided. Since Friday, she'd been pushing me to get this done before classes start, anyway. So I pulled out the essay questions and pasted them into a blank document.

Recount an incident or time when you experienced failure. How did it affect you? What lessons did you learn? What would you do differently now?

My cursor blinked back at me.

Now that I think about it, I have a couple of weeks to work on this. It's way more important that I get plenty of rest for my first day of school tomorrow.

Good night.

Lydia the Counselor's Fantastically Awesome and Insightful Questions for Lydia the Traumatized Young Woman

1. Barring the counselor/counseled relationship, would you do me? Would I do you?
2. Is it still as lame to start a movie with therapy as it is to end it that way?
3. How are you so awesome?
4. What do you see yourself doing in five years?
5. In ten years?
6. In a *hundred* years?
7. Why did you choose psychology as your focus?
8. Where do you think studying psychology will lead you?
9. Why is it important that you go to where that is?
10. Who will you meet there, if anyone?
11. Why can't you just stay home? Or why don't you want to?
12. Where is everyone else going?
13. If you're so awesome, why do you still feel so alone?

Chapter Seven
INTRO TO PSYCHOLOGY

I don't think I've ever been as simultaneously nervous and excited as I was the morning I started kindergarten. Mom didn't work, so I never did preschool or day care or anything like that. Kindergarten was really and truly my first day of school.

I threw up into my bowl of Trix.

Correction: I threw up the Trix I had just eaten back into the nearly empty bowl. Which meant I literally threw up rainbows.

That's how I felt when I woke up for my last first day of community college. Simultaneously so nervous and so excited that I thought rainbows could come erupting out of my mouth at any moment.

Just to be safe, I skipped breakfast and made it to my Intro to Psych lecture by 8:42 a.m. Eighteen minutes to spare. I was the second person in the room; even the professor (*Professor Latham*, I reminded myself, fully committed to this Prepared Student persona) wasn't there yet.

The lecture hall is one of the bigger rooms the school has, probably about eighty seats. Most of the classrooms fit twenty or thirty at most. Small class size is touted as one of the benefits to attending our community college. Seriously, it's all over the brochures. And it's something I used to love—not because we got more "teacher-student attention" (and ew, that sounds super gross now that I say it), but because you know everyone and everyone knows you. And, yeah, okay, it was easier to get everyone to pay attention to you—I won't deny it! Attention is nice. Or it can be.

But that's also one of the reasons coming back last semester was so difficult. Now, I'm glad to be taking a psychology class, but I'm also glad it will be a little easier to just blend in.

I pulled my blue spiral and a fountain pen out of my bag, trying to fill the silence of the room. Opening up to the front cover, I carefully printed:

INTRO TO PSYCHOLOGY, SUMMER 2013

Most of my notebooks for my previous classes have been filled up with whatever notes were on the board or PowerPoint, and doodles. Lots of doodles. I've gotten pretty fantastic at drawing spirally things that bleed into more spirally things. Too bad that's not something you can make a career of.

"Cool pen."

I raised my head to see the only person who beat me into class that morning.

A guy. A not unattractive guy. Maybe even bordering on, like, super cute and possibly even handsome.

Hey, I can take academia seriously, but I still have eyes.

He was turned around in his seat, looking up at me from a couple of rows ahead. Should I be sitting closer to the front? Would that show Professor Latham a dedication to the subject?

"Thanks," I said, looking down at my dad's fountain pen. I stole it off his desk—it's the most serious pen I know of. Serious pen for a serious student.

"Did you get the time wrong, too?"

"Huh? Oh, no," I replied. "I just . . . wanted a good seat."

"Cool." He nodded. "I screwed up and thought classes started an hour ago."

He had a half smile. So I half-smiled back.

"I'm new. Just fulfilling some requirements so I can change majors at my regular school."

"Makes sense," I said.

"What about you?"

"I . . ." was saved by a bunch of other people filing into the classroom. As the newcomers settled into their seats, scattering, chatting, the new guy kept his chair turned my way.

"I'm Cody," he said. "Would it be too soon to ask for your number?"

He must have seen my internal freak-out, because he held up his hands immediately. "I'm not hitting on you, I swear."

"Just so you know, when you have to tell people you're not hitting on them, it's kind of a given that you're hitting on them," I replied.

"You're the first person I've met, and you seem to know what you're doing," he said. I admit, I might have blushed a little. I guess this commitment to academia thing was really working for me. "It would be just in case one of us misses a class, or if we want to compare notes." He pulled out his phone. "Buddy system, you know?"

I hesitated. On the one hand, yes, it's totally valid to get assignments from someone if you're absent. On the other hand, I didn't want Cody to take my giving him my number as a sign to ask me out. But on the other hand . . . he certainly was cute.

On the other hand, I definitely only wanted to concentrate on school this summer. Apparently I have too many hands because when he offered his phone, one of them typed in my number and handed it back. Freaking hands.

"Well . . . 'Lydia,'" he read, and grinned. "It's nice to meet you."

That moment, a man about my dad's age, looking effortlessly uncool in a sweater vest and short-sleeved shirt, entered. Professor Latham.

"Here we go," Cody said, winking at me before turning back around in his seat and whipping his laptop out of his bag, ready to take notes.

A lot of other people took out laptops, too. And I would have joined them . . . if I had a laptop. Sadly, I'm stuck with my phone for most communication and my ancient, inherited desktop for typing up papers. Seriously, it's so old, it has a tower. And if you want to do something crazy like watch more than five YouTube videos in a row, the tower overheats.

But on the plus side, Kitty likes to sleep on it.

"I'm Professor Latham; this is Intro to Psychology. Now, who wants to learn how to manipulate people to do their bidding?"

Everyone in the room stopped talking and started paying attention.

"Or how about, you want to be an investigator and track killers and get them to confess their crimes?"

My eyes went wide. Yes, I wanted that. Without the whole having to hang out with killers part. But yes.

"How many of you just want to listen to another person's problems and help solve them?"

I immediately sat on my hand to keep it from waving around above my head like a dork.

"Believe it or not," said Professor Latham, "by studying the human mind, you are opening yourself up to all these possibilities. A research psychologist tries to direct people and study the outcomes. A forensic psychologist helps law enforcement dissect crimes and criminal intentions. And a psychological therapist helps people by listening and guiding their thought processes to helpful conclusions."

Where has Professor Latham been all my academic life?

Before, with math or history or whatever, I took down info and regurgitated it like one of Kitty's hairballs come test time. Here, I'm being given the chance to learn how to help people *as well as* manipulate them. Where do I sign up?

I looked around the room. No one else seemed as engaged as me. But they were probably here to finish out a credit requirement or kill six weeks, not because they'd found their calling, I thought, preening a little.

Professor Latham is going to love me. Just like Ms. W loves me.

"In this class we will discuss the different perspectives of psychology, such as psychoanalysis, behaviorism, humanism, cognition. We'll look at some tentpole studies of modern social psychology, like Pavlov's classical conditioning, as well as the Stanford Prison Experiment, the Milgram Experiment, the Kitty Genovese case . . ."

I was taking notes as fast as my dad's fountain pen would let me. Unfortunately, about six minutes into the lecture, the pen ran out of ink. I reached into my bag for one of my trusty gels, and that's when my hand brushed against my phone. Which was vibrating.

And I've been classically conditioned to answer my phone any time it buzzes (which I didn't realize until Latham got to that point in the lecture), so I didn't know how to stop myself.

He likes the sound of his own voice, doesn't he?

I looked down the stadium seating of the lecture hall through other students to Cody. I could see on his computer screen that he had his text window up. But to everyone else, he looked like he was just taking notes.

I frowned. But maybe because I found the class so interesting, I felt the need to defend it.

I started typing.

Some of us are actually trying to learn.

"Now, in this class you will be expected to complete an essay every . . . Excuse me, miss? You, with the red hair and the sparkle phone."

My head came up. Every eye in the room was on me.

"Yes?" I said, clutching my phone. I'd just hit send; I could see the message pop up in Cody's window three rows down, but he gave nothing away.

"What's your name?"

"Lydia."

Professor Latham ran his finger down a list on his podium. "Lydia . . . Bennet?"

"Yes," I replied, my throat suddenly dry. Like my body knew what this would mean before my mind did, because that's when I heard it. The whispers. *Lydia Bennet. The girl who . . . ?*

"No phones in class, Miss Bennet," Professor Latham barked.

"Sorry," I whispered, as I put my phone away.

He turned back to the board, the first slide appearing on the projector. A picture of a dog.

"Today, we'll start with Ivan Pavlov . . ."

But it was too late. The damage was done. Not only did my professor think I was a flake who texted during his lectures, but to the rest of the class, I wasn't just another student, lost in the eighty-seat classroom.

I was the notorious Lydia Bennet once more.

Chapter Eight

Coffee Shop Interlude

"Hey, how'd it go?" Mary said as soon as I walked in to Books Beans and Buds. She was behind the register, and for once was dressed appropriately for the world. Her black wardrobe had found its calling.

"Nuh-uh," I said. "That's not what you are supposed to say to me."

Mary sighed. "Do I have to? I've said it forty times in the last two hours."

"What did they tell you in your job orientation this morning?"

Mary's face didn't move as she recited her lines. "Welcome to Books Beans and Buds. Go, Pioneers. Can I interest you in a budding beverage?"

Books Beans and Buds is famous around here not just because of the name but because the owner, Mrs. B, is kind of super intense and makes her employees say the exact same thing to every single customer. Not in the "Welcome to McDonald's, can I take your order?" kind of way, either. When her employees don't say it, she knows. She always knows. Very few have glimpsed the infamous glare she's directed at (ex-)employees after creeping out from her back office—knowing, just *knowing* they'd failed in their duties—but it's practically become the stuff of legends.

Oh, and Mrs. B is a longtime alumni of our community college, and probably has more school spirit than . . . any human being who ever went to a community college.

Pretty soon, people from the school weren't coming in just for their caffeine or floral needs, but to hear the poor, pathetic baristas force-cheer for our very own Pioneers.

I didn't even know we had a mascot until I had a craving for a mochaccino.

"I'm afraid I'm going to need to see the hand gesture," I said.

"Oh, I have a hand gesture for you."

I cleared my throat.

Mary refused to look me in the eye as she clapped twice and raised her fist in the air, like the most depressed cheerleader of all time, and called out "Goooooo, Pioneers!" again.

I giggled. "Mochaccino, please."

"So, how did it go?" Mary asked again as she went about creating the frothy caffeinated goodness that would get me through the rest of the day.

"It went . . . okay," I said. And that was . . . an interesting interpretation of the truth.

Also interesting was the text Cody sent me afterward.

I packed up as quickly as I could once class was over. I saw Cody out of the corner of my eye trying to get my attention, but I avoided him. I got halfway down the hall when I felt my phone buzz from the back pocket of my jeans. Obviously, I assumed it was Cody. And on the chance that he was behind me in the hallway, watching to see if I'd grab my phone and what my reaction would be, I waited until I'd turned the corner and passed through the glass door to the front steps before even bothering to take my phone out.

> I'm so sorry. That was completely my fault. Let me buy you a beverage of your choice to make up for it?

I hadn't responded.

What should my reaction have been? I'm still not sure.

On the one hand, yes, it absolutely was his fault. On the other, it's nice he recognized that and was willing to make up for it . . . albeit in a manner that basically confirms he wants to be more than just study buddies. And on the other hand, if he really is a good guy, shouldn't he have owned up to his texting to Prof Latham?

Once again, too many hands.

"Good," Mary said. "Okay is good. Better than not okay, right?"

"Yeah," I said, still kinda wishing it had been better than okay. That my dreams of . . . I dunno, shining in academia for once hadn't gotten off to such a crappy start.

"So, you have Gothic Literature next, right?"

"Monday, Wednesday, and Friday," I said. For the next six weeks, I would be nose to the grindstone (no idea what a grindstone is or why you'd put your nose on it, but Lizzie used to say it all the time, so it must be good nerd vocab) three days a week, getting my course credits in order . . . and yes, kicking ass in academia, slow start or not. "I'll be here three times a week to bug you and listen to you clap and cheer for the Pioneers."

"Great," Mary intoned. "I'm sure Violet will appreciate that."

"Who's Violet?" I asked.

Mary rolled her eyes as she pointed toward the back of the coffee shop, where the bathrooms were. Just outside of them was the bulletin board, where people could sell couches or advertise basket-weaving classes at the learning annex. There, another barista was hanging up a new flyer.

"She's the assistant manager, but she's moving up to San Francisco in a couple of weeks, too," Mary said.

"Really?" I asked. Not a total surprise. No one our age stays in this town. It's either San Francisco or LA. North or south. They only migrate back when they want marriage and babies and weird stuff like that. "Why?"

Mary rolled her eyes in a very not-professional-barista way. "She's in a band. She says she's going to 'pursue her music.'"

My eyebrow went up exactly the way Ms. W's does. Mary must have been burned by Eddie more than I thought for her to not only be anti-dating, but anti-band.

But it makes sense. I mean, she didn't even bring her bass with her. And she loves that thing.

"Anyway," Mary said as the girl in question made her way back behind the counter, toward where we were chatting, "Violet, this is Lydia. My cousin."

"Hey," Violet said. "I see absolutely no family resemblance."

"I know, right?" I agreed. "Cool hair."

Violet had one of those faces that was completely blank—not that she was plain. But she just had normal features, nothing standing out. This meant she could do anything she wanted with her hair and it would work on her. She had this funky asymmetrical cut that was bleached blond and dyed purple on the ends, which I could never in a million years pull off.

"Are you the cousin moving to the city with Mary?"

"That's me." I'm pleasantly surprised that Mary had willingly revealed pertinent details of her life to a total stranger. Maybe we'll get her out of Jane's closet yet.

"Awesome—hey, you and Mary should come see our band play. We're doing a farewell show on Friday at Carter's. And one the next weekend. And maybe another after, we'll see."

"Yeah, maybe," Mary said. I knew she was being noncommittal for my sake. If it was up to Mary, she would have just said no outright, because going to a bar on a Friday is pretty much her idea of hell. But she was looking at me, trying to gauge how I felt about the idea.

I'd figure out how I felt about it later. Right then, the bell above the entrance tinkled, and the walking cliché of confused-looking white Rastafarians entered.

"Oh, goody, these guys," Violet said. "All right, Mary, gear up. Learning how to deal with these clowns is an essential part of Books Beans and Buds barista training."

I took that as my cue to take my mochaccino and get out of the way. As I started to shuffle back to a cozy table by the book section, I heard Violet address the newcomers.

"Welcome to Books Beans and Buds. Go, Pioneers We Do Not Sell Pot Here."

"Wh-what?" one of the guys said. His dreads smelled like Kitty's litter box as I passed by him.

"We do not sell pot here," Violet repeated, and then without missing a beat, "Can I interest you in a budding beverage?"

I settled into my table, looking at the time on my phone. I had about an hour to go before my next class. Forty-five minutes if I wanted to get to class early and get a good seat. This time I think I'll sit in the front row. And turn my phone completely off.

Still, with forty-five minutes to kill, I decided to do what Lizzie would do—get a jump start on being the smartest person in the room and do some of the reading for psych.

I pulled out my textbook and flipped to the right chapter. We'd spent most of the rest of the lecture talking about behaviorism and classical conditioning. You know, where you associate one thing with something else and it makes you react a certain way? (See: me and my phone.) So, the reading was mostly about this guy Ivan Pavlov, who would ring a little bell right before he fed his dogs. Eventually, he trained his dogs to salivate when they heard that bell, whether they got food or not. (Also, you know how he measured the amount of saliva they produced? He cut out a hole and put a tube in the dogs' cheeks! I would never do that to Kitty.)

The thing is, in class, the lecture was super interesting. But the reading? It was all numbers and charts about how much the dogs salivated versus when they didn't hear the bell ringing and it was *super* dense and boring.

This wouldn't be a problem, but Professor Latham said that more than half our grade would be based on our interpretation of the reading. How am I supposed to interpret the reading if I'm nodding off in my mochaccino as I read it?

This might be more work than I thought it was going to be.

I was saved from nodding off for the second time when my phone buzzed again.

> I totally get if you don't want to talk to me. But it doesn't have to be a beverage. It could be a foodstuff. Or a beverage/foodstuff combo.

That made me smile, just a little. Obviously he was really sorry about getting me in trouble. And I *am* going to have to be in a class with him for the rest of the summer. Better to let bygones be gone by. Or something.

> You're assuming I want to hang out with you . . .

I added his contact info into my phone right before it buzzed again.

> I hope you do. ;)

I slipped my phone back into my bag without responding. Too forward, too soon. Also, I have a super dense paragraph on Pavlovian saliva levels to read; I need to concentrate.

And besides, I hate winky faces.

Chapter Nine
GOTHIC LITERATURE

"Oh my God, Lyds, you're in this class, too? How . . . great!"

I hadn't been the first person to my Gothic Literature class. I hadn't even been the second. By the time I slipped through the door, there were limited seats left.

I blame Pavlov. If he and his saliva measurements hadn't been so snooze-worthy, I wouldn't have fallen asleep, and Mary wouldn't have had to wake me up five minutes before class began, and I wouldn't have had to sprint across the quad to make it to class on time. And this building was not easy to find. It's in the farthest corner from anything—totally missable if you don't know it's there.

So, not only was I almost late, I was out of breath and a little sweaty when I ran into the classroom and basically smacked into Harriet.

"Um, yeah," I said, a little flustered. "Like I told you yesterday?" She just looked at me as if the idea had never transferred into her brain. "Um, is that seat taken?"

Harriet looked over at the chair next to her, with her bag on it. She frowned. "Oh . . . sorry, I'm saving that for someone."

"No worries," I said, forcing a smile as I moved to the other side of the table, where the only other two open seats were.

Unlike the lecture hall for my psych class, this classroom was small, and all set up around one big table, like a conference room. There were only about fifteen students in the class, give or take. Apparently, this was going to be one of those "discussion" classes, where you don't get tested on the facts and stuff, but again, it's all about how you interpret the material.

Old, old material.

But I needed a class that would fulfill my English requirement before transferring to Central Bay College, and this was all that was open, so let's hope gothic lit is easier to interpret than my psych textbook.

"Hey, um, everyone?" said a tiny student at the front of the classroom. "We're mostly here, but I'll give it another minute before we start, okay?"

I was about to ask where the instructor was, but then I realized—the tiny student *was* the instructor. I realized this because she took a seat at the head of the table, and said, "I'm your instructor, Natalie."

Natalie. I've never called a teacher by their first name before. At least, not since kindergarten when the Blue Bugs classroom was led by Miss Judy.

Natalie looks like she's younger than me. I mean, I know that I can pass for a worldly twenty-four or -five since that's what my old fake IDs used to say (before I crossed the magic threshold into +21-dom, where I suddenly became legally able to hold my liquor), but this girl looks like she could still be in high school. It doesn't help that she's about the same size as her backpack—which she was currently unloading onto the table.

Excellent. This Natalie is going to love me, because I have all the books, too. *Dracula, Frankenstein, Jane Eyre, Wuthering Heights,* and a bunch of Poe. I'd actually gotten all the books from Lizzie—she'd given me her copies the second she saw the syllabus. They even have her notes in the margins, so it's like I have my own private tutor already.

I reached into my bag and started piling all my books on the table, too—until I noticed everyone looking at me like I was totally weird.

"Oh, Lydia," Harriet whispered across the table. "You don't have to show off. It's not like this is on camera."

Isn't it totally amazing how one simple sentence can make you feel like you're five years old and just got scolded by your parents? Harriet was looking at me with, like, the *deepest* concern, and it made me burn red even more.

I let my bangs fall forward, covering half my face, but snuck a glance out at the rest of the room. A couple of students were eyeing me, but most weren't, and Natalie hadn't even looked up from where she was unloading an entire library from her bag, until the door swung open behind her.

"Sorry I'm late," came a familiar voice from the door. Well, newly familiar. I brushed the hair back from my eyes to see Cody entering the room. "I got turned around on the quad."

His face lit up when he saw me. He mouthed, "Hey," as he made his way to my side of the table.

"Uh, Cody?" Harriet said, clearing her throat. Her eyes flicked to the chair next to her. The one she had been saving for someone. Guess that someone was Cody.

Although he must not have known his seat was being saved, because he hesitated, saw the instructor ready to begin class, and shrugged an apology toward Harriet as he took the empty seat next to me.

It all happened in less than a second. And it totally didn't mean anything. But still, watching Harriet's face fall made me feel a little better. So sue me.

"Good, we're all here now," Natalie squeaked from the front of class. The pile of books in front of her was practically as tall as she was, so she had to shift to one side to see over it. "These are all the books in our local library that qualify as gothic literature—all the books that have a heroine in danger from a dark and brooding man and a deep, sinister horror hidden in the past, or a scientific discovery gone awry, causing the creator to be doomed by his own creation."

"Ah, we're not going to have to read all of those, are we?" Cody asked, earning a couple of laughs—the loudest from Harriet. "I'm all for a good scare-fest, but we can Netflix some, right?"

Natalie smiled nervously, and I realized . . . it's possible that Natalie hasn't taught a class before. Ever. (Note to self: confirm theory and inform Ms. W about my rad observational skills at our next session.)

"No, we're only going to be reading the books that are on the syllabus—like yours." Natalie pointed to the comparatively microscopic pile of books in front of me.

"Great." Cody smiled at me. "At least one of us came prepared."

I felt myself smiling back.

"But you're right," Natalie was saying, "it is a lot of books. At the height of the Victorian era, gothic literature was the best-selling genre of fiction, even though snooty critics dismissed it as 'sensationalist.' But the popular stuff always is. There were more gothic books being sold than there are vampire YA books now."

Natalie chuckled at her own joke. The rest of the class just kind of . . . blinked.

"Um, anyway, I just wanted to illustrate a point. This genre was huge, and a lot of it survived, influencing storytelling to this very day. It was influential in its own time, too. Even Austen and Dickens both tried their hand at putting a little gothic into their stories. Any idea why?"

"Wasn't it just, like, totally popular? And they both liked money . . . so, they were following a trend," Harriet said.

"Yes," Natalie admitted, "but . . . think bigger. Any ideas?"

"Um . . ." I raised my hand. "I haven't done any of the reading yet, or anything," I ventured slowly. "But trends only happen in a moment, and then fade away. And things that last . . . they sort of tap into something true about everyone that we hadn't realized before. They say something real."

Natalie smiled wide. "Exactly. And we are going to spend the next six weeks figuring out what that is. We're going to draw a line straight from gothic's origins to *Wuthering Heights* to *Dracula* to . . . to modern dystopian novels like *The Hunger Games*. But let's begin at the beginning, with Walpole and *The Castle of Otranto* . . ."

As Natalie picked up one of the old paperbacks in front of her, jabbering on more and more excitedly about the themes that the writer Horace Walpole stole from medieval literature to create the first gothic novel, I snuck a glance around the table. Most everyone was taking notes. Except for two people.

Wanna guess who they were?

Yes, while Cody was trying to send me another wink (too many winks, dude), Harriet was looking at me like I was eyeliner that just wouldn't go on right and was messing up her whole vibe.

Well, I thought, so much for renewing *that* friendship. I did not sign up to be caught in the middle of some stupid love triangle this summer, but if Harriet's glare was any indication, I wasn't sure I had much of a choice in the matter. Guess our frenemy status was continuing to play out like a crappy TV drama after all.

*   *   *

It's still weird to me that there's no bell in college. No buzz over loudspeakers telling you to pack up your bags and go to your next class. And in this room, there's no clock on the wall, so when Natalie said, "Oh my gosh, I've been talking for an hour!" we were all kind of surprised.

I grabbed my bag and shoved my pile of books into it as fast as I could.

"So—" Cody started, but was cut off almost immediately.

"Cody!" Harriet cried, wrapping herself around him and sort of knocking him off balance. "OMG, when was the last time I saw you? Spring break?"

"Um, yeah, I guess," Cody said. "Good to see you, too, Hairball."

"Don't call me that," she said, swatting him playfully. Then, she turned her lips into a fishy pout. "I texted and told you I was saving you a seat."

"Sorry about that," Cody said. "Hey, do you know Lydia?"

Harriet just laughed. "Oh, yeah, we go way back. Everyone knows Lydia. Right, Lyds?"

"Um, yeah," I mumbled.

"Cody goes to school with my brother. We go way back, too," said Harriet.

"Right," Cody said, blushing a little. Then, taking a half step away from her, he turned back to me. "So, what are you doing now? I owe you a foodstuff/beverage combo, and probably some groveling."

"What?" Harriet said, and laughed, confused. "Why?"

"Sorry, I'm late for my next thing," I said. I didn't have a next thing, but I was feeling a little overwhelmed by the day. I was not up to a beverage or foodstuff, let alone a combo. And I admit, I was wondering if Ms. W was still at her office and if I could stop by for a sec. Just to . . . sort through my feelings, as Ms. W likes to call it.

"Okay," Cody said, a little deflated. "Next time."

"Well, you'll just have to grab a drink with me," Harriet said, pulling Cody away. "Have you been to Carter's yet? It's the only place in town with more than just Bud Light on tap. And it has a two-for-one special for opening day of the summer session."

Harriet had Cody halfway out the door, but he turned. "See you Wednesday, then?"

"Wednesday," I said.

"Bye, Lyds!" Harriet called out as they disappeared down the hall.

I waited. Counted to ten. Then I grabbed my bag and followed.

I didn't wait long enough, it seemed. Because as I rounded the corner, I heard them from the other end of the hall.

And sound carries really well in that hallway. I'll have to let Mary know about the acoustics.

". . . never called," Harriet was saying. "But I forgive you."

"Cool. It's good to have a friend in town," Cody replied.

"Right," Harriet said. " 'Friend.' "

"Speaking of, what's the deal with your friend Lydia?" Cody said.

"What do you mean?"

"She's, I dunno . . . interesting."

Harriet snorted. "Oh, yeah, she's interesting. Everything's total drama in her life."

"Why?" He sounded concerned.

Harriet laughed. "I don't know. Because she thinks she's *famous*."

Chapter Ten

DREAM

I have this dream sometimes. It's not like a crazy unicorn-riding, purple-octopus-eats-my-feet type of dream. It's more like a memory of something that never happened.

It's one of those dreams where you wake up and think everything is real. Everything feels real. My sheets. The sun in the window. The warm body against my back.

"Ly-dee-ah . . ."

I flip over. I don't see him at first. I feel him. How close his breath is to me. How warm he is, like an electric blanket, just covering me and making me safe. Then he comes into focus. His blue, blue eyes. His sleepy smile. The weird freckle on his shoulder that I told him he should get looked at but I secretly love because it's the one part of him that isn't perfect. He plays with the necklace he bought me, the one I still haven't brought myself to take off, even now.

"Hey, peach."

When I wake up, I tell myself I should have known right there that it was a dream, that this wasn't the real him, the real me. He never called me peach, not like he did with the other girls. Said I was more than that to him. But in the dream, he does. And I don't catch it until it's over.

"Hey," I reply, my voice weirdly echoey. Like I'm not really there, but actually in the next room.

"I haven't seen you in a while."

"I know. I'm sorry. That's my fault. I've been . . ."

But why haven't I seen him? I don't remember.

"It's okay," he says. "I forgive you."

"But we're together now," I say, smiling as he kisses my cheek, pushes my hair back behind my ear. I even feel his foot brush against my calf. "All I want is to be alone with you."

"But we're not alone," he says, laughing. "We're never alone."

"What do you mean?"

"Everyone else gets to see."

He nods over my shoulder. I turn my head. And everything in my body freezes.

The camera sits on the tripod, just . . . staring at us. Like the computer in that space movie Charlotte likes so much and tried to get me to watch. The red light on top glows, pulses a little. Recording everything.

Like it did when we . . .

That's about the time that I wake up. That warm body against my back dissolves, replaced by one that is fur-covered and purring. The red blinking light of the camera becomes the red digital time of my alarm clock. George isn't here. I'm okay.

I'm safe.

So why is it that all I want to do is crawl under my covers and pretend I don't exist?

Chapter Eleven

WITHHOLDING

"So how's it going? Still the star of your psych class?"

"Yep," I said, nodding, hoping my smile didn't come off as super false. "It's going great."

I was sitting across from Ms. W again, two weeks later. After my first day of classes, I made my way to her office, but the person at the desk told me she was out to lunch. So I went to my car and pulled out my phone, contemplating texting her a million times like my freaked-out self really wanted to. When she gave me her number and told me to text if I had any anxiety about classes, I thought she was overreacting. I thought I had moved on past this strange . . . panic.

I'm not used to panicking—not when it comes to what other people are saying about me. Because, come on, if they're talking about me, it means that I made some kind of impression—and that's all I ever wanted. For you to remember the Ly! Di! Ah!

But I didn't. Text her, I mean. I calmed down. On the drive

home, I turned the radio way up, sang loud enough for the cars who pulled up next to me at red lights to appreciate my spot-on rendition of Taylor Swift (you're welcome), and felt better by the time I got home to find Mom in the kitchen, putting actual icing on actual cupcakes to celebrate my first day of school.

Just like she did when we were little.

After a couple of cupcakes, I decided I was okay enough to wait until my special Tuesday appointment with Ms. W. Because when faced with Mom's cupcakes, anything Harriet Forrester could possibly say just sort of fades into a buzz of nothingness.

I decided it isn't a problem, Harriet filling in Cody about my past. Someone was going to do it eventually, anyway. Besides, he must have caught my last name when Professor Latham super unfairly yelled at me. Google is no longer just the tool of the stalkery—it belongs to all of the mildly curious masses.

Nor is it a problem that I made a bad first impression on one of my teachers (oddly, Natalie seems to like me. Even though she wasn't the teacher I set out to impress, I'll take what I can get). First impressions are just that . . . first. Not last, not deepest. Just an initial blunder. And in no way an indicator of what a person is like. Trust me, I've spent plenty of time watching my sister Lizzie figure out that little life lesson.

Second chances are key. And I was totally certain that someone who had dedicated his life to the study of the human mind would understand that.

That's what I told Ms. W, at our session the next day. Or at least, that's what I intended to tell her.

But something weird happened.

"It went great," I'd said. "Seriously, best class ever."

I don't know why I did that. Maybe we'll eventually get to a section in psych class on overcompensation. But in that moment, with everything Ms. W had said to me in the session before, with everyone wanting me to do well . . . I just wanted to do well, too. So when she looked at me with that patient expression she has down pat, I just told her what she wanted to hear.

Or, what I wanted her to hear.

"And the other students?" she'd asked gently.

"There's not a whole lot of people in class who I know." I'd shrugged, not lying, but not exactly telling the truth.

After that, we talked about the questions I'd written for myself as if I were my own therapist, how my application for Central Bay College was going, and how Pavlov's experiments were really about the digestive system and he sort of fell into behaviorism. Then, my hour was up.

I know I'm not supposed to lie to my counselor. Kind of a waste of the school's resources, right? And my time, too, I guess. I told myself I'd ease into the truth at the next session. Besides, the whole thing would probably have blown over by then. I wouldn't be the girl texting in class, I'd be the girl who did all the reading and had all the answers. And Harriet would have given Cody all the sordid details on my life and he most likely wouldn't even bother with buying Drama Girl her foodstuff/beverage combo and just leave me alone. Everything would be totes back on track to be exactly the hardworking summer I had planned.

Wrong.

*   *   *

It was psych class that Wednesday that messed things up. Or, messed them up more.

I did the reading. I did it twice—because it was in another freaking language.

Why can't scientists ever express themselves normally? Say, "We did this, thought it was going to do that, but it ended up doing this other thing, which means something else." Instead, it's all hypotheses, objectives, outcomes, and "corollary and causative effects as shown on this four-hundred-point graph of disparate data."

Sorry, scientists, but in my twenty-one years of experience, human nature can't be reduced to data points.

But regardless of my determination to completely understand the text (which was even more of a chore considering I spent half the time trying to get my ancient computer to stay connected to the Internet so I could Google the definition of every third word), it was all for nothing. Because on that Wednesday, when discussing the reading, Professor Latham didn't call on me once.

My hand was up. A dozen times. But there was always someone else to call on. And there are totally valid contingent factors (thank you, online dictionary spiral). It's a big class, lots of other students. Also, I sit a couple of rows up, and the lights are a little lower, so it's entirely possible he didn't see me. Plus, we had to move on to the lecture on the Milgram Experiment, so good-bye, Pavlov.

Still, I couldn't help but feel like an idiot, with my hand raised but still ignored, every time. And somehow I couldn't ignore the little nagging voice in the back of my head (the voice always sounds like Lizzie, btdubs) that said, "He's made up his mind about you already."

And then I started having the dream again.

I hadn't had it in months. Not since right after everything happened with the website. Ms. W told me a long time ago that dreams like that are normal—after all, my mind was still trying to process everything.

But it's so cheesy and lame to dream about George now! I thought I was way past this stage. But it's like I'm trying so hard to move on from that chapter of my life and there's one tiny part of my brain that just doesn't want to let go.

But I didn't end up talking about that in my next therapy session, either. Because I skipped it entirely.

Before you get all disappointed, I had a completely legit excuse. It's all because my mom took up tennis.

"And then the instructor said I had the best backhand he'd seen since he started at the club and how is it that I never played before," my mother had been saying, her arm in a sling. "And the very next serve this happens! I've never been more mortified in my life!"

Mom recounted her trauma to us over breakfast, the morning after it happened. I'm pretty sure I caught her practicing her rendition in the mirror not fifteen minutes before, but knew well enough to look super interested and horrified.

"Was your mortification because of your serve or because the tennis pro at the club happens to be exceptionally handsome?" my father asked with a smirk.

"Oh, you." She'd swatted his shoulder with her good hand. "But the bigger tragedy is your father won't let me drive until I've had this checked out. I keep telling him it's just a case of tennis elbow. . . ."

"Yes, and the dent in the front bumper was just a case of restless leg syndrome," he'd replied, and disappeared back behind his paper.

"We have an appointment tomorrow, but I need to run some errands this afternoon. . . ."

"I'll drive you, Mom," I'd said. "No biggie."

"Are you sure?" she'd asked, her eyes sliding to Dad's.

"Yeah, it's fine."

So I skipped, and drove my mom to and from the grocery store. I was sure one of them knew about my therapy session, but neither said anything. I texted Ms. W; she said it was cool. And I got to slide another week.

*　　*　　*

So here I am two weeks later, and Ms. W doesn't know about my dream, or Harriet, or Cody, and has spent two weeks thinking I've been killing it in psych class.

"I have to admit, Lydia, I'm impressed," Ms. W said with a small smile. "I remember my first couple of classes—all those case studies and scientific language was impenetrable."

"Well, it's not easy," I admitted. "But I'm getting there. I just turned in a paper. On the Milgram Experiment. And I totally rocked it."

This, at least, was the truth. Or I hoped it was. I wrote that paper and rewrote it just to make sure it was bulletproof. I cited the text. I used *footnotes*. Which means I finally had to figure out what footnotes *are*. If that doesn't get Latham's attention, I don't know what will.

"Wonderful! This makes me feel like you're well prepared for the transfer to Central Bay College," she noted. "But more importantly, how does it make you feel?"

"Did you really just ask, 'How does it make you feel?'"

"Yes, and mocking it doesn't make it any less valid of a question," she said.

I hedged. "It makes me feel . . . okay, I guess."

"Can you expand on that?"

"I . . . I know it's not the *norm* that I do well in a class, but this is what I want to be doing, so, shouldn't I be at least a *little* good at it?"

"Of course," Ms. W said gently. "But I'm sensing a little defensiveness."

"Just not used to it, I guess," I said.

She eyed me. "Lydia, you realize that when you graduate from here, our therapy sessions will be over."

My head shot up. "They will?"

"Counseling through the school is only available to students. Besides, you'll be moving."

"Yeah . . ." I said, not entirely sure what she was getting at.

"So, I want us to make the most of the time we have. If there's anything you want to discuss . . ."

It was weird, but I hadn't thought about therapy ending. I thought about school ending, and about moving up to the city with Mary, but never these Sunday sessions ending.

I should've been using the time better. Ms. W was right. I don't know why I wasn't telling her the truth. Telling her that Professor Latham has been patently ignoring me. Or telling her that I was going cross-eyed on the reading. Or about Harriet and Cody. Or my dreams coming back. Basically, about anything.

But if Ms. Winters and I are only going to have the next couple of weeks together, I want her to think she did a good job, I guess.

"Honestly, I'm great." I shrugged, putting on my best "I'm Lydia, Bitches, I Don't Care" posture. "I'm totally feeling ready to move up to San Francisco. Just these two classes and I'm gone."

If Ms. W suspected something, she didn't say it. She just kept her face neutral.

"Two classes and your application," she amended.

"Right. Which is almost done."

"Almost?" Her eyebrow went up. One thing Ms. W does not do is judge. It's one of the core rules of being a therapist. But that eyebrow felt judgy. "Isn't the deadline—"

"I've still got a little time. I'm just putting the finishing touches on it. Want to make sure it's perfect before I send it in." The eyebrow stayed up. "It's basically completely filled out. I'm just dotting t's and crossing i's."

It's at least kinda true. Most of my application is finished. Name, date of birth, social security number—I'd even found two professors at my school who don't completely think I'm a lost cause to write letters of recommendation for me. It's just those pesky essay questions giving me trouble.

Recount an incident or time when you experienced failure.

Well, it won't be now. I might be covering a little, but I'm actually doing fine. Maybe not as stellar as I've been making it out to sound, but I'm getting it done. I have two classes to pass and I'm gone. And I still have a couple of weeks before my application is due. I have a reminder set up on my phone. And I wrote it in my day planner, too—which turned out to be from two years ago, so I also put it on a Post-it and stuck it to my computer monitor. There's no need to worry.

And that's exactly what I told Ms. W.

"Don't worry about me, Ms. W. I'm fine."

The Milgram Experiment
By Lydia Bennet

Summarize the experiment.

The Milgram Experiment was a psychological behavior experiment conducted in the 1960s, around the same time that Nazi war criminals were being tried for their actions in the Holocaust. This is relevant, because Dr. Stanley Milgram wanted to see if it's possible that people would be willing to do terrible things simply because they were ordered to by someone in charge, like their boss or an authority figure. So Dr. Milgram set up an experiment where volunteers were told they were supposed to teach a set of vocab words to another volunteer, who was located on the other side of a wall. If the person learning the words got one wrong, the teaching volunteer would have to administer an electric shock to the learning volunteer, to "help" him learn. With each word he got wrong, the voltage of the shocks would go up.

An overseer in a white lab coat would be watching the teaching volunteer, to make sure the experiment ran properly.

What they didn't tell the teaching volunteer is that the other volunteer was just an actor. And he wasn't getting electroshocked, he was faking being more and more hurt. But that didn't matter, because the teaching volunteer *thought* he was shocking the other person.[1]

If the teaching volunteer ever wanted to stop, or questioned what was happening, the overseer in the white lab coat would tell them to continue. And a lot of the time they would, all the way up until they

---

1. The person told him that he had a heart condition, too, so this experiment might kill them. If it were real.

delivered a massive 450-volt shock to the other person, which would likely be fatal.[2]

This experiment has also been run many times since Milgram, in many different cultures, with consistent results.

What conclusions can we draw from this experiment?

We obey people who have authority over us . . . or those who at the very least seem to. After all, that white lab coat wasn't worn by someone with a medical degree, it was worn by someone who was paid to be in that role. But that lab coat conveyed knowledge—and when in doubt, we trust the people who know more than us.

Obedience and trust are twisted together—when you find yourself in a situation where you are the less experienced, you automatically trust the person who seems to have more experience. Or even just the person who speaks the loudest. This effect does not need clinical experiments to be shown. It's observable every day: My father trusts the mechanic to fix his car and not knowingly cause it or him any harm. We trust the police officer guiding traffic in the middle of the street to do so fairly and safely. I trust my friends to have considered my well-being when we go out and not make me eat pickles because they are disgusting. We trust people. But we especially trust people who need us.

The experimenter needed the teacher to shock the other person. That's what they were asking. We are conditioned to do as we are asked—especially in pressured situations, where the person asking has the appearance of control.

The fact that this experiment has been conducted multiple times in many different situations—some of the people tested had higher levels of education, some were poor, etc.—and that the results remain so consistent through the years is the proof that this is not a conditioning restricted to one social class or time period. This is

---

2. Again, if it were real.

much closer to human nature—and a kind of human nature that we all have to fight against to become better people.

In this situation, what would your reaction be personally?
I have enough experience defying authority that I absolutely would tell the experimenter to stop, and refuse to give shocks to the other guy. Because, come on. If you don't want to hurt another person, don't. It's that simple.

C. Good summary, but poor analysis and conclusion.

Chapter Twelve

CONFRONTATION

"Excuse me, Professor Latham?" I said, approaching the front of the room cautiously. Class had been dismissed for the day, and he was packing up his bag. I could feel Cody still in the room, slowly packing up his bag, too, wondering if he should wait for me. Then one of the other guys in class said, "Hey, Cody—did you get the notes from Monday?" And he was gone. Good. I didn't need an audience for this.

"Yes, Miss . . . Bennet?" Professor Latham said, only glancing up from his bag briefly.

"I wanted to ask you about my grade."

I never did this. Before last semester, I never really cared about my grades—but that was because I never really tried in school. Then, Mary tutored me in history, and I worked and worked at it, and ended up with an A-minus! But that was history class, where there are definite right and wrong answers. I never needed to have my grade explained to me before.

"I have office hours Tuesday mornings if you want to discuss your grade."

He zipped up his bag and started for the door. I stepped in his path.

"I'm not here Tuesday, and I just . . . I got a C?" I said, holding out the paper to him. And there it was, in bright red Sharpie with a circle around it. C. Like, Copyright You Screwed Up.

He sighed deeply, but then put his bag down and took my paper from my hand. He glanced at it for three seconds before giving it back to me. "Right. It was a C paper."

"But . . . I worked really hard on it . . ." My voice trailed off, tiny. I hate it when my voice gets tiny.

But the way Professor Latham was barely looking at me and my paper made me feel even tinier. So I drew myself up straight, and pretended I knew what I was talking about.

Oh, all right. I pretended I was Lizzie.

"Professor Latham, I'm planning on transferring to a four-year college and studying psychology to become a therapist. So if you could tell me where I went wrong, I would really appreciate the guidance."

Professor Latham stopped and looked up at me—and actually saw me this time.

"Your summary was fine. You tone is a little too conversational for the subject, and you need to include more of the hard data in your analysis rather than trying to tie the concepts of obedience and trust together, but your real problem is your answer to the last question."

I glanced at it. *If you don't want to hurt another person, don't. It's that simple.* "What's wrong with it?"

"It's a complete fallacy."

"No, it's not," I said. "I totally wouldn't shock someone for not knowing vocab words!"

"You like to think that. We all like to think that of ourselves, but that's the point of the experiment. To state definitively that you would defy the authority figure is complete hubris."

Okay, I would have to look up "hubris" later for the exact definition, but I got the gist. Still, I argued, "But it wasn't like the lab coat was holding a gun to the person's head. He just told him to continue."

"He didn't need one. Do you think anyone *wanted* to shock another person? Not recognizing the effect someone with authority has over your actions tells me that you didn't really understand the experiment."

"I understood it," I said. "But you asked what *I* would do, and that's what I would do. I don't like hurting people."

"No one does," Professor Latham said, his tone patronizing, like when Lizzie tries to explain something to me that she thinks I don't know. When Lizzie does it, it pisses me off. When my professor did it . . . it felt different. "Do you honestly think you would invite that kind of confrontation? Or would you just go along—no matter how uncomfortable it made you?"

I paused. Considering the swirling nervousness in my stomach right now when I was only asking my teacher about a grade . . . maybe I wouldn't? Maybe I would just do what felt easier. More often than not, I do what's easier.

Because it's not like I stood up for myself when George challenged me to "prove my love" for him.

"If you're going to spend the better part of the next decade studying psychology, then you need to not only write more scientifically but learn to think analytically about the subject and how you relate to it." Professor Latham glanced at his watch. "Now, if that's all, I have another class to prep for."

"Yes . . . thank you," I said, distracted. But then, as Professor Latham headed up the steps . . . "What do you mean, the better part of a decade? I should have enough credits to transfer into my next school as a second-semester junior. That plus a master's is only, like, four years tops."

"Yes, but if you are taking Intro to Psych now, you will definitely be behind on your required classes for your undergraduate degree. You'll probably have to take freshman-level courses. Plus, if you want to study clinical psychology, you might even have to go for your doctorate. That's a lot of time." He gave a pained smile. "Trust me."

He left, and suddenly I was alone in the middle of the lecture hall. Alone with a C paper, and feeling like I got hit by a truck.

* * *

"So how do you feel about living with someone else?" Mary asked, putting a mochaccino down in front of me and a black coffee for herself.

I nearly knocked over my drink. "What?"

"I've been looking online, there's no way we can afford even a one-bedroom on our own in San Francisco. So what do you think about looking for roommates?"

"Oh," I said, my heartbeat slowing back down to seminormal. "Fine with it, I guess. Though I can't believe you of all people are suggesting cohabitation with other not-us humans. Who were you thinking about? Violet?"

"No," Mary said, taken aback. "Why would you think that?"

"Well, you know her and she's moving to San Francisco, too," I replied. "Don't you like Violet?"

"No!" Mary said. "I mean, no, she's okay, I guess. For someone who's basically my boss. But she'll be living with her band, and I don't want to live with people playing instruments all the time. Do you?"

Ah. The band again.

"Well . . . I sort of will be, assuming your bass makes the trip to the city."

"That's different from living with a *band*. I'm not going to make my living at it. It's not exactly practical. I still can't believe Violet's going to try to live off her music, with no backup plan."

"Did I hear my name?" Violet came up to our table. She was bearing carafes of milk and a new bag of fake-sugar packets to refill the condiment station.

Mary looked like she'd just gotten caught doing . . . something, so I was left to answer. "Just talking about moving to the city. Do you know when you're going?"

Violet shrugged. "A couple of weeks, maybe? We want to do as many farewell shows as possible, and I can't leave Mrs. B hanging until she hires someone to replace me. Sure you don't want the assistant manager gig?" She looked at Mary as she said it.

Mary hid her face with half her hair. "I'm sure. I've got a job waiting for me, remember?"

"When are you guys heading up?" Violet asked.

This time, Mary was the one to pipe up when I got a little tongue-tied. "Once Lydia's done with her classes here."

"Right," Violet said. "You're going to Central Bay College—that's a great school, congrats on getting in."

"I . . ." I hesitated. "I'm not exactly 'in.' I mean, my counselor and Darcy—he's my sister's boyfriend—they called in favors on my behalf, but I still have to do some stuff to qualify."

"Like these courses?" Violet asked.

"Exactly," I replied. And fill out an essay application that is sitting on my desktop at home like a particularly judgmental Jiminy Cricket. "And after that, it's a lot of stuff, too. Like, years of school."

I glanced over and saw that Mary was looking at me funny. But she didn't say anything.

"Oh, trust me, I know," Violet was saying. "I majored in psych at NAU—going down the postgrad path just wasn't for me."

"NAU?" I asked.

"New Amsterdam University—in New York City. Man, I loved it there—and I'll be paying it off forever. Unless we hit the big time with the band, of course." She looked dreamy, probably imagining her rock-star life. "Fingers crossed. But it was worth it. The program is spectacular; I learned so much."

"Then why'd you stop?" I asked.

"Because one of the main things I learned was that I didn't want to keep doing it. What psychology helped me do was become a better songwriter—get in touch with my emotions, you know? What drives people?"

Made sense, I guess.

"If you weren't already going to Central Bay College, I would say you should check out NAU. But more importantly, you should check out our next farewell show." She grinned as she reached into her back pocket—no easy feat considering all the stuff she was carrying—and pulled out a flyer.

"Carter's, tonight," she said proudly. She turned to Mary. "I know you couldn't come to the last one, but this one's going to be awesome."

It's not that Mary *couldn't* come last time. Last weekend, Mary spent her Friday night on her computer, doing sample budgets for Lizzie's as-of-yet-unnamed company. I know, because *I* spent last Friday night in the next room trying to read *Frankenstein*. Who knew Frankenstein's monster was so talkative? In the movies he barely grunts.

So going to Carter's wouldn't have derailed anything exciting.

I opened my mouth, curious to ask how this farewell show would be different from the *last* farewell show, but Mary cut me off.

"Hey, Violet, I've got like seven minutes left on my break, so . . ."

"My bad." She shook her head. "Enjoy your coffee."

She moved off, and the minute she did, Mary's shoulders relaxed. It's weird. Mary is way too good an employee to be afraid of her supervisor. Especially a supervisor as nice and personable and purple-haired as Violet.

But maybe Mary wasn't uptight because of Violet. Because the next thing she said to me was . . .

"What's wrong?"

I dodged it. "What do you mean?"

"You've been a little distracted since you came in here. And when you were talking about school . . . you just sounded a little weird."

"I'm fine," I replied, knowing I sounded totally fine. Because I was getting really good at pretending I was.

"You're not. I've never heard you be down on deciding to go to Central Bay before."

"I wasn't down," I said. "I was just . . . my professor said something to me that made me think, is all."

"Think?" Mary asked. "As in *rethink*? You're not backing out, are you? We have a plan, and I need—"

"No!" I replied immediately. "I'm sorry. I got a C on my paper and it's put me in a bummer mood."

"On your paper on the Milgram Experiment? You worked really hard on that!" Mary said, angry. Which made me smile. Mary was going to defend me to psychology professors worldwide, even if my paper turned out to be a C paper.

"I know. It sucks."

"Damn straight it sucks."

I shrugged. "I guess I'll just have to double down on my studying. I've got to do a big paper on the five stages of grief this week."

"Which stage are you on now for your Milgram paper?" Mary asked, almost smiling again.

"Denial. Obvs."

Mary snorted into her coffee.

"Maybe I could help you study," she offered.

"This isn't your major like math was," I said, shaking my head. "You never took psych."

"Yeah, but I can read the textbook, quiz you."

"While you're working here, and working on Lizzie's company from home? Do you plan on giving up sleep?"

"It was just an idea," she said, a little stiff. I immediately softened, afraid I'd insulted her. For someone normally so steely, she has a surprisingly mushy center.

"I know. I just . . . don't want to do that to you. This is my problem."

"Okay," Mary said.

"Maybe Violet could tutor me, though."

"Violet?" she repeated, surprised. "Why?"

"Um . . .because she majored in psych?" Come on, Mary; keep up here. "Why are you so touchy about her?"

"I'm not," Mary replied. "She's just basically my boss, so it's weird that she wants to hang out . . . and invites us to her 'farewell' shows. All forty of them. Not that I want to go, of course. To any."

"Of course," I said, as deadpan as Mary. "You know, Violet's only going to be your boss for a couple more weeks, and I'm only going to ask her for some tutoring help. She has a psychology degree. And she seemed to really like getting it, too. I mean, she went to school in New York. That qualifies for a 'wow.' "

"Yeah, wow," Mary said. "She went to school in New York—the most expensive place on the planet—and is using her degree to write songs."

She paused. Spun her coffee cup on its saucer.

"You know, you're super anti-Violet's band for never having actually heard them," I pointed out. "I'm willing to bet they're pretty good. Or her lyrics, at least."

"Yeah . . . they're not bad," she mumbled.

"What?" I asked, not convinced I'd heard her right. "You've listened to them?"

"Mrs. B lets Violet sell her CDs at the register. She gave me one—in case someone was interested, so I could help sell them."

"And they're good?"

"They're really good," Mary relented. "Except their bassist, who could use some clues on rhythm. But, I have to admit, Violet's really pretty . . . good."

"Even though she's only using her degree to write songs?"

"Talk a little louder, why don't you, so Violet can hear you," Mary said to me, then lowered her voice. "I hesitate to suggest this, but . . . what if we went to the show tonight?"

My head whipped up. "What?"

Mary? Suggesting attending a social event? Violet's band must be much more than "not bad" for it to have come to this.

"Hear me out," she said, taking a deep breath. "You've been working so hard. Maybe you need a night of not psych to help you clear your head so you can work on all the other nights of psych."

I looked at Mary. I looked around the coffee shop. I did not find any hidden cameras within my view.

"Is this a *Freaky Friday* situation?" I asked. "Did we switch bodies and I missed it?"

"I'm talking about one night—not every night. One Friday night, two drinks and one pretty decent band. And . . . you saw, she's being pretty insistent, for some reason, so if I have to go eventually, I'd rather get it over with, and have you come with me. And it would probably go a long way with Violet, if you do want her to tutor you, if you would go to one of her shows."

I stared down into the foamy remains at the bottom of my mug. I was still a little crushed by my grade—and by what Professor Latham had said to me about how long I'd be in school. Because that's a lot of school—and while I had budgeted for my credits, I hadn't budgeted for my major. That scares me. I mean, I thought I was gonna be done by the time I was twenty-five. I didn't envision spending all of my twenties in school. I barely made it through my teens.

And how am I supposed to be a serious student for the next six to eight *years* if I can't manage to not party three weeks into the semester?

And yes, there's a part of me—large and looming—that's sort of scared about the idea of going out. People I know will be there . . .

and people I don't. But the one thing they'd have in common is that they know about me. Thanks to my social-media-star sister. And my own online activities.

I just don't feel like being judged anymore.

"My break's almost up," Mary said to me, finishing off her coffee in one giant gulp. "So . . . I can't believe I'm saying this, but . . . tonight? Carter's?"

For some reason, Mary really wanted to go—even though she seemed to be having such a hard time admitting it. Which is proof enough of her need for a non-awkward wingman.

That must have been the tipping point, because somehow words I'd never intended to say again (at least not for the six weeks I was in school this summer) popped freely from my mouth.

"Tonight. Carter's."

Chapter Thirteen
ONE NIGHT ONLY

"Woo-hoo! Carter's!" I yelled as we pulled into the lot behind the bar. Mary put the parking brake on and turned to glare at me. "What? I'm out of practice and just trying to get into the spirit."

The glare continued.

"Woo . . . ?" I tried, this time with a small Books Beans and Buds–style fist pump. That got her to crack a smile.

When we told my parents we would be going out that evening, they didn't even really blink an eye. I totally expected more along the lines of concerned furrowing of the brows. Instead, my mom and dad were just sitting, holding hands in my dad's den.

"That's nice, dear," Mom said.

She must have been a little distracted, because she didn't seem to even be looking at me. If she had been, she absolutely would have noticed that I looked different.

I'd dug out my purple sparkly eyeliner and my leopard-print top, which I wore under a black leather jacket. I debated for a whole thirty-seven minutes about wearing it, but it's the only rock-band-worthy outfit I could pull together. I mean, Mary's got the black-and-gray aesthetic covered. One of us has to be visible to the bartender, and she's basically a shadow.

But when I looked in the mirror, I didn't feel like I was wearing a cotton-spandex weave and drugstore-bright makeup. I was going into battle in Lydia-armor, wearing my old self on the outside to help steady my new, more wobbly self.

And I think it was a good decision, because the minute we pulled into Carter's parking lot, my stomach started flipping over like I'd just done a dozen cartwheels. Hence my "woo-hoo!" as an attempt to cover up said flipping.

We climbed out of the car and rounded the building to the front of Carter's.

"Whoa," Mary said.

"Whoa" was right. The line was out the door and halfway down the block. I've never seen the place so packed, and I had been a regular at Carter's during Swim Week.

Aaaaand there's another flippy-floppy stomach moment. Thinking about Swim Week. And who I met during Swim Week at Carter's.

Of course, he was into my sister Lizzie then. So he didn't really look at me. And since Lizzie was into him, I didn't really look his way, either. I just remember thinking, *He's hot. And he's nice, being all chivalrous and covering my sister's wet barstool with his swim jacket so she could sit. How did Lizzie get so lucky?*

Then, months later, he did look my way. And I started to think, *How did I get so lucky?*

The fuzzy memory made me feel stupid standing there, staring at the line outside of Carter's in my leopard-print top and purple eyeliner.

Dammit, this is exactly what I didn't want to happen. I wasn't here to reminisce. I was here to clear out school-related cobwebs, cut loose for one Friday night, two drinks and a relatively decent band. Nothing more, nothing less.

I grabbed Mary's hand. "Come on," I said, marching to the bouncer at the door.

"Hey, Mike," I said breezily as I barreled past him. Or tried to.

"My name's Chris," he said, barring my path.

"Chris, right. Sorry, you looked like Mike."

"No one who works here is named Mike."

"Right, so, Chris," I said, flipping my hair back and accidentally hitting Mary in the face with it. (Sorry, Mary.) "How much?"

"Cover is ten bucks. Line is back there."

"How long is the line if I give you twenty?" I asked.

Chris didn't even look at me. "It's ten per person, so the line would be the same."

Mary just hid her face in her hands. "Lydia . . ."

"I've got good door karma, just wait," I whispered to her. Or at least I used to. Squaring my shoulders, I fished in my pockets and turned back to Chris.

"What about"—I covertly counted my cash—"thirty dollars?"

"Don't insult me."

"Come on, thirty bucks, for like . . . thirty minutes? We just want to see the first couple of songs from the band. Violet's a friend of Mary's and—"

"Mary . . ." Chris checked his clipboard. "Mary Bennet?"

"Uh . . . yeah?" Mary said.

"You and your guest are on the list." He unclipped the rope—seriously, who was Carter kidding, getting a velvet rope—and let us past.

"See?" I said as we entered. "Still got it."

It was just as crowded inside as it was outside, but with the humid stickiness of lots of people corralled into a tight space. We wedged our way through the crowd toward the back, and miraculously found a high table with two barstools by the wall whose occupants were in the process of putting on their jackets. I can only assume the Karmic God of Bars (Matthew McConaughey) called one in for us, because we swooped in and took it the second the other people stepped away.

"Thank God," Mary said, practically throwing herself on the table.

"I know, right? I've never seen it like this." I knew Mary could tell what I was thinking. Violet's band must have been more than pretty decent.

"I don't even think I can cross the room to get to the bar," Mary said.

"Let me—I have skills."

"Skills like you had with Chris the bouncer?"

"Exactly," I said as I slipped away into the crowd. Thing is, I do have excellent crowd-management skills, and it applies well to everyday life.

Last year, I went to visit Jane when she was living in Los Angeles and she took me to all the touristy places I wanted to go—the Walk of Fame (I totally thought I was minutes away from getting my own star), Grauman's Theatre to see if my feet were bigger than Marilyn Monroe's (seriously, everyone's feet are bigger than Marilyn Monroe's). We were walking back to our car when we realized they were having a movie premiere at the ArcLight—which happens every five minutes in LA, Jane told me. But instead of walking four blocks around to get to the parking garage, I just grabbed Jane's hand, and ducked and weaved us through the crowd, getting us to our car in record time.

I credit my Just Dance moves. I can anticipate the change-up. (This skill is also good for malls at Christmastime.)

I quickly charted a path through the crowd, and was halfway to my goal of Carter and his extensive collection of microbrews when I dodged right instead of left and ended up bumping right into Cody.

"Lydia?" Cody asked, his face breaking out into a smile. "What are you doing here?"

And Harriet.

"OMG, Lydia," Harriet said, flipping her fat brown waves so hard I think she might have committed assault. She smiled tightly. "I totally never thought you would have come out to Carter's!"

"Really?" I said, my smile just as tight. "Why not?"

"Um . . ." Harriet's smile faltered. "That is a super-cute top, I've always loved it on you."

"Thanks. Well, I've got to grab some drinks, so . . ." I let that dangle as I weaved my way back into the crowd. I thought I heard Harriet's high-pitched laugh, but I couldn't be sure.

God, it's weird when you used to be friends with someone and then it suddenly becomes clear you never were. Why did Harriet even start hanging out with me last year? Boredom? My videos? So she could get a free ride to Vegas over New Year's?

I made it to the bar and squeezed in between two guys debating local brew types. I ordered my beers, paid, and shot a quick glance over my shoulder at Cody and Harriet. Harriet was saying something, but Cody wasn't paying attention—because he was looking directly at me.

Our eyes met. Oh, crap. I'd just accidentally given him the non-verbal green light to come over and talk to me.

He must have been skilled in the crowd-dodge, too, because he was next to me as soon as he could squeeze in.

"Sorry about Harriet."

"You don't have to apologize for her." You don't have to hang out with her, either.

"I was gonna ask you to come out to the show, but you got tied up with Latham. And Harriet said you wouldn't want to come out to Carter's, anyway," he said.

"Did Harriet tell you why?" I asked. I was done with talking around things—and I hadn't even had my first sip of beer.

"She . . . maybe alluded to stuff. . . ."

"Cody." That forced him to look at me. "Harriet doesn't know everything."

His eyes sparkled. "Yeah, I didn't think she did. There's always more to the story. Which I'd love to hear sometime, if you want to talk about it."

Definitely don't want to have that conversation. At least, not now. "Trying to analyze me?" I gave him my flirty smile instead. "This isn't psych class."

"Speaking of, how bad was your grade on the paper?"

I froze. "How bad . . . ?"

"It must have been bad to make a girl like you pounce on Latham after class."

I just shrugged. No need to share my disappointing C with anyone else.

"What do you mean, 'a girl like me'?"

"Someone who's generally . . . cooler about stuff. Was it at least a passing grade?"

I nodded.

"That's all that matters. It's community college, Lydia. No one's going to care. You can relax about it."

But what if I don't want to relax about it? What if *I* wanted to care?

Even though that's getting harder by the class. Especially knowing that I'll have to care about it for such a long time.

He must have read how I was feeling on my face because . . .

"Oh, shit, I did it again." He shook his head. "I stepped in it with you. I apologize. Let me pay for your beers to make up for it."

My beers arrived, and there was a line of people behind us, waiting for access to the bar.

"They're already paid for," I replied. "And you can't keep offering to buy me beverages when you think you've screwed up. It can't be fun, always being in someone's beverage debt."

"It's an admittedly weak way to try and make up for putting my foot in my mouth, but it's all I have." He let the side of his hand brush against my arm, resting against the bar. "Wanna come and stand with us? We got a pretty good view of the stage."

I grabbed the beers and pointed across the way to where Mary was defending my barstool with her death glare and combat boots.

"Thanks, but we got a table."

"Wow, how'd you swing that?"

"I'm Lydia Bennet. I have natural bar karma. Enjoy the show."

I left him standing at the bar with his mouth hanging slightly open. The trip back to the table was easier, because all the human traffic flowed toward the bar, not away from it, so I made it to Mary with only minimal spillage.

"Thanks," she said, moving her feet off my seat and taking a sip of her beer. "Who were you talking to?"

"Who?" I echoed, all casual. "Oh, Cody? He's in my psych class. Both my classes, actually."

"Uh-huh. And he's friends with Harriet?"

"Friends with her brother, I think."

I followed Mary's gaze to where Cody and Harriet were in the middle of the crowd. He wasn't looking at me this time, but he was talking in her ear—in that yelling whisper you have to do in crowds. She was giggling at whatever he said.

"They seem pretty tight."

"Whatever, the band's about to start," I said, pulling Mary's attention back up to the stage.

Violet and her band members had come out and were tuning their instruments. The murmurs of the crowd immediately shifted from normal, lazy bar chatter to "ohhhh, something's about to happen" chatter.

Violet said something to her drummer and then turned around to face the crowd.

"Violet!" I called out.

We were positioned well enough that she could hear me, and her hand came up to shield her eyes from the stage lights, so she could see out into the crowd.

"Wave," I whispered to Mary. Mary let her bangs fall in front of her face, but she held up her hand in a small wave. "Jeez, do I have to do everything?" I said, taking Mary's hand again and waving it, and mine—the world's biggest fangirls.

"Hey!" Violet waved back, her face breaking into a wide grin once she spotted us.

Violet looked different onstage. First of all, she wasn't in her barista uniform of black jeans, a ball cap, and an apron. But it wasn't only the rock clothes, or the guitar strapped across her body. It was something about the way she stood. Just completely owning the stage.

"Hello, Carter's!" she battle-cried into the mic. The crowd screamed back in response. "We are the Mechanics—let's get to work!" And they slammed into their first song. Super loud and super fast—just the way I like it—but with this total pop vibe.

Just the way I love it.

"Wow," I yelled over the music. "They are good!"

"I know, right?" Mary yelled back.

While I rocked out with the rest of the crowd, putting my hands up and moving to the beat (from my chair—there was no way I was moving my butt off the seat), Mary rocked out in her own way . . . which consisted of watching the stage intently and barely moving her head in time to the music. But I could tell she was totally into it. Which is good. Eddie and his roadkill songs don't get to take everything from her.

Violet and her band ran through their opening number and

slid directly into their second. It was slower and deeper, but I still dug it.

The marginally calmer music made the crowd less headbanging, and let someone slip through a little easier.

"These are for you," said Chris the bouncer.

On a tray he carried two beers. We were only half done with our first round, so this was surprising. Also surprising was the idea of table service at Carter's.

"O . . . kay," I said, wary. "Um, thanks? Is this to say sorry for trying to block us on our way in?"

Chris had a glare Mary could aspire to. "They're not from me. They're from him."

He pointed into the crowd, where Cody was watching us out of the corner of his eye. When he saw us looking in his direction, he raised his beer in a toast.

"He grabbed me from the door and paid me an obscene amount of money to deliver these to you. And to say the following." He cleared his throat and looked like he would rather be doing anything else. "He says he is happy to be in your beverage debt."

I raised an eyebrow and glanced over Chris's shoulder to Cody again. "Okay. Could you tell him—"

"No." Chris held up a hand. "I'm not a singing telegram. If you want to tell your boyfriend anything, do it yourself."

And with that, Chris put his tray under his arm and went back to being miserable at the door.

Mary looked from her half-drunk beer to her new, full one. "Anything I should know about?"

I took a sip of my new beer, even though the old one was right there, and let my eyes slide back toward Cody. "Not yet."

The band played for the next hour without stopping. And Mary and I rocked out (in our own ways), just drinking our beers and enjoying ourselves.

And God, how long had it been since I'd just enjoyed myself?

Lost the noise of everybody and everything and just existed in the here and now? It was amazing to completely forget about psych class and gothic lit and Ms. W and applications and my sisters and apartments and just . . . breathe, you know?

Mary was right. I needed this.

By the time the Mechanics took a break, Violet's clothes were sticking to her skin and she'd gone through two bottles of water, layers of tank tops, and popped a string off her guitar.

"All right, everyone! We're going to fix our instruments—and dry off—and we'll be back in a few!" Violet announced before the band waved to the crowd and headed off the stage. They were all as in need of a recharge as Violet was, given the way the bassist leaped from the stage and ran to the back. But even though she must have been worn the eff out, Violet still scanned the crowd, found us, and waved to Mary.

"I know you think she's an annoying boss, but she's super cool," I said.

"I don't think she's annoying," Mary protested. "But . . ."

"But what . . . ?"

"I dunno. She's my boss. And I've never had a boss before who wanted to hang outside of work. And she's . . . she's just Violet. Like, so nice it's weird. She even invited us backstage."

A very high-pitched noise vibrated in my ears.

It might have been me.

"We get to go backstage?!?" I squealed.

"Well, we could." Mary seemed to consider it for a second. But then she just shook her head. "But we'd have to give up our table . . ."

"Mary, I have never ever been backstage at a rock concert and you will not deny me this!" I grabbed Mary's hand and pulled her through the crowd and toward the back.

Turns out, backstage is really just the supply room off Carter's kitchen, next to the walk-in freezer—which must have been running at full blast. I was so, so glad I'd brought my jacket with me, even though it forced us to abandon our claim on our miracle table.

We slipped into the room and stood next to the boxes of frozen buffalo wings, completely unnoticed.

Unnoticed because Violet and her bassist were having a surprise shouting match.

"That was complete bullshit—you started on the one when I told you to start on the three!" the bassist yelled.

"Duke, we've always started on the one. Always. You can't just tell me to start on the three five seconds before—"

"It always sounds shitty on the one! If you were any kind of musician you'd know that—"

"And if you were any kind of professional you'd play the gig and let us work this out in rehearsals!"

"Just because I don't want to sound like crap when we play *I'm* unprofessional?" Duke said. "You know what, princess? Screw you."

And with that, Duke stormed out, shouldering me on his way to the back door.

"Hey!" I cried. "Uncool, Duke!"

And then everyone was looking at us. The two randos standing by the spiced chicken parts.

"Hey, Mary, Lydia," Violet said, distracted. "Sorry, um, things are a little . . . dodgy right now."

"Totally get it," Mary said, backing away from the buffalo wings. "Come on, Lydia." But as we backed out of the supply room, the drummer, who I remembered being introduced onstage as Genevieve, came up to Violet.

"That jackass. What are we gonna do now?" she said.

"Duke will be back," Violet replied. "He's just being a prima donna. As per usual."

"Before we have to go back out there?" Genevieve pointed her thumb toward the hall to the stage. Behind Mary and me, we could hear the beginnings of a low rumble. One that grew into a chant.

"Me-chan-ics . . . Me-chan-ics . . ."

"Whoa," Violet said. "Shit. Gen, go out back and grab Duke—once he hears that, he'll chill out. I've gotta fix my G string."

Mary tugged at me. "Lydia, *let's go*. We shouldn't be here."

But just that second, Gen zoomed past us again.

"He's not there."

"He's not out back smoking one of his stupid cigarillos?" Violet's head came up.

"No. And neither is the car."

Her eyes went crazy wide. "He took the car? *My* car? Shit. Shit, shit, shit." She began to pace in time to the chanting, which was growing louder and louder. "What are we going to do? We can't go out without a bassist."

"Mary can do it."

Every single eye flew to me—and the fastest was Mary's.

"Mary?" Violet asked.

"She plays bass guitar."

"Not, like, onstage!" Mary said, going pale. Well, paler.

"She's really good, though. And she knows all your songs. She's listened to your CD."

"That's right, you would have!" Violet replied, swooping over toward us and grabbing Mary by the elbow.

"But . . . I'm not . . . No, this isn't a good idea," Mary protested, her voice shaking a little.

"We only have three songs in our encore," Violet was saying, her eyes glued to Mary's. "And all the chords are super easy and on a four/four. It's nothing crazy—you'd totally be able to follow along. It's just for tonight. To save our asses."

"I . . . well, I . . . guess?" Mary squeaked.

Violet grabbed Mary into a rib-crushing hug, as the rest of the band swooped around her. "Gen, show her the set list. Jones, grab Duke's bass, make sure it's in tune, and give it to Mary. Come on, guys, we've got ninety seconds before that crowd loses it."

I jumped up and down, clapping with glee. Mary sent me a look of sheer terror, but I gave her the world's biggest thumbs-up. "I'm gonna go get a good spot. Break a leg, Mary!"

"I don't want to break a—" I heard her say before she got swallowed up by the rest of the Mechanics, and I squeezed my way back into the barroom.

As suspected, the miracle table had been taken over by a couple of frat bros high-fiving over their good luck. But that was cool; I wanted to be standing in the crowd for this. I wanted a good spot from which to witness Mary's debut.

Less than a minute later, Violet and her bandmates reemerged from the back . . . including Mary. Who, to her credit, did not look like a deer in headlights. She looked like a deer that had actually gotten hit by the car and was walking away, stunned.

The crowd roared as they came out. But there was no way they could drown out my screams.

"WOOOOOOOOO, MAAAAAAAARRRRRYYYYYYY!!!!!!!"

From her expression, I'm pretty sure Mary heard me.

"Y'all want more?" Violet said into the mic. "Careful what you wish for—one, two, three, four!"

And they launched into their song. For the first minute or so, Mary looked like she was playing catch-up, watching Violet and Jones (the other guitarist) for her cues, but soon enough, she relaxed into the gig. Started listening to the music she was playing.

Ten seconds later, Mary had a crazy smile on her face.

It was like seeing the yeti.

I whipped out my phone. Why hadn't I been videoing this from the beginning? I held it up, turned it on, and . . . nothing.

"Crap!" I swore to myself. "Battery's dead."

Then, I spied another phone in the audience. Harriet's. She was standing next to Cody, and annoyingly taking a selfie with him in the middle of Mary's moment.

But it gave me an idea.

I wedged my way through the crowd over to them. Harriet just looked at me, dismissed me, and turned back to watch the band. But whatevs, she wasn't my object.

"Hey, Cody—let me borrow your phone. Mine's dead."

He turned to me, blinked twice, then handed it over.

"What do you need it for?" he whisper-yelled into my ear.

"My cousin—" I said, pointing. "Look!"

He found Mary in the back of the band, jamming away. "Awesome!" he said. "You have to get that."

I held up his phone and hit record. Holding a phone steady above the waving hands of other partygoers while moving along to the music yourself is not easy, but I have skills.

"Oh, look at Mary!" Harriet said from Cody's other side, suddenly remembering my cousin existed and also trying to bring his attention back to her. "Are you going to put her online again, Lydia? It was always sooooo funny when she didn't want to be on camera—"

"No," I said, shutting her up. "This is just for me. And her."

Harriet's jaw clamped shut. Then, her voice turned all sickly sweet. "Hey, Cody—I'd love another beer."

"Oh, great. Me, too." He fished a bill out of his pocket. "Thanks."

Harriet had no choice but to stomp over to the bar, leaving us in the crowd, swaying to the music as the band transitioned into a slower, more mellow song.

"You're being kind of an ass to her," I said.

"She's been kind of an ass to you," he replied. "I know she left you in Vegas and everything."

I tried not to let the cold dread slide into my stomach. Vegas. Yeah, last New Year's, Harriet and I went to Vegas. We were supposed to hang out, but she and some other people abandoned me. And I ended up running into George Wickham.

Among other happenings.

But the only way Cody could know that is if he watched my

videos from last year. Those pesky things that keep retelling their history to everyone who wants to listen.

"Maybe you shouldn't have brought her out here tonight then."

"Maybe," he conceded. "She's okay. But I chickened out on asking the person I wanted to."

"That's a shame," I replied.

"What do you think that person would have said?"

"That person would have told you to take a hike." Out of the corner of my eye, I watched him break into a grin.

He leaned into my ear. "I like you, Lydia."

I felt his hand on the small of my back, just a light touch.

"I'm not sure if I like you yet," I replied. "But you're growing on me."

* * *

After the band finished their encore, they swept offstage like they were just declared the winners in the Battle of Being Awesome. I let Cody email me the video I took, but then I slipped backstage to hang with Mary before he could do or say anything else.

It's okay. He had to take Harriet home. Besides, I didn't know how I felt about what he said to me. All I know is that the night was awesome, with this buzzy energy that made everything better. So I'd think about that stuff later.

"That was amazing!" I said, grabbing Mary into a bear hug. "Ewww, you're all sweaty. I don't care, though." And I hugged her again.

"Yeah, Mary, you really saved our butts," Violet said, grinning wide. "Didn't she, guys?"

Genevieve and Jones nodded, shaking Mary's hand. "You did good, Bennet," Gen said, while Jones winked at her. Which made me grin like an idiot at a blushing Mary.

"Yeah, yeah, guys, give her some air," Violet said, shooing them away. "Now, um, I hate to ask this, but . . . those guys are going to take the equipment in the van back to their place, but it's a pretty tight squeeze. Would you mind saving my ass one more time and giving me a ride home?"

We crammed into Mary's car about an hour later, after playing roadie and helping Jones and Genevieve load all the band's equipment into their van. Actually, it was a minivan. Midnineties model. Never let it be said the life of a rock band isn't the height of cool.

We waved to them as they drove off, then loaded into Mary's car.

We were all super amped after the show. Even Violet, who said she'd been up since four to open the coffee shop that morning, was riding an adrenaline high. We chattered on about nothing and everything, until we pulled up in front of an apartment complex near the community college.

"Thank you so much for the ride," Violet said, opening the door in the backseat, one leg out of the car. "And Mary, thanks again for tonight. I didn't expect someone who could actually play—you kept up with the changes, and on a minute's notice, too."

"Thanks," Mary mumbled, tucking her hair behind her ear. "I . . . had a not entirely unawesome time."

"Awesome." Violet grinned. "I'm so glad you guys came out."

And with that, Violet lurched forward and quasi-strangled Mary in a hug around the driver's seat. "See you Monday at work!"

We waited in the car until Violet waved to us from the door of the apartment complex, slipping inside. "Awww . . ." I said. "You made a friend out of your boss. Not bad for a Friday night, two beers, and a pretty decent band."

"Shut up," Mary said, rolling her eyes.

"And you totally rocked it out onstage."

"Whatever," she mumbled, totally trying to hide her smile by putting the car into gear.

"I have video, I'll prove it to you."

I pulled out my phone and plugged it into Mary's car charger. I waited impatiently for the poor, tired thing to light up and download Cody's email of the video.

Finally it opened to my home screen, and dinged.

But it wasn't the video. It was something else.

Reminder: Central Bay College application due! Midnight.

I froze. Every drop of liquid in my body crystallized and started to crack. It was due. My application was due. No, not due—*past* due. I glanced at the clock on the dash. It was way after midnight. My phone had been dead and I missed the alarm.

"What is it?" Mary asked, as she turned onto to the main street of our little town. "Is the video terrible? Am I gross-sweaty?"

"No," I said quickly. "It hasn't downloaded yet. I'll . . . I'll just show you tomorrow."

Mary shrugged and kept on driving, humming one of the Mechanics' songs under her breath.

Shit.

Chapter Fourteen

SPIRAL

I've never been able to get my hair to hold a curl. It's always just straight. Sometimes I can tease it out with entire bottles of mousse, get it to look semi-tousled, but there's no curl there. Ever.

I have chosen this topic to fixate on because the alternative is FREAKING OUT.

And I've already done that. All weekend.

When Mary and I got home on Friday after the show, we snuck in the front door—shh, parents sleeping!—and straight up to our rooms. Mary crashed immediately, coming down off her adrenaline high.

I didn't. Because, duh.

Instead, I spent the hours before dawn frantically checking to make sure this wasn't some horrific cosmic joke.

Nope. Today's date was circled in my two-year-old day planner.

And the Post-it on my computer had today's date on it, too.

And the date listed on the application was today. Although, since it was past midnight, it's more correct to say "yesterday," right?

Not that it matters.

I only managed to fall asleep once I made a plan. I would call Central Bay College's admissions office in the morning. I'd just explain that my Post-its failed me and my phone died and ask for an extension. Of my extension. No biggie, right?

Kind of a biggie. Because, turns out, the admissions office wasn't open on Saturdays.

Or Sundays.

So what the hell else was I supposed to do all weekend? Cue obsessing over my hair.

And when I ran out of mousse, I obsessed over whether I should get Kitty those claw covers that look like nail polish, and then I hopped back on Twitter just to read every tweet from Ke$ha over the past year.

Maybe I should redye my hair. It's way faded.

Seriously, how can the admissions office be closed on Saturdays? Colleges don't close on the weekends. I've been to more than a couple college parties, and that's when the best ones always are. If I worked in an admissions office, being there on the weekends would be a perk.

Even my school—my *community college*—is open on the weekends. I know, because I had to go there on Sunday. For my counseling session.

I could have skipped. Maybe I should have skipped. But if I did, Ms. W would have totally known something was up. And yeah, her insightful tendencies could also lead her to figure out that something's up, but here her therapy training failed her.

Because she didn't have a clue.

I must be a really outstanding actress. I mean, I didn't get cast as the lead munchkin in my fifth-grade staging of *The Wizard of Oz* without having *some* talent—I was the tallest girl in my grade.

"So, how was your paper?" she asked as we were sitting down.

"Paper?"

"On the Milgram Experiment?"

"Oh. That." God, my paper seemed like a million years ago. And a C sure as hell didn't seem like the end of the world anymore. Perspective, huh? "It was fine."

"Fine?"

"I told you, the professor loves me." I shrugged, crossing my arms over my chest.

I thought I saw her squint for a split second, but I must have been imagining it because she immediately continued on: "Well, that's good to hear. But—"

"Ms. W, do we really have to talk about my grades? I don't come to counseling to have you make sure I'm doing my homework."

"All right," she said, her voice doing that calm thing that normally actually calms me, but this time it just sort of made me more uncomfortable. "Last time, we were talking a bit about how you are going to transition to Central Bay College—you seemed very positive about it."

"I am." Yup, positive. Because it's totally going to happen. Once the stupid freaking admissions office opens in the morning. WHY AREN'T THEY OPEN ON WEEKENDS???

"And are you feeling equally positive about leaving home?"

"Duh."

"Hmm," Ms. W said, writing something down on her notepad. Which only made me feel more uncomfortable. "I mention it because sometimes students with as much drive as you have to move on to the next step . . . find the transition more difficult than they expected."

"It's not going to be a problem. I mean, I'm so ready," I said. "And shouldn't I be? I've been in community college way too long. I'm not going to miss it. I'm not going to get sentimental for the campus parking lot, or that weird shade of yellow in the hallways. I'm not even going to miss you."

Ms. W sat up a little straighter. "Me?" she asked, her voice completely neutral.

"Counseling," I corrected, although her expression didn't change. "I mean, I'm good. Honestly, I sort of feel like coming here today was kind of a waste of time. My classes are fine; my life is fine; things are so normal now it's boring. We've been over everything, and since we only have like, two sessions left after this, why even bother? Just rip the Band-Aid off already."

"That's an interesting choice of words," Ms. W said, placing her notebook aside. "So you feel that you are . . . healed, for lack of a better term?"

"Maybe? But if I am, isn't that a good thing? And you can put a gold star sticker next to my name and be the one who fixed me."

Ms. W leaned forward, putting her forearms on her knees and lacing her fingers together in front of her. She looked me dead in the eye.

"Lydia, the work we do in here is not about me 'fixing' you. Nor is it about you fixing yourself. It's about us exploring your feelings, and how those feelings influence your actions. Then, we can create methods that help you find balance between said feelings and actions. Does that make sense?"

I nodded.

"It's a process of learning. And while I know you currently feel that since we have so little time left, any effort we make might be futile, I hope you'll consider keeping your next few appointments. Even if you don't have anything you want to talk about."

I just nodded again.

I bought a new can of mousse on my way home.

From the school's website, I knew the admissions office opened at 8:00 a.m. I set my alarm for 6:45 a.m., so I could have some coffee, prepare what I wanted to say, know how to pitch my voice so I sounded super sweet and apologetic and responsible, just completely taken off guard by the due date, considering I only received the form a couple of weeks ago. The admissions lady would totally understand. And everything would be fine.

I was up at 5:00 a.m.

Kitty looked at me like I'd grown a second, slightly less adorable head. Which she usually does, but it seemed particularly judge-y this time. I threw her a catnip-laced squeak toy and watched her flip herself over and around on the floor trying to conquer it.

I know how she feels.

Four cups of coffee, a shower, three outfits, a lot of reading nothing on the Internet, and one last attempt to get my hair to curl (nope) later, the clock on my phone ticked over to eight o'clock.

Three deep breaths. Then dial.

Ring.

Ring.

. Answering machine.

Seriously. Answering machine. It's almost like the admissions office doesn't realize they have a potential student with her life falling apart on the line so they just take their sweet-ass time opening up the office for the morning.

It took three more calls before someone finally picked up, at 8:04 a.m.

"Central Bay College Admissions Office," a tired-sounding admissions lady said.

"Hi, my name is Lydia Bennet, and I'm a fall semester student?"

"Hold on, let me log in to my computer." I could hear shuffling. This was absolute torture. I could picture her. Middle-aged, wearing a terrible color combo, taking off her coat, throwing it over the back of her chair, and then straightening it out and picking the cat hairs off it. Then, finally, turning on a computer even older than mine and humming to herself as she waited for it to boot up.

Well, that part I didn't have to picture. I could hear the humming.

It didn't help.

"What was your name again?"

I told her. And as she typed it into her computer, I told her my whole story. I made it as sob-tastic as I could. I told her about how they actually *had* most of my transfer application on file. That I could kick myself for missing the original form, but I was *so* very grateful they had emailed it to me. But with so little time to complete it, and the fact I was finishing up my credit requirements, and I was working in a coffee shop—okay, that part I made up, but they'd never check it and desperate times call for the occasional white lie—I hadn't realized I'd missed the deadline to turn it in, and surely they could give me an extension? A small one?

"I'm sorry, but we can't."

I was pretty sure the floor fell out from under me. It felt like it. I had to look down to make sure it was still there.

"But . . . not even a week? A couple days?"

I heard her sigh. "There are a limited number of transfer spots available every year. And usually applicants have all their paperwork in by the spring. We'd given you the extension to last Friday because of the . . . quality of your recommendations," she said, and I knew she had gotten to the part of my file that mentioned Darcy. "However, the application process is officially closed as of this past weekend. The fall semester starts in a month. We simply cannot hold up the machine any longer."

"But . . . can't you squeeze me in?" I dug through my panicking brain for Lizzie-speak. "I guarantee you I will be a vital asset to your campus and an upstanding scholar."

"If we squeezed you in, we'd have to do it for everyone. And we don't have that much space. Now, if you had contacted us earlier about the delay . . ."

"You weren't open on the weekend!" I could hear the defensiveness in my voice, and I hated it. Admissions Lady hated it, too, because when she spoke next, it was basically like taking an ice bath.

"What I meant was, had you notified us earlier that the application would be delayed, we might have been able to assist you."

"I didn't know the application was going to be delayed, because I didn't realize the due date was so soon . . ." I took a deep breath. Three. Then, I just let all the crap fall to the side. "I screwed up. I know that. But is there anything I can do to unscrew it? If so, please tell me."

There was a long pause. I crossed my fingers.

"If you can send me the completed forms we are missing right now, then I can probably go into the system and 'squeeze you in,' as you put it."

"Right now?" I asked. "Not even one day . . . ?"

"Right now. Otherwise . . . you are welcome to apply for next semester, although there are far fewer transfer slots available in the spring."

"No, I . . . I got it. I'll send it right away," I said, adding, "Thank you," before I hung up the phone.

I just stared at the phone for a little while. I don't know how long, but I only looked up finally because Kitty was scratching at the door to be let out. I should be rushing to my computer, emailing the admissions office my forms, and breathing a sigh of relief.

But I can't.

Because it's still not done. The essay. And now, it never will be.

Why the hell didn't I do the essay this weekend, instead of obsessing about my stupid hair? I went through three cans of mousse! Why didn't I just sit my ass down at the computer and write? Write anything. You know what would be a good moment when I experienced failure to write about?

That time I missed my deadline for the application to go to college.

And not just college. A *good* college. A college where I wouldn't be a screwup.

Except I am a screwup. All over again.

I wasted this weekend. Hell, I'd wasted the last three weeks. Why didn't I just write the freaking essay?

Why couldn't I write the essay?

All of this throbbed in my brain as I went over to open the door for Kitty, and found Mary standing right there, hand raised to knock.

"What are you doing?"

"Good morning?" Mary said, bringing her hand down.

"Were you eavesdropping?"

"No. Were you talking?"

I forced the panic back down into my stomach from where it had risen in my throat. "Just, like, talking to Kitty. Stupid stuff."

"Right. Well, it would have to be. If you were talking to a cat."

"Whatevs, did you need something?" I said, leaning against the door. "I'm going to be late for class."

"I was wondering if you'd want to carpool."

"Carpool?" I said, crossing to grab my bag, heavy with books and notes. I just wanted to throw it across the room. "You work later than I'm in school."

"Yeah, but Violet said she could give me a ride after work. She doesn't live too far from us. You take the car home. This way we can save on gas money. Maybe we can afford an apartment with only three roommates instead of four?"

I had to choke down a burst of hysterical laughter. *God, Mary,* I thought, *if you only knew.*

What was Mary going to say when I told her? What was she going to do?

I should have just told her then. I should have just blurted it out, and let her know that *Lydia Did It Again.* I'd screwed up not just my life, but hers, too.

But I didn't.

"Fine," I said instead, throwing my bag over my shoulder. "I'm driving."

Chapter Fifteen
ROUTINE

Monday

"When we talk about motivation, outside of the primary drive we have to survive, we are talking basically about two things."

There's this weird thing that happens when everything falls apart. It's happened to me before, so I know. Your body, the normal one you live in every day, sort of starts to exist apart from you. You're still there, of course. Still hanging out. But it all goes on autopilot, getting you through the days while you . . . contract.

"Intrinsic motivation—which is internal—is the desire to do something because it inherently pleases you."

For instance, as I drove to school that morning, dropping Mary off at the coffee shop, I have no memory of taking the correct turns, or pulling into the parking lot. My body just did it for me. Because my mind was swollen, trying to process what the hell I was going to do now.

I do remember that I told myself I couldn't cry. Not in front of Mary. So I didn't. I turned it off. Autopilot took care of the rest.

"And extrinsic motivation, which is the desire to take action because of the consequences resulting from it. Either reward or punishment."

And Professor Latham? I know he was talking. I know he put up slide after slide on his PowerPoint. I couldn't tell you what was on them, though, even though I copied every word down.

If it's not important, it isn't getting in. Autopilot would handle it.

And I need autopilot today. Because everything going on in my head is nothing more than a dull noise.

God, I bought a sweater in Central Bay colors. What the hell am I going to do with the stupid thing now? Way to jump the gun there, Lydia.

And it's not like I didn't get accepted. That "almost" would have been better, somehow. I'd be able to say, *Oh, well, you tried your best; we'll figure it out later, but for now, enjoy your fro-yo and wallowing.* And what's more, everyone else would say that, too. That this time, I really did try my best. But . . .

This isn't that. Because with my Darcy recommendation, I had basically been guaranteed a spot. It was *mine*. I just . . . hadn't taken it. I had only tried to try. And that wasn't good enough.

Why? I mean, I wanted it. It was the only thing I wanted. To go up to San Francisco with Mary. To have a plan mapped out for myself, helping people. When someone asked, "So, Lydia, what are your plans for the future?" *to have an actual answer.*

. . . but if I wanted it so much, why didn't I just take it?

You know, why do I *need* to fill out a stupid essay application, anyway? Who cares about my failures? You know what would have made a far more interesting essay? My successes. They are cooler and way more rare. Don't colleges *want* people who are successful?

But failure . . . who wants to stare at their failures? Who wants to let other people read them, as a standard for whether you get into a school?

This was the constant loop running through my head when I felt my phone buzz in my pocket, temporarily breaking me out of my autopilot.

You ok?

I glanced up. Cody, three rows in front, had his computer opened and his back to me. I could see the IM box on his screen open and blinking.

Fine, I typed. *Why?*

I waited. He typed.

You seem a little off. Too much fun this weekend? ;)

I was so surprised, I didn't even care about the winky face. Out of everyone, how is it Cody who noticed something's wrong? Mary certainly didn't. She was her usual unchatty self as we drove in today, her head buried in a Neil Gaiman book. And my parents barely glanced at us as we came through the kitchen. My mom just forced food on us, as per usual, and my dad, who hadn't left for the office yet for some reason, told us we better "hurry along, or else we'll be late" from behind his newspaper.

But Cody was not so oblivious. Weird. And interesting.

Yeah, long weekend. That's all. What was yours like?

I waited. Cody sat up a little straighter, surprised when my message popped up on his screen.

Nothing as fun as Friday night . . .

I smiled. Just a little, and for the first time since the Friday night in question. It felt really, really good to let my brain do something else, even if it was just for a second.

A really short second.

"Miss Bennet, as I have said before . . ." Professor Latham said, breaking through my phone-focus (yeah, that's a phrase now, deal with it) and making me look up.

And making everyone else look up at me, too.

But this time, I just shrugged it off. I didn't care that they were looking. Autopilot was back on.

"Yup, no phones," I said, putting it away. Whatever. "Got it."

Wednesday

"Welcome to Books Beans and Buds. Go, Pioneers. We do not sell pot here; can I interest you in a budding beverage?"

Mary stared dead-eyed at the poncho-wearing stoner standing in line in front of me. Even if his glazed eyes and weird lean didn't give him away, his hemp necklace did. Way to be a stereotype, dude.

"Whuh . . . ?"

"We. Do. Not. Sell. Pot. Here," Mary said, making sure every syllable got into the stoner's brain. I rolled my eyes. Mary caught it and rolled her eyes right back at me. "Can I interest you in a budding beverage?"

"Um . . . I'll need a minute," the stoner said.

Mary looked around him to me. "Mochaccino?"

"Thanks."

She stepped away to put together my drink, leaving the stoner standing at the counter. Swaying slightly.

You know what's great about autopilot? You're so busy caring about one big thing, you stop caring about all the other little things.

Like rules.

"Hey," I said, low to him. "You looking to buy?"

He looked over at me, kinda suspicious, but his drug-fueled paranoia lost to his desire for more drugs.

"Yeah. You got some?"

"Not me, but . . ."

I nodded to Mary, where she was working the frothing machine like she'd been barista-ing for much longer than a month.

"But she said—" The stoner looked so confused. Poor stoner. Maybe some coffee would perk him up.

"You just have to know how to order it." I leaned in, like a conspirator in a spy movie. "Order a small coffee, black. Then put a twenty in the tip jar."

"And then . . ."

"And then . . . she'll give you the coffee."

Stoner's bloodshot eyes went wide. "Ohhh . . . she'll give me the 'coffee.' Got it."

Mary came back, my mochaccino in hand. "Here you go."

"Thanks," I said, and headed to the doctoring station. I didn't need to add any more sugar to my sugary drink, I just wanted a view.

"I'll take a small coffee, *black*," Stoner said, as he confidently deposited two crumpled ten-dollar bills in the tip jar on the counter.

Mary looked from the stoner, to the tip jar, back to the stoner again. "Okay, then," she said, wary. "One small coffee."

She went to go pour it out, and Stoner looked around like he'd just won the lottery. But then she came back with just coffee, and handed it to him.

"That's one twenty-five," she said.

"I . . . have to pay for that, too?"

"Yes. That's how this works."

"But it's in here, right? The . . . 'coffee?'"

Mary, still as apathetic as ever, took the world's deepest breath before she answered, "Yup. Put it in there myself. One twenty-five."

"Okay . . ." Stoner, looking a little lost, dug into his pocket again and pulled out what other money he had left. Then he took his coffee and hurried out the door with his contraband as I watched, smirking.

"I saw that," Violet's voice came from behind me. She was holding a mop, having just finished with a spill under a table.

"Saw what?" I asked innocently. "Oh, did I accidentally give that guy the impression that there was marijuana in his coffee? Oopsie."

Violet bit back a smile. "He's gonna come back here, demanding to know why he didn't get high."

"Please," I replied. "You're assuming he can *find* his way back here."

At that moment, Stoner guy was still standing outside the coffee shop, taking two steps one way, then two steps the other, trying to remember where he parked his car, probably.

"Fair point," Violet said. "But no more tricking the druggies."

"Hey, maybe he will get a high just because he expects to. Operant conditioning, you know?" I said, as I headed to my usual table. At least I was getting *something* out of psych class. Even though it was pointless otherwise.

"I don't think operant conditioning is the right methodology," Violet mused, coming over to the table. "Maybe expectancy theory?"

"I guess? We haven't gotten that far in class yet." Or we might have. But the past two classes, it's been a little hard to give a damn about what Professor Latham was saying. Today, I barely took any notes. I mostly doodled in my notebook.

I drew a lot of ponies. I wonder if that would mean anything to Freud or Jung. It could just mean that once I had a pony.

I miss Mr. Wuffles.

"I'd be happy to tell you all about it," Violet said, as soon as I sat down. "Mary mentioned you might need some psych tutoring? I can absolutely help—I even still have all my notes from my classes at NAU."

"Oh," I said, feeling my stomach drop to my shoes. "Um, I think I'm okay."

Violet's forehead wrinkled. "You sure? She said you had a paper that you worked really hard on but—"

"Yeah. But it's fine, now. I talked to the professor about it." The bell above the door tinkled as someone new came in. "And I'm totally getting assistance. Cody!"

At the sound of his name, Cody looked around the coffee shop and found me, waving him over.

"Hey, Lydia," he said, a little surprised.

"Cody and I are study buddies. I've got this psych thing covered."

"Okay," Violet said, turning from me to smile at Cody. "Just thought I'd let you know if you needed help—"

"No, I got it. But thanks so much for the offer. Super great of you."

Violet and her mop went back behind the counter.

"OMG, you just saved me," I said as he sat down across from me.

He looked over to where Violet was helping Mary make drinks. "Not into hanging out with the baristas?"

"Just . . . my cousin trying to help me. It's too much dabbling, you know?"

"Uh-oh . . ." Cody said. "I know what this is."

"You do?"

"Halfway through class, and all the gung ho you had at the beginning has gung hoed," he said, grinning at me. "Now you see it for the slog it is. I wouldn't be doing it if I didn't have to. Would you?"

"I . . . guess not," I replied. Before, I had been all about my classes, because they were going to be interesting, and they were going to get me to the place I wanted to go. Now . . . I'm not going to that place. And that makes them way less interesting.

"Now is when you start hearing that little voice inside your head saying . . . 'It's a nice summer day. Why am I going to Gothic Lit and not the beach?'"

"Well, do you have any advice for how to get that voice to quiet down?" I said. "You know, some extrinsic motivation to counter the intrinsic lack of motivation?"

"In my opinion? Listen to him."

"Oh, really?" I replied. "Voices in your head have that much sway over you?"

"I just respect the occasional mental health day." He leaned in to me. "I mean, after everything you've been through this year, don't you deserve a break?"

I considered it. It was a nice day out. A beach-worthy day. Even my paleness seemed, for once, too pale. And I'd bet Cody had a beach-worthy body under that plain T-shirt. But I looked over and saw Mary behind the counter. She glanced my way. Violet must have told her about the study-buddy comment.

Expectations. She had them. And so did I, sort of. Even though I don't really know what they are anymore.

Guess I still do care. Just enough.

"Nice try," I said. "But I'm going to class."

"I had to give it a shot." Cody stood, grabbing his bag. "Shall we depart?"

Friday

More ponies in psych class. I turned in another paper. This one on motivation. But hell if I have any. I'll get a C on that paper, too. I don't think Professor Latham gives out anything but C's, at least not to me. So why kill myself on it, right? There's no one to impress, I just have to pass. Not do well, not kick ass. Just . . . get through it.

I wished I was doing literally anything else.

Gothic Lit was more interesting. Not because of the subject matter, but because Cody sat next to me. Where his knee could occasionally bump into mine. Or our elbows might bump up against each other.

And Harriet, of course, was stuck across from us.

I know I said that I didn't sign up to be part of some angsty love triangle this summer, but if Harriet still thinks she's part of this geometry, the past couple of Gothic Lit classes must have killed that idea.

It wasn't just that on Wednesday—and today—we entered the class together, sat next to each other, laughing about stuff. She'd seen that before. But when he leaned over and said something to me while Natalie was talking, I might have listened more to him than I did the lecture on Poe.

Yeah, not a fan of Poe, anyway. The writer of dark, twisty stories is weird and pale and depressed in real life. Shocker.

Poe could have really done with some girl-power music and a day at the beach.

So could Mary, come to think of it.

But anyway, after class on Wednesday, Harriet came up to Cody, tried flipping her hair, gossiping about class, and there was nothing. He just said, "Ready to go, Lydia?" and he and I walked out to our cars together, Harriet tagging along behind us, totally hating every step she took. Cody and I loitered by our cars in the parking lot, and Harriet sort of hung out beside us, trying to jump into the conversation. Eventually, she just hugged her notebook to her chest and said a halfhearted "Bye, guys!" and wandered over to her car.

By the time she drove away, I almost felt sorry for her.

Almost.

And today after class, she didn't even try to talk to him. She just slid away in pre-defeat.

I fully expect the rumors about Stupid Whorey Slut Lydia Bennet will be back in action come Monday. But again . . . stopped caring.

However, after class today, Cody and I didn't walk out together—because Natalie pulled me aside and asked to talk to me.

"Want me to wait?" Cody asked.

"No, it's okay. See you Monday," I said, and turned back to Natalie. I was a little exhausted by Cody, admittedly.

"Is everything okay? You were awfully quiet in class," Natalie said as soon as the doors shut and we were alone. Actually, I hadn't been that quiet and felt a little guilty about that. I just hadn't been talking about Poe, or to the class at large. "I was hoping you'd weigh in on the reading."

"The reading?"

"'The Tell-Tale Heart,'" Natalie said.

"Oh, that," I said. "I, um, didn't really get around to it yesterday." I totally intended to read it at Books Beans and Buds in between classes, but I accidentally left my Poe book at home. Besides, Cody was there to distract me, so it's not like I would have gotten a lot of reading done, anyway.

"Well, that's a shame. I always look forward to your insights."

"You do?"

"Yes," Natalie said, laughing. "Why is that so surprising?"

I shrugged, unable to come up with a properly insightful answer. But the way Natalie was looking at me, like the class actually *mattered* and I was disappointing her, just made me feel weirdly guilty.

And I didn't really want to feel guilty.

"Well . . . if you do have any insights, you can share them on Monday," Natalie said.

"Uh-huh, okay, see you Monday!" I said as cheerfully as someone released from school on a Friday afternoon in summer can sound, and headed out the door.

Cody, as instructed, hadn't waited for me. So I threw on my shades, strutted across the campus to the power-anthem soundtrack playing in my head, climbed in my car, and drove home.

By the time I got there, the power anthems had died, and the quiet had settled in.

"Mom? Dad?" I called out. My parents weren't home, it seemed. No idea where they were or what they might be doing (ew, brain, don't go there), but having the house to myself was a rarity. I could pig out on leftovers in the fridge. I could watch soap operas. I could dig out some of Jane's old craft supplies and use her fancy scissors to cut decorative trim into all the papers on my dad's desk.

Instead, I went upstairs and rooted around on the floor until I found my big book o' Poe.

Wow, I really did feel guilty.

How is it that Cody is the only person to notice that I'm "off" and Natalie is the one person to give a damn about it? I cracked the book's spine and flipped through the pages to "The Tell-Tale Heart."

Oh, hey, a story about someone wracked by guilt and trying to cover it up. I'll have some *great* insights for class.

I threw the story aside before I'd gotten halfway through. It was super short, and I could read it on Sunday. Besides, too nice a summer day for the horror-movie vibe. Unless that horror movie is *I Know What You Did Last Summer*. Oh, I hadn't seen that in a while.

I was watching a bootlegged version of vintage Ryan Phillippe on my phone when a knock on my door made me jump out of my skin.

"Lydia?" Mary's voice came from the hall.

"Yeah," I called out, not moving from my collapsed position on the bed. Mary stuck her head in. "You're home early."

She came in and sat on the bed. Folded her hands in front of her. Uh-oh. This was serious Mary. The differences between serious Mary and regular Mary are hard to spot, but I'm trained in this sort of thing.

Serious Mary meant that she wanted to have a serious conversation. Which sent a twist down my spine.

Did she know?

"Violet said you turned her down when she offered to tutor you?" Mary asked.

"Oh, that," I said, breathing a little easier. "Yeah, it was totally cool of her to offer, but I'm good."

"You're good?" Mary asked. "Because last week you were freaking out about a C on your paper."

"Yeah, but the paper I turned in this week is way better," I lied. But I happen to lie really well. This past week, I've practically become a professional. "It's awesome you were looking out for me, but I got this, cuz."

Mary eyed me for a while, but then she just shrugged. "So, you don't need help? Because I was gonna offer to help you study, quiz you from the textbook, if you wanted."

"That's your idea of a fun Friday night?" I asked.

"No. And since you say you don't need it, I won't offer."

"Good. We should be doing something way better. Oh! Let's go to the movies. I really want to see the one about the a cappella girl-group killing zombies."

"As . . . deeply horrified as I am at the prospect of a zombie film featuring singing coeds, can we put it off until tomorrow?" Mary asked. "Since you don't need to study, Violet asked if I'd sub in on bass for the Mechanics' practice session."

"Sub in? OMG, are you joining a band?" I squeaked.

"No, I'm just subbing in," Mary said, crossing her arms over her chest in that way that means there's no wiggle room—at least not in her mind. "Apparently Duke's ditching rehearsals even though they have gigs coming up. They haven't decided if they're going to replace him—he's a founding member of the band—but in the meantime . . . still gotta practice."

"Wow. That's quite the justification for you fetching your bass from your mom's place yesterday."

"Whatever." Mary rolled her eyes. "Do you want to come? I'm sure Violet wouldn't mind if you hung out."

I thought about it, but the idea of sitting in a garage on a couch listening to a band by myself seemed way too . . . Mary for me.

"You know I'm your original groupie, but I think I'll skip it this time."

"You sure?" Mary asked.

"Yeah. But have fun."

"Okay. But tomorrow, girls killing singing zombies?"

"Singing girls killing zombies, but close enough."

Mary gave me a little wave as she headed out the door.

Leaving me alone again. Nobody but me and Kitty. And Poe on the floor. And Ryan Phillippe on my phone. But neither of those two guys really interested me right now.

I'm still not very good at being by myself. This is something Ms. W and I used to talk about a lot. My need for attention mixed up with my desire for independence. So I would try it. I'd go get fro-yo by myself, or I'd drive to the beach alone and just watch the waves. Figuring out what it was like to not have someone else to distract me from me.

I should use this time, I thought. Do some breathing exercises, feng shui my room. Try to focus on what I'm going to do when I graduate—and of course, I've been avoiding telling everyone what has happened. They'll be so disappointed in me, and angry, and I'll—

My phone dinged. Cody.

I didn't get the chance after class to ask you what you're doing this weekend.

I looked around my room. My cat, Poe, and moving furniture while trying to figure out my life were no longer the only options.

You're taking me out. Tonight.

Chapter Sixteen
BEER AND TALKING

I was totally up for meeting Cody wherever, but he insisted on picking me up, like we were in high school. Luckily, since my parents seemed to have abandoned the building and Mary was off playing bass guitar with her new friends, he didn't have to face family awkwardness.

Besides, this wasn't a date. It was . . . beer and talking. That's all.

"So, what's your pleasure?" he said as I got into the car. He'd dressed up in a button-down shirt with the sleeves rolled up, and his sandy hair was combed into that messy thing guys do when they're trying to look more casual than they actually are. It's cute when they make an effort.

"My pleasure?" I asked.

"Where do you want to go? I don't know the town that well. . . ."

"You've been here almost a month now," I replied.

"And yet I haven't managed to tap into the zeitgeist. To find the spots that only the locals know about."

"You've been to Carter's," I said.

"Yeah . . ."

"Then you're tapped in." I laughed. "There's not enough town for there to be more than one cool place to go."

He put his car into gear. "Carter's it is, then."

Thankfully, Carter's was not hosting another farewell show that night, so we didn't have to deal with a line, a velvet rope, or a cover.

In fact, since it was summer, and school wasn't in its normal session, it was deader than I'd seen it in a while.

Side effect of my recent absences from, you know, life.

We slid past Chris, who was at the door, checking IDs. He eyed me and mine, but ever since I stopped having to use fake IDs, I consider bartender/bouncer suspicions a compliment.

The inside of Carter's was warm and friendly, like coming home. Except better, because this home didn't have a messy room, a bunch of homework waiting for me, and only Kitty for company. Instead, it had people talking, the movie channel playing something from the eighties on TV, and every type of beer brewed within a fifty-mile radius.

Cody went to the bar to order while I found us a place to sit. With no stage set up, Carter had moved all the tables and games back to their normal positions—the pool table that's always occupied by those two guys who think they know trick shots, the Just Dance game, the vintage reproduction of Asteroids.

"Did you know they used to have Whac-A-Mole back here?" Cody said as he joined me at the table, two beers in hand. "Harriet was telling me about it."

"Uh-huh," I said. "Thank God they got rid of it."

"Why?" Cody asked. "Mallets and alcohol don't mix?"

I shrugged. Why not tell him? Who cares, right?

"Well, that. But also, the last time I played Whac-A-Mole here, I was with a guy, we overpartied, and I almost got kicked out of the bar."

His eyebrow went up. "I didn't know Whac-A-Mole was that dangerous."

"Oh yeah. Just imagine how terrifying it is for the moles," I said.

"I bet you've got a million stories like that," he said, nodding.

"Like what?" I asked.

"Having fun," he said. "Crazy stuff happening. You know."

I cocked my head to one side, half-smiling. "Hoping something crazy is going to happen?"

"On a date with you? I have no doubt."

"Oh," I said, my face becoming super serious. "Cody, this isn't a date."

"It's not?" he said. "I'm pretty sure you asked me on a date. I have the text message—exhibit A."

"It's not a date-date. It's a *study* date. I'm all about my studies, you know."

"Ah . . . I understand," Cody said, smiling. "So what are we studying? Psych? Gothic Lit? The Ly-di-ah?"

"Nope," I said, feeling a little wary for some reason. Maybe I hadn't had enough beer yet to be the topic of scrutiny. I took a sip. A big one.

I mean, I hadn't hung out with a guy since George. Maybe that's what made me nervous.

However, basic Dating 101 is "ask about the other person." Maybe that was true of study dating, too.

"Today's subject is Cody Whatever-Your-Last-Name-Is."

"Ask me anything, I'm an open book."

"Well, let's start with your last name and go from there."

He threw his head back in laughter. And I laughed a little, too.

* * *

We drank our beers. We talked. Cody's last name, it turns out, is James.

"Totally boring, right?" he said.

"Not totally boring," I replied. "Just, marginally boring."

"But it's not something that's going to stand out on a bookshelf."

"A bookshelf?"

"Yeah, I'm . . . going to be a writer. Studying composition and fiction writing," he said shyly, but not really shyly. It was a total humble brag, but I was willing to let it slide. Being a couple of beers in will do that to you.

"I wrote a short story for my fraternity's newsletter—just as a gag,"

Cody was saying. "But it turned out really good, and everyone really liked it. So I thought, I was always good at telling stories, you know? Just need to find a story to tell, and boom—you've got a career."

So Cody's a brain. Someone like my sister Lizzie. I mean, I always knew he was smarter than your average summer-school student, but my guy experience has mostly been limited to the jocks. The beach volleyball team. Swimmers. Even a figure skater once (it didn't last long). So it was a little intimidating to be hanging out with a guy who wants to have his name on a book's spine someday. Which meant it was weirdly comforting that he was in a fraternity.

"It's why I changed majors. And why I'm having to take summer classes to meet credit requirements."

"What was it before?" I asked. "Your major, I mean."

He rubbed his hand over the back of his head and mumbled, "*Fnh.*"

"I'm sorry, what did you say?"

He sighed. "French."

"*French?*" I repeated. Then I burst out laughing.

"Yeah, I know," he said, chuckling.

"Who majors in French? Where do you even use French, besides France . . . and Canada?"

"Yeah, I started to figure that out. I took it in high school; I have Google Translate; I'd been to Montreal, watched a lot of sad, artsy French films . . . I figured I was golden." He stood up from the table. "Another round?"

* * *

More beers, more talking. I don't know how it happened, but when I looked up, the bar was emptier than before. And when I looked down, the number of glasses on the table told me I was well over my two-drink limit.

I didn't care. Which was probably a result of all those empty glasses. But it was kind of awesome. Awesome to laugh at stuff I can't really remember after the fact. Awesome to lose the collar that's been around my neck. Awesome to bop my head to the music coming from the Just Dance game while people played.

Awesome to not worry about what was going on with Lydia Bennet, for once.

"So tell me about you," Cody was saying. I don't know if he'd had as many beers as me, but my giggle-meter was amped higher than his.

"Like my hopes and dreams?" I said, taking another sip.

"No, more like . . . your best story." He smiled at me. Cute guy has a cute smile. Awesome. "Everyone has a best story. Something . . . daring, different. Exciting. You probably have twenty."

I let my eyes drift over the rest of the bar, thinking. "How about . . . when I got the high score on Just Dance?"

He looked over his shoulder to the recently unoccupied Just Dance machine, in all its neon-flashing glory.

"You have the high score? When did that happen?"

"Right now," I said, grabbing his hand and pulling him up with me.

I flagged down Chris, now standing behind the bar. Guess when it's late enough bouncers don't have a lot of bouncing to do. "Hey, Chris, can I get some quarters?" I said, holding up a five.

Chris sighed deeply, which I was beginning to think was normal. "Last call's in fifteen, guys."

"Just enough time to destroy all the records on Just Dance," I said.

"Just Dance, huh?" he said. "We'll see."

I scooped up the quarters he put on the bar and danced over to the machine.

"Okay," I said, plugging my coins into the machine. The scoreboard popped up. "That's the person with the high score—CCH. That's who LBB has to destroy."

Cody's hand hovered over the start button. "CCH won't know what hit him. Ready?"

I nodded. He hit the button. "Go!"

The music began, the dance steps coming fast and furious. My sister Lizzie thinks she's good at Just Dance. I'm *actually* good at it. Even considering my vow of no-funsies/all-study, I still kept my dance joints limber by using our home game as my brain break when I needed one. So Carter's bar game? No problem. The trick is to be loose. Lizzie is never loose.

I danced. I hopped, turned, skipped, hip-thrusted, got low and groovy, and even once got en pointe. I was racking up points almost as fast as the computer could give them. And I was loose. Everything felt lighter, like the only think I had to worry about was the next step.

"You're almost there!" Cody said from behind me.

I moved my feet faster than I ever had. The machine flashed like a strobe light. I only had a couple hundred points to go . . . a couple dozen . . . and then . . .

The machine went dead.

"Wha . . . what?" I said. I hit the start button. All the other buttons. Nothing. "No. No nononononononononnnnnooo!!!"

"What happened?" Cody asked.

"I don't know. Did I break it?" It's entirely possible that my awesome dancing was too much for the poor machine, so used as it was to mediocre patrons sloshing their beer on the platform while they tried to two-step.

"Huh," Chris said, the door to the back swinging behind him. "Breaker must have flipped. It does that sometimes."

"No . . . you mean I lost my entire game?" I cried. "I was about to win!"

Chris just shrugged. "Sorry. Maybe next time."

"Wait a minute . . ." I said, my eyes narrowing. The shrug. The raising of stoic eyebrows when I told him I was gonna beat the record. The slight suspicious smile he had on his face at that very moment. "Chris! You're CCH! You had the high score!"

Chris just looked from me, to Cody, back to the machine. "Last call."

"Cheater!" I called after him as he shuffled back through the door. "I'll get you next time! I challenge you to a dance-off!"

But he was already gone.

"Well . . ." Cody said, coming up behind me. "It makes a good story."

"Not a *best* story, though. Come on! Did you see me? I was kicking that game's ass, like . . ." I spun around, doing the double step and the kick and then . . .

The room started to spin with me.

"Whoa," Cody said, coming over to steady me. His hands on my waist.

"Whoa is right."

"You know what you need?"

"For Chris to admit defeat to my smooth moves?"

"I was thinking some food."

"Last call. Kitchen's closed," I said. *Why is the kitchen closed on me?* I thought. *What kind of cruel trick is that to play on the intoxicated?*

"Well, I have some leftover pizza at my place . . ." Cody was saying, but then I saw a sign.

A busted, broken sign someone had crashed into long ago.

"OMG, Crash!" I cried, grabbing Cody's arm.

"What? Something crashed?" Cody asked, looking at me like I was a nonsensical drunk.

I guess to the uninitiated, I might have sounded a little crazy.

"Crash," I said, pointing through the window. "The diner."

He looked at it, his forehead squishing up.

Heh. Squish. That's a fun word. Squish squishy squish.

"Is it . . . uh . . ."

"Sanitary? Structurally sound?"

"Open, I was going to say."

"It's always open," I said, waving aside his objections. "Come on—you're the one who wanted to tap into the local zeit . . . zetgie . . . the local scene."

* * *

Coffee and a breakfast plate later and the world felt less spinny. Still fuzzy, but less like it was going to throw me off its axis with the force of its velocity.

What? I've read *The Little Prince*. I was always worried that the little boy was going to fall off a planet that small, so I looked some stuff up.

But as my head cleared, not even the fluorescent lighting in Crash bothered me. Nor did the bored waitress, who only had to deal with us and a couple of high school theater kids who made it their mission to drink coffee until dawn.

"I mean, it's summer, guys," I said to Cody. "Go get a tan. Please."

He snickered, eyeing the theater kids. "Ah, making fun of the other cliques. Brings me back."

"What were you in high school?" I asked.

"Pretty popular. Student council during the week, parties in the woods on the weekend. You?" he asked.

I opened my mouth to answer, but he held up a hand. "No, let me guess. Partier? Super cute and fun."

"Well . . . yes, but . . ." There was more to it. More to me. Wasn't there?

"My last girlfriend was a theater chick, though," Cody said, rubbing his chin. "Moved down to LA after our freshman year. Trying to act."

The way he rolled his eyes made my stomach start to flip over.

"Do you really want to talk about our exes?" I said. "Kind of a downer."

"No, you're right," he said. "Besides, Mindy doesn't have anything on yours."

I fell silent. I knew by now he'd seen the videos. They were the elephant in the diner.

"He must have been a total asshole," Cody said, gentle.

I looked down at my plate. Which sadly did not have a crack shaped like Kentucky. "It wasn't like that," I said, softly.

"You can tell me about it," he said, matching his pitch to mine.

But I didn't. I couldn't. I just shrugged. "Tonight's been too much fun to be about all that stuff."

"Okay," he said, holding up his hands. "But I just want you to know, not all guys . . ."

"Yeah," I said. "I know." I shook my shoulders back, smiling big. Back to being Lydia. Back to fun. "You ready to go? We're about to outlast the theater kids and I don't want to bruise their egos."

"Sure," Cody said, rolling with it. "Just let me hit the bathroom."

"Yeah . . . you don't want to do that."

* * *

A quick trip back across the street to Carter's for use of their bathrooms (we made Chris open up for us; whatever, he owed me), and we headed home. Pulling up outside of my house, I could see Mary's car parked behind my parents'. Everyone safe and asleep as the sky gradually got lighter behind the house.

"So . . ." Cody said, leaning over.

"So . . ." I replied, not moving.

"I . . . guess I'll see you Monday," Cody said, watching me. Specifically, my mouth.

I rolled my eyes. And pulled him to me, tasting beer and coffee and some breath spray he must have snuck in while in Carter's bathroom.

I know I didn't *have* to kiss him. But at some point you gotta put a guy out of his misery.

"Wow," he said, when I finally let him go.

"Yeah," I said. "As far as first kisses go, I'd put it above par."

"Indeed." He exhaled. Then frowned. "Wait, do you mean it was good or bad, because technically above par in golf—"

"Cody," I said. "See you Monday."

I got out of the car and waved good-bye to Cody. He drove off before I'd reached the front door. Which I decided was okay. If either of my parents or Mary were waiting on the other side, I didn't want them to see the evidence of my evening in a silver Toyota Corolla driven by a dude.

But as I stepped back in to the house, I sort of wished he had hung out, for just a second or two more, because then I could look back out and see my awesome night of awesomeness. Instead, as the door swung shut behind me, I was overwhelmed by the silence of the house. One that quickly filled with voices, asking me how I could have screwed up. Telling me exactly what I did wrong. And wondering why I went out with Cody instead of feng shuiing my room.

But I wasn't going to think about that now. Nope, I refuse. Because I still had a little bit of an alcohol glow, and a fabulous kind of adrenaline-tired I hadn't felt in a while that just made me want to collapse.

Chapter Seventeen

NEXT . . .

"Lydia?"

Someone was pounding on my brain. No . . . they were pounding on the door. Either way, not cool.

"What?" I croaked, and immediately put my head under a pillow. I thought that after black coffee and some greasy breakfast food I should have been able to snooze relatively hangover-free. But noooooo . . .

My body was out of practice at having fun and being a normal human being, I guess.

The door creaked open—I need to WD-40 that door—and Mary's voice came from the other side of my pillow.

"Lydia? You okay?"

Okay, breathe. Breathe. Hold it together, and one, two, three . . .

"I'm fine," I said, throwing the covers back, and trying super hard not to cringe in the sunlight.

"You sure? You don't look fine."

"I might be coming down with something," I said, coughing for pity.

"You were already asleep when I got home last night," Mary said, taking another step back toward the door. For as low-key as Mary is about most things, she's weirdly germaphobic. Hey, it kept her from looking at me too closely. But still, it took me a minute to remember that I had stuffed my bed with pillows the night before, in case anyone came to check on me.

Yes, I know I'm twenty-one and an adult, blah blah blah, but old habits die hard.

"Yeah," I said, coughing again—this time to clear the fuzz from my throat. "When did you get in, anyway?"

"Late. Like midnight," Mary said. "But I looked up times for the movie."

"Movie? Oh, right," I said. The idea of a dark room appealed, but loud zombie snarls did not. "I don't know if I feel up to a movie today. Maybe I should just . . . sleep a little."

Mary watched me, and seemed like she was going to say something. But then she just shrugged. "Okay. You sure?"

"Yeah," I said. "Tomorrow, though?"

"Don't you have therapy tomorrow?" she asked.

Yes, I did. And my weekly paper for psych, and I probably should read that Poe. *Dracula* is coming up, too. Oh, and figure out my life.

But man, did I not care about any of that.

"It's okay. Ms. W doesn't mind," I said.

But Mary just kept watching me. "Let's see how you feel tomorrow. I don't suppose you want breakfast. Your mom made eggs over easy."

My stomach turned over—and not easily. "No, I'm good."

"Okay," Mary said, watching me as she went back out the door—using her shirtsleeve to hold the knob. She was definitely going to go disinfect her entire body after this. "I'll check on you later. Or, you know, text you."

"From downstairs?"

"Uh-huh, okay, feel better." And the door clicked shut—loudly—behind her.

I pulled my comforter back up over my head—and then put it back down again. The air under the sheets smelled like stale beer—not great for my queasy tummy.

But neither is the weird quiet.

I have nothing to do. No, not true—I have plenty to do. I just don't care about it. It's not that I'm blowing it off, or avoiding it. I just . . . don't care. About anything. Not my homework. Not what happened the night before with Cody. Not whatever's going to happen next.

And that's the weirdest thing.

I always care. Okay, yeah, I didn't always care about my classes—but I always looked forward to going to school. To putting on my latest cutest outfit and hanging with my friends, and seeing what new drama there was to gossip about. When I first got my smartphone, the most exciting part for me was the calendar. Yes, the calendar. Because I could fill it up with parties and half-off fro-yo Fridays and people's birthdays and get excited about what comes next.

I'm Lydia Bennet. I always look forward to tomorrow. Even when I didn't have a plan for my future. Even when George left and I felt like the world was crashing down around me. Half of what got me through that time was knowing that tomorrow couldn't suck any more than today.

But now . . . there's nothing.

I have nothing to look forward to.

. . . Yay.

Texts with Ms. W

Lydia: Hey, Ms. W—I'm super sorry but I'm not going to make it to our session.

Ms. Winter: I'm sorry to hear that. Is everything ok?

Lydia: Oh, yeah. I've just got to drive my mom around again because of her elbow.

Ms. Winter: All right. I think it would be a good idea to schedule a midweek session. I have time Wednesday and Thursday.

Lydia: I'll look at my sched and get back to you. Thanks, Ms. W, you're super sweet to let it slide. Byeee!

Chapter Eighteen
BRING IT

Okay, I would never say this out loud, but life is *so much easier* when you just don't care. Stroll in two seconds before class starts? Don't care. Teacher and other students eyeing you like you're the bad Chinese food they forgot was in the back of the fridge? Don't care. Your cousin/bestie watching you hang out with the guy you snuck out/made out with in the coffee shop? Don't care.

Although said cousin/bestie might care a little for you.

"What's the deal with Cody?" Mary asked. "Are you dating him now?"

It was Wednesday, and she'd cornered me the one time of day that my powers of avoidance are in a slightly weakened state—during our morning drive. When I have to pay attention to the turns and signals (autopilot no longer being on, but hey, who cares?) and I don't have the advantage of weirding people out with eye contact, it's hard to not be vulnerable to an attack of Driving Honesty.

Seriously, if I didn't have to carpool with Mary, I might have skipped school today. Or all this week.

"No," I said. Probably sounded a little too defensive. "Just hanging out. Study buddies. You know."

"You weren't studying when you guys were in the coffee shop on Monday," she said. Okay, yeah, there might have been some close-sitting, a little under-the-table flirting, but I thought we were being totally discreet. Guess not.

Whatever. Don't care.

"Not dating him," I said. "Not *not* dating him. Just hanging out."

Out of the corner of my eye I could see Mary's mouth squish into a hard line. "Okay, that's cool. I think it's a good thing you're interested in dating again."

Oh God, was this going to be "the talk?" Not the sex talk, which occurred when I was nine, and my mother sweatily showed me what happens between men and women using my collection of My Little Ponies. You think she would have been an old pro at the talk, three girls in, but from what Jane and Lizzie told me, the ponies had been an improvement.

No, the talk Mary was going to give me was the "It's so awesome you're getting back out there!" talk. The one where you get praise for having the inner strength to carry on living. And that's fine, but it's not something I was up for during morning talk radio.

But once again, Mary caught me off guard. "But is it a good idea to be dating someone now?"

"Why not?"

She sighed. "Because we're going to be moving soon. You're working so hard to transfer schools, I just don't want him to . . . distract you, is all."

I almost said, "Distract me from what?"—stupid Driving Honesty. But we pulled into the parking lot in front of Books Beans and Buds, taking my attention and giving me time to answer.

"He's not a distraction. I mean, is playing in Violet's band a distraction for you?"

"No," Mary said. "And I'm not playing in the band."

"Not officially, duh, but you still practice with them, and—"

"They only have one more farewell show, tomorrow. And Duke's playing the show. So I'm not even their practice bassist anymore."

"Oh," I said quietly. "I'm sorry. I know you liked hanging out with them."

"It's fine. It's not like I was ever going to actually *be* their bassist. I was just helping out for a minute." Mary shrugged. "But you're right. I've got too much to do to play in a rock band."

She said "rock band" like most people say "hair scrunchie"—a total disbelief that such a ridiculous thing even exists anymore.

"But I'm ready for when we get out of here," Mary said. "I can only make so many double espressos while working on Lizzie's stuff at night."

"Right," I said, guilt creeping in. Mary handles everything with a shrug and just gets it done. It hadn't occurred to me that she might be under pressure of her own.

Nope, go away, guilt. Don't care. Do not care.

"Anyway, see you after psych," Mary said.

She got out of the car and waved good-bye.

Leaving me with a heaviness in my chest.

Dammit, for the briefest second, I was caring again.

* * *

When you're gliding through the easy life of not caring, everything tends to bleed together. Days of the week, classes, hours. What episode of whatever show you're watching. It's all the same. So it's hard for things to stand out.

Everything is just . . . fine.

The only bright spot of any day was Cody. Chances are he'd

text with me during psych, and make me snort-laugh at something while Professor Latham was going over the subject of our next paper. Which I'll get a C on.

Or we'd be in the coffee shop, and Mary would watch us. But then, all I had to do was say Violet probably needed something and Mary would go and see what was up with her. No big deal.

Even Gothic Lit—which Cody totally should have been paying better attention to, given the fact that he's a writing major—was a chance to dust off my flirt skills. So what if Mary thought he was a distraction? He was—and a distraction was the only thing keeping me going at this point. Even though I'd read "The Tell-Tale Heart"—mostly because it was super short and Kitty ran down the battery on my phone by making me play her ocean sounds all night—and I was totally able to be insightful for Natalie's sake, I was still way more interested in Cody's knee pressed against mine than I was in starting the discussion on *Dracula*.

Not caring set me free. Not caring let me breathe easy. And not caring meant that if you wanted to be a bitch to me like Harriet was in the bathroom, I could take it.

It was after Gothic Lit. The mochaccinos had hit me mid-class and I'd had to pee for the last twenty minutes. When I came out of the stall, Harriet was standing at the mirror, reapplying her already perfect makeup.

"Oh," I said. "Hi."

I had two choices. Unfortunately, the leaving immediately one involved me being gross and not washing my hands, so I had to suck it up.

As I approached the mirrors and turned on the faucet, she kept her gaze locked on her reflection as she put on a coat of peach lip gloss.

"Oh, wow, your new boy toy let you out alone?" she said. "He should be more careful. Never know what Lydia Bennet will get up to."

I could have gotten sad. I could have gotten defensive. Instead,

I was the bigger person—not literally, Harriet has shoulders like a rugby player—and remained silent.

"Do us all a favor and bang *before* you come to class, okay? It's kind of disruptive when you guys go at it at the table."

Okay, first of all, I haven't slept with Cody. We'd barely kissed. But a little flirting isn't a crime, even in the middle of class.

And B . . . well, there's only so long you can be the bigger person.

"You should be careful with that shade of lip gloss," I said. "Doesn't exactly go with the color green."

"Please," Harriet replied. "I'm so much better off. I mean, if I'd known Cody was only into damaged chicks, I could have told him about that time I got mugged at the mall."

"He's not into damaged chicks."

She looked at me, with the kind of pity that just pissed me off. "Please. He told you his major, right?"

My eyes narrowed. "What does that have to do with anything?"

Harriet gave her reflection a small smile.

"Ever ask yourself what he wants from you?"

I smiled as sweetly as I could manage. "I just know he doesn't want it from you."

She turned so red under her foundation, I wondered if she needed another layer.

"Whatever," she said, straightening her shoulders and turning back to the mirror. "I can't wait to get out of this stupid town. Get down to LA and USC where I belong."

She threw her makeup in her bag, swinging it over her shoulder as she stalked past me for the door.

"Harriet. You weren't mugged. You dropped your shopping bag in the middle of the department store, and *thought* you got mugged. They had it waiting for you at the lost and found, with your name on the receipt and everything."

"How'd you know that?" she asked, shocked.

I snorted. "*Everyone* knows that."

She took a deep breath through her nose, all huffy. Then she shoved the door open with her hip, and left.

Leaving me alone, with the running faucet echoing off the tile.

She didn't realize it, but Harriet had managed to twist the knife Mary accidentally plunged in that morning. She was ready to leave town and go to LA. Mary was ready to head up to San Francisco.

Me? I'm not going anywhere.

Okay, maybe I cared about that a little.

* * *

But if I thought I was going to find any comfort at home, I was mistaken.

I was doing my normal Thursday routine. Which, two weeks ago, would have been rereading my psych textbook, making sure I understood it completely. Now, it was mostly watching nineties sitcoms on Netflix. I thought I was home alone, but then, suddenly my mom appeared in the living room.

In her nightgown.

At one o'clock in the afternoon.

"Mom?" I said. "I thought you were out?"

My mom is usually the first person up. More often than not, breakfast would have been made, cleaned up, and the living room floors vacuumed by the time any one else managed to get in line for the shower. I'd just assumed I'd missed breakfast because I got up so late. And the vacuuming, because Kitty was nowhere to be found.

"Lydia! I could say the same thing about you," she said, clutching her robe closed around her neck and madly fixing her bed head. "Don't you have school?"

"Not today."

"Well, still," she fluttered. "I would have thought you'd be out studying, or working on one of your papers."

I shrugged. "Just being a little lazy today."

"Are you hungry, honey? Can I fix you something?"

I held up my bowl of cereal. "I'm good, thanks."

"That's not a real breakfast," she said as she moved to the kitchen. I could hear her clanking pots and getting the cutting board out. I got up off the couch and followed the sounds.

"Mom, are you feeling okay?"

"Of course!" she said, a pot of water landing on the stove with a thud. She turned the burner on high. "Why would you ask such a thing?"

"Um, because you're in your nightgown in the middle of the day."

She just looked me up and down. Yes, I was still in my pajamas, but that wasn't the point.

"Well, perhaps I wanted to be a little lazy, too," she said. "I occasionally could use a break from having to do everything around here. A morning where I sleep a little later."

"Okay." Sorry. Didn't mean to strike a nerve.

"Honestly. I sleep in once, and it's an inquisition! What do you think I did before I had you girls to look after?"

"I . . . dunno." I'd never really thought of my mom before us.

"I had fun, that's what," she said, smiling at me. "Your father and I stayed out late, we slept in. Now that you're moving out soon, I thought I might give it a try again."

That knife—the one Mary plunged and Harriet twisted? Basically my mom was twirling it around like a baton.

"You're excited for me and Mary to leave, huh?"

"Honey, aren't you?" she asked. "You must be so bored, sitting here just watching television. If I were you, I'd be itching to get out of the house, get started on my new life. New people, new places . . ."

"Yeah, no, you're right," I said. "I'm really not that hungry. I think I'll take a shower."

"Okay, sweetie." The water had started to boil. "Lunch will be ready by the time you're dressed!"

Nothing like realizing that even your parents want you gone to make you feel like hiding in your room.

Which I did for approximately the next six hours.

But hey, I actually did my psych reading. And watched more nineties sitcoms on my phone.

I was drifting into a boredom coma, dreading Friday and the classes that were going to come with it, when there was a knock on my door.

"Hey . . ." Mary said, wearing a suspicious amount of eyeliner. "You're not ready."

"For what?" I asked.

"The last Mechanics show?" She crossed into the room. "You said you'd go with me."

"I did?" One side effect of actively not caring and letting everything bleed together was that you totally forget when you promise people things.

"You're not sick again, are you?" Mary asked, inching back toward my door.

"No!" I said, sitting up. "I'm totally down for going. I just . . . I didn't think you'd want to, considering Duke and everything."

"I dunno," Mary said, stubbing her toe against my carpet. "I figured I should go anyway. Support Violet. And Gen and Jones. But if you don't want to go you don't have to. I understand if you need to work."

"Nope," I said, hopping off the bed so fast I scared Kitty out the door. I started pulling an outfit together. Something bright and fun and awesome. "I'm in."

"Are you sure? Like I said, I'd understand—"

"Mary, please. Lydia Bennet is always ready for a party."

Chapter Nineteen

LAST LAST SHOW

The line at Carter's was, somehow, even longer than it was at the last Mechanics show. It's like the fact that they had already played a dozen "farewell shows" this summer had completely escaped everyone.

Then again, there really was nothing else to do here.

There was another bouncer-looking guy walking up and down the line while Chris, as always, guarded passage to the door. Wow, hiring extra help? Violet's band was probably the biggest business Carter's had ever seen.

We cut to the front, gave our names, showed IDs, the whole routine, and Chris waved us through the door. Fortunately, Mary was also busy looking at her phone, or she might have noticed his offhand comment about seeing me a lot lately.

C'mon, Chris. Discretion.

"Texting Violet?" I asked, squinting as my eyes adjusted to the darkened room.

"No," Mary replied. She rocked up onto her toes and scanned the crowd of people mingling before the show started. Her eyes locked on one spot and I followed her gaze.

"Denny!" I squealed, half running, half skipping to the boy coming toward us. I threw my arms around him. "Mary didn't tell me you were coming!"

Denny Reyes was Mary's former coworker back at the pizza place and, as far as I had been able to tell, only friend. Besides me, of course. And now Violet.

I'd been slightly interested in him prior to George, but it wasn't something that had any chance of working out.

"I wasn't sure I was going to make it," he replied, tossing a friendly head-nod and a smile in Mary's direction. He was way more respectful of her boundaries than I was. "Josh and I had plans, but he got called into work last-minute, so . . . here I am!"

Josh, aka Denny's boyfriend. Yeah, he had a pretty valid excuse for not falling victim to my adorbs.

Still, once Denny and Mary started working together, the three of us hung out a lot when I was visiting last fall. But as I'd been sticking close to home since, well, George, I hadn't seen him in ages.

"Where have you been?" he prodded. "I've sent you like thirty Facebook messages trying to keep in touch."

I knew he knew about everything that had happened, and I actually had never been worried about what he would think—once I got past the initial stage of worrying what literally everyone, even Kitty, would think—but communication was just a thing that had fallen to the side the past few months. Particularly through social media, where everything just felt like a constant reminder of the past.

"Pfft, Facebook," I scoffed. "Who even uses that anymore?" Everyone. "Well, we're all here now. And you totally won't regret making the trek down. Not only do you get to hang out with us, which is super mega awesome—duh—but the band is actually really good."

"Speaking of—" Mary finally piped up. "We should grab drinks and find a place to stand before the show starts."

"Definitely drinks," Denny agreed. "We have time, though. The guy at the door said some other band is playing first."

"Wow, an opening act," I said. Carter's really was pulling out all the stops. I didn't know of any other local bands off the top of my head, but if they're good enough to open for the Mechanics, this was looking to be a pretty sweet night.

Denny started leading the way through the crowd to the bar. I may have been good at ducking and weaving through large groups, but having a tall guy disperse the crowd for you is always a better option. Less chance of some dummy spilling a drink on you. Plus, it made me feel a little like Moses parting the Red Sea (Jane went through a *Prince of Egypt* phase — I've seen that movie way too many times).

Especially the part where the sea came crashing back down on the Egyptians. Because suddenly, mere feet away from our destination, Denny stopped, and I ran right into him, and Mary ran right into me.

He turned around, a strange look on his face. "You know, actually, we probably don't need to get drinks right now."

"What are you talking about? Let's get this party st—"

As I moved to push past him and order a delicious beer, I caught sight of what made him stop.

I turned back and faced both of them. "On second thought, we don't want to be *too* drunk for the show, right?" I grabbed Mary's hand again with the intention of yanking her away before she could see what Denny and I had seen, but it was too little effort, too late as a conversation happening at the bar made itself heard:

"No, *you* listen, brah. I am talent. I shouldn't have to pay for this shit."

If the bright blue blazer and dark, over-gelled hair hadn't given it away, I'd still have recognized that nasally voice. And clearly Mary did, too.

"Eddie?" she croaked, clapping her hand over her mouth after the name slipped out.

Yep. Eddie.

As in dumped-Mary-for-getting-in-the-way-of-his-roadkill-music Eddie.

Awesoooome.

He spun around at the sound of his name, his face lighting up in recognition as he saw all of us.

"Mary Bennet," he said. "What a lovely face to see before our first show tonight."

"You're playing?" I blurted out in surprise. I knew Mary had heard them play in Eddie's garage, but to my knowledge, nobody else had. They were practically the unicorn of bands. Well, except nobody knew or cared about their potential existence. And, by all accounts, they sucked.

"Right-a-roo." Eddie grinned. "Todd's pop knows some people who know some other people who hooked us up. Figured it was high time to stop being selfish and share our melodies with the world. Isn't that right?"

Eddie cocked his head toward the pastiest boy I had ever seen, looking nearly translucent in the shitty bar lighting. And his dull orange hair practically made me look like a brunette.

The guy, who I assumed was Todd, nodded slightly, refusing to look at any of us. He stared straight ahead just . . . staring. Between the two of them, any band posters featuring their images would undoubtedly fit that eclectic indie pop vibe they seemed to be going for.

"You guys want drinks? We drink free, talent and all," Eddie offered, eliciting a gruff "No, you don't" from Carter as he poured someone else's glass. "Might as well share the love with our biggest fans, coming out to support us."

"Actually, we're here for the Mechanics," Mary corrected.

"Right," said Eddie, smiling with disbelief.

"Yeah, Mary's friends with them," I added, backing her up. The last thing this night needed was Mary's weirdo ex thinking she was here pining over him. Man, what happened to party night?

Fortunately, that thought led me to realize this situation would be much better with the helping hand of—you guessed it—beer. I turned back to the bar and placed the usual order for all three of us ("Yes, Carter, I know the beer isn't free") as Mary and Denny continued fending off conversation from the unexpected acquaintances. Or rather, just from Eddie, as Todd had yet to so much as open his mouth. Or alter his eye line.

Carter handed me the drinks, which I put on my card with the instruction to keep the tab open. I saw Mary side-eye me, and I knew she was questioning the wisdom of me paying for all of our drinks.

But hey, it's not like I have a big move to save up for anymore, ami-right?

Drink up, Lydia.

I passed the remaining beers to Denny and Mary, who both looked relieved to have something to briefly distract them from this unfortunate turn of events. Poor Denny, I could tell he was looking for an opportunity to casually suggest we all go our separate ways, but Eddie was rambling on about their "process" and how he doesn't revise his lyrics—he just writes the words that course through him like a raging wildebeest. I wondered if it would be easier to take him seriously if he ditched those silly hipster frames. Or at least actually put glass in them.

And poor Mary. I'd hate to be stuck talking to my ex on what was supposed to be a fun night out. Even if said ex was more on the an-noying side of the spectrum rather than the exploitative, borderline-criminal one.

I had resolved to burst into the conversation with the insistence that we hunt down a table elsewhere, no matter how interruptive or awkward it might end up being, when Violet showed up.

"Mary!" she exclaimed. "Didn't think you'd be here. We've been stealing all your time lately. Hey, Lydia!"

"Hey," Mary said, looking like a cross between relieved and ap-prehensive. "What are you doing out here? Won't you get mobbed?"

Violet motioned to the beanie hiding all her hair from view. "Keep the hair tucked in and they don't know any better. It's kinda magic."

Eddie coughed loudly into his fist, eyeing Mary.

"Oh. Violet, that's our friend Denny." She pointed to the only guy in this bizarro circle we actually liked. "And this is Eddie, and . . . Todd." Yeah, thrilled was certainly not the word to describe Mary's tone. "Apparently they're opening for you guys tonight."

"Oh, right!" Violet exclaimed. "I'm sorry, what were you guys called again?"

"Eddie. Todd." It was Eddie who spoke, of course. I was beginning to think Todd either had no voice or was hiding multiple rows of tiny, sharp teeth behind his lips and just never opened his mouth so as to keep his secret safe.

"No, like, your band name," she clarified.

"We don't believe in names. It detracts from the music."

"Uh-huh." I could see Violet's confusion, and Denny's stifled laugh, even though I was more focused on Mary's eye-rolling. Which quickly turned into more of a deer-in-headlights kinda face after Violet's next question:

"So how do you know Mary and Lydia?"

I glanced behind me and nodded to Carter that I needed another drink. Yes, already. This was going to be a loooong night.

"Mary and I used to be a thang." Eddie twanged the last word, drawing out every letter in it. This kid was always strange, but I do *not* remember him being this annoying. I would never have been so giddy for Mary when they started dating if he had been like this. Right? So much of that year is a blur.

"For like, a second," Mary quickly interjected.

"True," he agreed. "It was that magnetic attraction between musicians. Powerful like a dissonant chord, but when you're resolving the progression, you just gotta let it go."

I don't know music terms, but between the looks on both Mary's and Violet's faces, I'm guessing that was a pretty douchey thing to say. At the very least, it sounded bizarre and hipstery and pretentious.

"Well, your . . . band missed out on a chance for a kick-ass bass player," Violet finally said, throwing a smile at Mary.

"Oh, no, no. We don't bass. We synth."

"Both of them," Mary added.

"Right," Violet said.

I exchanged glances with Denny. We were basically just playing a two-person audience to the most uncomfortable improv ever.

Three-person audience. Todd. Wow, he was even easier to forget about than Mary.

"Well, it's really cool of you guys to come open for us. We're calling this the 'No, really, it's seriously the actual last show' show before we *finally* leave for San Francisco," Violet said, then turned to us. "Carter pulled out all the stops on a Thursday because we actually have a gig in the city tomorrow. So we really are leaving. Promise."

"Wow, that's awesome! The gig, I mean. Where is it?" Denny said, trying to help steer the conversation away from Eddie. Although Eddie steered it right back.

"Yeah, me and Todd thought about San Fran," Eddie said, shifting the conversation to himself again. He was really good at that. Actually, I wonder if that's part of why Mary used to like him. She hates talking about herself. "But it's a little played out. Figure we'd head straight for the City of Angels."

"LA." Violet nodded. "That's cool. You got anything lined up?"

"Well, see, we aren't going yet," Eddie backtracked. "Todd's brother's out there hustlin' his own deals in the biz, so we thought, hey, let him do the legwork, we'll stay here and hone our craft, and once he's in, we'll just ride along on those coattails, right up to the top."

"Wow, sounds like you've really thought this out."

"Gotta have a plan." Eddie tapped his pointer finger against his temple. "I'm the brains, Todd's the connections, and we're both the sweet, sweet talent."

"Yep," Mary muttered into her drink before downing another gulp. I watched Violet's eyes dart toward my cousin and then back to Eddie.

"Hey," she said. "Aren't you going to warm up, or . . . ?"

"Naw. We like our sound to be fresh." He wiggled his fingers. "Being a performance artist is all about being raw and exposed, you know?"

"Bold choice."

The already dim overhead lights dimmed even further, and the stage lit up.

"And that, gentlepeople, is our cue," Eddie said. "Todd."

I swear, Todd's eyes did not change direction whatsoever as he followed Eddie off toward the stage. Come to think of it, I'm pretty sure he didn't even blink.

Maybe he had truly become one with the music. Or the synth.

Carter, another drink, please?

Nobody said anything for a moment as the two guys pushed their way toward the stage.

"So that's your ex?" Violet finally broke the silence, her voice doing a poor job of hiding her amusement. "I mean, I know I told you how weird my last girlfriend got when she decided to go on her vegan-hippie-commune-cult kick, but that guy takes 'eccentric' to a whole other level."

I grabbed my next beer from Carter as Mary fidgeted and shrugged uncomfortably.

"He was cute, and he was in a band," she mumbled.

"Oh, is that all it takes with you?" Violet teased, and I swear even with the crappy lighting, I could see Mary get a little bit redder.

"He wasn't that . . . *that* when we dated," Mary continued. "He's gotten douchier."

"Way douchier," Denny confirmed.

"Ah," Violet said. "Yeah, I get that. That's pretty much where we're at with Duke now."

"Duke? Are you saying he used to be less sucky?" I asked. He seemed pretty one-note to me.

Violet smiled, a little sadly. "He's been a pal for a while. He's always been kind of hotheaded, but he wasn't always . . ." She paused, chewing on her lip as she thought. "Well, he used to go by Justin, his actual name, if that's any indication of how far we've come. Sucks that he's let even moderate success go to his head."

"Well, if he starts trying to get you to call him Emperor, I just so happen to know another bassist who is super fine with just being called her given name," I said.

Yes, I was not-so-subtly pushing my cousin on her. So sue me. Mary's talented; I know she likes playing with these guys even though she doesn't want to admit it . . . so someone's gotta point out the obvious.

"It's too bad we can't have two bass players," Violet said, smiling at Mary.

"Well . . ." I trailed off, nodding toward the stage.

Eddie and Todd had finally shoved their way up front and gotten their instruments—not only two synths, but *identical* synths—plugged in. And with no introduction whatsoever (though, how do you introduce your band without a name?), they jumped into their first song.

I've never heard what a meteorite crashing to earth and obliterating an entire village sounds like, but if you could translate that into music, I'd imagine this would be the result.

Actually, scratch that, you wouldn't even need to translate it into music. It's just this.

"Not a compelling argument for double instruments." Violet cringed. "And a very good one for warming up. So I'm actually going to go round up the gang and do some of that."

"Nice to meet you, Violet," Denny said.

"Likewise. I can easily say you are my favorite of the three people I've met so far tonight," she joked. "Oh, I almost forgot. There's a reserved table up front. That's for you guys. If anyone's there, just get Chris to yell at them."

"I thought you didn't know we were coming?" Mary asked.

"Well, yeah, but I hoped you would," Violet said. "See you guys after the show?"

She squeezed her way through all the people and we grabbed another round of drinks before committing to doing the same. And then, realizing that it had gotten even more crowded, we grabbed an extra round so we wouldn't have to fight our way back quite as soon.

For those of you playing at home, that's:

Denny: Rounds 2 and 3

Mary: Rounds 2 and 3

Lydia: Rounds 4 and 5

But beer basically doesn't even count as alcohol anyway, so why keep track?

We finally made our way up to the reserved table. Pros: no one had ignored the sign and tried to sit there, so we didn't have to get Chris. Plus, it was literally right by the stage. Cons: it was way too far from the bar than I enjoyed . . . and we had a front-row seat for Eddie and Todd's show. Which is undoubtedly why Mary took the seat that let her face the exact opposite direction to talk to us.

"So now that we're done with that sidetrack extravaganza, tell me everything!" Denny said. "I can't believe you guys are getting out of this godforsaken place."

"You don't even live here," I pointed out, even as my heart pounded at the turn the conversation was taking.

"This town, my town . . ." He waved it off. "Everything in this area is all the same. I can only pray I make it out one day, too."

You know those cement trucks that are just constantly turning and turning so the cement doesn't dry out as it's being transported?

Yeah, pretty sure one of them was driving around in my stomach.

"Well, we're looking for a third roommate, if you feel the inclination," Mary suggested.

"Ha. I wish. Maybe someday," he said. "Anyway, seriously, tell me all your plans. I want to hear everything."

I was really glad Mary actually liked Denny, because that meant she actually talked. Which meant I could actually get away with not talking. First, the last thing I wanted on a fun night out was to be constantly reminded of all the things I had planned on but wasn't going to be able to do. And B, I had enough of a buzz going that I was worried if I tried to join the conversation, I'd let the truth slip.

Maybe beer does count as alcohol.

And maybe I shouldn't have skipped dinner.

And maybe I should've actually not screwed up my life.

Here we go again.

Rather than tuning out Mary and Denny completely, which would have probably resulted in having to listen to the galactic warfare that was Eddie and Todd's synth duo "music," I came up with an absolutely flawless plan during their conversation.

"San Francisco?" Drink.

"Lizzie?" Drink.

"College?" Drink.

"Plans?" Drink.

"Future?" Drink.

"A," "the," "of," "and," "but"—drink.

I suppose you could call it a drinking game, but I preferred to call it Lydia Bennet's Miraculous Method of Coping with Inevitably Disappointing Everyone Yet Again.

Hey, it did the trick. And so did the alcohol.

By the time Mary was telling a surprisingly intrigued Denny about the pros and cons of the various neighborhoods in San Francisco, I was way less tense and a little more fuzzy-headed, but the cement truck rolling over my internal organs had given up, which was nice.

"So Violet's moving up to San Fran, too?" Denny asked.

"Yeah, the band is going to record. Expand their audience. All that stuff," Mary said.

"Uh-huh," Denny said. "Well, it's cool you guys are moving to the same place."

"We're not— I mean, it's not like that, it's just this weird coincidence," Mary stuttered.

"It's a cool coincidence, then," Denny amended. "You'll have someone to hang out with."

"I already have Lydia," said Mary.

And the truck sputtered back to life.

I think Denny said something else about Mary hanging out with Violet, but I'd mostly stopped paying attention.

Because that's what it came down to, didn't it? I was letting Mary down both financially and in terms of having a roommate she knew wouldn't cannibalize her in her sleep, but I was also letting her down as her friend. Yeah, she might hang out with Violet, but . . . she *knew* me. It was different. And I just tugged that rug right out from under her.

Except she still didn't know it.

"Um, so, about that . . ." Mary started.

"I'll be right back," I announced, abruptly pushing my chair back. "I just remembered I was supposed to call Cody about an assignment. Anyone want another drink?"

I looked down at the table. They were both on their first of our double rounds, whereas my beer bottles were both empty.

"I think we're good," Mary said. "Everything okay?"

"Yeah! Totes!" I hoped my voice didn't sound as high-pitched out loud as it did in my head. "I'll be back before the band comes on."

I didn't wait for a response before taking off and heading straight for the bar. Even with a little bit of fuzz in my brain, I ducked and weaved like the pro I am, making it to Carter in record time.

"Same?" he asked when he saw me.

I really did want to step outside for a second, get some air, and I didn't feel much like shotgunning a beer, so I ordered a shot of tequila instead. The party liquor, right? How do we turn this into a party? Gotta shake this stupid guilt off before the band comes on (the real one, that is), and I don't know any better way to do that than alcohol.

I threw back the shot and let the liquid burn as it slid down my throat. It felt nice. Not caring is nice. Not being emotionally invested is nice. Letting go of my emotions and resolving to just not have them is nice. But everyone has to feel *something*, and if that something for me is alcohol, well, that's . . . nice.

The distinct lack of sweaty body scent and shitty cologne once I made it back outside was also nice. The air was crisp, like it might rain any minute. There was no loud, crappy music from Eddie's band. No unwanted body heat pressing in toward me from the tightly packed crowd. No Mary, explaining the future we weren't going to have.

I sat down, tucked in an alcove on the other side of the line of Mechanics' fans.

I sat down, and my resolve to avoid everything that was proving unavoidable tonight came down with me.

I have to tell Mary. I have to tell Mary, and I had to tell my parents, and Lizzie, and even Jane, and Ms. W. I messed up, and the clock is running out for me to tell them myself before we get to the awkward "Oh, the car is packed? Great. Um, no, I'm not bringing anything. Ha-ha, yeah, that is weird. Actually, you know what's even weirder . . ." stage of the whole thing.

Suddenly, everything I'd been putting off for the last ten days hit me all at once.

When should I tell them? And how? And what will I say when they ask what I'm going to do next? Am I going to apply for spring transfer? Do I even want to major in psych anymore? My grades are so mediocre, and they were even when I really *was* trying my hardest. And if I can't even get higher than a C—if I can't even write a stupid application essay—how could I possibly finish a psych major? Grad school? All the things that come after? How could I help anyone?

I sat there, bombarded by all these questions, until my head ached from the mental exertion. And yes, maybe a little bit from the alcohol.

A million questions, and no answers.

Well, no answers except "not tonight" and another beer waiting for me inside at the bar.

"Hey," a voice barked out, startling me out of my (increasingly fuzzier) head.

I looked up quickly enough to notice the parking lot was spin-

ning. Was that another new feature they added for the Mechanics'
shows?

Crap. The show.

"You can't sit out here." I finally realized the voice talking to me
was the other bouncer who had been working with Chris earlier. I
squinted at his name tag, trying to make out the letters and finally
coming up with *Scnnholh*. "Gotta get up."

"Just taking a breather," I mumbled, steadying myself before putting forth the effort to try to, you know, stand.

"Yeah. Can't do that," probably-not-actually-Scnnholh repeated.
"Cops come by, they think drunks are hanging out in the parking
lot. Doesn't look good."

"I'm up," I said. It was half-true. I think. At any rate, at some
point within the next second or five, I was full-fledged standing.

I headed back toward the bar, hoping I hadn't missed too much
of the show and that Mary wasn't pissed. Not that it really mattered,
considering how pissed she was going to be at me forever and ever
amen once she found out the truth. But if I was going to reveal all
in the somewhat-near future, then tonight I was still going to party.
I need more drinks.

I felt this new bouncer stick his arm out in front of me and block
my way into Carter's. Didn't see it. But that must've been what it was.

"Line's back there." He nodded toward a group of about a dozen
(okay, somewhere between three and twenty) people who were still
waiting to get in.

"Are you serious?" I asked, dumbfounded. "I was just in there.
You just saw me."

"Yeah, then you came out."

"So you're not going to let me in?"

He gave me his best *Are you deaf?* look and my shoulders sagged.
Or they may have already been pretty sagged. Come to think of it,
I wasn't even sure they were still attached to my body. Limbs are
weird.

It was almost laughable. I couldn't get into college, and now I couldn't even get into a stupid *bar*.

I shook my head, slowly, so irritated with myself, and tried to consider my options when Chris popped his head out the door.

"Let her in," he said. "She's with the band."

"She's drunk," Scnnholh replied.

"Better drunk inside with her friends than drunk wandering outside alone." At least Chris had some common sense. I decided he was half-forgiven for screwing me over with Just Dance. Besides, maybe karma would have pity on me if I bestowed forgiveness on someone who had wronged me once everyone else found out how I had screwed up.

Smiling my thanks at Chris, I squeezed past him and Scnnholh and back into Carter's.

The Mechanics show was in full swing, but I had no idea how far into it they were. I made my way back toward our table, grabbing an abandoned half-empty drink off the bar as I went. I didn't have the patience to wait for Carter; what's it matter whose beer I'm drinking, anyway? I got closer to the front, catching glimpses of Violet's hair and Gen's metallic-wrapped drumsticks, Duke's stickered bass and . . . well, I'm sure Jones was up on the stage somewhere, maybe blurring together with one of the others—yeah, I think I saw a hint of white shirt—and finally made it to where I'd left Mary and Denny.

"Everything all right?" Denny yelled over the music.

I nodded and took a swig.

Mary frowned in my direction. "You missed like half the show. What happened?"

"I told you, I had to talk to Cody."

She rolled her eyes. "Right. Cody."

And just like that, I felt my attitude shift from worried that Mary would be upset with me to annoyed that it was the case.

"What does *that* mean?"

"Thought you wanted to come to the show and hang out, that's all."

"I'm here, aren't I?"

"Are you?" she shot back. I got why she was upset, and I also knew that she'd drop it if I did. But somehow my irritation with myself got mixed up with unwarranted irritation with her for being irritated with me for the same reasons I was irritated with myself.

"I didn't *have* to come out tonight, did I? But I did. Because *you* asked me to."

Mary lifted one shoulder and turned back to the show, but I was already locked in. Too late.

I moved closer to her so she'd have to pay attention to me and not the song.

"Look, I'm sorry I wasn't here for the whole show. I'm sorry the night hasn't been as super fun as we wanted it to be. I'm sorry I was outside, *talking about my schoolwork*"—the lie didn't even faze me as it shot out of my mouth—"instead of in here listening to you drone on about the safety ratings of a neighborhood 3.2 miles away from Lizzie's office. But sure, get mad that I can't do everything exactly as according to some half-imaginary plan."

"Forget it," she said.

"Forget what? That you're upset with me over something stupid? That I 'screwed up'?" Okay, maybe I was mixing events together in my head now. But like I said, I was fuzzy, and I was on a roll that, apparently, couldn't be stopped. "Party girl Lydia. Disappearing Lydia. Worst cousin Lydia. That's what I do, right? That's why you're upset? I didn't live up to your expectations, even for the night? Maybe I'll just drop out of school and do something as 'frivolous and immature' as your BFF Violet." I threw back what Mary had once said about the idea of pursuing songwriting, before she actually started hanging out with the band.

Something snapped in Mary when I said that. Her eyes flashed, shot to Violet rocking out onstage, before she grabbed me by the arm and pulled me away from the front.

Whoa. Slow down there. Drunk girl walking.

She stopped in the mouth of the hallway to the back—just private enough that she could yell over the band and actually proceeded to do so.

Yep. Mary yelled.

"What the hell is wrong with you tonight?"

I shrugged.

"Forget Cody for a second. Forget running off and disappearing and, honestly, making me kind of worried about you. Why'd you go and drag Violet into this?"

I shrugged.

"Lydia, seriously, what's going on with you? This isn't like you. Not the you I've come to know lately."

I didn't shrug. But I didn't speak, either. I didn't know what to say. I was afraid of what I might say.

"You're 'sick' all the time, you're skipping therapy—don't think I didn't notice you've had like three times as much to drink tonight as Denny and I have—I don't know what you're thinking, but you know you can't pull this shit when we move, right? Not as my roommate, not as a serious college student—"

"Well, good, because I'm not going!"

It just fell out of me. And I couldn't take it back.

Not in front of the whole bar.

Mary and I were yelling because the band was really loud, but then the song ended abruptly and things got a little too quiet, with the exception of my voice, which was still quite loud.

I felt a dozen pairs of eyes swing in our direction. More. It was like that day in psych class all over again, only . . .

Did I care?

Really, did I?

I couldn't even tell.

But maybe that was because I refused to look at the only pair of eyes that actually mattered. Mary's.

I could feel them. But I wasn't going to look.

Through a haze, I heard Violet clear her throat into the microphone.

"We've still got a few more songs for you guys . . ." she went on, as if nothing had happened.

But everything had.

Chapter Twenty
RAINFALL

The windshield wipers squeaked back and forth for a long time. The rain was steady enough to keep blurring up the window in between, but not enough to drown out the sound.

We'd left the bar pretty much immediately, ditching Denny. I'm sure he'll understand. I hope he will.

Mary didn't say anything the entire drive home. Neither did I. I only managed to glance at her once we pulled into the driveway.

Mary didn't look at me, but I saw her jaw shifting. Chewing on words she hadn't decided to spit out yet.

And, quite suddenly, I felt sober.

I wished I didn't.

"Are you telling the truth?" she finally asked, her voice low and controlled. Her eyes still watching the rain beat down and get wiped away.

"Yeah."

She inhaled deeply, and it very well may have been the first breath either of us took in the past minute. Her hand reached up and turned the key in the ignition, stilling every sound except the rain. Tapping against the car over and over. Like a million people all trying to get our attention.

Why did you do it, Lydia?

What's Mary going to say?

What's everyone going to think?

Do you have anything to say for yourself?

Have you learned nothing?

Taptaptaptaptaptaptaptaptaptaptap.

"So that's . . ." Mary started, stilling the fake rain voices inside my head. "That's it? No school. No transfer."

I nodded even though I knew she wasn't looking at me.

Taptaptaptaptaptaptaptaptaptaptap, filling the silence.

"I'm sorry, Mary, I know you waited and planned everything around—" The words rushed out from my mouth all at once, only to be cut off with a shake of her head.

"It's fine."

"No, it's not fine. I promised you—"

"It's fine. It is what it is." Mary sighed. "I'm sure you did your best."

I sat there, unsure how to respond. I don't know exactly how I thought this revelation would go—I never really let myself think that far ahead—but I knew this wasn't it.

"Let's go inside before this rain gets any worse."

Rain. Right. I nodded. "There's an umbrella in the door." Before I'd even closed my mouth, Mary reached down, grabbed the pink polka-dot umbrella, and tossed it in my lap. Her car door opened and slammed shut again just as quickly, leaving her on the outside.

I followed, opening the umbrella and making the short trek from the bottom of the driveway to the front steps. Mary fumbled with the keys, slippery from the rain, her clothes dripping water all over the doormat.

She took off her soaked Converse wordlessly and left them by the door. I waited for her to go up the stairs first, alone. She obviously didn't want to talk to me. Not that I blamed her.

I decided to go into the kitchen and get some water before heading upstairs. The lights were off throughout the house, so I moved quietly, not wanting to wake my parents. I would tell them. I knew I had to. But it could wait until the morning. One weird confrontation was enough for the night.

"Eep!" I screeched as I turned on the kitchen light. "Dad! Oh my God, you scared me."

My dad was sitting at the kitchen table. In the dark. Like some creepy old statue.

"Sorry, honey," he murmured.

"What are you doing? It's like midnight." I grabbed a glass out of the cabinet and an unwanted thought snuck into my mind. "You weren't waiting up for me, were you?"

The idea that my parents possibly still didn't trust me was not a pleasant one. I mean, it was super valid, obviously. But it still hurt. I knew I'd been irresponsible lately, and Mary knew, but *they* didn't know. Yet.

"No, of course not," he replied.

I sat down across from him with my water and watched him massage his temple with his fingers. I realized his eyes were red, and he looked tired.

"Is . . . everything okay?" I wasn't sure I wanted to ask.

He looked up suddenly, as if just fully noticing I was there.

"Oh. Everything's fine, sweetheart," his tone changed as he reassured me. "I just couldn't sleep, and I didn't want to wake your mother." He smiled at me and I tried to believe it. "How was the show?"

I shrugged. "Mary's friend is a good singer."

"Good. Good. I'm glad you're going out again." I swallowed my guilt. Guess they hadn't noticed me sneaking out after all.

He got quiet, and I thought about telling him then. Ripping off the Band-Aid, all at once, tonight. But I looked at him again and saw how genuine the smile on his weary face was and decided to just let us both get a few hours sleep before I broke open that can of worms.

That's kind of what it felt like. A bunch of worms crawling

around my stomach, making me queasy at the thought of letting the rest of my family know I'd messed up. I thought telling Mary would make it easier, but it really just put me in a holding state, the in-between before everyone knew.

Tomorrow.

Tomorrow.

"It's late, peanut. Are you heading to bed soon?" Dad asked.

"Yeah," I said, pushing my chair back as I stood. "I'm gonna go upstairs now. Are you . . . ?"

"I think I'll just stay here for a few more minutes."

I wrapped my arms around his neck and hugged him.

"Do you want the light on?"

"No, that's all right. I don't want to wake your mother," he repeated. I flipped the switch and left for the stairs.

A minute later, I reached the second floor and saw that the light was on in the upstairs bathroom, and the door was open. I saw Mary's shadow moving across the doorway, and I walked toward it.

She stood in front of the sink, wringing her rain-drenched hair out with a towel. Her eyes caught mine in the mirror, unsurprised, and she didn't look away.

"Are you still going?" I asked her.

"I have to," she replied. "I already have a job waiting. I can't stay here and do nothing."

"I understand if you're mad at me."

"I'm not."

"Why?"

A sigh. "I'm just not."

Mary put the towel down and turned to face me, finally.

"Is that why you kept telling me to hang out with Violet? So I would know somebody in town and you wouldn't have to feel guilty about bailing?"

She didn't say it in an abrasive way, but it still took me by surprise.

"No, of course not." I hadn't even thought about that. And I wasn't entirely sure why Mary had, either, to be honest.

She studied me, and I found myself studying her right back. I had no idea what was going through her mind. This whole thing was . . . strange. Stranger than I'd thought. Less explosive than I'd expected. Less . . . anything, really. It felt flat. Hollow. And confusing.

"Okay," she finally said.

"Okay?"

"Yeah. Okay," she repeated. "Look, I'm tired, I'm going to go to bed. Tell your parents tomorrow, all right? You have some stuff to figure out. We all do."

"I will," I promised.

She brushed past me and headed for Jane's old room.

"Mary," I called out, stopping her. "Are we good?"

"Yeah, Lydia. We're fine."

I stood in the bathroom doorway as Mary shut the bedroom door behind her. Tomorrow was going to suck. Today sucked. Most of everything had sucked lately. And as things sucking was becoming the constant state of life, that turned into "fine." That was the most "fine" anything seemed to be.

So, really, I guess tomorrow would be fine. Everything would be fine. Just perfectly fine.

Chapter Twenty-one
The Pre-Fuckup

I didn't tell my parents the next day. The only thing I did was drive Mary to Books Beans and Buds for her last shift.

There's no reason for her to stay anymore, like she'd said. She isn't waiting for me to graduate, so why spend another two weeks down here when she could be up in the city? The past week or so she'd spent a couple of hours a day after her coffee shop shift on the phone with Lizzie, working on stuff, so obviously she's needed more there than here, pouring my mochaccinos.

After I dropped Mary off, I . . . didn't do anything. Didn't go to class, didn't go home and snuggle Kitty. Didn't get on the Internet and go to the CBC campus map and torture myself. Again. I just drove around, ending up at the beach.

I told myself I was gearing up to tell my parents.

In reality, I just fell asleep in the sun.

I thought this would be easier, now that Mary knew. But it wasn't. It just . . . it sucked.

When I woke up, I was hungry, so I drove back into town and bought myself a burger at Crash. Then, my car wouldn't start.

No, really. Just another thing to add to the crappy pile. I could have called a cab. But I decided to use the bathroom first. So I crossed the street.

Well, it would have been rude to use Carter's bathroom and not order a drink, right? And I'd need a little courage to talk to my folks.

It was dark by the time I got home. But that didn't mean people weren't out and about. Specifically Mary, who was outside in the driveway, trying to squeeze all her belongings into the back of her car.

"Lydia!" she said, as the cab pulled up. "What happened to your car?"

"Wouldn't start," I said, a little bleary as I got out.

Mary crossed over to me, got way too close to my face. Extreme close-up Mary. "Are you . . . are you *drunk*?"

"Not really," I said, as I dropped my keys. Bending down to pick them up, things got a little spinny.

"Shit—no wonder you took a cab."

"It's not that bad." I rose back up to standing. And it didn't even take three seconds before I had to fling myself at the hedges to puke.

Stupid Crash burgers.

"Oh, crap," Mary said, coming over to help me up. "Okay . . . okay, let's get you cleaned up."

"My parents . . ."

"Aren't here. They had a thing at the club." She took my sleeve and used it to wipe my mouth, started to lead me into the house.

I felt so stupidly relieved. I wasn't going to have to talk to my parents yet.

"My car really wouldn't start," I slurred.

"Uh-huh," Mary said as she took me inside, changed my clothes, and tucked me in. "I told you to figure your stuff out," I'm pretty sure I heard her mutter, "and this is how you do it?"

"I'm sorry," I said.

"I know," she replied. "I don't know why I expected anything else." I heard her sigh. "Dammit, how am I supposed to leave now?"

You have to go, I thought. *Lizzie needs you. You have to go, and I have to stay.* I didn't want to stand in her way.

That's what I thought. But that's not what I said.

"No one wants you to stay. Just . . . go already," I said, slurring as sleep overtook me.

And she did.

Mary left the next morning. By the time I'd woken up, she was already gone.

I don't know if she's ever going to speak to me again.

Chapter Twenty-two

THE TOTAL FUCKUP

I'd like to think this is my low point. That I'm never ever going to do anything again that makes me feel like this. Not the drinking/puking/morning-hangover-from-hell feeling (repeat two times now!), but the other feeling. The I-fucked-up-and-don't-know-how-to-fix-it feeling.

But unfortunately, that wasn't now. The low point would come later this evening.

"I can't believe Mary had to head out so soon—I feel like she just got here!" my mom said that morning at breakfast. I was trying to swallow some eggs. It wasn't going super well.

"Yeah, well . . . she had to jump at that apartment opportunity, you know," I lied. Mary was going to be staying on Lizzie's couch until she found a place to stay long-term. But since she wasn't going to be making a ton (until Lizzie's company got some rich people to invest in it) and I was no longer going to be there to contribute some of my student loan money to the rent, she was probably going to end up renting a closet in a house with ten other people.

Again—sorry, Mary.

"Well, at least you'll have a place ready when you move up." Mom plated an omelet and slid it to my dad under his newspaper. "Mary's coming down for your graduation, right? I hope so, so you two can drive up together. I do not like the idea of that old car making that long drive."

This is the point where I could have come clean. I could have said, "Mom, Dad, I have to tell you something." And I almost did.

"About that. Actually—"

"But of course you're going to *have* to take your car," my mom continued. "You have to get to campus somehow."

My dad looked at me over the top of his paper. Then he laid the paper aside. "But first we have to get it fixed. Now, I called the tow company first thing this morning. Your car is already at the repair shop. They'll have it right as rain. Is that what you're worried about, peanut?"

"I mean, the car is a problem, but . . ." I said, pushing my eggs around on my plate.

"Well, consider it taken care of," Dad said, forking up a piece of his omelet but still looking at me. "Soon enough, you'll have much more interesting things to worry about."

"And we won't have anything to worry about at all." My mom smiled at my dad, who frowned back at her.

Mom, Dad, I have to tell you something.

"Right," I said. And left it at that.

* * *

If I was going to chicken out on telling my parents the truth, I suppose I'd have to do something else with my Saturday. Luckily I had experience with this.

List of Things Lydia Bennet Would Usually Do While Avoiding Her Parents on an Average Saturday

1. Go shopping at the mall.
2. Tweet.
3. Vlog.
4. Cut up Dad's newspaper for papier-mâché.
5. Glitter something.
6. Groom Kitty.
7. Bandage scratches from Kitty.
8. Practice French kissing with stuffed version of Mr. Wuffles. (Note: this practice stopped upon my first real French kiss in eighth grade. Stuffed Mr. Wuffles couldn't compete.)
9. Hang with sisters.
10. Get kicked out of sisters' rooms.
11. Put together killer outfits for whatever party was happening that night.
12. Answer texts from a guy.

Unfortunately, most of those either don't apply anymore or aren't things I really wanted to do (especially grooming Kitty—she can sense when the nail clippers are coming), except maybe that last one.

Cody: Hey, what happened to you yesterday?
Lydia: Nothing. Did I miss anything in class?
Cody: Nothing. But I'll share my notes with you if you want.
Lydia: God, I'm bored.
Cody: I can fix that. ;)

You might be thinking that, considering how last night ended—and the night before—going out was the last thing I needed. And I totally agree. Last thing I needed.

Only thing I wanted.

Lydia: Pick me up at 8.

*　*　*

"OMG, I'm soooooo glad to be out!"

I rolled my shoulders back the second we walked into Carter's. I was so done tiptoeing around my house. Walking by Mary's/Jane's empty room is like, "Way to be reminded of your total failure in life, Lydia."

I didn't need to be reminded. I just wanted to have fun. Again.

"Wow, it's crowded," Cody said as he entered the bar behind me.

"Duh, it's Saturday."

"Right." He nodded. "Just want to make sure we can get a table. But you know if it's too crazy for you, we can always go back to my place . . ."

"Cody. It's never too crazy for Lydia Bennet." I pointed to the seating area. "See, a table just opened up."

"Oh, cool—I'll grab it; you go get drinks?"

Cody shuffled over to the table before I could say anything. Okay, then.

I elbowed my way to the bar, knowing to stand by the pass because in three . . . two . . . one . . .

"Chris!" I said as the bouncer stepped through the pass to begin his bartender duties. "My adversary. We meet again."

"Lydia. What can I do for you?"

I gave him our order.

"So," he said, pulling the taps for our chosen microbrews. "Third night in a row?"

"Um, yeah, I guess," I said, frowning a little. "Is that a problem? Afraid I'll beat your Just Dance record? *Again?*"

"Nope." Chris shook his head. "But . . . what are you doing, Lydia?"

The question wiped any trace of a smile from my face.

"I'm just having fun, Chris." And I would. If it killed me.

"Uh-huh," Chris said, and slid the beers across the bar to me.

I picked the money out of my pocket (no way I was gonna run a tab if Chris was going to be all judge-y) and headed back to the table.

"Man, a chick who asks me out and buys the beers. I think I'm enjoying this whole feminism thing," Cody said, raising his glass to me before taking a big swig. I sort of toasted him back and took a smaller sip of mine.

It tasted funny.

Not in an "Oh my God, someone spiked my drink" kind of way, but in a "This is not nearly as satisfying as I want it to be" type of way. Like, something sour on my tongue was getting in the way of enjoying my delicious beverage.

Or something sour in my brain.

It was as if there was an echo in my head. Things I'd managed to hear but not really absorb all decided that now was the time to worm their way into my brain.

"I knew there was something interesting about you the second we met," Cody said.

"Hmmm . . ." I replied, taking another sip of my beer. Maybe this one would be better. . . . Nope. Darn it. "What do you mean?"

"Oh, now you're just angling for praise."

That's when I heard the first echo. And it sounded like Mary.

I don't know why I expected anything else.

I wanted to be so mad when she'd said that. Mad because she was leaving, and mad because she'd said it. But I was too tired. Not because of being drunk and nearly asleep, but because . . . I don't know why I expected anything else from myself, either.

But I had. I'd expected more from me.

Why had I stopped doing that? Why had I just . . . given up?

"I don't want to be all psychoanalytic," Cody kept talking. "But you have a little bit of player in you, don't you?"

"Player?" I said, tuning back in to my date. Yup, date. I was on a date. Pay attention to him. Not to the refrain of my cousin's voice in my head. "Okay, you're gonna have to clarify that one, and no, I'm not just fishing for compliments. If I was, I'd direct your attention to my pretty eyes." I batted my eyelashes at him, and he laughed.

"You're determined. Determined to be yourself. To have a ball. To not let crap from the past get you down."

I was? Then why had I just given up?

That's when I heard the second voice.

And this one sounded like my dad.

Is that what you're worried about, peanut?

I was worried. About something. I thought I was worried about not getting into school and having to tell my parents and Lizzie and everyone else, and what I was going to do with the rest of my life. But was that *actually* what was getting to me?

At that second, with sour beer churning in my stomach, I'd have to say no. Because what was worrying me was that Cody thought I was only determined to have a good time. No matter what.

And yeah, maybe I came into this bar for that reason tonight, but . . . stupid voices in my head were getting in the way of that with their morals and their questioning.

"I don't think I'm really like that."

Cody leaned in, sincere interest on his face. "You're not? So . . . the past does get you down sometimes?"

"Umm . . ." I replied, not really sure how to answer that. "Oh, hey, look! The pool table is free! Let's play!"

I jumped up, pulling Cody off his barstool. He didn't really have a chance to object.

I was more than happy to give ignoring the voices in my head one last-ditch effort. And it worked. For a little while.

We played three rounds of pool, which was all we had the quarters for (hey, I just blew all my cash on those beers). But at the end of them, I felt a lot better. Maybe it was the fact that I didn't scratch on the eight ball and Cody did—twice (his face got sooooooo red the second time). Or maybe it was the beers he had to buy me after each lost round, which were tasting progressively less sour. But by the time we were forced to give up the table to the next set of quarters, I was pink in the face and laughing.

"Woo-hoo!" I cheered, flush with victory and beer.

Amazingly, my bar karma had remained and our table was still vacant—or vacant again; the place had thinned out a bit.

"Yeah, yeah," Cody grumbled. "You have better cue-handling skills than me. Not a shock." `

I frowned. "What's that supposed to mean?"

"Nothing," Cody backtracked. "Are you going to ask me what I mean all night?"

"Only when you're being weird about stuff."

"I suppose that's fair." Cody winked. "Didn't mean to guy double-speak you, like others have."

I didn't have to ask what he meant by that. "I . . . don't really want to talk about my ex. It's not relevant."

"I know, but . . . it has to be on your mind a little, right? Going out with someone new is always hard, brings up bad memories."

I just looked at Cody. Really looked at him, for the first time all night. Maybe the first time since we met. His body was leaned forward in that way Ms. W does when she's trying to pull something out of me. The only difference is, Ms. W is my therapist. Our relationship is all about us getting to the bottom of things.

My relationship with Cody is . . . not that.

You know what his major is, right?

Harriet's voice burst into my head.

"But for you it has to be extra weird because you filmed the whole thing. You're essentially famous for having a bad boyfriend. What was his name? George?"

I flinched. Who is this guy? Why is he even here with me?

"It's kind of weird for me, too," he said when I didn't speak. "If that helps at all. Dating a girl with that past."

And then . . . I started to really listen to what Cody was saying.

"You can tell me what it was like. It's . . . safe. I'm a good guy, you know?"

Here's the thing about good guys. They don't tell you they're good guys. Much like when we first met, Cody told me he wasn't hitting on me when he asked for my number. The winky faces that followed said otherwise. And everything Cody was saying, all the prying, was really starting to make me uncomfortable.

It was becoming stupidly obvious that this was the Worst Date Ever.

And Lydia Bennet doesn't do bad dates.

"Yeah, I said I don't want to talk about it, so we're not talking about it." My expression went pure bitch-face, which every girl needs to have in their repertoire if they don't already.

"Come on, Lyds—"

"I said no. You should get used to that."

And then I hopped off the barstool, and I walked out the front door.

God, I thought, breathing in the cool night air, when had I become so . . . weak? So distracted by everything that I let myself get lost in a little guy-attention. I'm not that person. I'm someone who can stand on my own two feet and handle myself.

I'm Lydia freaking Bennet.

And I'm done being lame.

Or so I thought.

"What the hell, Lydia?" Cody's voice came from behind me, the door to Carter's swinging shut behind him. "You're just gonna walk out?"

"I told you I was uncomfortable with the conversation, but you just kept going."

"You have to talk about it with someone."

"I don't have to talk about it with you." I crossed my arms over my chest. "But because you have big eyes and a soft voice you expect me to be sad and quiet and vulnerable. To pour all my secrets out to you?"

"Come on . . . I know you were hurt, Lydia."

"Right—and that's *the only thing* you know about me." I turned on him.

"What are you talking about?" he said. "You're drunk."

"No, I'm not," I said. The beers I'd had were quickly wearing off and things were becoming very clear. "You don't know anything about me. You never wanted to. You only wanted the gory details about my ex—'It must be weird coming back here to Carter's, Lydia' or 'My ex doesn't have anything on yours—tell me about it' and just now, you were all 'What was it like, being recognized? Must be weird. Especially being famous for having a bad boyfriend.'"

"You don't get to be mad at me for looking you up online," Cody said. "You left all that stuff up there."

"Yeah, and the second you found out about it, you started salivating. Like one of Pavlov's dogs," I said. "Now, I don't know if you're interested in me because you like damaged girls, or you think because I had a sex tape I might be an interesting fuck, but I don't care to find out."

His eyes got super dark. And scary. More scary than I'd ever seen.

"What the hell is this?" he said. "I thought you liked me. I take you out; I'm a nice guy! And now you're shoving me off?"

"Yeah, I'm shoving you off. Because you don't give a damn about me. You just want to tell your frat brothers about how you dated that crazy chick from the Internet over the summer, and then maybe write a story about her for your next composition class. Guess what: my life is not your story, jackass."

He looked down and away, for just a split second. But I'd been paying enough attention in psych class—and in my sessions with Ms. Winters—to know what it meant.

One last voice in my head. Cody's.

Just need to find a story to tell, and boom.

"Oh, so that's what you think of me?" he blustered, totally lying, totally caught. "You think because you got used before that I'm going to use you? God, take some responsibility for your own actions. You're just like my last girlfriend—such a pathetic victim, all the time. Stuff always happened *to* her, it was never her fault."

"Oh, I absolutely consider it my fault," I said.

He cocked his head to one side.

"That I hung out with you in the first place."

His eyes went dark again. But this time he wasn't just scary. He was angry. And I saw it—the second before he did. He was going to reach for me. Try and grab me—and what the hell was I going to do to stop him? I didn't have pepper spray or even my own car here. I could scream, though. I sucked in my breath and—

"Hey!" a voice called from the side door of Carter's.

Chris was standing there, his huge bouncer body blocking the light from the doorway.

"Lydia. Been looking for you. The Just Dance machine is free," Chris said, his eyes staying on me. "Everything okay?"

"Everything's fine, buddy—" Cody said, but Chris cut him off.

"I don't know you. So I wasn't talking to you." He kept his eyes on me. "You want to come back in? Dance battle?"

"Yeah," I said, backing away from Cody. "I think that's a good idea."

As I moved quickly to Chris, I could hear Cody muttering "Crazy bitch" under his breath as he stalked toward his car, got in, and screeched the tires on his way out of the parking lot. Yep, that's me. The crazy bitch who decided to stand up for herself. The crazy bitch who was over being super lame. The crazy bitch who didn't even consider putting pepper spray in her purse before this farce of a date.

The crazy bitch who was a little more wobbly at the moment than she let on.

"Hey, Chris," I said, following him inside. "Thanks, but . . . I'm a little too tired to dance battle right now. I think . . . I'm just going to go home."

Chris nodded. "Want me to call someone for you?"

I shook my head and held up my phone. "No, it's okay. I got it."

"Okay," Chris said, leading me into the storage room, aka backstage.

I nodded. "Thanks. For, um . . . all of that."

Bouncers, in my experience, aren't really big into displays of emotion. So if he felt anything at all about having just saved my ass, it didn't show beyond his blushing a little and mumbling about having to be back at the bar before shuffling out.

I didn't know my hand was shaking until I sat down and started to go through my contacts. I didn't have cash left on me for a cab. Even if I'd had my car here it wasn't drivable—still in the shop. And I didn't have a ton of friends in town. Mary was gone. There wasn't a lot of choice in who to call.

And for a split second—less than a heartbeat—I wanted to call George.

Yes, George. Because at one time, he would have held me until I felt safe. And once I felt safe, he'd make me laugh about it.

But I knew he wouldn't pick up now. I'd dialed that number until it disconnected.

I hated that I was thinking about him now. And I hated the hollow feeling in my chest whenever I did. I knew better. My head did, at least.

So instead, I called a man—the only man—I knew I could trust. "Hi, Dad? It's Lydia. . . . Um, I need you to come get me."

Chapter Twenty-three
COMING CLEAN

The drive home was quiet. My dad had left the house so quickly, he was still in his blue bathrobe and slippers. He'd pulled up outside of Carter's, and if I hadn't been at the front door waiting for him, I'm sure he'd have rushed inside like that.

It was a long time before he said anything to me.

"We didn't know you'd gone out."

"I know."

"When the phone rang it scared your mother."

"I'm sorry."

We drove on a little more.

"You know, you don't have to sneak out. You're an adult; we trust you."

"Yeah," I said, playing with my hands. "I just didn't want you to think I was being irresponsible."

"Why would we think that?"

He said it so softly, I barely heard it. And I didn't know how to answer.

"I screwed up," I said finally, just as softly. "I'm not going to Central Bay College. I missed the application deadline."

My dad was quiet as he turned onto our street. Then, he sighed. "Well. I thought it might be something like that. Mary leaving and all."

"I'm sorry."

"Yes," he said, parking the car in the driveway. "I imagine you are."

His voice was so quiet, so resigned . . . it just made me feel worse.

"I know you must be unhappy . . ." I began, but another sigh from my dad stopped me.

"I could be," he said, tired. "But what would the point be of that? Life . . . life is too short."

He opened his car door, climbed out. I followed him.

"Go get some sleep, Lydia," he said, letting me in the front door. "I'll tell your mother. We'll talk more in the morning."

I watched my dad, hunched over as he went back to his and Mom's bedroom. For the first time, my dad looked old to me. Like, grandpa, ear-hair old. Tired-old. And with my latest screw-up, I could see I'd just added more weight to him.

I went upstairs and flopped onto my bed, scaring a sleeping Kitty. She hissed at me. But I understood—I wanted to hiss at myself.

* * *

It wasn't just my parents who I had to come clean to. I owed others an explanation.

I sat in Ms. W's office, twisting my fingers, having just spilled my guts, waiting for her shock, her horror, her . . . however therapists tell you they're disappointed in you.

But Ms. W challenged my expectations.

"Oh, Lydia. I knew."

My eyes flew up. "You knew? How?"

"You started acting somewhat . . . defensively around the time I knew your application was due. Then you missed another session, and . . ." She sighed. "But I'm very glad you told me."

"Finally," I added. Then I waited.

And waited.

"Well . . . ?" I said.

She blinked at me. "Well, what?"

"Don't you want to know how this all makes me feel?"

"All right." She smiled. "I'll play along. How does it make you feel?"

"Like . . ." I searched for the words. "Like I've been wasting your time."

"My time?"

"All these months, we've been trying to put my life together. But nothing's changed."

Ms. Winters leaned forward. She didn't even glance at her notepad.

"What hasn't changed?"

"*Me*. I'm still *her*. The screw-up. The asshole-magnet. The traumatized chick with a sex tape." I sniffled, trying to suck up that sting in my nose that felt suspiciously like I was going to cry. I hadn't cried in months. And I hadn't cried in therapy *ever*. "I just thought she'd be gone by now."

Ms. Winters took a deep breath, then let it out slowly.

"First of all, the fact that Cody was . . . less than a gentleman is his fault, not yours."

I had to stop myself from rolling my eyes. She'd said the exact same thing about George, a million years ago. I don't know if I believed it—then or now. People will do what you let them get away with, you know?

"Second, you can't erase your past. And I don't think you actually want to."

I just shot her a look from underneath my bangs.

"If you did," she continued, "I imagine you would have taken down your videos from the Internet."

Okay, fair point.

"I wouldn't want you to change completely, either," Ms. W was saying. "You just have to find a way to reconcile your old self-image with your new objectives. Integrate old Lydia into new Lydia, as it were."

I just kind of . . . grimaced at that. Does she want me to end up some weird Lydia hybrid? Two personalities, one body? I mean, split personalities *look* like fun in those made-for-TV movies, but probably a little less awesome in reality.

"But still," I said, squirming a little. "I had this goal . . . this totally achievable plan, and I had you and Darcy calling in favors for me—and the second things got tough, I just gave up. And I mean, I don't even know if I want to study psychology anymore—which I guess is a good thing because I'm not going to get the chance."

"Hmm," Ms. Winters said. "Let's put your transfer and whether you want to study psychology aside for a second. You know what I find interesting? That you *didn't* give up."

I snorted. It was the only appropriate response.

"You didn't," she insisted. "You could have stopped going to classes. Stopped turning in your papers. But you kept on doing the work. Maybe a little less enthusiastically than before, but . . . you kept going."

I thought for a second and . . . yeah—last Friday aside, I did do all my schoolwork and go to all my classes. Even though there were times I *really* didn't want to.

"That's perseverance. And that's not something you can teach. That's something that you have." She smiled at me. "And you have intuition—which is how you were able to recognize Cody as a negative influence before you got more involved with him. Those two together, I have no doubt you'll succeed at whatever you choose to do."

"Not if I'm getting C's in psychology."

Ms. Winters leaned back in her chair, her arms resting open on the armrests. Like a noble something-or-other. The royal, benevolent therapist.

"Lydia, this is our last session. You have finals this week and then you'll be done. So I want to give you one last assignment."

"Okay . . ." I said, skeptical. "'Cause homework is something I'm totally going to be into."

She laughed a little.

"Be kind to yourself. When you get your associate degree, find a way to celebrate it. I know it feels like a small thing right now, but it deserves recognition."

Those words stayed with me long after I left Ms. W's office for the last time.

I mean, be "kind" to myself? I was pretty much under the impression I'd spent the last couple of weeks being way too easy on myself. Blowing off life never struck me as the harder path. And how was I supposed to celebrate getting my associate degree when I had no idea what to do with it and no idea what came next?

But then again, it wasn't exactly kind to beat myself up over my failures. And I'd been the one doing that—not my parents, not even Mary.

I'd expected more. I'm the one who let me down.

But an assignment from Ms. W is usually worth giving a try.

Be kind to myself. Celebrate. Never thought anyone would ever have to tell Lydia Bennet when and why to party, but there you go.

I guess some stuff has changed.

But before I do, I have to get through my finals.

Dracula, by Bram Stoker
(or, Seriously, Victorians Were Lame)

Dracula isn't a very good book. There, I said it. Even though it didn't "invent" the vampire, it is notable for popularizing vampires in culture and literature. So if we really wanted to, we could blame *Twilight* on Bram Stoker, but really I think we have to blame the late nineties and its fascination with body glitter more. But *Dracula*'s biggest problem isn't that it's an epistolary novel, written as a bunch of letters and diary entries, making it hard to follow (and seriously, who writes diary entries that perfectly describe events and conversations in a linear way? No one, that's who), it's that Dracula isn't a very good villain, because he's not a bad guy. He's just a whiny guy.

When we meet Dracula, Jonathan Harker is going to his castle in Transylvania (which is in Romania now—I looked it up) because he's a London lawyer and Dracula is buying a house somewhere and needs some paperwork filed. Then, Dracula won't let him leave and won't sign the papers, and Jonathan meets "the sisters," who are this threesome of women who want to consume him, and Dracula just leaves him there to be consumed. Because now that he had the paperwork for his new digs all worked out, and he'd seen a picture of Jonathan's fiancée, Mina, Dracula didn't need him anymore.

Let's discard for a second the morality lesson presented where if one gets bitten by Dracula they turn sexy and lustful. Presenting sexy as a bad thing (women have sex? Shocker! Someone fetch whatever smelling salts are!) is just what Victorian guys had to do because they couldn't handle women being awesome. It's pretty much still in effect, too, so thanks for that, Victorians.

Instead, let's focus on what Dracula does to Jonathan. He imprisons him. Jonathan can't be seduced by Dracula, and can't be driven crazy like Renfield, so Drac locks him away. To be fed to the sisters or to waste away. Kind of passive for a mega-evil vampire, don't you think? Strike one against being a decent villain.

So Dracula goes to London—after eating an entire ship full of sailors on the way (except for that captain, who is tied to the ship's helm and *how* did he write a captain's log while tied to a helm?)—kills a girl named Lucy, and stalks Jonathan's fiancée, Mina (again, behind the scenes—passive evil).

When Mina is being influenced by Dracula, she's in a dreamlike state, and starts to empathize with him. In the movies, this is presented as a seduction, as "love." And that Dracula can awaken a part of his victim that's missing.

But the thing is, that's not what Dracula is about. Mina and Lucy might think that they want what he has—that he can feed their "hunger"—that he's freeing them from it. But really, they're being enslaved by it. And it's sad. Because I bet if asked why he did this, Dracula wouldn't be able to answer, other than it's the only thing he can do. At least in the movie they gave him Winona Ryder, a wife who he loved and was searching for and avenging. In the book, he's just something that can never be filled. And he whines about it. Like it's the most terrible thing ever. More terrible than having cancer, or no Wi-Fi.

Because *of course* he wouldn't do those things if he didn't have to. If he didn't need to drain people's blood, everyone would be happy and pumping a full ten pints. But here's the thing: he *doesn't* have to. Really. He doesn't have to exist that way—if he truly felt bad enough about his actions, he could stop doing them. Yes, my theory might be flawed because this would result in Dracula's death, but he's a paranormal creature who shouldn't exist in the first place, so this would simply be the restoration of the natural order. Also, this is fiction. But if he wasn't supernatural, if he wasn't a vampire—if he was just a guy who wouldn't see past his own wants and needs—then you don't need him. People will only do what you let them get away with.

If I could, I'd like to talk to Lucy and Mina for a minute. Ladies: stop looking around for the exciting thing. I get it; I really do. You look around and sometimes wonder, *is this it? There has to be more.* And then this guy shows up and he tells you he's crazy about you but it's driving him mad and making him act the way he is. And it's exciting, and scary, but ultimately, that kind of drama will just leave you drained—and in your case, literally.

You've both got decent men who want to create lives with you. Lucy, you have three! Pick one! Personally, I'd have gone with the cowboy, so much cooler than the fancy British guys. They won't try to control you (beyond the usual "You're my wife, so please do as I ask you in these old-fashioned, non-women-voting times") and they won't try to use you for their own ends. Don't waste your time with crazy-makers like Dracula. Avoid it completely: just don't invite him in.

Come see me after class! —Natalie

Chapter Twenty-four
GOOD-BYE TO ALL THAT

"Excuse me, Natalie?" It was Friday. I hung back while everyone else packed up, taking my time, fidgeting with my pencil case. Back to fidgeting again. Back to caring.

Not a bad thing, of course. But when your teacher writes "Come see me after class!" (exclamation point included) just when you've started caring about your grades again, it does inspire some mild freaking out.

"Lydia?" Natalie blinked at me as she lifted her massive backpack onto her tiny shoulders.

"You wanted to talk to me?" I asked, holding up the paper. When she'd handed back the papers at the beginning of class, everyone was doing the usual showing of their grades to everyone else. Except for me. Not only because my paper didn't *have* a grade, but because I didn't have anyone to show it to anymore. On Monday, Cody had pointedly walked in late, and pointedly sat not next to me but in the empty chair next to Harriet.

Or at least, he tried to sit next to Harriet.

"Sorry, I'm saving this seat for someone," she'd said, placing her bag there before he could sit.

This left Cody with the option of sitting next to me (and you bet your ass I placed my own bag on the chair immediately) or wedging into the other empty chair in the back next to the broom closet.

As Cody made his way to the broom closet, Harriet flicked her eyes up at me with the tiniest of smiles. She didn't know anything of what happened over the weekend, I'm pretty sure. She just knew he was a jackass.

Cody had been much easier to avoid in psych, as he was three rows in front. I watched him play solitaire on his computer while the rest of us copied down a flurry of notes, reviewing what was going to be on the final. Not a single text buzzed my phone.

Good riddance to that. I know that the past couple weeks of slacking off had been my own doing, but I have to give Cody some credit—it's a lot easier to give up when there's someone giving up beside you.

But as soon as I smiled back at Harriet, her face went stony again, and she was back to focusing on her manicure.

But that was Monday. Wednesday we turned in our final papers. Today was our last class. Mostly, Natalie had spent it talking about conclusive themes in gothic literature, and what she hoped we'd gotten out of the class. Most everyone else snuck glances at their phones, or doodled.

But me? I got to spend the whole hour worrying about the "See me after class!" on my paper.

"Oh, yes!" Natalie's face lit up as I came forward. "Thanks for waiting."

"Uh-huh," I said, before rushing into the speech I'd been preparing all class. "Listen, I know that my work hasn't been really focused lately or up to certain standards, but I worked really hard on this essay, I read the book and the study guide. If you need me to rewrite it to get a passing grade, or to do extra credit work, I absolutely can—"

"Lydia, what are you talking about?" Natalie said. "I just wanted to tell you in person how much I enjoyed your final paper."

"You . . . enjoyed it?" I said, feeling the rushing tingles of relief all through my body. Or maybe it was disbelief. I'd been afraid the last hour that I hadn't gotten a passing grade on the final paper—which meant I wouldn't have gotten a passing grade in the class. Which would mean that I don't graduate. Which would mean that not only am I a non-Central-Bay-College-attending failure, but I am a spectacular mondo-failure of epic suckiness.

In order to avoid that fate, hell yes, I'd do extra credit. But it looked like I might not have to.

"Of course I enjoyed it! Why do you think I gave you an A?" Natalie replied.

"You did?" I flipped the paper over, looking for my grade. Nope, not there.

"Oh! Did I not write it on the paper?" she said, taking it from me and, very quickly pulling out a pen, planted a big, fat "A" at the top of the page. "I'm so sorry. Can I tell you a secret?" She leaned in. "This was the first class I ever taught."

"You're kidding," I said, trying to keep my face as stoic as possible.

"Yeah." Natalie giggled. "But that's probably why I enjoyed your paper so much. I don't know any better. You straight-up gave me your opinion, and laid out your argument. It was so refreshing after ten papers on how Dracula embodies nineteenth-century fears about colonialism."

"It was?" I'd have thought that anyone who taught gothic lit would have been all about boring stuff like colonialism, but what do I know?

"Yes, and I love that you wanted to give the characters advice. And not bad advice, I may add." She started to head for the door, and I followed her out into the hall. "Having been one of those girls myself, I could have used a good talking-to at that time."

My head snapped up at that. Little Natalie had a wild past with a bad boy? I just hope he wasn't a vampire (although it would explain her teaching gothic lit).

"Well, I'm glad you liked it," I said. "It's funny, in my psych class essays, the professor never liked it when I gave my honest opinion."

"Who'd you have?" Natalie asked as we walked out the front doors and got blinded by sunlight. "Professor Latham?"

I nodded.

"Oh, yeah. Word around the faculty lounge is that he's a stickler for the textbook, and that's all. Makes grading tests and papers easier."

"Yeah, I figured that out in time for the final. We just took it this morning."

I'd spent the whole week studying like crazy. I made flash cards—and I didn't even use a glitter pen. When I sat down to take the test, I knew pretty much every question—or if I didn't, I knew enough to guess well. I think I might have even broken my streak of C's with a B.

"Good. But it's too bad Latham wasn't testing you on your analysis skills. Because I think you could have saved Lucy and Mina some serious heartache. And beheading."

I said good-bye to Natalie and headed for the parking lot. A big red "A" on my paper added a little skip to my step. And so did what she'd said. About my being good at analysis. What had Ms. W called it? Intuition?

It made me feel just a little bit more like maybe psych wasn't *not* the path for me.

I'd been so down on psychology since learning how long it would take me to get my degree(s). And since realizing I had missed the deadline. Giving up had meant giving *that* up, and I hadn't cared, because it wasn't like the class was epically awesome. But now . . .

Maybe it's something I wouldn't be that bad at, after all.

Too bad I screwed up my chance.

＊　＊　＊

Community college graduation isn't like regular college graduation. At least, mine wasn't. There are no caps and gowns, no speech, no ceremony. Not for the summer session, anyway. What we got instead was a letter in the mail with our final grades (A for Gothic Lit . . . and a B- in Psych!) and an offer to order a copy of my associate degree on a real fake-leather backing for only $59.99.

I should probably order it. It's the only degree I'm likely to get, and Ms. W told me to celebrate my graduation. Although I'm not sure real fake leather qualifies as celebratory.

But even given my colossal screw-up, my mom wasn't about to let the occasion go unmarked. So, we got all dressed up and went out to dinner.

My mom, my dad, me, and Lizzie, who'd come down for graduation.

Just Lizzie. No one else.

"You must be so relieved," Lizzie said after the waiters had placed a piece of cake with "Congrats!" scrawled in chocolate sauce on the plate in front of me. I admit, I was a little disappointed. I expected some singing from the waiters. "To finally be done. I know I was."

"Oh, yeah," I said, plastering on a fake smile. "Super relieved."

"Lizzie, next time you drive down all the way from San Francisco, tell that *gorgeous* William Darcy of yours that I expect him as well," Mom said, casually swiping a bite of my congrats cake. "I don't like you on the road that long by yourself."

"I will," Lizzie replied. She was way more at ease with Mom's prying into her love life now that she had a love life to pry into. "He wanted to come, but something happened with his Domino project that he needed to fix."

"Besides, it's not like this is a big deal," I said under my breath. I knew if my mom heard me she'd be hurt. Granted, she didn't plan a big, elaborate meal and spend the entire day in the kitchen, but she's way more into the celebratory thing than I am right now. She's on her third glass of wine. And for Mom, that's like swilling a fifth of whiskey.

"Of course it's a big deal," Lizzie said to me, equally low. "Do you . . . do you have any idea what you want to do now? You can still apply at Central Bay College for the spring semester, you know. Darcy would be happy to call again—"

"Hmm," I said, not wanting to say anything. The truth was, I didn't know if I wanted to go to CBC. In my mind, it would always be the place I failed at. But it's also the only school where the Darcys have a building named after them (I think it's a pagoda), so my getting into any other college without the help of my sister's super-rich boyfriend is not exactly probable. Secretly, I was really glad Darcy had AI issues with his latest app and had to miss dinner, because how do you apologize to someone for not making good on the help they gave you?

But Lizzie was currently staring at me, so I took a sip of water and changed the conversation to the only thing I could think of. Which wasn't much better than what we'd been talking about before. "How's Mary doing?"

"Great!" Lizzie said, but then tempered her enthusiasm. "I mean, good. She's streamlined a lot of my work—the financing stuff I have no idea how to do. She's got me applying for small-business licenses and finding office space."

"Office space? Darce couldn't lend you a cubicle at Pemberley Digital?"

"Well, he could, but we are a separate company. So far we've been working out of my apartment. Which isn't even really mine. Plus, Mary's crashing there, so it can't be much fun for her, working where she sleeps."

"And where you sleep," I said.

"I think . . . you should give Mary a call. She'd probably really like to hear from you," Lizzie said, hopeful.

"Hmm," I said again.

"I'm very glad you're here, Lizzie," my father said, thankfully drawing my sister's attention to him. "Even though it's only for a short time. I'm hoping you can talk some sense into—"

Maybe I did want to call Mary. But if she couldn't come down for my graduation non-ceremony, then she pretty obviously doesn't want to hear from me. Which is fine. She's got her big new life, and I . . . I have congrats cake.

Although, not so much.

"Oh, honey," Mom interrupted whatever Dad was whispering to Lizzie, slurring slightly. "Can you find the waiter? I think we should have another slice of cake brought out for Lydia."

I looked down at my plate. The chocolate "Congrats!" was smeared into oblivion. And the cake? The cake was completely gone.

Mom wiped away a bit of frosting from the corner of her mouth. "You must be hungrier than you let on, sweetie."

※   ※   ※

We got home late enough that it kept Lizzie from asking me any more probing questions. Once we walked in the house, Dad put our cake-and-wine-filled mom to bed, and then went to sit in his den and . . . do den things, I guess. Lizzie had woken up super early to drive here today, so she pretty much crashed immediately in her old room/Mom's meditation room/aquarium/whatever. And that just left me.

I'd spent a lot of time alone this summer—but this is the first time it had felt like a void.

There's nothing on my calendar anymore. No Sunday sessions with Ms. Winters. No classes Monday, Wednesday, Friday. No date set to drive up to the city with Mary, or to register for classes. I might have a dentist appointment sometime in October, but that's it.

Lizzie had asked it, I'd ignored it, but in reality, it was the only thing I was thinking. *What am I going to do now?*

I could get a job. There was that opening at Books Beans and Buds left by Mary. And Violet. I could totally be a minimum-wage server at the coffee shop near my old campus—because that's not the most depressing thing ever.

I could try and sell my stuff online—but while my fashion sense is epically awesome, I don't think there are a lot of people who could pull off my style. And besides, who'd want to look like Lydia Bennet? The associate-degree-having, no-career-planned, still-living-at-home-with-her-parents loser (there, I said it) Bennet sister?

It's times like this I really wish I had a better computer.

No, really, because then I could go online and bliss out on blogs, or pirate movies, and not worry for a week, or three—and not go cross-eyed (not a super fetching look) staring at my phone screen. But as it was, my computer could barely open my email, which is what I was forcing it to do at that moment.

The second I did, glitter and cats rained down on my screen.

It took me a second to realize my computer hadn't exploded, and I was, in fact, staring at an e-card. Kinda the most perfect e-card ever.

There was only one person it could be from.

Happy graduation, Lydia!

I tried to call you a couple of times, and I sent a package, but it won't get there for a few days. But I wanted you to know TODAY how proud I am of you.

Miss you more than you know!

Love, Jane

Only Jane would manage to find the e-card with the most cats and glitter of all time because a present she sent will be late and she couldn't get through to me on the phone.

Speaking of, why couldn't she get through on my phone? I rolled my eyes as I checked it. Dead again. I have got to get better about charging it after Kitty's white-noise sessions.

I plugged it in and waited for it to glow on.

Five voice mails from Jane. And one from . . .

Ricky Collins. The weird guy who used to live across the street when we were kids, and went to school with Lizzie. And somehow kept finding his way back into our lives.

"Greetings, Miss Bennet! I do hope this message finds you in good health and good spirits. However, I wished to personally call and apologize on behalf of Collins & Collins, Winnipeg, for your . . . unfortunate circumstances. As someone on intimate terms with your family, I consider myself honor-bound to look after the Bennets, should a situation requiring as much arise. So it is my pleasure to offer you a position here, if you choose to come visit the magnificent province of Manitoba. Of course, you have no qualifications, but we do always need people to start at the bottom and work their way up to midlevel positions. In fact, we've been considering hiring a sign-spinner. My employees suggest this would not be beneficial to us, but I intend to bring the best of American marketing techniques to this glorious nation. How are your spinning skills? Nevertheless, should you wish to come be a part of our remarkable company, please feel free to give my assistant a call at—"

The message kept going as I took the phone away from my ear, staring at it for a couple of minutes. Ricky freaking Collins just offered me a job. As a sign-spinner. In Canada. In the most annoying way possible.

Now I know why Lizzie turned him down last year, I thought, laughing.

Then, I kept laughing. Because come on—Ricky Collins! Thinks he has to look out for me! And it's weirdly sweet, or sweetly weird, I can't decide. Oh God, wait till I tell Lizzie or Mary or . . .

Or Jane.

God, I miss Jane. Lizzie would get totally enraged by Ricky's proposal, Mary would shrug and ask if I got benefits. And Jane . . . Jane would just say it was nice of Ricky to offer, and then laugh with me.

Miss you more than you know!

Oh, Jane. I miss you, too.

So why not visit? a little voice inside my head whispered. I don't have anything on my calendar. I have a little money saved up, too. You know those videos I never took down because they represent a painful relationship and having them up seemed better than lying about it? Yeah, those have advertising on them. And apparently, some people are still watching.

Ms. Winters told me to celebrate my achievement. I can't think of anything more celebratory than going to visit Jane in New York.

And who knows? Maybe some new people and new places are exactly what I need to figure out my life.

I fell asleep planning my adventure. What to wear, who to see, what I'll do in the Big Apple.

New York City won't know what hit it.

Chapter Twenty-five
CENTER OF THE UNIVERSE

New York City! People rushing madly to and fro! Giant billboards! The guy peeing on the escalator!

And that was all before I left the airport.

"Lydia!" I heard a high, sweet voice. Someone was madly waving at me and holding a sign with the name BENNET on it, decorated with sparkly unicorn stickers. Jane.

"It's so good to see you!" she squealed as she wrapped her arms around me.

"You, too!" I squealed back.

"Hi, Lydia." A shy voice and accompanying wave popped into my view.

"Bing!" I cried, and jumped up on my tiptoes to hug him, too. He seemed surprised. Which is fair. While Jane's boyfriend and I have always been on decent terms—except for that time he left town without telling anyone and broke my sister's heart for a couple of months before he realized he was being an insane idiot and begged to get her back—we'd never really been on huggy terms. But hey, if he was willing to follow my sister to New York so she could pursue her career while they worked on their relationship, he's entered the hug zone in my book.

"Good to see you, Lydia," Bing said, his breath a little tight. Oopsie. I let his neck go. "Is this all your stuff?" he said, pointing to the carry-on at my feet.

I snorted. "No. I had to check the others."

Bing glanced at Jane.

"Lydia, how many other bags did you bring?" Jane asked sweetly.

"Just three," I said. What? I've never been to New York before, I wasn't sure how to dress. I need all of my cutest outfits on hand, and all of my outfits are freakishly cute.

If anyone would understand this, it would be Jane.

"All righty," Jane said, smiling after a moment. "Let's go get your bags. New York City awaits!"

*　　*　　*

This is the way to make an entrance to a city.

Town car? Check.

Little bottles of water in the cup holders if you're thirsty? Check.

Sunroof I can stand up through while we zoom down city streets looking for landmarks? Well, the sunroof was there, but the driver yelled at me the second I tried to stand up. (And besides, I guess it wasn't much of a *sun*roof considering it was already night by the time I got to the city.)

But the city lights were bright, and the landmarks didn't disappoint.

"What's that?" I asked.

"That's the site of the 1964 World's Fair," Jane replied.

"And that?"

"That's where the Mets play."

"And that?"

"That's . . . I think that's a retirement home."

"So, Lydia, how is everyone?" Bing asked, from Jane's other side. "Your parents?"

"They're good," I said. "You know. Normal."

Although I think normal for Mom and Dad shifted sometime recently, because before I left, something seemed . . . off.

Case in point: I had thought that my parents were going to be severely anti-NYC for me. I was partly right.

"It's about time you're up," my father had said as I came down the stairs the morning after my graduation dinner. "You missed your sister."

"Lizzie left already?" I plopped down into my seat at the table, still barely awake.

"She had to get back, sweetie," my mom said.

"I still don't see why she had to leave before dawn," Dad grumbled. "I'd liked to have had a chance to talk with her, at least."

"Honey, she had an important meeting and a long drive. I told her she didn't have to wait around for something as silly as breakfast," Mom said, as she placed a pot of sweet, sweet coffee in front of me. "Especially when I can make her a nice boxed lunch for the road."

"Still," Dad said, then turned his attention back to me. "I suppose you deserved to sleep in on your first day after graduating," he said, winking at me.

"Actually, it wasn't that," I said, taking a deep breath. "I was up late planning my trip to New York."

Both my parents looked up from their breakfasts as I laid out my scheme. I'd found a really cheap flight through a last-minute booking site, and had already talked to Jane (it's three hours later there, but I still caught her before she was awake). I was going to go explore the city, take in some of that culture everyone always talks about, and visit my sister as a sensible, responsible, associate-degree-having person would do.

Neither of my parents' expressions changed for a good thirty seconds. Then, my father sighed.

"I'm sorry, peanut. This isn't a good time." His shoulders slumped, as his eyes shot to my mother. "I wish your sister was still here, because there are some things that we need to discuss about what's going to be happening now—"

So this was it. I had graduated, gotten to sleep in, and now my dad deemed it time to talk to me about the future and my plans. I expected this. I mean, I was a little hurt by it, but I had arguments ready to go (I was going to be with *Jane*, the best argument I could possibly make) when—

"What's going to be happening now is Lydia is going to New York!" Mom butted in, a bright smile painted on her face. "I think it's a fine idea."

"Marilyn, this can't continue—"

"Tom," she said, warning him. And that shut Dad right up. My mom never called my father by his first name. We lived in a world of "honeys" and "sweeties," and occasionally "muffins." "It's only for a little while. Lydia is an adult and can make her own decisions, just like you and me. Why, she's already bought the ticket—haven't you, honey?"

Actually I hadn't, I was waiting to talk to my parents (like a sensible, responsible, associate-degree-having person would do), but you bet I nodded like I'd already checked the no-refunds box and hit buy.

Argument: ended. My father, displeased, kissed my head and grumped off to the den, and my mom was happy to shove me out the door and off to the airport.

Which sort of felt weird. Because she didn't even send me off with any messages or packages for Jane. I know that they were excited to be empty nesters, and my not moving to San Francisco with Mary put the brakes on that, but . . . this just gave me the sense that I was not wanted. Anywhere.

But I didn't tell Jane that. Being in New York cleared all that stuff away. I'd spent six hours in a middle seat on a plane without Wi-Fi and now half an hour in a car on traffic-jammed streets, so by all accounts I should have been feeling pretty bitchy. But I wasn't. I felt . . . new. Everything around me was new, and I was new to everything. Every city block we drove, I could feel more and more of the weight of the last six weeks—expectations, essays, congrats cake—lifting off me.

I could be anything here. I could be *anyone*.

I could be anywhere. Seriously, by the time we pulled up in front of a flat-fronted building somewhere in Brooklyn, I could have been in Timbuktu for all I knew.

"Where are we?" I asked. "Is this where Bing volunteers?"

Before coming to New York, Bing had decided that his path did not lay in being a doctor to rich hypochondriacs, but instead in working with the needy. But I didn't think they were *this* needy.

"No, silly." Jane smiled. "This is my place."

"Your place?"

"The neighborhood is up-and-coming."

It had a lot of up to come, if the middle-aged drunks on the corner were anything to go by.

"It's nicer on the inside," Jane said, and then made goo-goo eyes at Bing. "We can handle the bags, you've already been so helpful with everything."

"Four flights of stairs? Are you sure?" he asked.

"Umm, four flights of stairs? As in walking up them? With all these bags?" I looked back and forth between Jane and Bing.

Bing smiled. "Maybe I should go ahead and help."

*   *   *

Far too many steps and much wheezing later (on my part, anyway—massive amounts of stairs aren't really part of my daily routine), we finally made it to Jane's apartment.

"Are you sure you don't want to come in for tea?" Jane asked Bing as he set my two biggest suitcases down.

"I'm sure you two have a lot of catching up to do," he said. "Besides, the driver is still waiting for me downstairs."

"Thanks for helping." Jane smiled.

"Anytime," he replied, and then, like, waited for the earth to finish rotating before he finally tore his eyes away from her. "Lydia—hope you enjoy the city. I'll see you both soon?"

I nodded. "Def. Thanks, Bing!"

He waved and disappeared back down the steps.

"Let's get you settled in," Jane said, pushing open the door to the apartment.

NYC apartments on TV are always really cute and spacious—turns out, that's a total lie. Well, not a total lie. Jane's apartment was cute (duh, it's *Jane's*), but spacious . . . not exactly.

"Oops, sorry," I said as I banged one of my suitcases against the wall. We were both inching down the narrow hallway toward the rest of the apartment sideways.

"Allison, this is my sister, Lydia," Jane said as we finally made it into the slightly wider space of the living room.

My eyes darted around the room, mentally matching things up to the pictures we had all insisted Jane send us, and finally landed on a girl who looked to be about the same age as my sister, curled up in the corner of a cute black-and-white-striped couch with a book in her hands.

"Lydia! Oh, I've heard so much about you!"

Allison's smile took up half her face as she walked over and shook my hand. One of those weird super eye contact–y handshakes where my hand ends up sandwiched between both of hers.

"Allison . . ." I started. "You're the one who works in PR, right?" I looked to Jane for confirmation, but Allison nodded her head enthusiastically.

"That's me! Shea's off in her room studying—" She turned to my sister and lowered her voice. "Shocking, I know."

Shea. That's the grad school roommate. Jane's never talked much about either of them—everything we talk about is always work, Bing, work, Bing, and asking about how all of us at home are, of course—

but those are the two facts I do know. Anything else would be new and surprising, just like everything else here.

"We're going to toss Lydia's stuff in my room real quick," Jane said.

"I was going to watch a movie in a few minutes, if you two would like to join? There's a documentary about the Manson Family on demand," she continued.

"I don't know . . . Lydia's probably pretty tired—" Jane replied. But I knew that tone. That wasn't the "I genuinely think you're tired" tone so much as it was the "We need to talk" tone.

And talking, I knew, would have to happen sooner or later. It's just that I would much prefer it be later, is all.

"Actually, that sounds great!" I interrupted. "Let me just get changed out of these gross airplane clothes."

"Are you—" Jane started.

"Who can say no to a family-friendly documentary?" I said, grinning, and started dragging my stuff past Jane toward another smaller hallway. "Which one's yours?"

"To the left."

I steered myself over that way but heard a door creak open from the other end of the hall behind me.

"I heard Allison say you guys were watching a movie?" a voice said quietly. I turned around and saw a girl who definitely could have walked straight out of that a cappella zombie movie appear in the doorway of one of the other rooms.

"Yeah," Jane said, equally hushed. "Don't worry, we'll keep it down, I know you're working. Shea, this is—"

"Lydia," she cut her off. She looked me up and down before nodding her head at me. "Hi."

"Hi . . ." I said back.

She turned her attention back to Jane, shooting her a questioning look.

"Just text me if we're too loud."

"Thanks," Shea replied, and before I even noticed her move, she was back in her room with the door shut securely behind her.

"Friendly," I murmured once we'd gotten into Jane's room.

"She's great," Jane countered. "Just busy. Living with other people requires . . . compromise."

"Hey, I just lived with Mary all summer, you don't have to remind me," I joked.

Mary.

Right.

Another thing I didn't want to think about tonight.

Fortunately, I wouldn't have to. Not yet.

"So, how about that movie?"

Chapter Twenty-six
WELCOME TO NEW YORK

I had one of those startle-y moments when I woke up the next morning—the kind where you slightly panic for a minute because you don't know where you are. And no, it wasn't just because Allison's documentary turned out to be about a murderous cult rather than a sweet, adorable family. There were cupboard doors banging closed in the kitchen and I must've been sleeping more lightly than usual, because I came to immediately, thinking Kitty had knocked something over in my room. But then I remembered Kitty wasn't there, because I was sleeping on Jane's couch, and the other side of the living room wall was the kitchen and that's where the sounds were coming from.

That never happened. I was used to waking up on our couch, or in Lizzie's room, or on a friend's floor, or in a boy's bed. It never fazed me.

But I guess I hadn't woken up anywhere but in my own room since George.

It seemed like such an insignificant change—being startled by unfamiliar surroundings when you never used to be. But something about it scared me, the second I realized that's what had happened. Like my eyes were suddenly brown, or my elbow wasn't double-jointed anymore.

That was the second slight panic within the first few moments of waking up this morning.

The third came when a high-pitched whistle cut through the apartment.

I figured out pretty quickly that it was a teakettle, but yup, awake now.

I shook Jane's blanket off me and sat up. The whistling stopped, thank God, and I heard whoever was in the other room start to walk toward this one not too long after.

"Hi! I hope I didn't wake you up!" Allison said, heading toward the couch. I barely had time to move my feet before she sat down on the far end.

"No, I was up," I lied.

"Do you mind if I turn on the TV?" she asked, already pressing buttons on the remote. I nodded, fairly certain she wasn't looking at me as she barreled on. "I just have to watch *Meet the Press* with my tea. Ooh, sorry, I'd have seen if you wanted any but I thought you were still asleep."

"That's all right," I said, and yawned. "Is it okay if I hop in the shower?"

"Oh, of course! Jane's towels are the purple ones on the second shelf in the cabinet," Allison said. "Fair warning, the hot water runs out pretty quickly, and there are three more people, so . . ."

I nodded through another yawn, grabbing my toiletries and some daytime-appropriate clothes from my suitcase in the corner, and shuffled toward the single bathroom.

After about twenty minutes and an annoyed realization that I had forgotten my face wash and had to borrow Jane's, I felt way less yawny and more ready to go out and finally see the epicness that is supposed to be New York City.

"What do you want to see first?" Jane asked, pouring me a cup of coffee in the kitchen. She had gotten up while I was in the shower and made tea for herself and coffee for me and a "hi, bye" Shea passing through the living room on her way to the library.

"You mean you don't already have an itinerary planned out?"

"I may have jotted down some ideas," Jane admitted.

I grinned, knowing that even if it wasn't a full-blown schedule, that was only because Jane had been super busy. Lizzie may be the nerd, but Jane is organized and prepared for all situations.

"I'm totes down for whatever you wanna show me," I told her.

"Perfect!" Jane smiled. "We can do the sightseeing stuff today and then get you a little more acquainted with the local places after that. Sound good?"

I nodded. "Let's tourist it up, sis!"

"I just have a few emails I have to deal with from work before we head out. Give me ten minutes?"

I waved her away and sat down at the kitchen table to finish my coffee while she went back to her room.

I pulled out my phone and idly checked my text messages. Nothing new, but I scrolled down to my last conversation with Mary and stared at the screen for a few seconds, my thumb hovering over the virtual keyboard.

How's SF? I finally typed after considering a few options. *I'm in New York!* wouldn't have provided a question; *What's up?* is too general; and *Hey, I'm really sorry I screwed up, are we good yet?* is too much for 9:00 a.m.

Crap, 9:00 a.m. Which means it's 6:00 a.m. on the West Coast. Mary is an early riser, but nobody gets up that early on a Sunday. Hopefully my text doesn't wake her up and prompt crankiness. That would not be a good way to start talking again.

Either way, I probably have a couple of hours before she maybe decides to actually respond, so that means I have a couple of hours before I can get anxious about her maybe not responding. Hypothetically. I've never been good at waiting.

At least I'd get to spend the day distracted by my adventures with Jane and not have to think about all the messes I temporarily left behind. This trip isn't about that. It's about taking a break and regrouping. And, at least for a few more minutes until Jane finishes up work duties, it's also about beating Lizzie at this pop culture trivia game on my phone.

* * *

Ten minutes turned into thirty, which turned into an additional twenty when Jane got a work call as we were walking out the door, but after that, we finally got the tourism started.

"Keep your purse in front of you and make sure it's always zipped up," Jane told me as we pushed through the turnstile in the subway station. "The train gets really crowded and you have to be aware of your surroundings at all times."

"You sound like Mom the first time she let me walk to school by myself," I said, rolling my eyes.

"I'm serious! Bing's already been pickpocketed twice."

Somehow, it didn't entirely surprise me to hear that Jane's very smart but also somewhat naïve-seeming boyfriend had fallen victim to subway theft on multiple occasions. But it's also kind of ridic, because everyone who knows Bing also knows that if any stranger just asked him for money, chances are he'd whip out his wallet and ask if they preferred twenties.

But I did what Jane said anyway, and soon understood why it's so easy to get stuff stolen from you. Sweaty bodies pressed up against mine as we all crowded onto the 2 train—not even in a creepy grope-y way like I'd heard happens on public transportation, just in a "well, crap, there's not enough room for everyone" way. I sucked it up and clenched my fist around the metal bar above my head as the train tried to toss me even further into strangers, thankful for the hand sanitizer I would be making generous use of once we got aboveground (seriously, Mary would freak). I was in New York City; I was going to do things the New York City way. Hey, nobody ever said Lydia Bennet wasn't ready for an adventure.

I thought we'd go see the Statue of Liberty, picnic in Central Park, climb to the top of the Empire State Building (if *only* for the Jay Z song, to be totally honest), and zip back to Times Square for an expensive, overrated dinner and a Broadway show.

Turns out, not only is tourism in New York City dirtier than I'd imagined, it's also significantly more time-consuming.

After a long underground commute and more walking than I'd done in a while (at least Jane had also warned me to wear comfortable shoes), we'd hopped onto a ferry, which took us to tourist stop number one, the Statue of Liberty.

"I'm so excited to get to take you to all these places for the first time!" Jane whispered to me as we stood in the outrageously long line to actually go up to the top of the crown thingy.

I'd been debating whether it was worth it, considering how much longer it was looking like it was going to take—on the one hand, the Statue of Liberty! It's in so many movies! But on the other, the middle-aged couple in front of us wearing matching I ♥ NY shirts had been discussing the possible meanings behind the discoloration of their chiweenie's poop for the past twenty minutes—but Jane's excitement sealed the deal for me. If Jane wanted to be here, I wanted to be here.

Fortunately, though the long wait in line would have been an easy place to corner me to talk about everything that had happened this summer, Jane knew better, and we mostly talked about her job (with several phone/email interruptions regarding it), and Bing's work at the center, and what kind of things we might do around the city. Getting to the Statue of Liberty came and went during the conversation, and it wasn't underwhelming, but it wasn't overwhelming, either. It was just . . . whelming? Is that a thing? But Jane was still happy, and I was glad to be here with her, so it was all right.

*   *   *

Finally, by late afternoon, and after an abbreviated stop at the Metropolitan Museum of Art, we found ourselves walking through Central Park. My feet were *dying*, but at least it was alive with things to see. We passed musicians and mimes and kids throwing pennies into a fountain. I told Jane I wanted to see *everything*, but she just laughed and told me the park may be a little too big for that, but maybe I could come back one day next week while she was at work and mosey around.

After about an hour of walking, I convinced her that *one* little snack from a street cart wouldn't ruin dinner, and we snagged a couple of overpriced pretzels before settling down on a cute wooden bench next to the water.

"This isn't *real* street-cart food, you know," Jane said. "It's like the food you get at a convention center. There are a lot of authentic street carts outside of touristy areas—we'll have to try some while you're here."

"'Real' street-cart food," I said, mocking her, and stopped devouring my pretzel long enough to throw air quotes up around my head. "You're so New York now." It was true—Jane had always been the most stylish sister ever—but now she has this polish, like moving so fast through the streets tumbled her surfaces shiny and smooth.

"I just want you to be able to experience the things you wouldn't be able to experience in other cities!" she protested, still sweet as ever.

"Sure," I said. "Can't wait for you to come back home and start pushing people off the sidewalks because they aren't moving fast enough."

She shoved me with her shoulder and shook her head. It's

strange that no matter how old we get or what happens, Jane and I always fall into the same big sister, little sister routine. It's nice in that "some things never change" kind of way, which is good when things keep changing around you.

"You're checking your phone a lot today. Waiting on something?" she asked.

I was confused for about half a second until I looked down and realized my phone was, in fact, in my hand. I guess I'd been taking it out subconsciously throughout the day, waiting to see if Mary would text me back.

Nothing yet.

"Just habit," I said.

Actually, no one had texted or called except for Lizzie, who scolded me for not letting her know I got to Jane's safely. Usually when I left town, I'd get a call (or twelve) from Mom making sure I was okay, but nothing so far. I shot Mom a text saying as much anyway, and wondered if this meant my parents now trusted me, or if they were really this ready to have the house to themselves.

"Speaking of phones . . ." Jane stood up, looking at the screen on hers. "This is work, I have to take it."

Before I even got a chance to nod, she had taken off down the path we'd used to get here, answering politely with a "This is Jane Bennet."

I slipped my phone back into my pocket and continued munching on my pretzel and let myself marvel a little. This really was a beautiful park, even if it was a little hot in the summer and a little crowded on the weekend. I turned my attention toward the water, watching the ripples from the slight breeze pass through it. The spot we'd found was a bit off the trail, and this was probably the first quiet moment I'd had all day. God only knows I'm not usually much for quiet, but maybe that's because it's all I'm used to being around in the suburbs. In a bustling city, it's kind of nice.

Naturally, as I was thinking about how peaceful it was, I heard the sound of sneakers scratching across grass nearby and turned just in time to see some guy in a gray shirt and black skinny jeans plop down in the grass a few feet away and open up what looked to be a giant sketchbook. My eyes darted between the water and this new arrival as he started to draw, trying not to be too awkward about it, but wondering why exactly he was sitting so uncomfortably nearby.

I thought back to something Jane had told me earlier, when we'd been listening to a middle-aged man warble out some song while hitting a cup against the pavement. It hadn't been good, but it had been attention-grabbing enough to make us stand there for a minute and watch.

"If you stop, you should put something in," she had said after dropping a dollar into the coin-filled mug the "singer" had set out next to him.

I checked the ground around this younger guy, but I didn't see any mug. He had, however, taken off his hat and laid it on the grass.

Hats were for money, too, right? I'm pretty sure I saw that on *Law & Order.*

I stared at him for a minute, considering my options.

"If you want money, I don't have any," I finally said.

The guy kept drawing for a few seconds and then looked up suddenly, as if he'd heard me on a delay.

"What?" he asked.

"Are you one of those people who does like art and stuff for everyone to watch and then we're supposed to give you money?"

"Me? No." The amusement was perfectly clear in his expression, as he went right back to sketching.

I frowned. I didn't necessarily want to keep talking to him, but it felt super awkward sitting this close and *not* talking. Was this how people in New York always did things? A city so crowded that sitting down next to people and not acknowledging their existence was the norm?

But the park wasn't crowded, and he had still sat down here.

And he didn't seem to be hitting on me, either, so . . .

"Is it like some weird performance-art thing, then? Sitting really close to strangers and seeing how they react?"

His smile continued, though he didn't look up at me this time. "I've been drawing that bridge all afternoon. Got up to stretch my legs, came back, and you were sitting there. I'm sorry if I made you uncomfortable. Trying to get done before the sun sets is all."

"Oh," I said, feeling a little silly. That made sense. "No, it's okay."

He didn't say anything else, so I reached into my pocket and pulled out my phone to try to entertain myself.

Only to have it immediately die.

Seriously, this is getting ridiculous. I have got to get one of those battery packs Jane has.

Twisting in my seat, I looked around for Jane, finally spotting her pacing up and down the path nearby. She threw me a quick wave but immediately continued what looked to be a really intense conversation.

So, no, not on her way back to rescue me from awkwardness and boredom.

I slumped back down onto the bench and found my eyes wandering toward the non–street artist's sketchpad.

"I think you're drawing upside down," I called over to him.

"I could be, I guess," he agreed. "It's the reflection, see?" He took his pencil off the paper and pointed the eraser end at the water, where I could see a wobbly image of the bridge reflected back upside down.

"Are you doing a landscape thing?"

"Nah. Just the bridge."

"And its reflection?"

"Just the reflection."

"Why would you only draw the reflection?"

He opened his mouth but snapped it back shut again, looking me over. "You ask a lotta questions."

"You don't give very good answers," I fired back, frowning.

"If I spent all my time talking, wouldn't get much done, huh?"

"Hey, sorry about that." I looked up and saw Jane walking toward me, phone actually not glued to the side of her face. "There was a . . . fabric situation."

"Sounds dire," I said, trying not to let my vague annoyance shine through too much.

Jane looked over to the weird drawing guy, who was, of course, already right back to drawing. But she must have noticed we'd been kind of mid-conversation when she got back, because, being Jane, she ducked her head down in an attempt to catch his attention.

"Hi! I'm Jane, Lydia's sister."

He glanced up ever so briefly. "Hello."

"What was your name?"

Oh, Jane. I stood abruptly and linked her arm in mine. "He doesn't like questions."

"Okay?" Jane squeaked out as I pulled her along with me. "It was so good to meet you!"

"Same to you, Jane," I heard him call out from pretty far behind us. Looks like I've already picked up the city dweller's fast-walking habit.

"Lydia, that wasn't nice," she scolded as we slowed down to a slightly more casual pace.

I shrugged. "I wanted to spend more time with my sister. Is work stuff done?"

She shot me a look, and I immediately felt bad for the slight guilt trip.

"I'm sorry I keep getting pulled in for that," she said, sighing. "I want to have today with you, but—"

"Sometimes life happens. It's all right. You're stuck with me for a whole week, anyway. So . . . where to next?"

"Well . . . Bing wants to take us to dinner in about two hours—"

"He does?" I squealed. "Ooh, is it someplace fancy? I've always wanted to go to a classy restaurant in the city. Can it be just like the movies?"

"Slow down," Jane said, grinning. "I think you'll like it. That's all I'm going to say because it was supposed to be a surprise, but I don't want you stuffing down any more pretzels before we get there."

"No more pretzels," I said. "Promise."

"Good." She tilted her head up toward the sky, past the trees. "It looks like the sun is going to be setting by the time we make our way back out of the park. . . . Wanna just walk around a bit before we go meet Bing?"

Oh, goody, more walking.

But my mind was already drifting away to expensive bottles of wine and filet mignon—pronounced by a waiter who sounded like he'd come out of the womb speaking French, obvs—as Jane led me down a new path and onto a bridge.

The same bridge, I realized, we'd been looking at from the park bench. I squinted in that direction and saw a faint person-outline in gray and black sitting where we'd left him. I briefly wondered if he'd catch me and Jane walking across in the reflection, and if we'd end up part of his weird backwards drawing.

Chapter Twenty-seven
CHANGE OF PLANS

Dinner with Bing was super fancy and expensive, just as I'd hoped. And he insisted on paying for everything, just as I'd hoped. And he and Jane were adorable all freaking night, just as I'd hoped.

Except I'd also hoped my phone wouldn't be dead so I could sneakily take photos of them being all googly-eyed and send them to everyone in our family.

It was refreshing to see two decent people in love and actually getting along with each other. Bing and Jane were a perfect match. Just like Darcy and Lizzie, in their own weird way.

And me and Kitty.

Not that I don't enjoy being single. I really, *really* do. No more relationships for a while. I need to figure out my own stuff first, and obviously what happened with Cody told me I am not ready for that yet.

Whatever, I'm good alone.

And I told Bing as much when he tried to horn in on my dessert.

"Are you going to eat all that cheesecake, or—"

"Bing, it's my first trip to New York. I am having this slice of New York cheesecake. By myself." Bing blinked, shocked by the shutdown. But I'd become protective of my sweets since the congrats-cake fiasco.

Jane had stepped away to take yet another phone call. It's obvious she loves her job and is a godsend to her employers, but still, it would be nice to go three minutes without her phone ringing.

But as Jane walked back to the table, I could see there were tears in her eyes.

"What is it?" I asked. "What's wrong?"

For a second and a half I thought something devastating had happened, like Bing had broken up with her again, leaving her heart in a puddle on the floor dusted with snickerdoodle crumbs. But then I remembered that first, Bing would never in a million years do that again if he wanted to avoid death-by-Bennet-sister, and B, Bing was next to me while Jane took the phone call.

"Cecilia broke her ankle!" Jane said, as she plopped back down into her seat.

"Oh no," Bing said, putting his hand over Jane's, and handing her his napkin to wipe her eyes.

"That sucks," I said. "Who's Cecilia?"

"She's a coworker," Jane replied, sniffling. "And she was supposed to go to Miami this week for me, but now there's no backup. I have to put together a gift basket for her. She likes *Doctor Who*—do you think I can get a TARDIS at this hour?"

"Explanation, please? About Miami, not *Doctor Who*."

It turns out Jane was supposed to go to Miami this week for a fashion exhibition. But since I called last-minute and said I was coming, she convinced the office to send her coworker Cecilia in her place. But Cecilia broke her ankle this afternoon while rock climbing at Chelsea Piers, so good-bye, Miami.

"Since it's so last-minute, they don't have a choice. They have to send me." Jane was saying. "My flight out is tonight . . . I'm so sorry, Lydia, all I wanted to do was spend this week with you. . . ."

"Jane, it's okay," I said, trying to be all casual about it. "I completely get it."

"Do you?" she said, biting her lip. "It is only three days."

"Know what? Those three days you were going to spend at work most of the time, anyway. Basically, we're missing out on three evenings of Netflix after you get home from the office so beat you don't want to do anything."

Jane sniffled through her smile. "Thank you for understanding."

"Well," Bing said, signaling the waiter, "if your flight's tonight, we'd better get you packed and to the airport."

"I could make you a list of things to see on your own," Jane said, as she was throwing clothes into a suitcase. Although, Jane's version of "throwing clothes" involves folding everything neatly into their own perfectly fitting compartments. "I'll do it on the plane and send it once I land."

"Sure," I said. "Sounds great." In reality, I was a little more waffly.

There are lots of things I want to see, but I don't really want to do it by myself. Not that I'm afraid of getting lost in the big, bad city—please, Lydia Bennet adapts quickly and flawlessly. It's just more fun to experience things with other people. Namely, Jane. The actual sights still haven't been as great as I'd hoped. The great part was seeing them with my big sister.

But I wasn't about to let Jane know that. She already felt guilty enough.

"Or, if you want company, I'm sure Bing would be happy to take you to the center with him. The kids he works with are really lovely. And Allison and Shea will still be here."

"Uh-huh," I said. "Don't worry. I'll find something to do tomorrow. And a lot of it is probably going to be sleeping, because I'm beat. Touristing is exhausting."

"Your feet are not going to be happy in the morning. It took a couple of weeks before I got used to it," Jane said, with an apologetic smile. Then, as she clicked her suitcase shut, her smile turned serious.

"I don't mean to be a spoilsport, but . . ." She took a deep breath and fixed me with her best "concerned big sister eyes." And if you know Jane, you know they're good ones. "I'm sorry to be leaving, because I was hoping we'd talk about everything that's happened this summer."

"I'm sure you've heard it all," I said.

"Probably," she agreed. "But that doesn't mean there's nothing to talk about."

"We can worry about that when you get back." I shrugged it off.

"Okay."

I blinked.

That was it? No concerned Jane gently pressing me to get to the heart of the issue? About what I'm doing next? I don't have an answer, sure, but I was still surprised she'd let it go that easily.

Then again, Bing was waiting to take Jane to the airport, so she probably didn't have the time for an hours-long heart-to-heart.

"Have you talked to Mary lately?"

"Uh-huh." Once Jane and I got home and she rushed to start

packing, I rushed to get my phone charger. Once my poor baby had some juice, I had found a text waiting for me:

Not bad. Sorry, been working all day.

Yeah, of course she's busy. I get it. I texted back, and told her I was in New York.

The three little loading dots tortured me for a couple of minutes until—

Neat. Say hi to Jane for me.

I could have responded, but it felt weirdly distant. Talking to Mary is hard enough; it turns out that texting with her is even more emotionless. Or, now it seems to be, anyway.

"I think that's it," Jane said, grabbing a sun hat off a hook. She came over and hugged me. I inhaled her Jane smell. "I'm so sorry I won't get to see you."

"You will in three days. Don't worry," I said, and then gave her one of my brightest smiles. "I mean, Lydia Bennet loose in New York City? What could possibly go wrong?"

Chapter Twenty-eight

ALONE

Jane was *not* kidding about my feet. The minute they touched the creaky floors next to her tiny bed this morning, they transformed from regular feet to swollen stubs.

The throbbing paired nicely with the throbbing in my head.

It had nothing to do with last night's wine. I barely had one glass. No, it had to do with the construction crew jackhammering the sidewalk, starting promptly at 7:00 a.m. I think I'll have to resign myself to never getting a good night's sleep here. But hey, for the next three days, at least I'm not out on the couch.

Deciding a shower could wait, I grabbed the essentials (my phone and Jane's personal laptop she said I could use while she was away), hobbled into the kitchen, and brewed a pot of coffee.

I grabbed my phone and pulled up the notifications.

I'd slept past multiple Jane texts (*Just landed! Check your email for that list!*; *Morning! Sleep ok?*; *Oh, I forgot, there's some construction on our block. Just so you know!*), a couple of Lizzie's (proddy about having Darcy talk to Central Bay again, ugh) and . . . even one from Mary.

Any thoughts on what you're going to do after New York?

Yeah . . . I might need more coffee to respond to that one.

Because, what are my plans? Now that I'm here, I've gotten to the end of any previous planning. There's this great big question mark that can't be ignored much longer. And since Mary asked the question, and Jane is expecting a conversation when she gets back, I should go into that conversation with some ideas.

Hey, I could still move to Winnipeg and spin signs while standing in three-foot-deep snow most of the year. Epic career plan.

If there was ever an argument for finding a way to get into a real school, that's it.

"Hey." A raspy voice drew my eyes away from my phone and toward Shea entering the apartment and looking more asleep than I felt prior to coffee.

"This coffee claimed?" she asked, pointing to the pot.

"All yours," I said.

She swung her backpack down on the floor next to the table before rummaging through the cabinets for a coffee mug, and I realized she was dressed in the same clothes she was wearing when I'd seen her briefly last night.

"Fell asleep at the library," she said, noticing my stare.

"They just forgot you?"

"School library's open all night," she explained, pouring coffee into a white mug with hipster glasses and a mustache on it. "Everyone's got too much work to do for it not to be."

"That sounds awful."

"It is. You dodged a bullet missing that transfer deadline."

I swept past the (totally logical) realization that Jane must've told her roommates about me, because I didn't want to think of what else she might have told them. This is New York. I'm New York Lydia here. Looking forward.

"Do you regret grad school?" I asked.

Shea swirled her coffee around in the cup. "No," she finally answered. "But I jumped right into it from undergrad. Sometimes I wish I'd taken a breather. But I didn't, so . . . more studying." She grabbed her bag off the floor and left the room.

So that's one vote for finishing college, one against.

Maybe it's time to do some research of my own.

I flipped open Jane's laptop and started typing "cool jobs you can do without a college degree" into the search engine.

Dental hygienist . . . ew, no . . . *cosmetologist* . . . I'd be stellar, but pass . . . *court reporter* . . . bor-ing . . . *refrigerator mechanic* . . . okay, seriously?

Surely a bunch of people I went to high school with opted out of college; I could see what they're doing. I directed the browser to Facebook for the first time in ages (seven new messages from Denny—oops, sorry, Denny) and started going through the list of old classmates I haven't talked to in years.

After scrolling through a number of profiles featuring colleges and marriages and babies—seriously? We're barely past our teens, guys, enjoy it while it lasts!—something caught my eye.

Casey, a girl I went to high school with and had known since our Girl Scout years, was living in New York. I checked her page—her occupation was listed as freelance, but all her pictures were of really cool parties, so she had to be doing something right to make it in NYC.

I jotted out a quick message:

> Hey, Casey! We haven't talked in forevs, but I'm in New York visiting my sister and I've got some free time. Wanna catch up?

I was about to close the window when I saw the indication that she was typing a response back.

> For sure! Are you around tonight?

Well, I don't have Jane. Shea's a library zombie. Allison's . . . somewhere. Might as well do something, right?

It wasn't long before we'd come up with a plan to meet, and I shut Jane's computer, pretty pleased with myself. While I knew going back home with even some sort of vague life plan was unlikely, this was at least one step closer to figuring out what I could do as a maybe-non-college-grad (besides sign spinning).

And I was certain that had earned me the rest of the day off watching Netflix. My feet would thank me.

Chapter Twenty-nine
CASEY

It took me about three minutes into drinks with Casey to remember why we'd never really hung out past Girl Scouts.

I couldn't freaking stand her.

We'd agreed to meet at this place in the East Village, near Alphabet City.

"Wait, is Alphabet City the name of the restaurant?" I'd murmured to myself as I put the address in my phone before leaving the apartment. In my mind, they probably served a lot of soup.

"It's the name of the neighborhood," Allison said from the couch. She was simultaneously reading a book and watching something about insect mating habits on the Discovery Channel, but managed to tear her eyes away long enough to roll them at me with pity. "You know, because the avenues aren't numbers there, they're letters?"

"Oh," I replied. "Got it. Do you know the best way to get there? I'm meeting a friend from high school."

"Planning on a late night, huh?" She flashed me the exact same smile that I'd seen from her before.

"Probably not, but I don't know."

"Well, try not to get into any trouble. Jane would have my head if anything happened on my watch." Her smile didn't budge. "Or, if you do, just . . . keep it out of the apartment. The less I know the better."

"Sure," I murmured, turning toward the door again.

"Oh! Um, did you bring anything less . . . princessy with you?" I frowned as Allison looked over my outfit. I wasn't even wearing sparkles. "I think you look impeccably . . . cute, but New Yorkers can smell an out-of-towner a mile away. Better if you can blend in a little bit." She laughed, and I wasn't sure why.

I nervously smoothed out the blue dress I was wearing. "This is Jane's dress," I said. "I stole it from her closet."

Allison's head cocked to the side. "Jane's in fashion," she said by way of explanation.

I don't know what she meant by that, but I ducked back into Jane's room and grabbed a cardigan before I finally made for the door.

"Lydia," a voice emerged from the shadowed room of Shea. She blinked into the outside light. "Take the G train to the L, it'll drop you off on First and Fourteenth. The G and L suck, but that's the closest stop."

"Thanks," I said, surprised. But I don't know if she heard me because she re-turtled herself back into her darkened room-shell.

That was enough of the roommates, I thought, as I made for the train.

I got to the restaurant where I'd agreed to meet Casey ten minutes early, but the waiter refused to seat me until my "whole party arrived," so I sat down on a bench outside and resisted the urge to play battery-sucking games on my almost fully charged phone, instead imagining what Casey's deliciously vague freelance job description meant.

Freelance what? Freelance writer? Freelance designer? Freelance *assassin*?

"Lydia?"

I recognized Casey approaching me, though if we hadn't planned this and I'd just seen her on the street, I may not have. Gone were the spaghetti-strap tops and brightly colored jeans, traded in for a decidedly more New York wardrobe of slim clothes in dark colors.

"Hey! It's so good to see you," I said, doing my best Jane impersonation as I got up for the obligatory greeting-hug.

"Look at you!" she squealed. "I can't wait to catch up, come on!"

This was a level of enthusiasm I was unprepared for.

She pulled open the restaurant door and we walked in, ready to actually get a table this time around, thank you, Mr. Waiter.

It was a trendy place with dim lighting and lots of artwork that was clearly done by locals on the walls. Everything in the East Village seemed a little grungy, but expensive grungy. We passed the bar at the front and ended up at a small booth in the center of the restaurant. Everyone was a little crammed in, so close you could easily touch fingertips with the people across the aisle, but nobody seemed bothered by it.

"So how have you been?" Casey asked as the waiter dropped off two glasses of iceless water. "You said your sister's living here now?"

"Jane," I replied. "She moved here for work a few months ago. Fashion stuff."

"That's a tough industry, but hey, she's trying."

"She's doing pretty well," I said.

"A lot of dreams don't go anywhere." She sighed.

"Anyway, what about you?" I continued, dodging the original question. "I saw on Facebook you're freelancing . . . ?"

"Yeah, just, whatever, here and there, you know," she replied dismissively.

"Must be some impressive 'here and there' if it's enough to live in the city," I said, determined to coax my potential future out of her.

She shrugged. "Last job I had was PAing on a reality show. That was almost three months ago. I'll have to get another one when my funemployment runs out."

"So you . . . work in TV?" I said.

"Sometimes. I thought I'd be an actor but . . . it's a lot of work, you know?"

"And you can be a PA without a college degree?"

"A PA just stands around all day with a walkie telling people where to go. The day you have to go to college for that? Although . . ." She leaned in super close to me, excited to share a secret. "Don't tell my résumé, okay? It thinks I graduated early from Georgetown."

Wow. Okay, not the glamorous freelance life I had pictured. Or the glamorous TV life. Or the . . . anything.

Casey's life seemed to be put together piecemeal. And the work she was doing, she was super down on. Yeah, there was a time that "funemployment" might have put dollar signs in Lydia Bennet's eyes, but now . . . to work just long enough to collect on it seemed weirdly hollow.

"My parents keep threatening to cut me off, because they don't get how much work it is to make it in this city. But soon, I'm not going to have to worry about all that, because I have the perfect gig coming up!"

I perked up. "Really?"

She nodded enthusiastically. "I met this guy, he's an animal wrangler. And it seems like the easiest job, because he just has a lizard. Put the lizard in a tank in the background and he gets paid for it. So I've started training my two rats—"

"Rats?"

"I figure every movie shot in the city needs a rat or two to run down the street, for grittiness? And I won't have to do anything, the rats do all the work."

"Wow, that's . . . something."

"Would you like to meet them?"

"Your . . . rats?"

"We can head there after dinner."

"Um, I don't think—"

"Or tomorrow?" Casey said, hope drenching every syllable. "What are you doing the rest of the week?"

Not meeting your rats, I thought.

"Just, things . . . Do you keep up with anyone from our class?" I asked.

"Not really," Casey said, grimacing. "People sort of fall away, you know? It's why I was soooo glad you reached out on Facebook. There's a ton of people in New York, but so few of them seem worth knowing. So, tomorrow? There's this spoken-word poetry thing at the bar next door, it could be fun. . . ."

I wish I could tell you how the rest of the conversation went, but I was mostly zoning in and out after that, considering the possibility of a future featuring me, two rats, and spoken-word poetry. Oh, and no plan for my life beyond freelancing and lying on my résumé.

"I'll be right back," I said, standing up suddenly and taking off for the restroom without waiting for a response.

If the restaurant was tiny, the bathroom was even more cramped, featuring only one stall and a sink/counter combo that took up half the space on its own. The stall was occupado, but at least I had the sink area where I could shuffle/pace, wondering how my trip had become such a bust so quickly.

The way I see it, I have two options. I can suck it up and listen to Casey talk about trying to get a book deal from training rats to do tricks on camera while contemplating the likelihood of a depressing and unfulfilling future. Or I can come up with an "emergency" and go watch insect documentaries with Allison. While contemplating the likelihood of a depressing and unfulfilling future.

At least that one includes TV.

I heard the toilet flush and I turned toward the mirror, pretending to check my reflection so it didn't look like I was just casually hanging out in a bathroom. Which, of course, was exactly what I was doing.

A girl maybe a little bit younger than me with super on-point dark curly hair walked out, and I jumped back toward the wall to avoid getting hit by the stall door.

She moved to the sink, forcing me to squish up against the corner. When she saw I didn't move to take the stall, she glanced at my face and smirked.

"Avoiding someone?"

Guess I was pretty obvious.

"Old high school friend. Who I no longer have anything in common with. And who doesn't seem to realize that."

"Sounds like a good time."

"So good I could cry," I monotoned. "Hey, how well do you think 'Shit, I totally forgot I have this other random vague engagement right this second' holds up as an excuse to bail?"

She snorted and slowly shook her head. "That one's pretty hit-and-miss."

I groaned.

"It really that bad?"

"Yes. No. This is just . . . not turning out to be the awesome first trip to New York I had hoped it would be. Sorry, I'm compounding various disappointments. And venting to a stranger in a tiny bathroom."

"What are tiny bathrooms for?"

I tried half a smile, but it probably came out as more of a grimace.

"Guess I should go test my excuse in the real world," I said, pushing myself off the wall. "Wish me luck."

A minute later, I was back at the table with Casey, who immediately picked up her story where she left off.

"So, where was I? Oh, yeah, I had one audition for a commercial, and I thought, I don't want to be in commercials, I want to be on the stage. I walked out before I even read—"

"I'm so sorry," I interrupted. "I totally forgot I'd made plans with a friend who's in town. She leaves first thing tomorrow, otherwise I'd reschedule, but . . ." I trailed off, hoping she got the point.

"Oh. What time are you meeting her?"

Dammit, I had no clue what time it was, and pulling out my phone to check would be too obvious. Let's see . . . I met Casey at seven thirty, it definitely has to have been almost two hours at this point, so maybe . . .

"Ten?"

Casey pressed a button on her phone and my heart sank as it lit up on the table in front of us.

"Perfect!" she said, smiling. "It's only eight fifteen. We've got time for at least another drink."

"Actually—" I rushed, as she started to stand. "I'm meeting her back in Brooklyn." *What parts of Brooklyn are far away? Think, Lydia! Stupid city I don't know well.* "Um, like pretty far away . . . in Brooklyn—"

"Sorry I'm late." It took me a second to realize the voice that spoke was both nearby and connected to a body that had stopped right next to our table. And that it sounded familiar.

I looked up to find myself staring at the face of the guy from the park.

The one with the upside-down bridge.

He recognized me, but recovered more quickly than I did.

"I'm Milo," he said, extending his hand toward Casey. "Lydia's boyfriend."

Lydia's *what*?

"Um . . ." I started. "This is Casey, Milo."

"I wanted to let you guys finish chatting," Milo(?) said. "But Kat swears we'll be late if we don't leave now." He jerked his head toward the bar, and I swiveled around in my chair to see the girl with the dark curly hair from the bathroom waving at us.

"Oh . . ." I said, finally catching on. "Right! She's right. We were just having such a good time, I was hoping we could get in just one more drink. But she's definitely right. Darn."

I stood up, fishing my wallet out of my purse and pulling out enough money to cover my half.

"No, no, no," Casey protested. "My treat. Or my parents'."

"No, that's really—" I started.

"Nice of you," Milo cut me off. "And it was very nice to meet you, Casey." He slid his arm around my waist, barely touching, and started to guide me down the walkway away from the table.

"Okay?" Casey replied, a touch of confusion still lingering. "Maybe I'll see you again before you go home?"

"Yeah, I'm pretty busy with Jane, but we'll talk on Facebook!" I called back as I followed Milo's lead. I think she said something else, but we were already at the door.

Milo dropped his arm as Kat joined us.

"You looked like you needed some help with that," she whispered to me.

"Thanks."

I stepped out onto the sidewalk and paused, trying to reconcile my surroundings with my memory of getting here.

"You taking the subway?" Kat asked.

"Yeah, I guess so," I said.

"Lexington line is this way." Milo nodded toward the direction I'm pretty sure I didn't come from, but the subway's all connected somehow, right?

"Do you just go around pretending to be random pseudo-strangers' boyfriend often?" I asked, quickening my pace to keep up with them.

"Yes, actually," Milo said.

I opened my mouth to start to pry further, but changed direction. "Sorry, I forgot you don't like questions."

"It's not that I don't like questions, just that I like bridges more," he said.

"Am I missing something?" Kat asked, peering around Milo to glance back and forth between us.

"Your latest rescue was watching me sketch in the park the other day."

"I wasn't *watching* you—you sat down right in front of me. I tried to be polite and make conversation."

"Well, we're making conversation now, aren't we?"

"I didn't mean for you to track me down and pretend to be my boyfriend."

"Hey, that was Kat's idea."

"Not that I'm ungrateful for the out, but this is starting to feel more and more like some bizarre con-artist situation," I pointed out, quietly feeling alongside the top of my bag to see if it was zipped.

"It's just something we do sometimes," Kat said. "Usually on the subway or something, when a guy is clearly bothering some girl, you go act like you know her so he'll go away."

"That's . . . cool of you," I said, thinking back over all the times that would have come in handy at Carter's. Some drunk dudes cannot take disinterest at face value.

"There's a lot of shitty people around. Gotta watch out for each other."

"Well, Casey's not shitty, just . . . boring."

"I'm sorry, do you want to go back?" Milo teased, pointing back to where we came from.

"Only if you get me really drunk first," I said, then realized how that sounded. "Not that I want you to get me drunk. Or that I want you to take me back. I'm good right here, and . . . sober."

"If you say so," Milo agreed.

We crossed the street and I realized we'd already made it to the subway station. I looked at the sign as I followed them down the steps.

"We're headed south. You?" Kat asked.

"North, I think," I said, knowing that much even if I was a little iffy on the rest. I'd figure it out. Hopefully. "Thanks again for the save."

"No problem," she said.

"And good luck with your bridges," I told Milo.

He nodded. "Tell Jane I said hello." Wow, good memory for names.

"She had to go out of town for work," I replied before wondering why I felt the need to tell him that.

"While you're visiting?" he asked.

I shrugged. "Yeah, spur-of-the-moment thing."

We stood there for a second, and Kat's eyes moved from Milo to me.

"You know," Kat started, "we're going to a party. Nothing crazy, but it sounds like your bar for fun in New York is pretty low right now. Wanna come?"

I know I kind of swore off partying for a while after the whole Cody thing, even if not in quite so many words. And running off with strangers while alone in a big city probably isn't the most advisable thing. Especially after that documentary. But my other options at the moment suck, and it's not like we're in the middle of a dark forest where it would be super easy to chop me up into little pieces and go all cannibal on me or anything. Right?

"Um, okay. Hold on." I held my phone up and clicked a quick photo of them. "Collateral," I explained, typing out my email address and sending a copy of the picture to myself. "If I go missing, the police will hack into my email and see that you guys were the last people to see me."

Kat laughed. "Can't argue with that."

"Well, there goes our brilliant kidnapping scheme," Milo said, and Kat smacked him in the arm. He winked at me as he swiped his MetroCard and walked backward through the turnstile.

It took me the entire subway ride to remember I'm not supposed to like winky faces.

Chapter Thirty
SOMETHING DIFFERENT

Not gonna lie, when they said we were going to a party, I expected somebody's dorm with frat boys doing Jell-O shots out of girls' belly buttons. Sure, I knew college had to be a little bit different here, but I just thought that meant maybe the frat boys would be wearing hipster glasses and doing Jell-O shots off other dudes rather than girls.

Instead, as we got to the eighth and top floor—via elevator, thank *God*—of a building on a quiet street in what Kat said was the financial district, I got a little nervous when I realized there was no music noticeably pumping out from behind any of the doors, signifying where the supposed party was happening.

Reassuring myself my photo-if-kidnapped plan was foolproof, I let them lead me to a door at the end of the hallway, where Milo paused.

"We should probably warn you, it's kind of a themed party."

"Themed?" I asked, glancing over my clothes and then at theirs.

I certainly wasn't dressed appropriately for any kind of theme, and neither were they, as far as I could tell.

Before she could answer, the door swung open and a small brunette (also dressed in totally normal clothing, phew) appeared in the doorway.

"You made it!" she squealed, reaching forward to hug first Kat— "Well, you always do"—and then Milo—"but you haven't been around in ages."

"You know how weekends are at work," he said. "Yet somehow these things are always on Saturdays."

"Oh, you mean when normal people have parties? Never mind, I'm glad we were able to do a last Monday hurrah before classes start back up."

"Uh, some of us already had classes start, thank you?" Kat said, but the girl waved her off as she thrust her hand out at me.

"Hi! I'm Stephanie," she said.

"This is Lydia," Kat introduced me before I had the chance. "New friend."

"Cool! Good to have new people for this."

New people for this? Is this some sort of weird sex orgy party? Is it really *a murder cult?* I tried to peer around Stephanie into the apartment to see if everyone else was naked or chanting in Latin or something.

But out loud I just said, "Hi."

"Now . . ." Steph said, reaching into her back pocket and bringing out a notepad and pen. She ran the pen down the page slowly, glancing up at all of us critically every so often, finally making three quick strikes across the paper. "Mmkay."

She moved to the side and Milo took one step into the apartment, leaning down for Stephanie to whisper something into his ear. He nodded and took another step forward so Kat could do the same. It came to be my turn and I hesitated.

"Have they told you the rules?" she asked.

"Not yet," Kat said.

"They will," Stephanie said. "Just remember the name I give you and don't say it to anyone."

I crinkled my forehead as she whispered a name into my ear.

"The theme this time is Disney," she said to all of us. "There's paper by the window. You guys know the way. And don't forget—phones off once you get to the roof."

The apartment was mostly empty as we made our way down a narrow hallway (much the same as Jane's place) and into a huge living room (at least twice the size of Jane's place). We stopped in the kitchen.

"First of all, phones off," Kat said, taking hers out and shutting it down. "Rule of the party is socializing, not social media. Asami—that's Steph's roommate—is really strict about it. Anyone using their phone up top gets put on immediate cleanup duty."

I hesitated. A party without a phone? How were you supposed to take pictures? Or text when things got awkward? Or call for help when you were being murdered by a Disney orgy cult?

But cleaning sounded pretty horrendous, too, so I powered my phone down, whispering a silent good-bye to the Internet.

"Second, whatever name Steph told you, that's who you are tonight. You don't have to be constantly 'in character'—most people don't commit that hard, but you can if you want." She led us to a window by the far wall. I noticed it was cracked open and, as Steph had said, there were note cards and pens on the counter next to it, and she grabbed three of each. "Point is to live in your character's head, and at midnight we write down what we think our characters' deepest secret is and burn it on the roof. Which is . . ." She pushed up the window to reveal a fire escape. And the not-so-distant sound of music, finally. "This way."

"This seems weirdly complicated for a party," I said, following Milo out through the window. "Where I'm from, people just put out a keg and call it a rager."

"Steph's a theater student; this is an extension of some sort of acting exercise," Milo elaborated as he started climbing up a rusted metal ladder. "But we get to set stuff on fire."

"Isn't that . . . illegal?" I asked, looking down—and immediately wishing I hadn't.

"Maybe, but no one's ever stopped it," he said, stepping around to the reverse side of the ladder and dropping down onto the roof. As Kat and I did the same, I was very glad to be on solid ground again. I've never had a fear of heights, but . . . note to self: don't get drunk tonight or you will most likely fall and die.

Also glad Jane's dress was knee-length and I'm pretty sure I didn't flash anybody.

"It's mostly just an excuse for monthly parties people actually show up to," Kat said. "But it's kind of fun. Especially when some people take it *very* seriously. As you are about to see."

A large guy in a flannel shirt with stubble the same length as the shaved sides of his head came up to us. "Kat!"

"Hey, Jay, how's it going?" Kat said, smiling.

"Kat's my friend." Then Jay leaned over and proceeded to chew on Kat's arm like he was gumming corn on the cob. "World domination!" he cried, and then ran off.

As Jay left, we all looked at one another.

"Now I'm afraid I have rabies, so I'm guessing he's something from *101 Dalmatians*," Kat said.

"Dude," I replied, shaking my head. "World domination but with obvious affection for the dark-haired girl and an unending appetite? Stitch from *Lilo and Stitch*."

Milo touched his nose and pointed at me. Kat's eyebrow went up in appreciation.

"Welp, I think I need a vodka soda to deal with that for the rest of the night," Kat said, and didn't wait for us before taking off toward a big table of alcohol set up off to the side.

"What's your poison?" Milo asked me when we caught up with her. He picked up the bottles, reading over each of the labels.

"There's plenty to choose from." I glanced over the table. There was liquor, wine, beer, chips, cheese, and . . .

I snatched up a plastic fork and coughed hesitantly. "Yeah, look at this stuff . . . isn't it neat . . . ?"

Milo barely glanced at me as he poured himself a whiskey, but I saw Kat smirk at me and my awkward attempt to play along with this whole theme thing.

"So what ya drinkin'?" Milo asked again.

"I'm . . . good for now," I said.

The words shocked me, too. Don't worry. But strangers, roof-tops, fire, *no phone*, and the way this summer had gone left me strangely fine with that decision.

As Milo and Kat fixed up their drinks and filled plates with various meats and cheeses, I took the opportunity to look around. The roof was done up really cool—there was a string of bulb lights forming a rectangle around where the party area was, with chairs here and there in groups. But truth was the place didn't really need a lot of decoration, because it had the city in the background.

It was a clear night, but I couldn't see a single star (okay, I might have seen one but I'm betting it was a plane), but the buildings mapped the edge of the sky. Looking north, I could see landmarks (the Empire State Building—oh, and that one from *Annie!*) popping up at intervals, marking the length of Manhattan. To the south, if you peered around one of the sleek high-rises, you could catch a glimpse of water. And I realized I was just down there yesterday, at the Statue of Liberty with Jane.

"Yeah." Milo appeared next to me, watching me watch the city. "I've lived here my whole life, and it never gets old."

"Milo! Hey, man!" A guy hanging in a group a few feet away raised his cup in our direction, and Milo gave him a two-fingered wave in response before turning back to us.

"Time to go do the rounds. I'll meet up with you guys in a bit," he said, and spun around toward his awaiting friends.

"That guy is perpetually stuck in the catch-up phase," Kat said, shaking her head. "He's always working or at school or with his family. Me and his roommate are probably the only ones who see him more than seasonally."

"Are you guys dating?" I asked.

"Me and Milo?" Kat chuckled. "No. Sometimes people think we are. Guys and girls can't be friends, et cetera, bullshit, et cetera." She waved her drink around dismissively. "He was dating my cousin for a little while when I moved out here—I'm a sophomore; Milo's going to be a senior. I tagged along with them sometimes, and Milo and I just stayed close, even after . . ."

I nodded empathetically. I'd never been friends with any of Lizzie's or Jane's boyfriends, but when I was in third grade, my two best friends—Courtney and Blake—went steady for, like, three weeks and then broke up when he spilled apple juice all over her new backpack. Picking teams at recess was a nightmare after that.

"Anyway," Kat exhaled. "Let's go see how many people we can introduce you to before midnight. Parties where you don't know people suck."

She looked around the roof, before zeroing in on a group hanging out near the far corner. "C'mon," she said, and grabbed my hand, leading us through the small crowd.

*   *   *

I probably met twenty new people by the time Steph called for the burning ceremony to begin. And not just "Hi, it's nice to meet you" meeting people, but, like, really meeting them.

Turns out it's a lot easier to get to know people at parties when everyone isn't totally shitfaced from the start.

I met Carrie, a friend of Steph's from high school who had just moved to Queens a few months ago and was very passionate about belly dancing and Spanish.

I talked to Roni, a transfer student who served in the Israeli army before coming here, but was way more interested in discussing film history than anything else.

I listened to Jess recount several stories of acid trips with her ex-boyfriend, which hadn't happened anymore after a particularly bad one resulted in a jagged scar up her calf from a busted Coke can.

I saw all of Asami's dozen tattoos, and found out the meaning behind each one.

Meanwhile, I found myself telling them about my sisters; Kitty; Mary's dumb ex, Eddie; and even my failed plans to transfer to Central Bay College and study psychology. I didn't tell anyone about Cody, or Harriet, or especially George, but even saying as much as I did felt like more openness than I'd expressed to anyone besides Ms. W all summer.

And I learned that Kat goes to New Amsterdam University.

"New Amsterdam?" I said, nearly choking on my (nonalcoholic) drink. You know, the school with the fantastic psychology department Violet told me about way back when I thought I had my future all planned out? "Don't they have a good psych program?"

"Yeah," Kat said, surprised. "My roommate last year was in it. She said it was intense, but was really into the whole thing. How'd you hear about it?"

"A friend of my cousin's went . . . Recommended it to me."

"You should come check it out while you're in town," Kat suggested.

"I can show you around, if you want," Milo had cut in. "If you're . . ." He turned to Kat, and she nodded. "I'm usually around during the day."

"Do you go there, too?" I asked, stalling. I wasn't sure I wanted to think about future stuff right now. But at the same time, how often was I in New York? And wasn't I *in* New York to figure out future stuff?

Not that I'd ever thought about NAU when I decided to come

here. Honestly. Okay, more honestly, it might have been in the back of my mind, because Violet talked about it, but not as something serious. But Kat going there was like a weird fate-type thing. I've never been one to ignore weird fate-type things.

He glanced at Kat again. "Yeah. I go there."

"Then . . . that'd be great," I agreed before I could change my mind.

Just then, Steph called out to the party. "Everyone! It's time for the lighting of the ceremonial circle!"

We all shuffled around this freestanding firepit, which Steph lit with one of those barbecue lighters. It shot up fast, a blue flame dancing against the metal.

Jay, the guy who bit Kat, came forward first.

"My secret is . . . I tried to take over the planet, but I actually like it here."

Kat nudged me. "Classic Stitch," she whispered.

Another person stepped forward.

"And he's been working hard to please everyone tonight," I said. "Cinderella?"

I shook my head. "Genie."

I was proven right when he read, "My best friend only likes me for what I can do for him."

The circle continued, with everyone surprisingly respectful of the vaguely bizarre ceremony, and I found myself becoming more invested as each new person stepped forward with a new sentence to burn. Strangely connected to strangers telling secrets that weren't really theirs.

"I wanted more than I had, and I had everything."

"This hasn't been my home since my mom died."

"My only friends can't talk back to me."

I wondered briefly if this is how cults get their power, but dismissed the thought as the circle reached our small group.

"I'm not sure if my opinions are my own anymore." Kat.

"I'll never really fit in here." Milo.

And then it was my turn. I hadn't gotten around to writing any-thing down on the paper.

"I gave up my voice for someone I hardly knew."

I took a step forward and quickly tossed the blank paper into the bottom of the fire, waiting, and watching, as the flames found it and the glow blazed brighter, if only for a moment.

* * *

Rather than taper down, the party rolled on after that. Things felt easier then. The music got turned up, the alcohol somehow kept coming (although I still kept it strictly soda), and there was even a little dancing.

And by dancing, I mean mostly me and Milo making up really bad synchronized dances to nineties pop.

And by bad, I mean totally the most amazing thing you've ever seen. Obvs.

"White kids," I heard Kat mutter after our not-particularly-well-coordinated rendition of "Wannabe" by the Spice Girls.

"Hey now," Milo said, halting suddenly. "You know damn well that I am a certified"—he paused, taking a moment to shim-my—"go-go dancer."

"What?" I exclaimed, bursting out laughing.

"I am!" he said, feigning hurt. "I'm good, too."

"Wait, are you really a go-go dancer?" I asked.

"The Braveheart, every Wednesday, Friday, and Saturday."

"That's . . ." I shook my head, utterly taken aback by this news. "Amazing."

"You may think that now, but wait until you have to actually go watch him cover himself in body glitter and shake his ass in front of a bunch of college boys," Kat said.

"Hey, those 'college boys' tip surprisingly well. And some of them are kind of cute." He winked at me, and Kat rolled her eyes.

"Ah, shit," she said suddenly, glancing down at her watch. "I told my mom I was going out tonight—she'll throw a fit if I don't check in." Her hand went to her pocket before she stopped herself from actually pulling her phone out. "I gotta duck inside real quick."

She trotted off and disappeared down the ladder.

"So . . ." Milo started.

"You know what?" I said. "I think I changed my mind about that drink."

He smiled at me, and we headed for what remained of the bar.

"Do you think anyone ever says their own secret instead of their character's?" I asked.

He tilted his head toward me. "I guess it's possible. I never really thought about it," he said. "Did you? Tell your own, I mean?"

I held up the plastic fork I'd snatched from the table earlier. "Only if I'm a mermaid."

Milo laughed. "Figures Steph would give you the ginger princess."

"What about you?" I asked. "Who was yours?"

"Ah," he said, wagging his finger. "We're not supposed to tell, remember?"

"Well . . . your secret was you'll 'never really fit in here.' So, some might say Tarzan or something. But since Steph assigns things based on what she knows of the person, and you're a happy-go-lucky rescuer of girls on bad dates . . . I'm gonna go with Tramp, from *Lady and the Tramp*."

"You're good at this figuring-people-out thing."

"Or I've seen *Lady and the Tramp* a million times," I said.

"It's got great animation," he added. "I wish they still made movies like that."

"Hmm . . . nostalgic for traditional animation . . . sketching in the park . . . lemme guess, you're an art major?"

"Architecture."

"Architecture?" I repeated. "If they make you draw buildings up-side down, that doesn't make me feel very safe."

"They usually prefer them right side up," he said. "But when I'm on my own, I like to do things my way."

"And your way is—"

"Upside down, sometimes."

I stared, waiting for an explanation, and he finally sighed and reached back around the table to grab more vodka to pour into his cup.

"You ready to think I'm totally lame?"

"What makes you think I don't already?" I said, and Milo smiled.

"When you draw things different from how you normally look at them, it makes you actually pay attention to what you're drawing. You see things you wouldn't otherwise." He looked past me at some-thing and I turned to follow his eye. "Come over here." I felt him brush by me and I followed, reaching a walled area in the center of the roof.

He stopped, with maybe a foot of distance between us. "Look at my face. Tell me what I look like." He stood perfectly still, affixing me with a gaze that was troublingly difficult to look away from.

"Um . . . green eyes," I started before making myself look else-where. "Brown hair . . . your chin is kind of stubbly . . . not as pale as me, but not tan, either . . ."

When I didn't add anything else, he nodded, tucking in his shirt. "Sure. All true. But now—"

Milo bent down to the ground and set his cup to the side before placing his hands on the cement, doing a handstand against the wall.

"Come sit down. Tell me what I look like. My face."

I glanced around to see if anyone else was watching this

mini-spectacle, but everyone was doing their own thing. I kneeled down in front of him, playing along.

"Well, all the blood is rushing to your head, so you look a little redder . . ."

He shook his head. "Look harder."

Leaning in, I looked again.

I noticed the differences first. The redness, like I said. The veins straining against his forehead as he concentrated on holding himself up. But then . . .

"You have a scar on your forehead. Shaped like a V."

"Good. What else?"

"Your nose isn't straight. It goes slightly to the right."

"Anything else?"

I saw his green eyes, still staring into mine, with flecks of gold surrounding the center, a dozen shards of glitter looking at me looking at him.

"You . . . are about to fall."

And he did. Into a smiling heap.

"Told you," he said, wiping his hands off on his jeans. "You'd been looking at me all night and thought you knew what I looked like, so you didn't look any harder. But upside down . . ."

"I was not looking at you all night," I mumbled.

"You see my point, though," he said, grinning again. This time I noticed that he only showed two teeth when he smiled like that, with the smallest of gaps between them. "Yeah, I guess you're right."

Suddenly his eyes unfocused. As if all the blood that had been in his head rushed to his feet and back again.

"Whoa," he said, unsteady. "Mind if we get some air?"

"We're outside," I said, but followed him a couple of steps over to where he could lean against the railing.

From this angle, I could see new stuff on the skyline. "Which bridge is that?" I asked, pointing to the gap between two small buildings.

"The Brooklyn Bridge," he answered. "Have you been there yet?"

"Brooklyn? That's where I'm staying."

"No, the bridge."

I shook my head.

"You should. Go at night, if you can. With some friends or something. It's amazing."

"It looks it," I agreed. "I can't believe you can see that from here. All you can see from my sister's building is another brick wall."

"A view like this must cost a fortune," Milo said. "Even that sliver of it. Asami's mom is a big producer for some news station in DC; I think she pays for most of it."

"Must be nice to not have to worry about money," I said into my beer.

"Sometimes the cards just fall in your favor. Can't fault her for that." He tipped his cup toward the partygoers. "Besides, she's generous with what she's got. My experience is that it's hard to find generosity without flaunting."

"Some people surprise you," I said, thinking back to Darcy. But reminders of his generosity and exactly *why* he had to be so generous to me stirred up feelings I wanted to keep pushed down for now.

But as the nerves in my stomach began bubbling over, I knew things had shifted, and the temporary reprieve alcohol could buy wasn't something I wanted to delve further into tonight. Not with Milo and Kat and this really great time, or with Allison and her "request" to leave trouble behind before I come back to Jane's.

"It's getting pretty late," I said as casually as I could manage. "I don't want to wake my sister's roommates up at like three a.m., so I should probably head back."

"Sure," Milo said. "What part of Brooklyn are you staying in?"

"Umm." I realized I had no idea where Jane lived. I'd just followed her lead any time we'd gone out. "I have the address in my phone."

"D'you know the neighborhood?"

"Umm," I repeated, sounding like an idiot. "I know there's like, a deli down the street?"

I could see Milo doing his best to fight a smirk, and I admired his restraint.

"Don't feel bad. New York takes some time to get used to. Especially with the subways. People who aren't from around here get all kinds of mixed up 'cause you can't tell where you've gone once you're underground. I can take you back, if you want. Not that far out of my way."

I hesitated. I didn't want to get lost—and even I was willing to admit there was a pretty good chance that would happen trying to navigate the subway all the way back to wherever Jane's is—but I didn't want to give Milo the wrong impression.

He squinted at me over the top of his cup, finally setting it back down on the wall.

"Kat!" he yelled.

I saw a head of curly dark hair swivel toward us and Kat made her way over.

"You headed back soon?" Milo asked. "Thought we could all hit the same train. This one doesn't know the city yet." He nodded his head toward me.

Kat stared at Milo, then me. What was it about these guys that made me feel like they were constantly trying to stare a hole into my freaking head? Was this a New York thing?

"Sure," she said, her eyes sparkling. But that could have been the alcohol, because she kicked back the rest of her drink. "Let's roll."

Texts with Jane

Jane: Hey, I hope you're doing okay. I'm sorry I had to go.

Lydia: No, it's cool, I get it. How's Miami?

Jane: Sweltering. But it's nice to get to see it. What did you and Allison and Shea do last night?

Lydia: Shea had to study and Allison had some stuff to do, but it's okay, I met up with my friend Casey from high school for dinner.

Jane: Oh, good! New York is full of questionable strangers, I'm so glad you found someone there you know.

Lydia: Yeah.

Chapter Thirty-one
CAMPUS TOUR

I traveled to the New Amsterdam University campus pretty sure I was going to the wrong place.

Last night after I got back to Jane's I couldn't sleep, so I idly browsed her computer for a while (two Facebook messages from Casey, yaaaaay) and found myself on the NAU website.

I'd never actually toured Central Bay College. I just knew I could get in there, and that Lizzie and Mary would be nearby. But it looked really pretty on its website—although, that's sort of the purpose of websites, right?

Well, New Amsterdam University looked pretty, too. And pretty large. It turns out they had multiple campuses, with the main one being in the Bronx.

The only thing I know about the Bronx is that it's where the Yankees play (Mom has a thing for "that nice Derek Jeter"—and his butt) and that it's always where the perps come from on *Law & Order*.

Before we parted ways last night, Kat and Milo walked me to Jane's door, and we made a plan to meet up today for my tour of NAU, on the main campus. So this morning (okay, afternoon, I did get in really late) I'd hopped on the subway and rode it all the way from Brooklyn, through Manhattan, and into the Bronx. For over an hour.

Which meant one of two things: either I was going to the wrong place, or there was absolutely no way that I was "on their way home" when they dropped me off last night.

I got off at my stop, and super subtly checked my phone for the direction I was supposed to head. I didn't know what to expect. On the website, the campus looked like a park, with old, important buildings lined by trees. But here I was passing by regular buildings squished up together, a freaking highway, and finally turning left into . . .

Oh.

The beautiful park, the old buildings, the trees. They were all here, but with an iron gate separating this fairy-tale land from the city surrounding it.

"Hey."

I whipped my head around. Milo leaned up against the side of the gate. I relaxed and took my earbuds out.

"Hey. I was worried I was going to end up in the wrong place."

"Nah. You pick things up quick," he said. "Bet if we threw you in the ocean you'd figure out how to get across it, no problem."

"Um," I said, blushing. "Let's not test that theory."

"All right, now, before we get this started, you gotta be properly outfitted."

"Outfitted?" I scanned my clothes. I thought I was New York normal in jeans and a gray shirt (neutral!) with a yellow bedazzled tiger on it (okay, not neutral).

"You got your campus map, your official NAU water bottle"—he handed me a bottle of water with the letters NAU written on it in Sharpie—"and this wonderful souvenir bag from the gift shop."

"You mean this plastic shopping bag?" I asked, raising an eyebrow.

"*Souvenir* plastic shopping bag," he corrected, grinning at me. "You ready for your personalized tour of the wonder that is New Amsterdam University?" He held out his arm to me.

"Ready as I'll ever be," I replied, taking that arm and passing through the gates.

*   *   *

The campus, like the website pictures, was amazing. The buildings, cool in that crumbly castle kind of way. But the tour was . . . weird.

"There anything in particular you'd like to know?" Milo asked once we were properly on campus grounds.

"Um, I don't know," I said. "What happens on normal college tours?"

He cocked his head. "Mostly history stuff. Like that building was the first one built, in, uh, 1835." Milo pointed to a chapel-looking thing in the center of the quad. "This school was founded as a Jesuit college for training priests."

"Really?" I said, looking closer as we approached the building. "Because the seal says 'EST. 1904?'"

He leaned in and examined it. "Huh. It does."

"And on the website it said it was always coed. Nothing about priests."

"Oh, that. Yeah, that's when the *university* was founded. They had to reestablish it when they changed it over from a Jesuit college to a university. The website's just an abridged version, y'know. What d'you say we go check out the psych building?"

"Okay," I said, and made the sharp left turn to follow him to the other side of the quad.

"Can I see that map I gave you real quick?" he asked, and I

handed it to him. "I've never been to the psych department, just wanna . . . right, this one."

We came to a building, and he took out his student ID to swipe it to open the doors.

"I think this is the art building," I said, pointing to the stone above us, which was etched with the words COLLEGE OF FINE ARTS.

He glanced up. Then back down at the map. "Right. Well, we're cutting through is all. Psych building's on the other side, I guess."

"You guess?" I asked.

"We gotta get to the other side to find out." He smiled and swiped his ID.

And swiped it again.

"Let me try—I have a good door karma," I said, snatching the ID out of his hand and gliding it through the electronic thingy next to the door. Once, twice, three times. "Huh, it doesn't want to—"

I glanced down at the ID.

"This . . . isn't you," I said, eyeing him a little suspiciously. "It's Kat."

His lips tightened into a thin line. "Yeah, I lost mine, and Kat gave me hers for the day, so . . ."

"What is this?" I asked, taking a step away. My mind jumped into high alert because first, I was in the Bronx, which is filled with perps, and B, oh yeah, I only met Milo *yesterday*. Or a couple of days ago really, but still. "You don't know anything about the campus, and how does an architecture student not know where the art building is, and is this water poisoned?" I held up my bottled water, waving it so a little sloshed out.

"Okay, okay, you caught me." He held up his hands, a gesture of surrender. "But the water's not poisoned. I promise, see?" He took the bottle from me and took a swig. Okay. If the choice is poison or backwash, I'm fine with backwash.

He shoved his hands in his back pockets and sighed. "I don't . . . *technically* . . . go here."

"Why would you tell me that you do?"

"I thought I'd visited enough times to know my way around, and you kinda just assumed I did when we were talking last night, and—" He paused, reassessing. "Would you believe I just wanted you to like me?"

I frowned. "Lying is a pretty shitty way to get someone to like you."

He looked momentarily taken aback, like he was really considering that for a second before nodding his head.

"You're right," he said, chewing on his lip. "I didn't think about it like that, but you're totally right. I'm sorry."

"Are you even an architecture student?"

"I really am. I just . . . go to Columbia, not NAU," he admitted.

"Really?" I asked, not bothering to hide my disbelief.

"Promise," he said. He pulled his wallet out of his back pocket and dropped it open, flashing his student ID at me.

"Why would you want people to think you go to NAU when you go to freaking Columbia?"

He sighed. "The part of the city I grew up in . . . people treat you differently when they know you're going to a 'good school.' Doesn't matter they've known me my whole life. Just got into the habit of keeping it to myself, I guess."

"Are you telling me your parents don't yell it from the rooftops that you're in the Ivy League?" I replied.

"My mom . . . maybe." He shrugged. "But my dad would probably yell it from the rooftops if I joined the Teamsters. Architecture, Columbia . . . it's just not his world."

"Well, Columbia's impressive. And pursuing something you care about is never something you should have to keep to yourself."

He sort of smiled to himself. "Well, I'm sorry I ruined your fake tour of a great school."

"It's all right, I guess," I said, my smile a little sadder than his. "There's absolutely no way I'm getting into it, anyway."

"Why do you say that?" he asked.

I shrugged. "Admittance is probably based on, you know, grades.

And I didn't really do well in school. I mean, I did okay, but I never really tried until this past summer. And I only really tried because I finally found something I liked."

"Psychology," he said. "So what is it you like about it?"

"I dunno, I guess . . . people interest me. How their brains work. What makes them who they are. What breaks them. How to put them back together. That kind of thing." At least, that's what I'd thought. It seemed like the more times I said it out loud, the more vague it sounded and the less certain I felt.

But Milo was smiling at me in that way that reminded me of him being upside down last night. I had looked at him in a different way, and maybe he was looking at me in a different way, too.

"That's a better answer than I expected," he said.

"What did you expect?"

He just shook his head, still smiling. "No clue."

We stood there for a little while, letting the hot city air pretend to be a summer breeze as we watched the campus. School had started only recently, so half the students were wandering lost, looking at maps. Like me. But there was also noise, and excitement, and this vibe of anticipation. For what comes next.

After a couple of minutes, Milo let out a sigh. "Let's find the psych building."

*   *   *

"We should *not* be doing this," I said.

"S'okay," Milo whispered, ducking his head into the door. "This one's empty, c'mon."

We didn't need to use Kat's student ID to get into this building, since people were walking in and out, in basically a constant stream. Once inside, it . . . looked like a normal school building. Halls, doors, classrooms with desks, that sort of thing.

But then we stuck our heads into one of the lecture halls . . . and it was *packed*.

"We can slip in the back if you want," Milo whispered to me. But I shook my head. And even if I didn't really know why I didn't want to stay and listen, Milo seemed to.

"Okay," he said, narrowing his eyes, thinking. "Come with me."

He peeked into every classroom, until he found this one. An empty lecture hall.

Three times bigger than Professor Latham's classroom—and even empty, it was intimidating as hell.

"If you're gonna go to school here, you gotta be comfortable here," he said, dragging me down the steps to the podium at the center. "So, professor, get up there."

"Are you serious?" I asked.

"Sitting in the back of class is easy after standing up front." He took a seat in the front row.

I placed my water bottle on the podium, and promptly spilled it on one of the pads of paper resting there. A bunch of scribbles bled into nothingness. Great start.

"Um, how about we talk about . . . impulse control?" I said as I took the sopping-wet pad and put it in my plastic bag. I kept my eyes on Milo. Not the crazy big room.

"Impulse control?"

"Yeah, you know how some people make decisions spur-of-the-moment like idiots and think they'll work out, like idiots? Like . . . giving a tour of a school they don't go to, or giving a psychology lecture totally on the spot. My theory," I said, sort of getting into it, "is that impulsiveness is really a result of too much awesome."

"Awesome?"

"Yeah, that awesome feeling you get when something is about to happen. That buzz when you say, 'Screw it,' and jump in with both feet. Too much awesome just makes you want more awesome, which just leads to more and more impulsiveness."

"Your theory could use some work." A voice came from the side door. There, a skinny man with salt-and-pepper hair was leaning against the doorframe. He didn't look like he'd ever smiled in his life, nor like he was going to start now. "I'm Professor Malikov, and that's my podium you're littering."

"I'm sorry," I said, grabbing my water bottle and backing away from the podium. "We're just—"

"The 'awesome,' as you so aptly put it, is dopamine, and it's been shown to spike during reward-based behavior. You need to prove scientifically that impulsiveness is rewarded."

He didn't even look at me, but something about the dry way he spoke made me feel less like a kid caught at playing grown-up and more like someone who could debate him.

Stupid idea, I know.

"Isn't that the reward itself?" I asked. "The dopamine, I mean? You do stuff to feel better and—"

"Where's my notepad?" he asked suddenly. "There was a notepad on the top of this pile. It had all my notes on it for my next lecture. Where is it?"

Then he looked at me, and I knew that trying to engage him in debate was an impulsive decision that I'd regret.

"Sorry, Professor, we were just working on some fear-based issues, but come on, Lydia, time to go!" Milo grabbed my hand and we ran out of there before Mount Malikov could blow.

"That was . . ." I said between breaths once we made it out a side door of the psych building and back to the quad.

"Impulsive?"

"Should we go back?" I asked. "I have his notepad, it's . . . maybe dry now?"

"I think we let this one go," Milo replied. "C'mon—there's more fake tour to be had."

I expected him to hold out his hand to me, but he didn't have to—he was still holding mine.

＊　＊　＊

With Milo admitting he didn't know anything about NAU, it became a lot of fun making up what various things on campus were,
and helped forget my impulsiveness with Malikov. By the end of
the afternoon, our alternate-reality New Amsterdam University was
founded by Jesuit priests from Australia, who time-traveled here
from the future because the world would end unless they estab-
lished a school whose mascot was a manatee.

You kinda had to be there.

The sun was a low orange ball by the time we got back to the
front gates.

"So, what are you doing now?" he asked.

"Headed back to Brooklyn, I guess." I rolled up my campus map,
shoving it into my bag.

"Would you like to go to dinner with me?"

My eyes came up to meet his.

A date.

My heart started beating double-time. But I made sure I took
two breaths before answering. "I . . . I'm not really doing that right
now. Dating."

"Okay," he said immediately. "No problem."

"It's just . . . baggage."

"Lydia, I get it. It's fine."

"It is?"

He shrugged. "Everyone has baggage. I think it's a requirement
for living in New York . . . like you have to provide first and last
months' rent and at least one medium-size baggage." He paused.
"But I hope this doesn't mean you won't hang out with me and Kat
again—she thought you were really cool."

I warmed at the compliment, and at the relief of his accepting
my decision. "I'd like that."

"Lemme walk with you to the subway?"

"I thought you said I was a quick study. Throw me in the ocean and all that."

"I'm sure you can find your way back." He smiled, as we started walking. "I'm just not sure if I can."

* * *

When I got back to the apartment, I almost regretted saying no to dinner with Milo. But after Cody, it's crystal clear I'm not ready to be dating anyone, and I'm super committed to that. Besides, I'm only going to be in New York for a couple more days. Starting something with a guy that's just going to be hot and quick and then fizzle does not, for once, appeal.

At least not with Milo.

Besides, I should give hanging with Allison and Shea a chance.

Yeah, probably should have cleared that with Allison and Shea, because one was studying and the other had big plans to watch a Ken Burns documentary. Guess which was which.

So I picked up a sandwich at the deli downstairs for dinner and resigned myself to Jane's room and her computer. And once again, I found myself on the NAU website.

And idly clicking on "How to Apply."

Even if I'll never get in, and even if one professor might want to freeze me with his eyeballs, what's the harm in just seeing what the application looks like, right? No biggie.

Okay . . . it looked like it was all the usual stuff. Transcripts, recommendations, financial aid information, essay ques—

I froze.

Recount an incident or time when you experienced failure. How did it affect you? What lessons did you learn? What would you do differently now?

No.

Way.

How the hell is it possible that I'm being freaking stalked by this same stupid essay question?

Is the universe like, "We haven't tortured Lydia in a while, let's have some fun!"

I never really thought about it, but it must be a standard college application question. Which means I'm not meant for *any* college, I guess.

I closed the computer. My eyes fell on the plastic bag from the NAU gift shop, sticking out of my bag. Even if it was never serious, even if my tour included speculation about manatees and time travel, it was a nice dream to have for a day.

Guess that's all it's ever going to be.

Chapter Thirty-two

CENTERED

The next morning, I was barely awake and looking forward to hiding in Jane's room from my quasi-roommates when my phone buzzed.

"Hello?" I answered, groggy.

"Hey, Lydia!" Bing's soft and cheerful voice echoed in my ear. "What kind of bagel do you like?"

"Um . . . cinnamon raisin?"

"Great!" he said. "I got one of those. And coffee. You ready?"

"Ready for what?"

"I thought you'd like to come with me to the center today."

The center? But I had a big day of watching Netflix planned.

"Come on, Lydia, you didn't come all the way to New York to stay in and watch Netflix, did you?" Bing said.

Note to self—other people know Jane's account password and

can see when you're watching stuff. But still, the Teen Crisis Center where Bing volunteered did not exactly make for a vacation day.

"You keep saying that you want to help people," Bing said. "So let's get helping. Coffee and a bagel await you downstairs."

"O . . . kay," I said, leaning out Jane's window and peering down. Yup, one town car double-parked out front. One Bing, waving up at me with a bag of bagels in his hand. "I'll be down in ten."

"Perfect. If you're not down in ten minutes . . . I'll still be here, but I can't promise the bagel will be."

*　*　*

Nine and half minutes later, I had a bagel in one hand and a cup of coffee in another. Twenty-three minutes after that, we pulled up in front of a super nice brownstone in the nice part of Brooklyn.

"The brownstone was left to the center's founder in the previous owner's will," Bing said. "The neighbors don't love it, but the kids do—they feel a lot safer in this neighborhood."

We mounted the steps. The facade was like every other house on the street—except this one had a very discreet TEEN CRISIS CENTER painted in gold letters across the window above the door. But as unassuming as it was on the outside, the inside was like a beehive.

There were people in every room—some sitting at desks talking with kids, some sitting in groups and doing crafts. One group of teen girls burst out laughing as we walked past, and Bing stuck his head in.

"Hello, ladies," Bing said, smiling in that way that says he has absolutely no idea the effect being handsome, nice, and rich has on people. But these were a bunch of girls—teenagers. And yeah, while they were at a crushable age, they also seemed so much wiser than Bing. Not a fragile flower in crisis in the bunch.

"We were just saying you got a thing for redheads or what, Mr. Lee?" one of the girls piped up, causing the rest of them to start snickering.

"Careful, that's my future sister-in-law," Bing said, grinning, and angled me forward. "Lydia, the ten a.m. group session—group, Lydia."

I guess my coffee hadn't kicked in yet, because it took me a second to . . .

"Wait, I'm what?" I blurted out, but Bing was already halfway down the hall. I waved bye to the group and trotted to catch up to Bing, who was unlocking the door to a broom closet.

Except it wasn't a broom closet.

In it was a desk covered in papers, shelves full of binders, and not much else. Not much room for else, except for a picture of Bing and Jane at some party in the center of the wall.

"You have an office here?" I said. "I thought you just, like, volunteered."

"That's how I started," Bing replied, taking off his shoulder bag. "I did the counselor training, was working the crisis phone lines three times a week, and then . . . I just started coming every day. Doing what needed to be done. Dottie—she's the center's founder—saw that I was good at it, and gave me more responsibility. Then, when she found out about my family . . ."

"That you're rich?"

"More like, I have the right connections to put the center on the radar of influential people," he said, showing more self-awareness than I'd thought him capable of. "It's the first time that's ever really come in handy, so I don't mind using it."

Wow, self-aware and shrewd. Maybe he and his manipulative sister, Caroline, are related after all.

"But it's good experience, for when I open up a center of my own."

"You're going to open up a center?" I asked. "When? Where? How?"

"The 'when' is after I get my master's in social work—I'm planning to apply to schools next fall. My folks aren't exactly happy about replacing med school with social work, but Caroline says they'll come around."

He pulled a binder off the shelf, flipped it open. "The 'how' is trickier. But I have my money. And Darcy's already said that he'd be a primary donor, and could even tie it in to his company's charitable arm."

There's that Darcy again, I thought. Always coming to the rescue.

"And the 'where' is . . . wherever Jane's work ends up."

"Yeah," I said. "About that . . . you said something about a future sister-in-law?" I blinked at him innocently.

Bing blushed a little. "No questions have been asked, if that's what you're wondering. But I hope . . ."

He let his sentence trail off, because what else needed to be said? He hoped. And considering where they were six months ago—Bing coming to the city with Jane to repair a relationship that he'd almost screwed up permanently—that he had cause to hope was everything.

"Hey, um . . . could you do me a favor?" Bing was saying.

"Oh, I won't tell Jane anything."

"Jane wasn't my worry. But maybe don't mention it to your mother."

*　　*　　*

Once Bing got a bunch of papers and stuff out of his office—and ate his third bagel of the morning; where does that boy put all those carbs?—he gave me a proper tour of the center and what they do there.

Turns out they do a lot.

"We have a hotline for teens in crisis, and it's manned twenty-four/seven, so anytime someone calls, there's someone to talk to," Bing was saying as he dodged people in the halls. "We also have one-on-one counseling, and group sessions, like you saw." He pointed to a bulletin board. "We even have career counseling, and job placement services."

"Jobs? You mean like after school?"

Bing nodded slowly. "Sometimes. But often, these kids aren't in school anymore. Aren't living at home, or anywhere. They need a way to support themselves. Or, sometimes they just need a place to sleep for the night or a hot meal, and we do what we can to make sure they have that, too."

A rush of gratitude for my parents flooded through me. They were always, always supportive. Even when I screwed up . . . except maybe Dad when I said I was jetting off to New York for a week.

I shook myself free of that frowny thought, and instead turned a bright smile on Bing. "So, what do you want me to do? Man the phones? Sit in on a group? Oh! I could do crafts with them! Where do you keep the glitter?"

Bing smiled. "No glitter or group sessions for you. And to man the phones you have to go through the training, which takes a lot longer than an afternoon. But we could use extra hands in the kitchen making lunch."

Lunch? I was here to make *lunch*?

"Seriously?" I frowned. "But I'm really good at giving advice, my teacher said as much." Granted, it was my Gothic Lit teacher, but still. "I could, like, tell them about me and show that I re-late—"

"Lydia," Bing said, in his firmest tone. Which is kind of like a bunny being firm with you. "Like I said, you have to be trained to do any of that. But if you were going to talk to anyone, it's not about your story and relating to them. What most of the kids need here is someone to just listen to them."

"Oh." I looked at my toes, feeling kind of small. Of course it's not about me. I've spent so much time inside my own head the past couple of months, it's kind of hard to remember that. "So, what's for lunch today?"

I spent the rest of the morning preparing, baking, and serving massive trays of macaroni and cheese. Which I'm actually not bad at. I'm not my mom's chosen sous chef for nothing. But usually Mom's making a casserole for five people, so this was . . . different. Plastic sandwich gloves and aprons aren't exactly fashion-forward.

But I didn't mind so much. The other volunteers in the kitchen were nice, and worked together with a rhythm they'd perfected over time. I tried to do as I was told and not get in their way.

Bing popped his head in a couple of times—each time taking a double helping, seriously, where does he put it?—to make sure I was doing okay, and to talk to one of the fifty or so people who filtered through the dining room as we served lunch. And time flew by—not because carrying those trays from the hot oven to the front and then scooping them out and making sure the condiments and napkin dispensers were full was exhausting (now I know why Mary was always tired when she got home from a day at the coffee shop), but because I did what Bing said.

I listened.

I listened as Malik, the head cook, told his cousin Layna, the other cook, how his mom was doing in rehab. I listened as some of the girls from the 10:00 a.m. group came in for lunch, chattering about an upcoming dance. I listened as one incredibly skinny guy came in and asked if Bing knew how to tie a tie. He was going for an interview for city housing, and, if it went well, he would finally have a place to live.

And it made me realize Bing was right. How could I have ever thought that I could say, "Oh, hi, yeah, I totally get where you're coming from because once my boyfriend filmed us having sex and tried to sell it on the Internet," or "This one time I missed a deadline for an application, so I totally understand how hard your life is."

It also gave me a new respect for Bing. He often comes off as too nice and too easygoing, but working at a place like this wasn't for the faint of heart.

But was it for me?

I mean, my version of helping people sort of always involved my own swank office with vases of reeds and calming music in the waiting room. But this . . . this is helping people, too. And if I *did* want to try and go into psych again (which is in no way certain because . . . come on) this could be a part of that.

Although, right now, "this" is just rinsing out metal trays and taking the trash out. Not exactly advanced awesome helpfulness.

The trash bags were heavy, so I was dragging them out the front door. My back was kind of turned and I didn't see the girl at first.

She was sitting at the bottom of the stairs, curled into a ball. Her rounded back and green army jacket made her look like a turtle, turning her head and peeking at me from behind her shell. As I passed her to get to the garbage cans, I said, "Hey."

"Hey," she mumbled back.

"Are you here for . . . someone?" I asked as I closed the garbage lids.

"No," she said, bringing her head up, barely. She had her arms wrapped around her stomach, and for the first time I could see that it looked like she was pregnant.

And really young.

"Okay." I waited for some sign of what I was supposed to do now. "Um . . . we just finished lunch. But there's a bunch left over. I can get you a plate."

She shrugged, and I took it as a yes.

"Cool. I'll be right back." I jumped up the steps. "Don't go anywhere, okay? It's . . . really good mac and cheese."

I found Bing talking with Dottie, and pulled him away.

"There's a girl outside. I don't think she'll come in, but I said I'd bring a plate of mac and cheese out to her?"

Bing immediately moved to the front window and peered out, then nodded to Dottie. "Lydia, grab me that plate."

I ran to the kitchen, spooned out mac and cheese. By the time I brought it back, though, Bing was already sitting on the steps next to the girl.

"Go on," Dottie said to me.

I walked down the steps, clutching the plate. Bing turned when I cleared my throat.

"Thanks," he said, taking the plate from me. "Lydia, this is Vicki. Vicki, Lydia."

"I said I don't want to see a counselor," Vicki mumbled.

"Oh, don't worry, Lydia's not a counselor, either. So, we can't really do anything except sit here, eat some mac and cheese, and listen. If you maybe wanted to talk."

It took a couple of minutes of just sitting there, of Vicki picking at her food, then commenting on the crappy parallel parking job the guy who parked in front of us did, for her to start to talking. About the guy at school who got her pregnant, and how he's not talking to her now, and not having anywhere to go.

Bing was just a warm presence for her, an open space she could say anything to. He never jumped in with other stuff, or pressured her, he just let her tell her story.

By the time she got to why she ended up on the center's doorstep, she'd talked herself into coming inside. When we stood up to go in, Bing leaned over to me and whispered in my ear.

"Good job, Lydia."

"I didn't do anything," I whispered back, and he shook his head.

"You did more than you know."

Chapter Thirty-three
JANE RETURNS

"Jane!" I called out from the area just past the exit doors of the terminal, waving my sign bearing sparkly unicorn stickers and the name BENNET.

Yes, I recycled it. But come on, it's too cool not to be used again.

"You guys!" Jane waved back, rushing over. "It's so good to see you!"

She embraced me only briefly, but I'll allow it. She went starry-eyed when she saw Bing behind me, and I knew they wanted to get a little PDA action in.

I broke them up after an inappropriate amount of time. "Come on, guys!" I said. "I've been waiting three days to have my sister back in New York, I'm not wasting another minute."

* * *

In the town car on the way back to the apartment, Jane regaled us with tales of Miami, how it's even hotter there than here (impossible), and how she worked with the fabric dyers getting a perfect pattern to be featured in their winter collection. She told us all about everyone she met (wherever Jane goes she comes back with at least fifty new Facebook friends), all the delicious food she ate (she now has tamale recipes on her Pinterest) and about how she truly believes the tropical color scheme they came up with is going to dominate fashion next year.

But by the time we got back to the apartment, and Bing had walked us up the four flights of stairs again and taken some inappropriate PDA time again, Jane turned to me.

"So . . ." she said, plopping on the couch beside me. It was the middle of the day, so Shea was at the library and Allison was at work and we had the place to ourselves. "How have you been? Is there . . . anything you want to talk about?"

Oh no. Was she expecting to have the talk now? The "What are you gonna do with your life" talk?

Although I was a little better prepared than I was three days ago. Kind of. Maybe.

But what popped out of my mouth surprised me. "Not really."

Jane's smile faltered by a millimeter.

I could have told her. I could have said, "Well, actually, I'm thinking about school—but not in San Francisco. Guess where?!" And I could imagine her response: completely enthusiastic, totally wanting to help out in any way possible, and sharing the joy with Bing and everyone else of Lydia Having a Life Plan.

Which is great . . .

But what if it doesn't happen?

What if I screw up again?

What if that stupid essay on failure is going to be my nemesis forever?

I would let everyone down. Once again. So . . . this has to stay mine. Until I feel more sure about it.

It's different to share it with Milo and Kat. They don't have any expectations. The only thing they see when they see me is . . . possibility.

And when I'm hanging out with them, I can see that possibility in myself, too.

"Okay," Jane said, covering any feeling she might have with a bright voice and jumping up to head to the kitchen. "Want some tea? I brought back some delicious Cuban cookies called *torticas*."

Much like Mom, Jane both soothed and avoided via food.

"Sure," I said.

"Bing said you had a good time at the center," Jane called out as she put water on the stove.

"I did. They're a great group of people."

"They are," Jane agreed. "Bing said they liked you a lot, too."

Soon enough she came back with a pot of tea and plate of cookies—that were basically snickerdoodles with a little lime, but totally delicious.

"I know Shea's always studying and Allison's always working, but I'd hoped they'd be able to at least . . ." Jane looked a little disappointed, but then she covered it with a smile. "Anyway, I'm so glad you had your friend Casey to hang out with. I was afraid you would end up alone in the city or fall prey to strangers."

I started playing with the seams of the couch's slipcover. "Strangers aren't all bad, right?"

Jane just shook her head. "Of course not, but you have to be careful. I mean, Bing did get mugged—"

"—twice. Yeah, I know."

Awkward silence wormed its way into the room. I don't know if Jane noticed, because she just hummed a little to herself as she sipped her tea.

Then, suddenly—

"I have to do a couple of work emails, but the office gave me the afternoon off so we can spend the day together."

"Oh." I blinked. "Great."

"So what haven't you seen yet?" she asked excitedly. "Have you been to Macy's? It's huge, so much bigger than the one in the mall back home. Or what about the Cloisters? That's really pretty."

"Haven't seen either," I replied.

As Jane started tackling those work emails so we could enjoy an afternoon of shopping and cloistering, I smiled and played along, but I had this weird feeling in my stomach.

Now that Jane's back, it's like I'm back to being Jane's sister. Back to being the tourist, being shown around. Not that that's bad! But for the last three days, I haven't been a tourist. I've been part of the city. Part of a group.

I like that version of Lydia. But now that Jane's back . . . I have to go back to the old one.

Or maybe not.

Hey, what are you doing tonight? Milo and I are going to see Wicked with some friends and one bailed so we have an extra ticket. Interested? —Kat

A flutter went through my stomach. I'd love to spend one last night being that other Lydia . . . but I was worried things were left a little weird with Milo and the whole asking-me-out thing.

But then, another text chimed my phone.

You leave Saturday right? You can't leave without saying good-bye, anyway. Might as well do something fun :)

I did have so much fun at the party the other night. And on the tour with Milo, despite any weirdness.

"Hey, Jane," I called out, pulling her attention away from email. "Do you think we'll be out all night?"

"Um . . ." She squinted, considering, and I swear I saw her eyes flutter shut a couple of times. "We can if you want to be! Again, I'm so sorry I've been gone for half the week. . . . Was there something in particular you wanted to do tonight?"

You wanna know the truth? Old me—Internet-famous me—would have totally loved dragging my big sister out for a night on the town, playing her guilt over going MIA in my favor to party till 3:00 a.m. and sneaking into VIP lounges and whatever other stuff Jane would never want to do if I just asked.

But now, I wanted something else.

"No, it's okay!" I said. "Actually, um, Casey invited me to go see *Wicked* later. She's got an extra ticket. And we'll probably hang out after. Is that okay?"

Jane looked relieved as she said, "Of course! It sounds like fun. And it's a great show; you'll absolutely love it."

I grinned and typed out a quick message:

Definitely.

"But until then . . ." Jane hit a few last keys on her computer and stood up, grabbing her purse. "You ready to go? The continuation of our New York adventure awaits!"

Chapter Thirty-four
BRIDGES

We wrapped up our second-to-last day of sisterly sightseeing early (as expected, travel exhaustion hit Jane fiercely before dinner) and I met Milo at the subway stop near her apartment that evening.

"Kat's meeting us at the theater," he said, almost sounding apologetic. "She had a late class today, it was easier."

Any worries I had in that moment that hanging out with Milo on my own, even just for the subway ride, was going to be awkward or weird were quickly erased.

"So how're your feet?"

"My feet?"

"Your sister's back, right? Figured you continued your city tour."

"Oh, yeah. My feet are better this time," I said. "Getting used to walking city blocks."

"Good." He smiled. "Soon you'll be all assimilated."

"Does that mean that I'll be a speed-walking, neutral-color-wearing New Yorker before I leave on Saturday?"

"I hope not," he replied. "Saturday, huh? Did you make it to the Brooklyn Bridge in your travels?" he asked.

"No," I said. Truth be told, Jane had suggested it, but when I asked if we could wait and go tomorrow night, she put on her worried face and insisted it was much safer during the day.

So we didn't go.

"But I'm kind of burned out on the tourist stuff, anyway." I shrugged. "It's not as cool as I thought it would be."

Milo looked at me, remaining steady as I gripped the metal railing to avoid tumbling into him as the train began to slow down for the next stop.

"The touristy parts of New York are fine. You just gotta know how to look at 'em." He moved away from me, toward the door.

"This isn't our stop, is it?" I asked, looking up at the map to see where we were.

"It is now. Come on."

The door dinged open and he looked back to make sure I was following him before stepping out onto the platform.

A platform with signs pointing toward the Brooklyn Bridge.

We emerged into the slowly setting sun, rounded a corner, and there it was.

"I thought you said it's best to see it at night?" I asked.

"It'll be dark by the time we get across."

"Won't we be late?"

"Nah, we got time. Besides, this is important."

We started walking, the footpath in the center of the bridge crowded with people in suits headed home after work, families, tourists with cameras. Instead of doing the usual crowd-dodge (at which I am skilled), we strolled slowly, each step both wandering and deliberate. Kinda like our conversation.

"So bridges, huh?" I asked, looking around us as we walked side by side down the pathway. "What do you like about them so much?"

The view was pretty, all the cars trailing along below us, and the water flowing beside them. The tourists were fun to watch, eavesdrop on, just like they had been everywhere else. The bridge itself was neat, if a little old for my tastes. But so far, I didn't see why he thought it was the end-all-be-all of things to do in New York City.

"You know all that stuff you like about psychology?" he asked, and I nodded. "That's what I like about architecture. Figuring out how things are put together, how they get made."

"Bridges are people, too?" I teased.

"It's not just bridges," he said, delicately running his hand along the railing. "I like the idea of making something that's still gonna be around for decades, maybe even centuries. Places mean something, even if they just . . . blend into the background of a memory for most people. They're still part of it, y'know? I could make something that'd be a part of so many people's lives, even if they didn't know it. And maybe whatever happens coulda happened on another bridge or in another skyscraper or tunnel that somebody else built in that spot if I didn't do it—who knows, doesn't matter. What matters is I would know I did that."

"Lofty goals," I said, if only because I didn't know what else to say to something so . . . figured out.

"If you're gonna dream, might as well dream big," he said. "I think I read that on a coffee cup somewhere."

"Right," I said, smirking. "Anyway, if this"—I waved my hand around, indicating the expanse of the bridge—"is the backdrop to my memory of my last big night out in NYC, I think I should know more about it."

"Yeah? Like what?"

"Things an architecture student slash bridge enthusiast should know. Like . . . who built it?"

"I could just make up all the answers—I'm pretty good at that, you know."

"You could," I agreed.

He paused, and I saw the hint of a smile flash briefly before he nodded and answered my question:

"John Augustus Roebling. He designed the bridge. But like a thousand guys built it."

"When?"

"Finished in 1883."

"How? Did they even have cranes or whatever to move big stones back then? I'm assuming those tower thingies are made of really big stones, right?"

A grin spread across his face and I blushed, realizing I was shooting off a dozen questions in a row again. "Sorry."

"Don't be," Milo said, still smiling. "I like that you ask a lot of questions."

"I thought you didn't like questions when you could be looking at bridges."

"Might've changed my mind," he said, shifting his gaze from me to the sky.

I reminded the butterflies in my stomach that they shouldn't be there, couldn't be there.

"Stop here for a sec," he said suddenly, and we did. "The sun'll be behind the skyline in a few minutes, and this is the best place in all of New York to watch the sunset."

I frowned. "Aren't you supposed to go up to some high point to watch a sunrise or a sunset? Shouldn't we be at the Empire State Building or something?"

Milo laughed. "Why would you wanna do that when you can be right in the middle of it all? Just . . . watch."

So I watched.

I watched the sky separate into three distinct bands of blue, yellow, and pink as a little boy clapped his hands while his dad lifted him up onto his shoulders so he could see over the rail.

I watched lights flicker on throughout the city as a woman stopped her bike to take a selfie with the sunset, and then turned around and just looked at the sky.

And I watched Milo watch the sunset. I watched the open-mouthed smile on his face as he watched the last of the light hovering between the cables stretched out in front of us, reflecting off those golden flecks in his wide eyes.

He watched the sunset. I watched the people. But somehow, I think we still saw the same thing.

Either way, he was right. There's no way the bridge wasn't the best place in the city to be right now.

"Wow," I said as the sun disappeared behind the Manhattan skyline.

Milo forced his stare away from the sky and looked over at me. "Worth it?"

"Yeah," I said. "Worth it."

I'd been looking into his eyes, still bright even without light to make them sparkle back at me, but my eyes followed the same path the sun had just laid out in the sky behind him, drifting down the length of his barely crooked nose, past the day-old stubble underneath it, and landing on his lips.

I wondered if they were as soft as they sounded when he spoke of things he loved. I wondered if his fingertips were callused from long hours holding his pencil as he drew things the way only he saw them. I wondered, if he kissed me, if his hair would brush across my temple, tickling my skin enough to make me break away, giggling, until he pulled me back in.

I wondered if I had been wrong. If this was right, after all.

My gaze flicked back to his eyes, which were still fixated on mine, and I wondered if I should lean forward, if I should—

But then he looked away, so suddenly that the only thing I was left wondering was whether those few seconds had really happened at all.

"I'm really glad you got to see that," he said, picking up the walk across the bridge once again. "Wouldn't be a trip without it."

"Yeah. Me, too."

Chapter Thirty-five
No Good Deed

The sky grew darker and the city lights brighter as we crossed the rest of the bridge into Manhattan. We didn't talk much for the rest of the way—a surprisingly easy silence—before hopping onto another train that would take us as close to the theater as possible.

"Two missed calls from Kat," Milo said as we emerged from underground and back into the land of cell reception. "You?"

"One, and a text," I said, already flipping through my phone out of habit. "She says they left the tickets at will call for us because the show's about to start. Crap."

"It's okay, we still have a few minutes," he reassured me. "Kat gets paranoid about being on time for stuff. Looks like I've been getting *Where are you?* texts since half an hour before showtime. Oops."

He sheepishly stuffed his phone back in his pocket and picked up the pace.

I have to admit, part of me had been a little disappointed that this version of Lydia's last hurrah with her new friends was going to be spent doing something so very touristy and not just part of blending into the city, but first there was the bridge, and now even as we ran through the outskirts of Times Square—the most touristy part of New York—to get to the theater on time, that feeling had almost completely faded. Milo knew exactly where we were, exactly how to cut through the crowds and around obstacles, and I was right there with him.

We grabbed our tickets, snuck into the theater just as the lights were dimming, and made our way up to the balcony.

"Look who showed up," Kat whispered as we sat down in the seats next to her. A guy I recognized from the party leaned forward and waved at us from the other side of Kat, and I waved back, whispering to both of them:

"Sorry we're late, we—"

The sudden burst of sound from the orchestra cut me off as the show began. I shot a quick glance over at Milo, and at Kat, both already watching the stage. I realized even if this wound up being terrible and horrendously touristy, what mattered to me now was that I was experiencing it with people who made me feel anything but. I settled back into my seat, all misplaced disappointment having vanished as we got lost in the spectacle in front of us.

* * *

"Wow!" I said, twirling around on the sidewalk several hours later. "That was amazing. No wonder Jane loves it so much."

"The tourist *would* love *Wicked*," Milo teased, directing his comment over my head and toward Kat, who was walking alongside of me.

"Oh, don't start! I definitely saw tears during the last song," I pointed out.

"Hey!" he protested. "Yes, I cry at touching scenes. I'm man enough to admit that."

"You own the soundtrack," Kat said. "I've seen your iTunes."

"Fine, fine," he relented, smiling.

After the show, we'd said good-bye to Kat's friend and taken the train down to . . . well, I'm not totally sure where, but we just bought the best french fries I'd ever tasted and apparently there is the promise of a bar in our future. One that doesn't card, since Kat doesn't have a fake ID (super jealous her nineteen-year-old self lives near non-carding bars), hence why we wound up in yet another part of the city.

Growing up in a town with one bar, one diner, and one pharmacy/pet shop/school supply store, I was starting to wonder if it was even possible to see everything this city has to offer. People here must never get bored.

"I wonder how it'd go if they retold every story from the villain's point of view," I said, still on *Wicked*.

"Sure, but wouldn't you rather the bad guy just not be a dick?" Milo asked.

"So you're sure you're not the villain of anyone's story?" I asked him.

"Are you calling me a villain?" he teased.

"No," I said, shaking my head. "At least, not in my story. But there's no situation where you'd be cast as the bad guy? No one who sees you *differently* than I do, or Kat does?"

He appeared to catch my emphasis, pausing to think on it for a second. "Lee Newman. He'd been working up the courage to ask out this girl in our class since seventh grade, but the day he finally got the nerve, she agreed to go to homecoming with me. And we dated for two years."

"See? There you go," I said.

"Guess this is what we get for hanging out with a psych major." Milo laughed.

"Nah, my mom just watches a lot of *Days of Our Lives*. Everyone's always declaring their selfless love to somebody in one scene and plotting to kill someone else in the next," I said. A small part of my brain registered that he'd called me a psych major, and I didn't bother to correct him. I kind of liked the sound of it.

"Hey, Lydia," Kat said, stopping at a stand we were passing and snatching a hat up off the shelf. "I think you need a souvenir from this trip. Something fancy. This is so you."

She placed the hat on top of my head and directed me to a small mirror glued onto the side of the stand.

It was a furry headpiece that was meant to look like a white tiger. Long white-and-black-striped pieces of cloth hung down from the top part, and the whole thing felt itchy on my head. I looked in the mirror and laughed.

"Perfect, but I don't think anyone would take me too seriously as a college student if I wore this everywhere."

"You'd be surprised," Milo said. "Besides, it's too late, I already paid for it. This is who you are now. Tiger-hat girl. Girl of the tiger hat."

"Didn't realize we were close enough for nicknames," I joked.

"Oh, yeah, we're all best friends now, did you miss that?" Kat said, playing along.

I looked around us as we started moving again, taking in all the shops for the first time. There were a couple more stands like this one, some grungy clothing stores, and a lot of piercing and tattoo shops.

"Where are we, anyway?" I asked.

"Saint Mark's Place," Kat answered.

"My cousin would be so in love with this street," I said, grabbing my phone out of my pocket and snapping a quick picture of the area. "She's super into darkness and stuff."

I made Milo and Kat pause and do a quick selfie with a shop whose windows were covered in skull-and-crossbones decals, too.

"It's hard to imagine someone related to you and Jane being into 'darkness and stuff,'" Milo noted as I saved the photo.

I nodded. "Trust me, I know. But she's cool. Hang on, I'm going to send that to her real quick." As much as I loved texting and walking, I'd figured out the hard way that it wasn't particularly easy in a crowded city. I'd probably walked directly into at least six people since I'd been here, and one street sign.

Swiping through my photos, I added one from the theater to the text—Mary loves theater and art and all that stuff, so I was pretty sure she'd appreciate that—and another I'd taken of the skyline walking across the bridge earlier this evening. I tried to fight off the twinge I felt when I remembered I wasn't sure if she'd respond, and that even if she did, it would probably be something simple like *cool* or *okay*, and pressed send all the same.

"There," I said, lifting my eyes up from my phone screen and picking up the pace again. "Goth shopping street photo sent. I sent her that picture I took from the Brooklyn Bridge, too."

I saw Milo's face drop and knew immediately that I had said something terribly wrong, even before Kat slowed to a standstill and didn't turn around.

"You went to the bridge?"

It was silent for a long handful of seconds, everything moving slowly in our small bubble of the world even as everyone around us kept going at full speed.

Finally, she turned back toward us, skimming over me entirely and fixating on Milo.

Milo shook his head and took a step forward. "Kat, I'm sorry, I didn't mean for you to find out—"

"It's not about me *finding out*, Milo," she said, her eyes growing wider and her weight shifting backward, away from us, away from Milo. "You didn't tell me you were gonna be late. And you didn't answer my texts. For all I know—"

She cut her words short, swallowing hard and shaking her head.

Milo opened his mouth to try again, but Kat didn't give him the chance.

"I don't want to talk to you right now." Her voice was low and shaky, even as she tried to sound commanding. Still, it worked, because Milo shut his mouth and stayed where he was as she turned away from us and, very soon, had disappeared around the corner onto another street.

"What just happened?" I asked, almost more to myself than to Milo, who simply shook his head, raking his fingers through his hair. I watched his jaw clench, and he looked like he wanted to kick the brick wall next to us, but he didn't.

"Should we . . ." I looked off toward where Kat had gone, but when I looked back, Milo was still shaking his head, pacing.

"She won't listen to me right now," he said to me, and then to himself, "Should've known better."

"Hey." I moved closer to him and placed my palm flat against his chest, willing him to look at me. "I'll go talk to her. Okay?"

He worked his jaw up and down, and I thought he was going to speak, but finally he just nodded his head.

"Wait here."

*　　*　　*

Once I turned the block, catching up to Kat didn't take as long as I'd expected. She'd only made it up the street before settling down on concrete steps, pressed up against the iron railing alongside them.

I hesitated when I saw her. Saying I would come out here and talk to her seemed like the right thing to do at the time, but now that I was faced with actually doing it . . . I didn't even know what was going on, let alone how to fix it.

Closing my eyes, I took a deep breath, remembering my time at the center with Bing, and even my sessions with Ms. W.

I didn't have to fix it. I couldn't, most likely. That wasn't what I'd be good for here.

I approached slowly, so she could see me. She didn't look up even as I sat down silently next to her.

She was picking at the handrail, the paint coming off in small chips. It made the tiniest metallic sound every time she touched it with her fingernail. She was shaking, just barely, and silent. I kept my distance.

"You don't have to talk to me if you don't want to," I said quietly. "I'd like to at least just sit here, if that's okay. But if you do want to talk . . ."

Ting. Ting. Ting.

The gray metal underneath the black paint formed an abstract design, something that reminded me of the art Jane and I had looked at when we went to the Met. We had seen this one guy staring at a painting when we first walked in, and when we left, I caught a glimpse of him still standing in the same spot, looking at the same painting. It had seemed silly to me to look at one thing for so long, but Kat was fixated on chipping away this paint with the same intensity that that man had been looking at the artwork in front of him.

Finally, I heard the sound stop, and out of the corner of my eye, I saw her move her hands to her lap.

"My cousin was killed there."

My brain jumped into motion, doing its best to interpret what she was saying.

"Cousin"—the one that Milo dated?

"There"—the Brooklyn Bridge?

The place we went—the place we were late, when Kat couldn't get ahold of either of us.

I waited.

"There was another girl there, they said." Her voice was scratchy and she tried to clear it as she went, but it still shook. "Some guy was harassing her, and Nikki saw it when she was walking home. Across the bridge. She got in the way, tried to stop it. The guy stabbed her. Ran off. They, um . . . they didn't get help in time."

"I'm . . . so sorry," I said.

"I came to school out here because . . . I just always figured I'd go where she went. Couldn't get into Columbia like her and Milo, but I was still in the same city, at least. After she died, Milo was the only person I really knew here. And who got it. Who understood why I didn't want to be out at night, or by myself, or anywhere—*anywhere*—near that place, without acting all weird, like I was broken or something. Because he felt that way, too."

I thought of all the things I could say right then.

I promise I had no idea.

I'm sure he didn't mean to upset you.

We're fine, so everything's okay, see?

I know how it is to feel like everyone's looking at you differently.

But I kept my platitudes to myself and moved just a little bit closer as I put my hand on her shoulder.

She finally turned to look at me, and I saw the hint of tears in her eyes even though she was trying not to let them spill over.

"I'm sorry," she whispered, wiping at her eyes.

I shook my head deliberately. "Don't be."

"I just . . . feel like I should be past this now."

"Are you?" I asked.

She shook her head slowly, and I shrugged.

"Then you're not. That's okay."

"Thanks," she said after a moment, almost too softly for me to catch.

"What are friends for?"

I smiled. She smiled back. And we stayed there for a while, her telling stories about trouble she and her cousin used to get up to when they were kids. Me just listening.

"We should probably go find Milo," she finally said. "I want to apologize for flipping out at him. He shouldn't feel bad about going there, if that's what he wants to do."

"Kat . . ." I started as we stood up. "Maybe I'm way off base, but, if I'm not, maybe it wouldn't be the worst idea for you to go back there sometime, too. Make a new memory of it. One day, at least."

She bit her lip and looked off to the side, and for a second I was worried I'd said something wrong again.

"Maybe you're right," she said, nodding. Then she looked up a little higher. "I guess it isn't hard to take you seriously in that ridiculous hat after all."

My hands flew up to my head, touching the tiger hat, having totally forgotten it was still on my head.

I smiled sheepishly. "Oops." But I guess Milo was right.

Milo, to his extreme credit, was right where we had left him. He'd taken a seat on the ground against the wall, and stood up nervously as we approached. I couldn't see what Kat's face looked like, but I smiled, trying to reassure him that things were okay, and as I did, she threw her arms around him. He looked surprised, but adjusted quickly, letting her hug him, a quiet apology in the air between them.

I watched, and after he got over the shock, his eyes locked with mine, as sincere as I'd ever seen them.

"Thank you," he mouthed.

I smiled back at him.

Maybe I wasn't so unprepared for being helpful after all.

*　*　*

We decided to skip the bar and just call it a night, taking Kat back to school before riding the subway all the way back to Jane's apartment. She'd made me promise to keep in touch, and let her know if I ever came back to visit, or if I decided to move out here after all.

"I don't know what you did," Milo said, "but you did good. I've never been able to pull Kat out of her own head when she's gotten like that."

"I just listened," I replied.

He studied me before nodding. "I knew she was still upset about everything. Hell, I mean, I am, too. I know it's not the same, but . . ."

He shook his head, clearing it of whatever he was going to say. "I didn't know how to tell her I go back there sometimes."

"Why do you?" I asked carefully.

"I don't wanna forget it happened, I guess," he said after a moment. "It mattered. It's important to who I've become, who Kat's become. And . . . that's not the only thing that's happened there. I've had a lot of good memories on that bridge, too. Bad stuff happens all the time. But . . . as bad as it is sometimes, I can't let that stop me from living my life."

"You'd never even go on the subway," I agreed, thinking of Bing's pickpocketing adventures.

"Exactly. I just . . . I can't do that."

"I think she knows that," I said. "Sometimes there's just some space in between when you figure something out in your head and when you actually *get* it, you know?"

"Yeah."

We reached my stop, and Milo insisted on accompanying me back from the subway station.

"I don't live too far," he said. "I think I wanna walk the rest of the way, anyway."

I nodded, and we walked all the way to Jane's apartment in silence, the sounds of the city filling the spaces between our footsteps.

"Here we are," Milo said, stopping in front of the steps to Jane's building.

"Here we are."

"I'm very glad I met you, Lydia," he said. "Both times."

"Me, too," I agreed.

"And all that stuff Kat said, stay in touch, et cetera, y'know—if you want to."

"I do," I said. "I will."

"Okay, well, good night," he said.

"Good night," I said.

I walked up the steps and typed the door code into the keypad, wrenching the heavy door open as the buzzer sounded. I turned around, and Milo was still standing at the bottom of the stairs, watching me.

He waved.

I waved.

I wondered if I should say anything else, but I wasn't sure what else to add. It felt like an unsatisfying ending to a great adventure, but, to my constant dismay, life wasn't actually an epic musical, and maybe mutual waving was just how things ended sometimes in real life. The story a little bit bumpy, the people a little bit changed, but no orchestral finale to play us off after our last exchange of meaningful words.

I let the door shut behind me.

Chapter Thirty-six
LAST DAY

Unfortunately, Jane had to go back to work the next day. She apologized like fifty times, but I told her I still had some sightseeing I wanted to do, and it was fine.

And that was true. What's also true is that I want to see if I could at least kind of get around the city by myself after spending a week here.

I walked down Jane's street and got breakfast at a cute little mom-and-pop coffee shop I'd seen in passing a few times, but we'd never gone into. I sat by the window, watching kids walk by on their way to school, thirtysomethings walking their dogs, a musician I'd seen playing in the subway station lugging his guitar out in that direction.

I took the subway to Grand Central. I took pictures for my dad, knowing he'd probably blow one up to frame for his train room. When I'd gotten enough, I walked around for a while, keeping my pace up enough to avoid getting trampled by busy commuters, but still slow enough to take in everything around me.

I walked from there to the south end of Central Park, and then along the east side of it, watching the people, watching the birds and the cars, and looking up at all the buildings. I wondered who had designed them, when they had been completed, and what kind of memories people had made there.

My earbuds were in my purse, like they always were, a safeguard against any potential silence I might encounter on my journeys, but I didn't take them out.

I got as far as the Met, though I was surprised to find that I didn't recognize the surroundings as the place Jane and I had visited on my first real day here. If not for the giant banners out front, I wasn't sure I'd have known it was the Met at all. It looked different, somehow, though I couldn't recall what I'd thought it'd looked like before.

After that, I got back on the train. There was one more thing I wanted to do today before it got too late.

I wanted to go back to NAU.

＊　　＊　　＊

I got back into the psych building as easily as Milo and I had the other day (once we'd figured out where it was, of course), slipping in the door as the real students were traveling in and out.

I meandered through the building fairly aimlessly, checking things out but being careful not to wind up anywhere I shouldn't be. Fly under the radar; don't be noticed. I'd done a lot more of that this summer than I'd ever been used to, so it wasn't too difficult.

Eventually, I passed by a group of students sitting at a table in the center of an open room that seemed to be a study lounge of some sort, and overheard something that piqued my interest:

"I'm going to be late for Developmental Psych. Catch you later?"

I watched the girl walk down the hallway toward a lecture room and followed a few steps behind. Peering into the room after her, I saw maybe thirty students clustered in various parts of the room, chatting.

Milo and I would have managed to sneak into the other lecture because there had been so many people, but this . . . it wasn't the time.

I was about to peel myself away from the door and figure out if there was anything left to see when I knocked into someone.

A woman a little younger than my parents who was carrying a briefcase in one hand and a stack of papers in another, which promptly fell out of her arms at our contact.

"Sorry," I mumbled, bending down to pick them up for her.

"You don't look familiar," she said. "Are you a new student?"

"I . . ." My first instinct was to lie, to say that I got lost or was looking for my friend. "I don't go here, but I was thinking of trying to transfer next semester. I want to major in psych and I heard someone say this was a Developmental Psychology course, so I . . ." I what, exactly? What was my plan here? "I'm sorry if I made you late."

"We're mostly doing an overview of the upcoming semester today, but would you like to sit in on my class?"

"Really?"

"Yes, of course! If you're interested in coming to NAU for psychology, then I'm interested in you finding out if this is the right fit for you. Now, what's your name?"

"Lydia," I said.

"I'm Professor Cutkelvin; it's nice to meet you." She turned and marched into the classroom and I followed hesitantly. "Everyone," she said as she walked toward the table at the front. "This is Lydia. She's thinking of transferring next semester, so she'll be sitting in on the class today. Sit anywhere you like, but if you need to leave before the two hours are up, I'd advise you sit near the back."

A few students turned and nodded at me, and I settled into a spot on the aisle toward the back, just to be safe.

But only a few minutes after the lecture started, I knew there was no way I was going to leave before it was over. Professor Cutkelvin was so engaging, and the students so interested. It was much more give-and-take than my community college class. It was like a discussion, kind of the way Gothic Lit had been, and it was about things I immediately found I cared about. Problem-solving skills, development of morality, identity formation . . . it was everything I wanted to learn. Two hours flew by, and after thanking the professor for the opportunity to sit in, I knew that, as hard as the essay question might be, I had to find a way to get it done.

This is the place I want to be.

* * *

When I met George in Vegas—not the first time I met him, but after Lizzie, when we actually got together—he was a total gentleman. I was upset and alone and purposely reckless and drank way, way more than I should have.

There was some guy I'd been talking to on and off throughout the night, who kept buying me shots and hanging around. He was fun and cute and nice, I guess; I don't really remember. What I do remember, albeit vaguely, is his trying to get me to leave the bar with him and go back to his hotel room.

And George stopping him.

He figured out where my hotel was and took me back to my room, to my bed, and slept on the floor to make sure I didn't go out partying by myself again like I kept trying to.

At the time, I remember thinking that could have gone really bad. Not the George part, but the other. George did the right thing. He looked out for me.

That was the bar I set for him, and for our relationship: that he wasn't the worst person I met in Vegas. That he didn't take advantage of me being really drunk. So that if there was worse, that meant he was at least decent enough.

And sometimes, he was.

Sometimes, he wasn't.

But George and I had always existed in that little bubble, isolated from the outside world. In the moments we were together, everything became either/or. George, or that guy. Me, or Lizzie. My family, or our relationship. Our happiness, or his money and revenge.

We couldn't survive in a cohesive outside world because we had never been together in any world but our own.

I still didn't know why the bubble popped, not really. But I knew that I didn't want to live in one again.

Milo had looked at the sunset and the bridge the same way George had looked at me during the good times, when it had just been the two of us against the world. The same way Cody had looked at me when he asked about my past, caught up in his own head, thinking about this great hook for his novel.

Where they could only see what was right there in front of them, and no further than that, I thought maybe Milo could see a bigger picture. A bigger world, with more than just selfish ambition or codependence.

I wanted to see that, too.

*   *   *

So I called him.

I mean, no, okay, I didn't call him. I texted him, like a normal person would. I asked if there was any chance he had just a few minutes to meet with me tonight.

I'm on my way to work, but I can swing by your place—you home? —Milo

He showed up at Jane's doorstep at the same time I was getting back from the subway, out of breath and . . . covered in body glitter.

"Sorry," he panted, motioning to his all-over sparkle. "I usually put this on at the club, but it exploded at my apartment so I just kind of . . . went with it."

"You really did," I said, not bothering to hold back my laugh. "Wait—"

I dug through my purse and pulled out the white tiger hat from the other night, glad I hadn't thought to put it in my suitcase yet.

"Now we're even."

He smiled appreciatively. "So, what's up?"

"Why didn't you kiss me, back there on the bridge?" I asked.

"That's what you wanted to talk about?"

I felt a little silly, now, making him come all the way out here for this. But as much as I love texting, some conversations are better had in person, where you can read what a person's thinking on their face instead of trying to decode emojis. And this may be my last chance.

"Yeah," I confirmed. "Why didn't you? The bridge, the sunset, it all seemed . . ."

"Right? Yeah, I know," he said. "It would've been. For me, anyway. You said you didn't want to go out, so I assumed that included, y'know, kissing." He shrugged, kicking at a candy wrapper someone had left on the front steps.

I thought back to George, and to Vegas. Being decent wasn't good enough, but, as a start, it wasn't *not* good enough, either.

"The reason I said no to going out with you isn't because I don't like you. You know that, right?"

"You don't owe me any sort of explanation, Lydia," he said.

"I know. But, my last boyfriend . . ." I started, and then I remembered Cody and whatever this summer was between us. "My last real boyfriend, I guess . . . he wasn't who I thought he was."

I looked at Milo, waiting for his face to light up in anticipation the way Cody's had, or for a slight eye roll at the thought of another crazy girl telling a story about a supposedly shitty ex, but he just looked back at me, waiting, but not expecting.

I took a deep breath, not sure why I was telling him this, and realizing somewhere in the back of my mind that this would be the first time someone heard this story from me. The first time I told it and saw that actual initial reaction from anyone.

"We made a sex tape," I said, not bothering to mince words. "And he tried to sell it on the Internet. My sister's boyfriend stopped him, but . . ." I shrugged. "Everyone knew. And even if that wasn't the case . . . I'd trusted him."

Milo frowned, and didn't look anywhere but right at me. I felt like I should be holding my breath as I waited for his response, but I wasn't.

"That really sucks," he finally said, and I laughed in spite of myself, taken aback at how simple his response was.

" 'That really sucks,' " I repeated. "Yeah, it did."

His forehead stayed creased, his mouth set in a straight line until he spoke again: "I don't get what would make someone do something like that."

"Me, either." I blinked and shook my head. "But that's why I . . . or *part* of why I said I don't know if I'm ready for anything right now."

He nodded. "That makes sense."

"But . . ." I started, steeling myself. "I also don't want to let it stop me from making new memories, or from living my life. Even if the life I've had here is only for another twelve hours."

"So what are you saying? I mean, I can't very well take you on a date if you're back in California."

"No, not really," I agreed. "But I may not stay there. I don't know what's going to happen, and I don't want you to take any of this to mean that I do, but, in the meantime . . . what I do know is that as shitty as it looks, this apartment building behind us is very memorable. And there are totally at least three different colors of sky happening right now."

He looked up, the grin on his face growing even wider, and I saw that gap between two of his teeth like I had at the party. It seems so long ago, now. "Huh. I guess there are."

I stepped forward and lifted myself up onto my toes just as he was tilting his head back down from looking into the sky.

His lips weren't as soft as I'd thought they would be. And his fingers weren't callused on my neck. His hair brushed my forehead, but it didn't tickle hardly at all.

It felt right.

"Well," he said as we broke apart. "I'm gonna have to write whoever designed this building a thank-you note."

I smiled back, and leaned up to meet him again.

"Lydia?"

Or not.

"Jane!" I yelped, stepping back away from Milo.

She and Bing were standing a few feet away . . . watching . . . awkwardly . . .

The shock on her face lasted several seconds before she morphed back into sweet, kind Jane—or at least, an outward clone of her. Internally, I wasn't so convinced.

"Who's your friend?" she asked, moving closer to us, and inspecting him quizzically as she did. "Have we met?"

"Yeah, in the park, I'm—" I nudged him not too gently, but certainly not quick enough.

"Oh," Jane said, recognition washing over her.

He looked over at me, not sure what to do now, but finally just came out with it: "I'm . . . Milo."

"Milo. Right. Bing! Have you met Lydia's new friend Milo?"

Bing stepped forward and offered up his hand, completely friendly and not at all secretly hiding a layer of questions and anger under his smile like Jane very possibly was.

"Hello, Milo," he said.

"Hi . . ."

"You've got glitter," Jane said, her voice tight, looking at me. "On your face."

I swiped at my face. Of course I would end up catching glitter-face from a sparkly boy on my doorstep while my family watched in disapproval. So much for low-budget cable movies—this was turning into a weird YA novel. I wasn't sure which was worse.

"We should probably get inside for dinner," Jane continued. "It was so nice to see you, Milo."

She didn't wait for me to respond as she marched inside, Bing following along looking a little lost.

"Bye," I whispered to Milo, unable to stop the smile that flitted across my face despite whatever confrontation waited for me inside Jane's apartment.

"See you later, Lydia," he said, and I hoped he was right.

Though if Jane had her way, I may not see anyone ever again after tonight.

Chapter Thirty-seven
WE GET IT FROM OUR MOTHER

"Lydia, it's fine, really," Jane said as we entered her apartment. "I just wish you'd told me, is all."

"I don't see what the big deal is," I replied, stomping in after her. "Milo's nice. They're a good group of people—"

"Oh, so there's a group?" Jane asked, her smile tightening by the minute.

"Yeah, I've met a lot of really nice people," I said. "They're great. They . . ."

They what? Don't treat me like I'm fragile, for one. They accepted me straight off the bat.

Bing left us when we got to the door. Jane begged off from dinner, saying she was a little tired and wanted to spend this last night with her sister. Bing either took that at face value or was smart enough to realize the ruse. Either way, he left me to Jane's devices. Her sweet, overly concerned devices.

"I'm sure they are," Jane replied, reaching out to touch my arm. Then . . . "Would you like some tea?"

You know how I said Jane uses food to both soothe and avoid? We're in the avoid section.

"No, I'm good," I replied.

"I wouldn't mind some," Allison said from the couch.

Oh, okay. There was an audience for this. Granted, that audience was watching a political commentary show and reading her tablet at the same time, but I'm betting the sight of Jane even mildly disconcerted was more interesting than anything from the TV talking heads.

"Sure!" Jane said too brightly.

She rummaged in the kitchen for a couple of minutes, came out with tea for her and Allison.

"So," she said, sitting down at the tiny table. "Tell me about Milo. And his friends. You should have invited him up; I'd have loved to get the chance to talk with him."

"Why?"

"Because he's your friend, sweetie," Jane said. She hadn't stopped smiling since we got into the apartment. Not in the normal Jane "I'm so happy" way, but in a "My face is frozen because I don't know what will happen if I move it" way. "And I'm sure Allison and Shea didn't get to meet him, either."

She turned her weird smile to Allison, who shook her head.

Or maybe we weren't in the avoid section. We were in the passive-aggressive section.

Hoo-boy.

The thing is, Jane doesn't get mad. She doesn't fight. She just gets tighter and tighter until she looks like she's going to pop.

I didn't get why she was getting tight with me. And I didn't get was why she was getting tight with me *now*. Over this.

And quite frankly, it pissed me off.

"Yeah, but I don't need you to, like, approve my friends. And I don't need your roommates to approve them, either. Everyone keeps telling me I'm an adult, making adult decisions."

Allison *finally* cottoned on to the idea that there was a fight going on and rose from the couch. "Yeah, I'm going to finish watching this later. . . ."

But Jane didn't seem to notice as Allison walked not into her room, but into Shea's. "Of course you are. I just . . ." she said. "I really wish I hadn't gone to Miami."

"That doesn't have anything to do with this!"

"If I hadn't abandoned you, maybe you wouldn't feel the need to lie to me about your friends."

"Are you kidding me?!" I said. "You don't mean my 'friends.' If it was Kat—another one of my friends—downstairs with me you wouldn't have minded. It's the fact that Milo's a guy." A glitter-covered guy.

"Well . . . to be fair," Jane said, "you have to be careful. This is New York; it's a very intimidating place. It's safer if people know who you're with. And you haven't dated anyone since—"

"Since George?" I shot back. "Actually, I have."

"You . . . you have?"

"Yeah, I have."

"Okay," Jane said, putting up her hands. "So why didn't you tell me? About Milo or about this other guy, or about . . . anything? I thought you came here to—"

"I came here to see you, Jane. To figure out my life, but not to have you try and solve it for me. And not to have you pity me and pet me, either." I threw my bag on the couch. "Not everything gets solved by a cup of tea!"

"Okay . . ." Jane held up her hands again, her eyes wide. At this point, I'm betting she realized we were on the verge of a solid fight and, never actually having been in one before, was retreating.

I, however, was seeing red on the edges of my vision and, for better or worse (worse), dug in.

"And you know what? I *have* been trying to figure out my life—and they've been helping me do that. They're the ones who took me on a tour of the school, not stupid tourist attractions. They're the ones who made me feel welcome, not your roommates—definitely not the one who thinks I'm gonna call her for bail money."

A gasp sounded from Shea's room, but I couldn't care about that.

"Well, I'm sorry you didn't want to go see tourist attractions," Jane said, her voice breaking a little. "If you would have told me, we would have done something else. I just wish you would talk to me. I worry about you, Lydia. I'm not mad, I'm worried."

"Well I wish you would be mad!"

Now I was *sure* I heard whispering coming from Shea's room. But there was Jane sitting in front of me, looking like I'd slapped her. Or like I'd slapped her puppy.

"Why is no one ever mad at me?" I cried to the room. "You, Mom and Dad, Lizzie. Everyone's so goddamned *careful*. You sigh and are disappointed and sad and it's like you're climbing this mountain and you're carrying me but it's okay because you're used to it.

"You don't blame me! But I'm the one who screwed up this summer. I'm the one who didn't do my application. And I'm the one who made it so you just left—"

"I told you I'm sorry about Miami."

"Not Miami, San Fr—"

San Francisco.

I froze. Clamped my mouth closed, afraid more words would come spilling out.

She just left. Mary, I mean. I did something terrible to her, and she just left. She even put me to bed after I came home drunk, and didn't stay to yell at me in the morning. She just walked away. Disappointed. Sad. But not mad.

Even her texts—they're not angry, or stiff. They're just . . . resigned.

And if anyone deserved to get mad at me, it was Mary. Instead, she just moved on.

Over my dead body.

"Oh my God," I murmured, shaking my head.

"Lydia?" Jane's voice was small. "I'm sorry, but . . . I'm afraid I don't know what you're talking about."

"No, Jane, I'm sorry," I said, coming over to hug her. "I didn't mean to fight with you. In fact . . . I think I'm supposed to be having this fight with someone else."

She put her arms around me, a little hesitant at first, but then holding me fiercely.

We stayed there for a while; I don't know how long. Long enough for my breathing to go back to normal and my nose to start running with unshed tears.

Finally, I heard, muffled against my shoulder, "Do you think you'd like some tea now?"

I laughed a wet laugh. "Sure." I sniffled. "And I'll tell you all about Milo."

"And school?" Jane asked. "You said you went on a tour?"

"Yeah . . . um, I'm thinking about applying to New Amsterdam. They have a good psych department."

"So does Central Bay College," Jane said. And I don't blame her. I have a Darcy-shaped in there.

"Yeah, but NAU feels different." I don't know why it feels different, but it does. Maybe it's the city. Maybe because in New York, I could be something other than someone's little sister (even though Jane's here), or cousin, or charity case. And feel less like I'm being watched. The act of observing something automatically changes how that thing acts, after all. I want to be able to grow into myself, without all that. "It feels . . . more right for me, right now, than anywhere else."

"Well." Jane smiled—her real smile this time. "I can't wait to hear all about it."

Chapter Thirty-eight

HOME

Bing, smart man that he was, sent Jane and me in the town car to the airport by ourselves. He must have known that we needed our sister time.

We were silent for most of the ride, having talked through the night. About all the stuff that was going on, and also about a lot of nothing, and we drank our weight in tea. Instead, we just leaned against each other in the car. I kept my eyes out the window, watching the city go from bunched together to more and more spaced out, until we found ourselves pulling up to the curb of the airport.

"You got your bags?" Jane asked.

"Yeah, I'll manage," I said, hoping there was one of those carts, because four bags is no joke.

"So . . ."

"So . . ."

"I'm sorry that I lose it sometimes. I get that from Mom, I think," I said. Jane wrapped her arms around me.

"I'm sorry that I sometimes hold it in," she said. "I get that from Mom, too."

"I'm surprised she held in the fact that I was seeing Cody," I said, pulling back, brushing the hair out of my eyes. "I thought she would have gotten on the Bennet family phone tree with that one. Guess she wanted to not spread my disappointingness to others."

"Mom wouldn't do that. Be disappointed in you. They support you; you know that, right? No matter what." She hugged me one last time. "And so do I."

I had a long flight, and a layover in Denver, to think about what Jane said.

And it made me realize that Mary wasn't the only person I needed to talk to.

Luckily, when I walked through the front door of the house, before I even put down my suitcases, I had my chance.

"Baby, come here, let me look at you!" Mom cried, as I came in. She moved a little slowly, but once she negotiated past my bags, she pressed me against her.

"Hi, Mom. Where's Dad?"

"He's picking up your car, good as new."

Good. I was going to need it tomorrow.

"It's good to have you home," Mom said. "Kitty missed you. I kept trying to get her to come out into the living room when we watched TV at night, but she just wanted to sit on your bed and stare out the window."

"Awww, poor Kitty," I said, gently running my nails over her back as she purred her appreciation.

"She's going to have to be sad a little longer," I told Mom. "I'm going up to San Francisco tomorrow."

"Oh, wonderful! Are you going to see Lizzie?"

"Probably. But I need to talk to Mary about some things; I'd just rather do it in person," I said.

"Maybe you could tour the college while you're there? See if anything . . . clicks?" Mom suggested.

"Maybe," I agreed. "I don't know if I'm going to be there that long."

"Well, no pressure, dear," she said.

More eggshells. More dancing around what people really wanted to say to me.

I'm fully prepared to have it out with Mary when I go see her tomorrow. I know what buttons to push to get her to admit she's upset with me. But I don't want to do that with my *mom*. Making your parents upset isn't any fun.

And maybe my mom figured that making your kid upset isn't any fun, either.

"Mom?"

"Hmm?"

"I know you and Dad aren't exactly . . . pleased that I messed up going off to college this fall. Especially on top of everything else this year. I know you'd hoped we'd all finally be out of the house by now," I said quietly. "I'm trying to figure out what I need to do to make that happen."

I kept my focus on Kitty during my mini-monologue, petting up and down her back, up and down. Sometimes it's easier to say stuff when you pretend you're rehearsing. I rehearse a lot of conversations in front of Kitty, anyway. When I finally looked up, my mom was frowning.

"Lydia," she said. "Your father and I want you to do what you think is best for you. If that's more college, that's wonderful. If it's not, I'm sure, in time, you'll figure something out. You're a smart young lady. As long as grandbabies are somewhere in my future between the three of you girls, you know I'll be happy."

I smiled a half smile. "See, I know that. In my head, at least. I know you just want me to be happy, and that you and Dad will always support me. Which is why it was so strange when you basically pushed me out the door to New York. And Dad wasn't happy about it."

And you've been sleeping a lot, I wanted to say.

And Dad was sitting in the kitchen in the dark.

And you both kept disappearing, for "things at the club."

I'd thought they'd been avoiding me. That this was all about me. But once again, when I pick up my head and actually see outside myself, things fall into place.

"What's been going on, Mom?" I watched her closely.

She sighed deeply, and a second later her hand stilled my incessant petting of Kitty.

"Your father wanted to tell you, but I made him promise not to . . ." she began.

I shifted nervously. Nothing about that sounded good. "Tell me what? Mom, you're scaring me."

"Do you remember my tennis elbow? Well, when we went to have it looked at, the doctor noticed something . . . else."

"Something else. Something . . . bad?" I asked.

"Something else that *might be* bad. So they did some more tests, and some more tests, and . . . the week you left for New York, they needed to do some exploratory surgery." Her hand went to her side, holding it lightly.

"Mom!" I blurted out, stunned. "You had surgery? Why didn't you tell us?"

"You girls have all had so much going on, I didn't want my silly, old, aging body to get in the way of that," she said, retracting her hand from mine and busying herself straightening out the bedding underneath us.

"Mom . . ." I started.

"I know, I know." She raised her hands in defeat. "Your father disagreed with me. But we didn't know if it was anything, and I just wanted everything to be fine for a little while longer."

I softened. Guess my penchant for pretending everything is okay even when it might be crumbling down around me comes from somewhere.

"I don't like it," I said. "But I know what you mean."

Mom smiled, albeit a little sadly, understanding what I meant.

"Are you okay?" I asked when she didn't pick up the conversation again.

"I'm fine, sweetheart," she said. I looked at her, willing my stare to convey that I wanted the truth. No more appeasement or hidden truths. "I promise. The doctors assured me that everything's normal."

I breathed a sigh of relief.

But I couldn't stop my mind from drifting to the what-ifs. What if things hadn't been okay? What if they had found something that actually was bad? Would they have told us? Or would they just have kept pretending everything was fine until there was no more hiding that nothing was fine at all? And how could I be upset when she was just doing the same thing I had done? Kept doing?

At least Mom did something about it, I thought. She only kept the truth about not being fine from me and my sisters; she still got help. I, on the other hand, had lied to myself about everything, letting things eat me up from the inside like an unchecked disease until the symptoms became too obvious for the world to ignore.

A choice like that could've been dangerous for my mom, but I'm starting to realize how dangerous it could have been for me, too.

"We're not kids anymore," I said.

"No, you're not."

"Promise you'll tell me if anything big happens again."

She looked me in the eye, as serious as I've seen her. "I promise. Anything big happens, you'll be the first to know," she replied. "Besides your father, of course. But I need you to do the same."

Fair. "I will. No more secrets."

"No more secrets."

"Well, some secrets, because duh, you're my mom, I can't tell you *everything*," I quickly corrected myself. "But not big life-changing ones."

"That sounds good to me," she agreed.

"I love you, Mom." I reached across Kitty and pulled her into a hug. "I'm glad you're okay."

"I love you, too," she said. She pulled back and held my face in her hands. "No matter what. I hope you know that."

I nodded. I did—I do—know that. Mom may spend all of every dinner gossiping about the neighbors and wondering whether Jane and Bing or Lizzie and Darcy will be the first to tie the knot and will they have the wedding here or out where they live now—but it's dinner she's made for us, every night. The things she's always done to show me and my sisters that she loves us mean more than just saying it. And hopefully . . . hopefully every member of the Bennet family can get better at this whole communication thing. I feel like we're trying. Miracles don't happen overnight, you know.

"Now, you tell Lizzie I say hello when you see her." Mom stood up, straightening the wrinkles she had left in my comforter as soon as she did. "Mary, too. And make sure they're eating right. I hear kale is big in the cities nowadays, maybe some of that. And lots of water, the heat's been just awful lately."

She went on for a few more minutes about things I had to do to check up on my sister and my cousin—way too many things than I could possibly remember, but I promised to try my best—and finally left me and Kitty on our own.

* * *

I headed up to San Francisco first thing the next morning. I was still on NYC time, which meant I actually woke up before nine on a Sunday, and there just didn't seem to be much point to putting it off.

Most of the drive consisted of listening to the radio—something I had found I missed profoundly in New York without a car. But I also spent part of the time strategizing.

I didn't want to do any more dancing around with Mary, pretending everything was fine and we were just super okay. Because she would. "Fine" is her default mode. "Fine" is her not being angry I screwed everything up for her. "Fine" is her just leaving.

I needed to up the stakes. I needed to get Mary mad at me in order to get her to admit that she was already mad at me. Look, it makes sense if you know Mary. Which I do. And I know one of the best ways to irritate her is to invade her privacy.

So, four hours after leaving my house, I parked my car, marched up to the door of Lizzie's building, crossed my fingers that I hadn't somehow mucked up the address, and barged right into the apartment.

Right into . . . something.

Mary squeaked incoherently as soon as the door swung open,

rushing to disentangle herself from another body on the couch with her.

A body that was attached to asymmetrically cut bleached-blond hair with purple at the ends.

"Lydia!" Mary yelped, fumbling with the unbuttoned buttons on the front of her shirt. "What are you doing here?"

I blinked. And then I jumped back on track.

"Why aren't you mad at me?" I demanded. I saw Violet smoothing out her hair and looking intently at absolutely nothing on the side of the couch where Mary wasn't sitting, but I kept my focus on my cousin.

"What are you . . . What?" Mary started, confused. "What's going on? Why are— Wait, what the hell are you doing?"

Good. There was that break from the constant Mary Bennet deadpan. I'd need that to get anywhere with this conversation.

"I think I'm gonna bounce," Violet broke the silence, looking back and forth between the two of us. She turned back to Mary. "See you tomorrow?"

Mary nodded.

Violet leaned in toward my cousin but seemed to think better of it and instead stood up and walked all the way around the coffee table in the other direction. She made her way past me, offering up an uncomfortable smile as a wordless greeting and good-bye as she went. I heard the door shut behind her and I shifted closer toward Mary, who was standing now.

"Okay, so, what? What's going on?" Mary asked, shaking her head.

"You're supposed to be mad at me. Why aren't you?"

"Wait. You came all the way out here and burst into your sister's apartment to . . . try to make me mad?"

"What? No!" I responded. "Well, kind of. But just to make you talk. Where is Lizzie, anyway?"

"She's . . . out?" Mary said. Uh-huh. Later on I would take a quick glance in her fridge, but if it wasn't stocked with artisanal cheeses, then I'm guessing Lizzie doesn't *really* live here, and the pillow with her head dent is resting on Darcy's bed.

Mom's gonna flip.

"Okay," I said. "But where was I? Oh, yeah, me barging in to be mad at you for not being mad at me is not why you're supposed to be mad at me."

"I literally have no idea what you're saying."

I drew a breath and started in on the real issue at hand. "I screwed up. I promised you I would move up here with you, and instead, I messed up all your plans—our plans—and you didn't get mad at me. Why?"

Mary sighed and sat back down on the couch again. "Lydia . . . we've been over this. You've had a lot going on this year—"

"No! That's not good enough! I can't just have people make excuses for me all the time! Or make them for myself! I. Messed. Up. You have every right to be mad. Be mad at me!"

"Okay? I'm mad at you?" she tried. "I don't know what you want me to say."

"Anger is the second stage of grief, we learned that in class. Second, so you can't just skip over anger and move through the rest. That's not right. Something's not right. That's what happens when people screw you over. You get mad at them. There's something wrong if you can't get mad. Right? I screwed you over. It was my fault. So you're supposed to . . ."

I heard it as I was saying it. But at the same time, I think I knew it all along.

Yes, I wanted Mary to admit that she was upset with me and for things to get back to normal between us instead of all this uncomfortable distant crap.

But there was someone I was more upset with—me.

"Why can't I be mad at him, Mary?"

Her brows furrowed in continued confusion before I saw the realization sink in.

George.

"Everyone wanted me to be mad at him. I want to be. I think I should be. But I can't. I don't understand it."

All the muscles in my body that had tensed minutes ago in preparation for this argument went slack, and I slumped down onto the couch next to my cousin, who was probably suffering from emotional whiplash at this point.

"You don't have to feel any certain way," Mary said. "Everyone deals with grief differently—I'm sure you learned that, too. If you aren't mad, you aren't mad. That's okay."

I wonder what Ms. W would tell me in this moment. I wish I'd thought of these things before now, then maybe I could have talked to her about them. Not that I really let myself think of anything beyond schoolwork and Cody and how *fine* I supposedly was all summer.

"I feel like I'm supposed to be. I feel like . . . there's something I'm supposed to be feeling, something I'm missing, that I'm not."

Mary chewed on her lip. I could tell she was struggling to find something comforting to say. Something useful.

"When I found out you weren't coming up here with me, I wasn't . . . disappointed," she started. "I mean, I was, but mostly, I just felt like an idiot."

"Why?"

"Partly for believing our plans would actually work out. You were ditching me again, and part of me thought I was stupid to think you'd want to come out here and be my roommate and whatever—"

I opened my mouth to interrupt her but she cut me off.

"I know, that's dumb. I know. It's why I didn't tell you," she continued. "And another part of me felt stupid for not pushing you when you started flaking on schoolwork and counseling. I knew something was going on, but I don't think I wanted to know. And that's really shitty of me. And I think I was just too busy being mad at myself to think about being mad at you."

I thought about that for a minute.

I spent a lot of time being mad at myself for everything that happened with George. I . . . think I still am, in some ways. Sometimes I wonder if I should have seen it coming. I'd heard people say he was no good. I knew it was shitty of me to get with Lizzie's ex behind her back. I knew that some of the things he said and did felt . . . off.

Everyone says it's not my fault. Lizzie, Mary, Ms. W . . . okay, maybe not people like Harriet, but that doesn't matter. The people who count always say it's not my fault. And I know that's true. Logically, I know that's true.

But sometimes it takes emotions a while to catch up with logic, if they ever do.

I'd wanted to think I was done feeling this way, but it still creeps in.

Because sometimes I think about the good times. How when we were together, none of the warnings mattered. It was just us. And I loved the bubble we lived in together. Our own world.

I feel guilty about that.

It doesn't add up. The two George Wickhams. Because there were two of him. Two sides. And the side I spent most of my time with . . . it just doesn't add up, everything that happened.

Anger, guilt, confusion. I felt a lot of different things about our relationship, and the fallout I was left to deal with on my own. And I felt just about all of it toward myself.

But I hadn't really gotten a chance to feel it toward him, had I?

"I know where he is."

I heard her, but I wasn't sure. Or I didn't want to. I don't even know.

"What?"

"I know Darcy told him to stay away, but I wanted to make sure. I didn't want him to just show up back home or in New York and surprise you, even on accident. So I've been keeping tabs on him every once in awhile."

I leaned back against the arm of the couch. Too much was happening at once.

"Why didn't you tell me?" I asked, more buying time to process all of this than anything else.

"I wasn't trying to keep it from you," Mary assured me. "I just didn't want to bring it up and . . . set you back, I guess."

I nodded. That made sense. I know I need to move past George, and that means not thinking about him all the time or wondering where he is or remembering what we were. And yet . . .

I still do. He's still always there, isn't he?

That hasn't changed just because I don't see his face every day.

He's the one thing that changed my life more than any other. Everything I've done and learned for the past however long stems directly from knowing him. And I'd never be able to move on from him, if I didn't know . . . why.

"Where is he?"

She looked down at her hands, but I could see her brow furrow before she responded. "Lydia . . ."

"Mary," I kept my voice low, but steady. "I need to know."

Her eyes finally moved back up to mine and she nodded.

"About an hour north of here."

I know gasping at surprising information is such a cliché, but I did something close to that, at least. I couldn't help it. George had been that close the whole time? I tried to wrap my head around it. Why did he stay nearby when Darcy told him to leave? Why hadn't he contacted me? What was I going to do?

I straightened up, coming out of my thoughts. My eyes traveled up from the spot on the carpet where they had inadvertently fixated and settled on Mary.

"Lydia . . ." she started again, her voice holding a warning this time. I almost grinned. She knew me too well now. I didn't respond and she sighed. "Are you sure?"

I nodded. "I need to do this."

She raked her black nails through her black hair as she shook her head. "Your sister is going to kill me."

"This isn't up to Lizzie," I countered. "It's my choice. I need to do this."

"All right," Mary said, standing up. She snatched her keys up off the coffee table. "Let's do it."

I stared at her, and when I didn't make any move to get up, she kept going.

"What? I'm not making you go see that jackass by yourself. Come on!"

"I missed you," I said, unable to stop from breaking out in a smile for real this time. Mary was the weirdest cousin, but she was also kind of the best.

"Of course you did," she said, rolling her eyes.

"Ooh, careful, Mary," I warned as I pushed myself up off the couch. "You're sounding a little like *moi*."

She rolled her eyes. "You wish."

I grabbed my purse off the floor where I'd dropped it, and Mary yanked the front door open.

"I'm driving," she said.

"Sure." I stopped in front of her in the open doorway. "You might wanna finish buttoning that shirt up, though." Her face fell and I stifled a laugh as I left her once again fumbling with buttons behind me.

It's nice to joke around with Mary again. It's nice to joke around now at all.

Especially knowing that in an hour, the only joke will probably be on me.

Chapter Thirty-nine

GEORGE

Mary pulled the car over to an empty spot along the curb and pushed the gear into park.

We'd sat in silence almost the entire way here, Mary allowing the radio to meander through top forty pop hits and me compulsively checking the maps on my phone as if that would somehow make us arrive where we were headed faster. Or slower; I'm not really sure what I wanted. I'm still not. But here we are.

"It's the one up on the left, with the red mailbox." Mary pointed to a two-story house with cream-colored stucco and big windows that were rounded at the top.

"Wow, he bought a house," I murmured. The idea of George planting roots anywhere upset me a little, and I made a mental note to analyze the thought further when this was all over.

"Rental," Mary corrected, and I felt a little better. Then I remembered Mary had said he'd been here the whole time, and the uneasiness returned.

I had tried to think about what I would say on the drive up, but nothing I'd thought about seemed right. I'm usually pretty good at this kind of thing, but I guess I usually had people pretty well figured out, which always makes it easier to imagine their side of the conversation. I'd thought I had George figured out, but it didn't seem that way anymore. I just knew things about him, and that wasn't the same. You could only predict so much of the future with the past.

"Just because we're here doesn't mean you have to do this," said Mary. "We can always go back."

"No, we can't."

I unbuckled my seatbelt and got out of the car. Mary did the same.

"How far do you want me to come with you?" she asked.

"I'm not sure," I told her, pushing the passenger door shut. "I'll let you know."

She nodded and waited for me to lead the way. I stepped out into the street, crossing the pavement to his side. We reached the curb in front of his yard and I looked back at Mary, letting her know it was okay to wait here, for now. I eyed the door—so far away, it seemed—and thought of one more thing.

My hands shook as I pulled my phone out of my pocket. I swiped over the lock screen—the picture of me with Milo and Kat on my last night with them, that silly tiger on my head—and I remembered again how I felt when I was in New York. Unafraid. Unburdened. Unlimited. I wanted to be able to feel that all the time, not just when I was far away and mostly surrounded by people who knew nothing about me. I wanted to be free to be whoever I wanted, wherever I was. I needed this.

And I needed to include the other member of our relationship. The camera.

I tapped open the camera app and switched it to video recording. The phone chimed softly as I pressed the record button, and with one last deep breath, I started the walk up the path to the front door.

And stopped.

I saw his abs first, if you can believe it. The sun glinted off them like some commercial for men's cologne or gum or something equally ridiculous. He was walking toward me along the side of the house, watching behind him as he unraveled a garden hose.

My throat was dry, but I swallowed and readied his name. I wouldn't wait for him to see me; this was going to be on my terms.

"George."

His shoulders tensed. The hose stopped unwinding. He cracked his neck to the side like I'd seen him do too many times and he reached around for a white shirt on his porch I hadn't noticed before. He turned toward me as he slipped it over his head.

There he was. George Wickham.

He looked the same. Same hair; same body; same mouth; same eyes. Only his eyes weren't looking at me, like they always used to. He glanced past me, to Mary, and then . . . at my shoulder, or something. But not at me.

"You shouldn't be here," he said finally, no discernible emotion behind his words. He nodded toward the phone I still held in front of me, pointed at him. "What are you doing?"

"I thought you liked being on camera?"

The words came easier than I thought they would. George, on the other hand, said nothing, pushing his jaw around and still refraining from making eye contact.

"You never responded to any of my messages or calls or emails, so tracking you down was kind of the only way to get your attention."

"Still thinking of me after all this time, huh?" There was no teasing in his voice, no mocking. It felt rehearsed, back to being some late-night cable film, and the actors had better places to be.

I let it go, and waited for something more. George was like me, in that way. He needed to talk to fill the silence when it got uncomfortable. And if you talk too much, eventually something true is bound to spill out.

"Anyway," he continued after a moment, "I'm not exactly supposed to talk to you. Part of the terms of my deal with dear ole Darcy."

"You don't get to decide that," I echoed what I had said to Mary earlier. "Neither does Darcy. Or my sisters. Only I do."

"Yeah, because your decisions have always turned out to be just super." The sarcasm was there this time, strong, and it stung. I started to wonder if this had been a good idea after all, or if I was just hoping for closure I could never get.

But I had to know why. Why things went wrong. If there was ever anything or if everyone else had been right about us the whole time. If I should have been different. I had to know.

"Look at me."

George finally turned his eyes up toward me after a moment of hesitation. I stared him down, trying to find answers without asking for them.

"What do you want, Lydia?" I'd never heard my name sound so cold. *This was not the George I knew*, I told myself. And yet it was. Only now he was talking about me with the same voice he'd used when he talked about Darcy, or Gigi, or even Lizzie, sometimes.

"You left, with no explanation. You betrayed me, with no explanation. You want to talk about what I want from you, George? Start with that." I was quieter than I wanted to be. I wanted to be mad. I still wasn't mad. Why couldn't I get mad?

"Answers?" he laughed, and we stepped back into that stupid movie. "That's what you're here for? An *explanation*? *Justification*?" He exaggerated the words like I was nothing more than a silly child, and I almost felt like one. "Damn, I at least thought you'd ask for a cut of my money."

"I loved you."

I had this English teacher in high school who made us write an essay about a moment in which the entire world seemed to slow down to the point where we could make note of every detail around us—what the ground felt like, what the air smelled like, every sound that was idling in the background. It seemed stupid at the time, but now I understand the kind of moment she had been talking about.

I loved you—the words slipped out of my mouth unprompted, and everything stopped.

A car sped past on a street nearby. Someone a couple of houses over was barbecuing in the backyard. There was a small rip in the sole of my right shoe I hadn't noticed until now. George had a scar running across the backs of two of his fingers that hadn't been there before. And his eyes weren't leaving mine, not now.

His lips parted and I saw him swallow, saw his tongue move as if trying to push out a word lodged in the back of his throat.

I instinctively took a step toward him and the moment broke.

He shook his head, the coldness returning to his gaze. "And I used you. It's what people do. Get over it."

"I don't believe you," I said, as uncertain as I suddenly felt. "What we had—"

"I don't care about you! All right? This was never about you. Get it through your freaking head. You and me were done before we even started! I got my money. Darcy got to play hero and triumph over the big, bad villain. It's how the story goes. You got caught in the middle, but hey, even the damsel in distress gets a long-awaited reconciliation with her neglectful and distant sister. That's what you wanted, right? It's a win for everyone. Take it and move on."

I stepped back, thrown by the aggressive outburst. I expected him to keep messing around and dodging questions, but I hadn't expected this. At some point, I'd heard Mary step up onto the curb behind me, but she hadn't come any closer just yet. I tried to process his words, but something was off to me. Something was sticking.

By the time I'd refocused on the scene in front of me, George had moved back to the garden hose he'd dropped when he first heard me say his name.

"Good-bye, Lydia," he called out resolutely, clearly more of an attempt to get me to leave than an actual good-bye.

But then I realized what he'd said. A *long-awaited reconciliation*. The only way he could have known about that . . . is if he saw it.

I hit the record button on my phone, turning off the camera, and slipped it into my pocket.

"Why did you watch the videos?"

He slowed and turned again, just like before, and I wanted to yell at him to stop trying to leave and just have a stupid conversation with me.

"What are you talking about?"

"Me and Lizzie. You know what happened with us, after . . ." I still couldn't bring myself to say what he did out loud to him, and if what was happening right now wasn't more important, I knew I'd have been irritated with myself. "Why did you watch if you never cared?"

"I wanted to make sure my investment would provide a lucrative return," he said after a beat. "Get people invested in the outcome, they're more likely to buy, right?"

"Bullshit." I rolled my eyes. His jaw shifted and his muscles tensed under his shirt. I'd caught him now and we both knew it. And I know George, like I know myself. Prepping response for his deflection in three . . . two . . .

"Look, I don't have time for this middle-school confrontation—"

"You play the victim, like life has screwed you over, and now you're gonna do whatever you have to in order to get what you think it owes you. But you know what? There are more than just victims and heroes and villains caught up in the middle of some endless tragedy, George. People are just people. Trying their best to make something decent out of whatever crap has been thrown at them. Together. I hope you figure that out one day."

I knew him now. Not just what he'd done, what he'd been. I knew him. The immature boy who felt neglected and misunderstood by the people he'd once cared about, who couldn't own up to his own mistakes, who was too scared to think there'd ever be anything good out there for him so he decided to just commit to being bad instead. I always knew George and I were similar. And after everything, I'd started to worry our similarities went beyond what I even knew.

But George was stuck in the role he'd felt life had laid out for him.

I wasn't.

He shifted uneasily, eyes twitching to Mary, to the phone in my pocket, finally back to me.

"And here I thought I'd just get a good slap. It's what your devoted fans wanted, you know."

I crossed the ground that was left between us, realizing I'd moved closer at some time during all of this. I put my hand on his face, and he flinched. I remembered all the times I'd felt the scratchy surface of his skin under my palm, in a different context, different life, and I wondered if he was remembering all the times he'd felt the warmth of my hand on his face and realizing what he'd lost.

"That'd be easier, wouldn't it?"

He swallowed any words he might have had to say and reached out, running his fingers along the chain that dangled from my neck. He started to pull, to lift the rest of the necklace up from under the collar of my shirt, to see if it was his, I had no doubt.

I caught his wrist and his gaze shifted from the necklace back to my face. He was softer now. Curious. Lost. But it was too late for that.

"No. Now you're the one who gets to question everything."

I let his hand drop from mine, falling effortlessly back down to his side.

I turned my back to him, to his world, and this time, I was the one who walked away.

Chapter Forty

OKAY

I don't know what to say about all of that. I don't know if it was right, or if there is a "right" for something like this. I don't know if I'll regret things I said, or didn't say, in a week or a month or years down the road. I don't know if closure—if that's really what this was—is going to make much of a difference when I start dating someone else (for real, this time) or if things will just feel uncomfortable and a little scary until one day they don't anymore.

The only thing I know is that I feel kind of . . . okay.

For now, right now, I feel okay.

"Do you want to talk about it?" Mary asked after we'd been on the road for a few minutes.

"I don't think so," I told her. "Not yet. Thank you, though."

We drove along a little bit farther, no sound other than occasional music coming from other cars who passed us by with their windows down and their radios booming. Ours stayed off.

"You did good, you know," Mary finally spoke again. "It's fine if you don't want to talk about it. But you did good."

I smiled. "No pleading for my shitty ex-boyfriend to take me back, so call it a win."

"Those abs were like a beacon of danger, drawing sailors into a miserable death upon jagged rocks," Mary continued. "It takes strong willpower to resist."

"I think you're mixing your lighthouse and siren metaphors," I said. And hey, I totally just called Mary out on something having to do with reading and books!

"I don't know if I like this pays-attention-in-class version of Lydia," she said.

"Tough luck." I considered telling her about my plans for school then, but I wasn't sure it was a conversation I wanted to launch into right after dealing with George. I did feel okay, that's the truth, but I was a little exhausted. This joking around felt nice after those few minutes of confrontation and the hours of anxiety leading up to coming here, and coming to see Mary in the first place. College talk could wait for a little while.

"So . . . then . . ." Mary started hesitantly. "About before . . ."

I blanked for a minute, then turned away from Mary to hide the grin that popped up on my face. *Before*. Right. I was wondering when we'd get around to this.

"We just talked about George," I said, doing my best to sound confused.

"No." She sighed. "I mean . . . *before*. At the apartment."

"You mean our fight? We're good now, aren't we?"

"Oh my God, Lydia! Violet!"

"Ohhhhh, Violet." I saw Mary take a small breath of relief, thinking she wasn't going to have to spell it out for me after all. Sorry, cuz. "I'm glad you guys are still friends."

One of the stories we'd read in Gothic Lit this summer mentioned a basilisk, which is this super creepy snakelike creature that can turn people into stone just by staring into their eyes. Mary jerked her head toward me and I decided there was a pretty good chance her mom's side of the family may actually be descended from these creatures. Yeesh. Maybe it was time to stop messing with her.

"Wow, you just took your eyes off the road for like, three whole seconds. This must be serious."

She didn't say anything, refocusing on the road, and I felt kind of bad. I could see her eyes twitching toward me every other second, waiting to see what I would say next.

"Do you like her?" I asked.

"Yeah."

"Is she nicer to you than Eddie?"

"Yeah."

"Then, good."

I kicked my feet up on the dash and picked at some loose threads around a hole on the knee of my jeans. Mary paused, then glanced over at me. A much shorter, less stone-inducing glance this time.

"That's it?" she asked.

Crap, did I do that wrong? I made a big deal when she started dating Eddie, should I have made a big deal about this?

"I can do more if you want this to be like, a whole thing."

Mary shook her head. "No, that's okay, I don't, I just . . . it's not like a phase or anything."

I couldn't stop myself from laughing. Is that what she was worried about? That I wouldn't take her seriously? Well, any less seriously, anyway.

"Mary. You play the bass and just moved to San Francisco. I'm not assuming this is a phase."

"Stereotypes!" she yelped, but I totally saw her mouth kind of half twitch into a smile. And I mean, this is Mary we're talking about. That's as good as squealing in glee, really.

"When the combat boot fits . . ." I teased, and she rolled her eyes.

I'm happy for Mary. Yes, okay, a part of me is relieved that something turned out okay even after I abandoned her to move to a new city by herself, sure. But I'm also glad she's not holing up alone in a dark vampire cave crunching numbers and reading books until she slowly loses her mind and starts hallucinating demons as friends or some other completely likely scenario. My family might worry about me, but I worry about them, too. And Violet's certainly no me, but if Mary's added her to the very short list of people she can stand to be around without wanting to paint them into some grotesque murder scene diorama, then there's gotta be something good about her.

"You know I have to meet her now," I pointed out.

"You've met her a dozen times."

"First of all, today definitely doesn't count unless you consider her hand being up your shirt a casual wave in my direction—" Mary groaned and probably would have buried her head in the steering wheel if the earlier multisecond glance my way hadn't already fulfilled her reckless driving quota for the year. "And B, I need to remeet her properly, as your girlfriend. I have to give her the cousin talk."

"That's not a thing," Mary immediately countered.

"It is *so* a thing."

"Nope."

"Are you having safe sex?"

"Oh my *God*, LYDIA!"

The car swerved a little and I was glad the highway wasn't packed today. But . . . I was also glad to have provoked dangerous driving in Mary twice in one day. Imaginary self–high five!

"I know, like, everything about girl-on-girl sex. I can give you pointers, if you want," I continued, and Mary didn't even have to look at me for me to feel her confusion. "What? I got stuck on a weird YouTube spiral once."

"This was a bad idea."

"You love me."

"I'm reconsidering."

I dug my phone out of my pocket and quickly tapped out a text.

"What, no comeback?" Mary challenged.

"Pause," I responded. A second later, my phone dinged and I grinned. "Well, I hope you're also reconsidering my heart-to-heart with your new GF, because we are all meeting up at the Rusted Tip in two hours."

Mary groaned. "How did you even set that up? Wait." She glanced over at my phone. "How did you get Violet's number?"

"I took it from your phone before you moved, duh," I said. Seriously, how has she not come to expect this by now? "Don't worry, I've never texted her before. But you didn't think I would let you move to a new city without backup ways to contact you, did you? What if you disappeared and nobody knew where you went and it turned out you'd gone hiking and a bear had eaten your phone and you were trapped in a cave somewhere, camouflaging yourself to look like the rocks and the *only* person who knew where you'd gone was Violet? Hmm? How else would we ever find you again?"

"You took the whole band's phone numbers, didn't you." It wasn't even a question. Much better.

"Uh-huh!"

"And here I thought you'd at least vaguely deciphered the meaning of the word 'privacy,'" she complained, but I could hear the acceptance in her voice as well. Mary needed a little delving into her personal bubble, or it would always stay in place, protecting her from all the cool stuff in the world. Like me! And I was certain Violet had delved into her bubble, too.

Okay, that does not sound the same as it did in my head. Retract. Full retraction on that one.

"Sometimes a little invasiveness doesn't hurt," I responded. Then, after a beat . . . "You like Violet."

Mary grunted quietly, which I took to mean agreement.

"You like me."

"Debatable." That's a yes.

"So you probably want us to like each other," I concluded.

Mary sighed one of the most dramatic sighs I'd heard from her, and I knew victory was mine.

"Fine," she conceded. "But no talking about sex . . . girl-on-girl or otherwise."

"Yay!" I couldn't stop from clapping excitedly. "I will be on my best behavior. Promise."

"Why doesn't that reassure me whatsoever?" Mary muttered under her breath.

I reached over and flipped on the car radio, letting it land on an indie rock station. Mary let me have the music on the drive up, but I'm pretty sure she'll need her own jams on the way back. I wonder if there will be more for us to talk about later. Ooh, I wonder if she's told Lizzie. I'll have to find out. Someone needs to keep an eye on Mary when I'm not around, after all, make sure she doesn't get up to too much trouble. Or that Violet doesn't turn out to be another Eddie. What is with Mary and people in bands, anyway?

Better bands than swim teams, I guess.

I wonder where future architects fall on that spectrum of "people who turn out not being that good to date." Though it's silly to lump everyone from one activity group into one type-of-person group. There are probably overlapping traits that draw people to whatever activity, but there are more levels than that. People are complicated, and not all the same. Duh. But as shitty as it can be sometimes, it's kind of fun peeling back those layers and figuring out what and who they are, and even why.

And then? Well, then you're really getting somewhere.

"Hey, Lydia?" I turned toward her and waited for her to go on. I was getting too lost in my psychology thoughts, anyway. "I know today was a lot, but I'm glad you're here."

I shifted my gaze out the window and onto the road ahead of us. The sun was starting to set off to my right, and the sky was turning all sorts of amazing colors. I'd always loved the night—at home, it was the time for parties and secrets and things you could forget in the morning if you wanted, and in New York, it had been quiet and thoughtful—but I realized I'd never paid much attention to the transition the world took to getting there. It wasn't the same as watching the sunrise. But there was something just as beautiful about this.

"Yeah. Me, too."

Chapter Forty-one

RECOGNITION

By the time we got to the bar, we were half an hour later than I'd told Violet we would be, but it was still pretty early in the evening, so we grabbed a couple of drinks in record time compared to how long it always took at Carter's (I told you, bar karma), and made our way toward the back, where Mary said Violet was waiting for us. It was a pretty low-key bar. A bit more "private library" than Carter's, that's for sure. There was a small, currently empty stage over in one corner, and I wondered if the Mechanics played here sometimes. Oh, and if so, would we get free drinks for being with the band? That'd be pretty sweet. Definitely a point in her favor, if so.

I spotted Violet—or rather, I spotted her hair first, and then Violet—hanging by herself in a red leather booth underneath a creepy black statue of a horse head on the wall. She didn't notice us, or even seem to be looking around for us, and I couldn't decide if I disliked that she wasn't eagerly looking out for Mary to get here, or if I admired that she wasn't super clingy and/or was attempting to seem chill and not anxious about us hanging out.

"Hey," Mary said as we reached the booth. Violet looked up, finally noticing us, and grinned at my cousin.

"Hey!" she responded, moving over for Mary to scoot in next to her. "Sorry I didn't see you, I was going over some new lyrics in my head."

I stayed standing at the end of the booth, filing that reasoning under "maybe acceptable." Violet finally glanced away from Mary and up at me.

"Hi! I'm Lydia," I introduced myself, sticking my hand out toward the girl I had, as Mary pointed out earlier, met a bunch of times before. "You must be Violet."

Mary cut Violet off before she could do more than look suddenly and utterly confused. "She's pretending she's never met you before because she considers the you who worked with me at the coffee shop a different person than the you who . . . doesn't work with me at the coffee shop," she stumbled. "Just ignore her."

"Oh, okay, I get it," Violet said. "But there's a flaw in your logic. The me you met earlier today in Mary's apartment is the same" — she shot a look at Mary before continuing — "me who doesn't work at the coffee shop. So you've still already met me. And you didn't even introduce yourself."

I stared at Violet.

She stared back.

"I like her!" I announced, and slid into the seat across from them. "But you both have a weird hang-up about saying you're dating."

"So you told her," Violet acknowledged. "Cool."

"You didn't tell her you told me?" I asked Mary.

"I thought you did when you stole her number out of my phone and texted her to meet us here."

"First, I stole her number months ago, get it right. And B, this sounds like a communication issue," I pointed out. "Communication is crucial for a successful relationship."

"Oh my God, stop trying to analyze us." Mary groaned.

"Actually, she's doing it pretty well," Violet said, winking at me.

"I just want you two to have the best shot at making this work," I said.

"We aren't test subjects in your Intro to Psych class."

"Well, if you'd prefer, we can always talk about what I learned on a weird YouTube spiral instead."

"NO!" Mary yelped. I couldn't stop myself from grinning, and noticed Violet was doing the same.

"It's just so easy to get under her skin," I told her.

"That it is," she replied. "But it's cute."

Mary dropped her head onto the table in embarrassment and I could've sworn I heard a muffled "Kill me now" emanate from under the mass of dark hair and protectively shielding arms.

"So, Violet," I started again, ready to take full advantage of Mary's distraught and distracted state. "I know we've met before, both this incarnation of you and the previous one, but now it's time for me to really get to know you."

She turned her full attention to me and squinted, seemingly analyzing the situation.

"Okay," she agreed. "Lightning round?"

"Lightning round."

I settled in as Mary continued to groan in protest from her place facedown on the table.

"How many girlfriends have you had?"

"Three."

"Boyfriends?"

"One and a half."

"Is Violet your real name?"

"According to my parents."

"Have you ever been convicted of a crime?"

"Negative."

"Have you ever gotten away with one?"

"Couldn't say."

"Been involved in a pyramid scheme?"

"Only if you count cheating on a history test in fourth grade."

"What are your intentions with my cousin?"

"Okay!" yelled Mary, finally popping her head up. "That's enough."

"This is your second non-friend friend ever! As your cousin and your best friend, I have every right to pry," I insisted.

Mary raised an eyebrow. "Non-friend friend?"

"Well, I can't say second girlfriend because of Eddie, and I can't say second boyfriend, because, duh, Violet's not a boy. This is really complicated."

"Words are the complicated part," Violet interjected. "The rest . . . not so much." She put her arm around Mary and pulled her in closer, tickling her shoulder. I saw Mary blush, and believe me when I say it took all my energy not to squee at the adorbs. Mary had lightened up a lot after we started getting closer last year, but I could already tell this was a side of her I never got to see.

"All right," I conceded. "You passed the test. Just . . . don't be a dick, okay?"

"I will do my best," Violet promised.

I turned to Mary. "That goes for you, too!"

"Hey!" she protested. "You're supposed to be on my side."

"Always," I reassured. "But I like her. Don't mess it up."

"She better not," Violet teased. "I don't want to have to replace another bass player."

"Wait, what?" I said. Mary smiled.

"I was planning on telling you tonight, but . . ." She shrugged. "I'm officially taking over Duke's bass duties."

"Oh my God!" I squealed for real this time. "That's so cool!"

"Thanks," Mary replied, putting her finger to one ear. I may have been a little overenthusiastic. It happens. But this is super exciting! "It'll be nice to do something other than just accounting. I like it, but it gets a little boring being on the computer all day."

My nerdy cousin wanting to do something other than just nerdy things. My, how far we've come.

"So . . ." I prompted, to absolutely no response. Or at least not one quick enough. These girls are way too chill in the face of awesome exciting things. "When do you play? Are you recording an album? Is there merch? You've gotta come back and do a show at Carter's!"

"One step at a time, Lydia," Mary tried to calm me down. As if. "I have to finish learning all the current songs, and once that's set, we'll all go from there."

"Oh, please," Violet said. "She learned all our songs in like a week. Mary is way better than Duke could ever hope to be. And that's not just me being incredibly biased in my girlfriend's favor. We're hoping to get a gig at Central Bay College next month during one of their fall mixers."

"That's fantastic," I said.

"I wish you were going to be there," Mary responded quietly.

"It's not far," I told her. "Obviously spontaneous road trips are kind of my thing, of course I'm not gonna miss you playing in a freaking awesome rock-and-roll band! I totally get to be one of those before-they-were-famous groupies."

"Cool." Just a word, but I know Mary well enough to know it meant a lot to her. Assuming I, you know, followed through. Which I would. No way was I bailing on this. Except . . .

"I should probably tell you, though . . ." I started. "I don't think I'm going to be around much next year."

"Oh?"

"There's this school in New York someone told me about"—I glanced at Violet—"with a really great psychology department. I checked it out while I was visiting Jane and . . . I'm going to apply for the spring."

"Really?" Mary asked. I could tell she was excited but a little hesitant. Can't say I blame her.

"Yep, I mean, I have to actually fill out the application. But I think I have a pretty good idea of what to write this time."

"That's amazing, Lydia!" Mary's enthusiasm shone through a little more now. Or at least whatever passes for enthusiasm when it comes to Mary.

"You know, they wear a lot of black there, so you're going to have to come visit," I said. "It's like, the call of your people."

"I'm planning a trip back in the spring, anyway," Violet cut in. "I'll do my best to drag Mary along. Assuming we haven't had some horrendously dramatic breakup that destroys not only our relationship, but the entire future of the band as well."

The color drained out of Mary's face as she thought that over for a second.

"Joking. Totally joking. Too far?"

"Don't worry," I told her. "She's always that pale. It'll work well when you guys are visiting me in the city."

"And on that note, I think I'm going to go buy the next round of drinks since the two of you seem to have a lot to celebrate," Violet said, motioning for a slightly recovered Mary to let her out of the booth.

"Plus you want me to like you, and the best way to do that is buying me drinks," I added.

She laughed. "Yes, I remember."

Mary watched her push her way through the crowd toward the bar, and I watched Mary watch her.

"You really like her?" Mary asked.

"Oh my God, you're so needy for my approval." She kicked me lightly under the table and we both grinned. "But yes, I do. You know perfectly well that you'll never hear the end of it if I don't."

"That's for sure." Mary swirled the remnants of the melted ice in her glass around with the tiny straw. "I'm really happy for you about this college thing, Lydia, if that's what you want to do. But a whole new city? Are you sure? New York is a big place."

"That's what I liked about it," I said, thinking back to all the cool stuff I'd gotten to see with Jane, and with Milo and Kat. And how much more there was still left to do. "Besides, Jane is there if I need her, and so is Bing. And I made a couple of new friends, too. Friends who just know me as Lydia, you know? Not the Lydia who lived in the same town her whole life, or even 'the Lydia Bennet.' It's kind of neat."

"I knew I recognized you!"

I turned to see a girl who looked to be a couple of years older than me step up to our table. She was wearing a Belle and Sebastian T-shirt and a string necklace with beads that read "P-A-R-I-S." I had no idea if that was supposed to be in reference to the city or if it's her name or if she just swiped a really crappy necklace from some kid she'd been babysitting, but regardless, I didn't like where this was heading.

"Lydia Bennet," she repeated as a guy with a button-up shirt and glasses that looked like my grandmother's came up behind her and snuck his arm around her waist. "Remember, Jordan? Duh nuh nuh nuh nuh nuh nuh nuh nuh nuh nuh, yeah!"

Wow, she actually just sang the theme song from my videos. I completely forgot I'd even had a theme song.

People from school knew I made videos, and so did other people in our town who already knew me or my family, but I'd never had someone *recognize* me from them before. A year ago, I'd have been totally eating it up. Now, it was kind of bizarre to be honest. Like opening up some time capsule buried in the backyard. And the contents are barely recognizable.

"Oh yeah!" Jordan said. "We used to watch your vids every week. I really dug the raw aesthetic. None of that overproduced, overstylized Hollywood bullshit that's infecting YouTube now. Just . . . raw, man. It was sick."

"Um, thanks," I said.

"Yeah, your last video was so . . ." the girl started, and I froze. Sad? Pathetic? Anticlimactic? I waited. Would they ask about George? Would they want to know why I didn't listen to what everyone online told me at the time? Sure, I'd faced my demons and whatnot today, but that didn't mean I was ready to air them out in front of an entirely random group of people at a bar. I wasn't a YouTuber anymore, after all.

". . . sweet," she finished. "It sucks that guy was such a dickbag. I hope you find someone way more deserving of 'the adorbs.'"

"Yeah," Jordan cut in again. "You know, my brother had a friend whose other friend dated a swimmer for like a week a couple of years back, and she swears it was the same guy. My brother's friend does, I mean. She couldn't remember his name, but he was a major asshole by all accounts."

"So tell us, did fame totally go to Kitty's head, or has she remained down-to-earth?"

I grinned. Maybe not everything about this whole being a former YouTube star thing was that terrible.

"What can I say? Kitty was born a star."

"Really? Don't lie to me about my favorite Internet cat."

"I feel like I'm late to the party," Violet's voice cut through the small blockade Jordan and maybe-Paris had formed at the head of the booth as they listened to me talk about my cat's fame. "What'd I miss?"

She slid back into the booth next to Mary, drawing the attention to that side of the table.

"Oh!" the girl exclaimed. "Mary! Cousin Mary from the videos! I didn't even see you there."

I stifled a snort to the best of my abilities and I saw Mary attempt to do the same with her classic eye roll. Violet handed her a drink and she went back to doing what she does best—ignoring other people exist. Or tried to, at least.

"Dude, is that a screwdriver?" Jordan pointed to the glass in front of Mary. "I thought you didn't drink."

"I drink, now. I don't get drunk," Mary said. "Overconsumption of alcohol destroys brain cells, and I happen to like my brain just the way it is."

"Still," he said, laughing, "bet there would be some disappointed straight-edge kids who used to look up to you."

"Well, maybe they should acknowledge that each of us can only know an extremely finite portion of any other human and, ultimately, consider forging their own paths and being their own 'role model' rather than asserting that title on another human being who will, inevitably, disappoint them, seeing as how both people and our knowledge of them are in a state of constant flux," Mary calmly rattled off. "Particularly people you only know via the Internet."

"Damn," he said, laughing. "You are exactly like you are in the videos."

This time Mary didn't even bother trying to hide her eye roll, and even Violet stared at the guy with more than a hint of incredulity.

Before one of us could break the awkward moment, someone waved at the duo from across the room and they took off with a "Nice to meet you" and a "Tell Kitty we adore her."

"Friends of yours?" Violet asked both of us after probably-Paris and Jordan were out of earshot.

"With that extreme lack of self-awareness?" Mary shot back. "Definitely not."

"Figured. So, Lydia," Violet transitioned, pushing the final drink over toward me. "I was thinking, my favorite professor from New Amsterdam just got promoted to head of the department last year and we still talk sometimes. I could put in a good word for you, if you want."

I took a sip of the drink: amaretto sour, just like my last one. If this wasn't just luck and Violet could identify drinks on sight, I was definitely making Mary keep her around. Any party tricks involving alcohol were the best kinds of party tricks in my book. And yes, I was stalling my response, which Violet seemed to catch on to.

"I don't wanna overstep any bounds," she went on. "I will take zero offense if you want me to stay out of it, promise. I just respect seeing people figure out what they want to do, and supporting it when I can. And from what Mary says, you're pretty smart at this kind of stuff."

I thought back to missing the deadline for Central Bay College. I didn't think something like that would happen again. Things felt different now. I felt different. Sure, it was just a feeling, but that's a start, right? But I couldn't help wondering if I had asked someone for help instead of hiding the problems I was having and pretending everything was fine—Mary, Ms. W, even Darcy—if things would have turned out differently. I wasn't sure I wanted that, not now, but I guess learning to ask for help was a lesson I needed to learn. Again. How many times do you have to learn the same thing?

Until it sticks, I guess.

And anyway, this wasn't asking for anything. Violet was offering. And I got the feeling it really wasn't out of pity or obligation to Mary or something like that.

"Thanks," I told Violet. "That would be awesome of you."

"Great!" she said. "Let me know when you're submitting and I'll let Professor Malikov know he's got an application coming his way he should pay extra attention to."

I groaned. "Professor Malikov?"

"Yeah . . ." Violet responded, clearly confused. "Do you know him?"

"It's a long story." I sighed. "Better if you don't ask.

"Now, I hate to be this person," I started, not giving them a chance to interject. "Actually, I don't. I love to be this person: I think this night deserves a toast!"

"Ugh, toasts are so lame and overtly cheerful," Mary said. "Can't we just show our happiness for you by buying you drinks?"

"Aw, you both know the way to my heart so well!" I said. "But no. This isn't just a toast for me. It's for all of us! There are a lot of epic new things going on in our lives, and we need to acknowledge them and celebrate. It won't kill you, Mary, I promise."

"She's right about that. I can't say I've ever heard of a toast causing anyone to drop dead," Violet said.

"See? Of course I'm right. And I'll start." I raised my glass. "To me for picking out a new college, and confronting my douchebag ex, and coming back from New York without accidentally joining a weird sex orgy cult while there."

Mary shot me a look but let it slide.

Violet lifted her glass up as well, adding: "To the Mechanics getting an awesome new bassist."

"To Mary dating someone who has way better hair than Eddie," I threw in, and she laughed.

"Seems like a general 'out with the old, in with the new' sentiment would've worked just fine for this whole toast, if you ask me," Mary pointed out.

"To getting rid of the old stuff that sucks and starting cool new adventures without ever forgetting the old stuff that's still pretty awesome to have around," I said, looking over at my cousin. She shifted uncomfortably as a smile forced its way onto her grumpypants face, and finally raised her drink as well.

"Yeah, I guess that's good enough," she agreed, and we all clinked our glasses together.

There was still a lot to do. Tomorrow, I had to go talk to Lizzie and tell her about George, about school, and do my absolute best to not tell her about Mary and Violet because that wasn't my place. I had to go home and do the same thing over with my parents. I had to spend the rest of the year figuring out a lot of things about my life and myself. And I had to actually, you know, write my application essay this time.

But it was nice to just enjoy this night. And for the first time in a while, even with so much to do, I didn't feel like I was burying my head in the sand and avoiding everything. Now when I thought to myself, *Tomorrow*, I didn't feel some looming sense of dread. In fact, I felt pretty freakin' excited.

＊　　＊　　＊

Recount an incident or time when you experienced failure. How did it affect you? What lessons did you learn? What would you do differently now?

I've tried to write this essay many times.

The first time I tried, I would have told you my failure was having judgment poor enough to not be able to see that somebody I trusted was only using me for his own game.

Another time I tried, I would have told you my failure was letting that situation impact me so deeply that I couldn't keep my life on track, couldn't even write this essay and get into college and move on from my past, and it cost all the faith other people had put in me.

A lot has changed since then. I've changed, even if you can't always see those changes on the outside.

I'm writing this essay now, aren't I?

I can be loud, and obnoxious. I enjoy partying, occasionally too much, and I don't always avoid trouble very well. I nag on my sister, and my cousin, too, and sometimes I forget that the world doesn't revolve around me. I think I'm getting better at that.

Sometimes I'm afraid I don't have the right thing to say. Sometimes I try anyway, and I'm right. Other times, I'm wrong. I'm learning that sometimes, the best thing to do is to say nothing at all.

Everything that I am is made up of both my failures and my successes. My attempts and my stumbles. I've learned that in order to rise up from failure, and move forward, you have to acknowledge when you've failed to begin with.

But here's the thing about all of those failures: they're mine.

The person who betrayed my trust did so because he'd already betrayed himself years ago, by not examining his own shortcomings, and still refusing to, even when they stand in the way of his entire life.

That, and everything else he did that hurt me, was not my failure. It was his.

It sounds obvious, when you lay it out straight on paper like that. It's basic sentence structure—the subject verbed the object. But sometimes what seems really obvious in hindsight is impossible to see when you're in the center of it.

I know that now.

And I know that, for all the things that are within my control, this wasn't. This was not my fault. And taking it upon myself didn't change anything, it couldn't. It isn't something to be fixed, it's simply something that has been, and is now a part of me.

My greatest failure was the time I tried to hold myself accountable for somebody else's failures. My greatest failure was the time I failed myself.

I've learned to ask for help. I've learned falling down doesn't mean you can't get back up again.

But as for that relationship, I wouldn't do anything differently, because I wasn't the reason it failed.

If you Google my name, you'll find my story.

Lydia Bennet.

I don't tell you that so you'll feel sorry for me, or so that you'll think I have some sort of extra insight because of the things I went through.

In fact, I'd rather you didn't. Not because I'm ashamed of what you'll see. But because that's not who I am anymore. It's a part of me, and it always will be, but it isn't *me*.

But you can if you want.

Because another thing he has failed at doing is taking my identity, and taking my voice. Those are mine. And with them, I can always turn my failures into strengths.

That's kind of the point, isn't it?

The Epic Epilogue

"Welcome to Books Beans and Buds. Go, Pioneers. We. Do. Not. Sell. Pot. Here. Can I interest you in a budding beverage?"

"I'm not here for pot, dummy," Mary said, staring at me.

"Really?" I asked, all innocent. "The twenty you're going to put in the tip jar says otherwise."

Mary just crossed her arms over her chest. "Why on earth would I do that?"

"Because I'm your cousin, you love me, and you happen to be in the unique position of knowing how much I get paid."

Hey, you know how I said that the idea of working in a coffee shop on the campus of the community college you graduated from was really super depressing?

Actually, it's not that bad. Sure, I have to say the stupid line, and sometimes people look like they recognize me, but then I realize I just had psych class with them or saw them around campus over the summer.

But now that it was the holidays, people kept filtering back in who might recognize me from other things. And might think it's depressing to be working in the coffee shop on campus.

But hey, all the mochaccinos I can drink.

"Black coffee. And please tell me you're not really selling pot."

I just gave her a patented Mary-stare. Of course I wasn't. But the funny thing was, some of our customers didn't seem to know that. About once a week or so, someone would come in, put a twenty in the tip jar, and order a small black coffee.

I have to ask Mrs. B what she puts in the house blend.

I'm working here to pump up my savings account, but it (and other things) also helps pass the time. While I wait.

"Are you excited?" Mary asked, as I poured her coffee.

"About your bass rendition of 'Jingle Bells' this year? Of course. It's gonna be epic," I said, nodding. "Especially since you brought a collaborator."

"Temper your expectations, please," Mary said, blushing. Aw, she and Violet have been dating for months now and she's still blushing. "Vi's not getting here until tomorrow, so you'll have to wait. I meant are you excited about NAU?"

My stomach flipped over as she said the letters. "I haven't heard anything yet."

"Yeah, but you're going to get in."

"We don't know that." And this time I'm not getting my hopes up. I mean, yeah, Violet put a good word in for me with her old professor. And Darcy placed a call (even though he's not a benefactor of NAU), and Bing did, too (he managed to leverage his contacts to get the Teen Crisis Center a write up in the *Times*, so he figured why not use it for me, too), *and* Ms. W cold-called their psych department, but I have no idea if it did any good. The only thing that's going to really get me in are my transcripts (eep) and my application.

And if I don't, it's not the end of the world—this time. There would be a plan C. Don't know what it is yet, obvs, but this time, I know I've done absolutely everything I can.

So yeah. Waiting. And making coffee. Because that's what you do while you're waiting.

"So did you come straight here or stop at the house?" I asked. "Because Mom was on a present-wrapping binge this morning, and if you walked in on that I fear for your mortal soul."

"Nah, we knew better and came straight here."

"We?" My head came up as I was getting Mary's change (sadly, she had not tipped me a twenty). "I thought you said Violet wasn't coming until—"

"Hey, sis!" Lizzie's voice rang through the shop as she walked in. "Good to see you!"

"Lizzie!" I squeed. "You weren't supposed to come down for two more days!"

"Well, I gave my CFO the time off, so I figured, why couldn't I take it, too?"

If there wasn't a refrigerator case full of holiday-themed cake pops in our way, I would have hugged her. As it was, she hopped up on the counter to quasi-strangle me.

"Darcy isn't going to come through the door, too, is he?" I asked.

"He's coming down with his sister, Gigi, tomorrow. I need a night to prep Mom—you know, get her to lay off any marriage and kids talk," Lizzie replied. "So . . . are you excited? NAU?"

"I'm excited for you to order a coffee," I said, and nodded to the line forming behind my sister.

"Oh, right! Sorry," she said sheepishly, and put in an order for a peppermint latte—someone was getting in the holiday spirit. Then she stepped aside to let the line progress as I made her drink.

"So . . . have you heard anything? Mom said the admissions office told her that they'd be sending out acceptance or rejection letters this week."

My mom called the admissions office. And told everyone. Of course. "Nope, haven't heard," I replied. "Man, all we need is Bing and Jane and we'll have hit the worry-button trifecta."

"Well . . ." Lizzie said, her forehead wrinkling in an attempt to make her look innocent.

"No. Way."

"They're getting in tonight. Sorry, we're just all excited."

"There's nothing to be excited about," I said. *Yet*, my brain whispered.

Stop it, brain. You're getting ahead of yourself again.

"At least we can engage in that most Bennet of traditions tonight," Lizzie offered. "Eating our feelings while watching bad movies. Usually romantic comedies, but you can pick."

Mary looked at Lizzie, horrified. "Please don't make me watch a romantic comedy."

"Can't tonight," I said. "I'm on duty."

"On duty?" Lizzie's forehead wrinkled. If she kept doing that, there would be sad, sad consequences.

"At the crisis hotline," I said, and watched Lizzie's jaw drop.

"Since when have you been working at a crisis hotline?"

I shrugged, super nonchalant. "The past couple of weeks. It's kinda cool. I like it."

I did like it. Bing's boss, Dottie, set me up with them. It's a national hotline, but it has local centers, so you're talking to people who are from your same area, and the one I report to is about a half hour away. I had to go through sixty hours of training (seriously, I don't think I've done anything for sixty hours total, unless you count sleep, school, or shopping), and I finally started taking call shifts about two weeks ago.

And it's felt really good. Really . . . right. Which makes me all the more nervous about NAU, because now I *know* this is the path for me. And of course I'm trying to not think about it, which makes my cousin and sister really, really annoying.

I love them, but . . . annoying.

"That's so awesome," Lizzie said, and I could see the telltale sheen of moisture in her eyes that she was going to start sniffling. Oh God.

"Seriously, it's no big deal." I rolled my eyes over to Mary . . . but she had a suspicious sheen in her eyes, too.

Thankfully, the guy behind Lizzie cleared his throat, hoping to move the line along.

"Right," she said. "We'll just go . . . grab a table. Give Mom time to finish up her wrapping fest."

I was happy to take the next guy's order, and the one after that, and the one after that. I find foaming milk to be very soothing. A mindless task, it let me push the nerves down in my stomach, until I almost forgot about them.

Almost.

Hey, heard anything yet? —Milo

My phone buzzed in my back pocket right as I was headed to the back to get more whipped cream for the canisters out of the fridge. So I was semiprivate as I answered his text (you have to be super on the lookout for Mrs. B. She doesn't like phones while on the job and her spies are *everywhere*).

Lydia: Oh God, not you too.
Milo: Hey, I just want to know when I should make reservations
      at your favorite pretzel stand in the park.

I couldn't help my smile. Since I came back home, Milo and I have been texting. Nothing serious, nothing even romantic. But just . . . friendly. And if I thought about him more than I thought about most of my friends (man, I still owe Denny like seventeen emails) well . . . it's a possibility.

And I like there being possibilities. I haven't had possibilities in a while.

Maybe I needed to plan a trip to visit Jane, regardless of any news I may or may not get in the near future.

But when I came out of the back, new whipped cream canisters in hand, I immediately forgot about the phone in my pocket, and the line of customers about to swallow my coworker Harrison whole, because standing in the doorway of Books Beans and Buds were my parents.

That's right. My mom was standing in the middle of Books Beans and Buds, wearing her favorite Christmas sweater and clutching her purse like she'd walked into a den of thieves and hippies, my dad guiding her by the elbow.

Her face broke into a relieved smile when she saw me, and rushed forward. I came out from behind the counter.

"Mom, Dad, what are you doing here?"

"So this is where you work, honey? Oh, I just had to see it. It's so . . . earthy."

She gave a startled little laugh, and my Dad held her steady. "Sorry, peanut, but we couldn't wait."

"Wait?" I asked, alarmed. "What's wrong? Did you have a doctor's appointment or something?"

"No, no, nothing like that. . . ."

"Mom? Dad?" Lizzie said, coming up behind them. "What are you doing here?"

"Lizzie! Oh my goodness, why are you here? I didn't expect you until Wednesday, and oh—your room isn't ready!" Mom said, hugging her.

Perfect, now we were four—no, wait, Mary came, too, so five—people standing in a group in the middle of the coffee shop. Harrison sent me a *What the hell is going on?* look.

I would like to know that, too, buddy.

"Okay, Mom." I cleared my throat. "Why are you here?" I doubted she'd had a sudden urge for a book or a flower arrangement.

"Well, honey, we had to come as soon as the mail arrived," my mom answered.

"The mail . . . ?"

And she reached into her bag, and produced an envelope. An envelope with the return address of New Amsterdam University.

For some reason I couldn't feel my feet anymore. This wasn't a huge issue, but just something worthy of note. I took the envelope from her, held it in my hands, felt its weight.

"Wow, real mail," I said softly. "I thought they would have sent an email."

Is that a good sign? Like, a real-mail envelope comes with paperwork you need to fill out and send back, right? But then again, an email would do that, too, wouldn't it? Plus, was this envelope big enough for a bunch of paperwork? Or was it a one-page rejection letter? It was impossible to tell.

"Well?" Lizzie said, leaning over my mom's shoulder, each with an identical eager expression. "Open it!"

I took a deep breath. Two. Here goes nothing, I thought as I slipped my finger under the flap.

It took me a minute to figure out what the words on the page said. But it started with "Congratulations."

"I . . . got in," I said, finally bringing my eyes up from the page.

The cheers of my family around me deafened me. Probably deafened the entire room. But it was really hard to care. Because come the spring semester, I would be a student at New Amsterdam University. I was going to go start my new life. I was going to get that pretzel from Milo. And it all started now, in this coffee shop surrounded by my family going nuts—seriously, my mom was running from table to table showing people the letter—and a bunch of strangers wondering what the heck was going on, who slowly started clapping their epic congrats.

Which kind of made sense. Everything's been a total whirlwind in my life, why not have a crazy finale to it all?

But that's how it is when you're Lydia Bennet. For better or for worse, just about everything winds up being some kind of adventure. And when all is said and done, I don't think I'd have it any other way.

I like the person I'm becoming.

I like my family, my friends, my life. My future.

I'm ready now to see what lies ahead. Things haven't always gone according to plan—actually, they rarely have—and this may not, either. But I think I'm learning to deal with that better. Roll with the flow or whatever. What's important is putting one foot in front of the other and only looking back to learn from where you've been.

And right now, one foot is leading me to New York. And all its possibilities.

What an adventure that'll be.

Acknowledgments

The Epic Adventures of Lydia Bennet is the direct result of people caring about a secondary character so much, she needed the chance to tell her own story. Thus, everyone who tweeted, tumblr-posted, or said anything about how much Lydia's story meant to them is the reason this book exists.

Special thanks go to our editor, Lauren Spiegel, for having faith that Lydia's story could be a book, and Annelise Robey, for being our representative and cheerleader the whole way. As well as Kate's husband, Harrison, and new baby—the latter without whom this book would have been done a lot sooner. And Rachel's friend Lars, because *du jour* means sanity maintenance against all odds.

We also must acknowledge the amazing team behind the web series *The Lizzie Bennet Diaries*, and specifically the actors whose characters appear in this book: Ashley Clements, Laura Spencer, Briana Cuoco, Christopher Sean, and Wes Aderhold all created people we cared for and cared to know more about.

Finally, Lydia would not exist without the talent of Mary Kate Wiles. She took a character that most people dislike in *Pride and Prejudice* and made her alive and adorbs. Her voice played in our heads as we wrote, and we hope we did her Lydia justice.

The Epic Adventures of Lydia Bennet

Inspired by Jane Austen's timeless novel, Bernie Su and Kate Rorick created a modern-day *Pride and Prejudice* with *The Secret Diary of Lizzie Bennet*. Now, Rorick and Rachel Kiley tell the story of Lydia Bennet, never before explored in the Emmy Award–winning YouTube series.

Before her older sister, Lizzie, started her wildly popular vlog, Lydia was just a normal twenty-year-old obsessed with partying, shopping, and getting away with doing as little work as possible while still having maximum fun. But once Lizzie's vlog turned the lives of the Bennet sisters into an Internet sensation, Lydia quickly realized that all the attention coming her way as people watched, debated, tweeted, and blogged about her life was not always good. . . .

After her ex-boyfriend George Wickham exploited her newfound web-fame, betrayed her trust, and destroyed her online reputation, naïve, carefree Lydia was no more. Now she must work to win back her family's respect and find her place in a far more judgmental world.

For Discussion

1. This novel expands on storylines documented in *The Secret Diary of Lizzie Bennet* and the YouTube series while retaining the plotlines and character archetypes from Jane Austen's *Pride and Prejudice*. Discuss how the authors make Lydia's circumstances contemporary while still drawing on source material from the nineteenth century.

2. Think about Lydia's attraction to psychology, taking into account her eagerness to be respected by her professor in class, as well as her relationship with her therapist, Ms. W. What do you think draws her to this field? How does she apply the concepts she learns (for instance, Pavlov's dogs and the Milgram experiment) to her own life?

3. Why do you think Lydia does not try to take down the incriminating videos of her past? Do you think it's possible to "rewrite your history" in this day and age? How does the permanence of the Internet affect our society? How has it affected your life?

4. Discuss Lydia's relationship with her parents. How do you think their support helps or hinders Lydia's journey? How is Lizzie's relationship with her parents (from the previous book) like and unlike Lydia's?

5. How do Mary and Lydia act as foils to each other, particularly in social settings? How do they complement and push each other to grow as people? Give a few examples from the text.

6. Lydia is grappling with her identity after hitting rock bottom and is newly motivated to be a hardworking student. However, this role is still very new to her, and she is alternately disappointed and heartened by her performance in different classes. Talk about a time when you decided to change your life — how easy was it to enact new goals and ambitions, and how did you overcome hurdles along the way?

7. At a party Lydia attends in New York, guests adopt the personalities of different characters for the entire evening and, at the end of the night, share their characters' secrets and then burn them. How is this both therapeutic and cathartic to Lydia? How does it parallel the new "character" she is trying to be in her own life?

8. On page 92, Lydia says, "There's this weird thing that happens when everything falls apart. [. . .] Your body, the normal one you live in every day, sort of starts to exist apart from you. You're still there, of course. [. . .] But it all goes on autopilot, getting you through the days while you . . . contract." Discuss how detachment and self-sabotage come into play while Lydia tries to reacclimate herself to the real world after this traumatic event. Can you relate to Lydia's feeling of sometimes being on "autopilot"? How so?

9. In *The Secret Diary of Lizzie Bennet*, which takes place before this novel, older sister Lizzie feels that she has failed Lydia, realizing after she learns of her sister's sex tape "that Lydia has never been told that she is loved exactly as she is." Now seeing

the story from Lydia's perspective, how much of this still rings true? How does Lydia crave love, and how does she receive it from her parents, Lizzie, and Jane?

10. Discuss how Lydia is manipulated by the men in her life, Cody as well as George. Lydia declares on page 155: "Here's the thing about good guys. They don't tell you they're good guys." How is this true or untrue in your experience? How are Cody and George harmful to Lydia in their own distinct ways?

11. Lydia realizes that there are so many people in the world who know her from her sister's vlog and her tape scandal, and yet these commenters are faceless to her. What do you believe is the function of anonymity on the Internet, especially in commenting communities? What are the positive and negative possibilities for anonymous communication online?

12. Think about Lydia's relationship with Lizzie and with Jane. Lizzie is absent for much of this novel, yet Lydia often compares herself to her. Alternatively, Lydia seems to blossom in a new way when she visits Jane in New York. Discuss the ways Lydia compares herself to her sisters—is it internally or externally motivated? If you have siblings, do you relate to Lydia's relationships with her sisters?

Enhance Your Book Club

1. Watch a few *Lizzie Bennet Diaries* YouTube videos and then have a look at the comments below. Discuss in your group how comments can be constructive or destructive, and how they act as a form of instant feedback.

2. Try making a YouTube video with your group! React to the book and speak to the ways vlogs and social media impact the narrative. Invite your friends to join in the conversation!

3. If you were going to write a book from another *Lizzie Bennet Diaries* character's point of view, whose would it be? Bring in a chapter to share with the group.

A Conversation with the Authors

Why did you decide to continue the Bennet story beyond *The Secret Diary of Lizzie Bennet*? What was it like to delve into territory not previously covered in the web series?

> **Rachel:** We told Lydia's story alongside Lizzie's for certain parts of the web series with her own series, *The Lydia Bennet!!* We actually had one more set of her episodes written that wound up not being shot for various reasons, so her arc always felt like it had been left somewhat incomplete. Personally, a lot of the writing I did on the show was for Lydia's series, and most of that was just made up outside the confines of adapting *Pride and Prejudice*, so expanding her story from there into a novel (which included some of the things previously written for the episodes we didn't shoot—the scene between Lydia and Wickham, for example, is almost identical to one of the unshot episodes) wasn't very different from what my work on the show had already been. Just more novel-y.

Why did you choose to focus on Lydia in this story, rather than continue with Lizzie's perspective? Did you research any real-life events to create Lydia's storyline in this novel?

> **Kate:** When we finished the web series, everyone's story had been neatly wrapped up. Except for Lydia's. When we leave her at the end of the series, she's still in the emotional aftermath

of the sex tape. There was a vague sense that she was going to be all right, but we didn't know how she would get there. When we talked about the idea of doing a sequel to *The Secret Diary of Lizzie Bennet*, Lydia was the first and foremost on our minds. Plus, her voice and personality are such a standout that of course she has to get her own story! As for drawing from real-life events, Rachel and I drew a lot of inspiration from our own lives. We both spent years in New York City. And I did have a Gothic Literature class in college. I never really understood the lure of *Dracula*.

The subject matter (particularly the sex tape) in *Epic Adventures* is extremely relevant to readers now—how difficult was it to incorporate elements from *Pride and Prejudice* into this very 2015 story?

Kate: In *Pride and Prejudice*, Lydia causes a scandal by eloping with George Wickham, which causes a rift between Lizzy and Darcy just as they are getting close. In modern times, eloping with someone is not necessarily scandal-causing. We needed a public scandal that resonated for today—and since *The Lizzie Bennet Diaries* was informed and influenced by the fact that it was happening online, having the scandal be on the Internet felt right.

However, we've always said that the biggest change we made with the storyline was not the sex tape, but the fact that we actually liked Lydia. We related to her better in *LBD* than we did in *P&P* because she's closer to Lizzie/y. We watch her be vulnerable and get her heart broken in a way that the brash Lydia from *P&P* never shows.

At one point in the novel, Lydia expresses her anxiety about all the people in the world who now know her from her sister's vlog

and her sex tape scandal. Have you ever felt vulnerable or excited putting a piece of work online, knowing it will receive an immediate response? How do you feel about the anonymity of the Internet community?

Rachel: A lot of what college/general writing experience teaches you as a writer is to accept and withstand criticism, but it seems like everything online now becomes so personal. It's not just "This piece of work sucks, here's why," but instead often turns into "YOU ARE THE LITERAL SCUM OF THE EARTH FOR WRITING THIS." We (and by "we" I mostly mean me since I was the only one dumb enough to pay attention to things online) dealt with that on *LBD* to, I think, a much lesser extent than I've seen TV writers deal with it, and watching writers I admire on shows I watch get responses like that is terrifying. I don't read stuff about my writing online anymore because even more than sometimes turning into personal attacks, which you can eventually learn to shrug off, it also sometimes makes you question what you're writing, and if you're in the middle of a story, changing it as you go to react to one fan's criticism here or another fan's criticism there just muddies everything up. It's a weird balance to try to navigate.

Kate: Rachel is absolutely right in that to be a writer you have to be able to take criticism—and that was true long before the Internet. But the Internet does make it more immediate, and often true criticism gets lost in the noise. You just have to know that you can't please everyone, and if you try, you'll drive yourself crazy and probably harm your work. To be on the Internet in any capacity now, you have to have a very thick skin—which was something Lydia had to develop once the sex tape happened.

Both of you were also writers on the *Lizzie Bennet Diaries* web series. How is writing the Bennet story in a novel format different from writing a web series?

Rachel: You go from having talented actors who can convey the emotions and layers you're trying to get across in a scene to actually having to find the words to do it yourself, which, after years and years of training yourself not to use adjectives or get too descriptive in sentences (aka screenwriting), can be very daunting. I've hardly written any prose since probably middle school—all my experience is in screenwriting, or really crappy poetry in high school—so having Kate there was incredibly helpful in the whole process since she knows what she's doing. Plus the web series was literally just people talking to a camera, which is a whole separate beast from most storytelling of any type.

Kate: I've written both books and TV screenwriting for a while now, and I've actually come to the conclusion that they aren't as different as we think they are. When I'm trying to put together a scene, I hear the character in my head, I play out the scene, I notice what they would notice. The novel is of course much longer—a lot less white space on the page—but you still have to justify every word you put down, every scene driving the story forward.

Now that you've explored the perspectives of two Bennet sisters, which one do you think you relate to more and why? Are you like Lizzie in some ways and Lydia in others?

Rachel: I kind of talk like Lydia (possibly a product of writing for her for so long), but I don't particularly relate to her too much. There are always small similarities you find as a way to delve into every character you write, but I've always probably related most to Mary, Darcy, and, in certain non-creepy ways, even Wickham.

Kate: I'm a straight-up Lizzie. While there are certain things about our Lydia I definitely relate to—her tendency to pretend everything is okay, for example—I've been an Elizabeth Bennet wannabe since I was fifteen.

Do you have any plans to continue telling the story of the Bennet sisters beyond this book, whether in the form of a novel or a continuing web series?

Rachel: I don't know what Pemberley Digital has in store, but personally I feel like Lydia's story has gone as far as we can take it without beating a dead horse (sorry, Mr. Wuffles). At a certain point, you have to say good-bye to your characters and let the rest of their lives be left to the imagination. Or kill them off, but that would probably be an odd twist in this genre. (Or would it?!?)

Kate: I can't speak for what Pemberley Digital has in mind, either, but I'd like to think that if we left our characters here, we know that they're going to be okay, leading happy, fulfilling, and slightly wacky existences. And in the end, that's what we want from a story, right?

About the Authors

Kate Rorick is the coauthor of *The Secret Diary of Lizzie Bennet*. She has written for a variety of television shows, including *The Librarians*, *Law & Order: Criminal Intent*, and *Terra Nova*. In her spare time, she is the bestselling author of historical romance novels under the name Kate Noble. Rorick is a graduate of Syracuse University and lives in Los Angeles.

Rachel Kiley has written for *The Lizzie Bennet Diaries* and its spin-off, *The Lydia Bennet!!*, and might eventually write more things. She lives in Los Angeles with her dog, Bumper, and a cabinet full of red Solo cups.

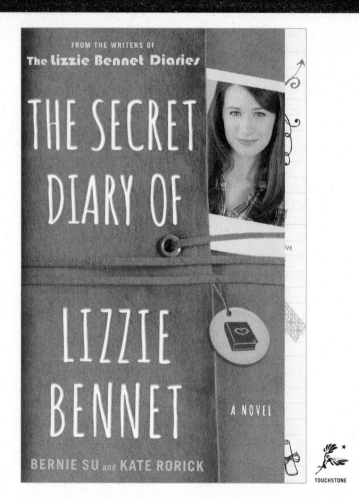